Bodies in the Bay

by

Richard Albion

Bodies in the Bay

Contact Information: info@thewildrosepress.com

Cover Art by *Abigail Owen*

The Wild Rose Press, Inc.
PO Box 708
Adams Basin, NY 14410-0708

Visit us at www.thewildrosepress.com

Publishing History
First Scarlet Rose Edition, 2019
Print ISBN 978-1-5092-2788-4
Digital ISBN 978-1-5092-2789-1

Published in the United States of America

Dedication

To the Mistress of all—she knows who she is.

Acknowledgements

Frances—Editor extraordinaire,
keeping me on the straight and narrow.
Cover artist Abigail Owen

**Complicated love, kinky sex, and
intrigue in San Francisco...**

Once I'd surveyed the entire house, I methodically went through the premises, carefully starting in the office. Her laptop was closed on her desk. I opened it using a pen. The screen blazed to life. "Any idea on a password?"

"No, but it won't take me long to get in. Let me sit. You go sleuth elsewhere." She noticed me regard her. "I have a good idea what she'd use."

"Great. Let me know when you're in. Look for anything in her e-mail for threats or anything travel related."

"Threats? You think something's happened to her, don't you?"

"Could be." I answered her with a look that said more than I intended. "We need to contact her employer and find out if she's traveling, or whatever. We'll also contact the police when we're done here. Covering bases."

Somberly, Sophie turned back to the laptop. I went into the bedroom, starting with the nightstand. Not much in the bottom drawer. The next was more interesting—several sex toys, dildos, a vibrator, and several types of lube. *No condoms. Solo show. To each his own.* The top drawer had several more items of interest—handcuffs, and good quality ones at that, leg cuffs all with keys attached, and two sets of nipple clamps. This was turning out to be a very interesting day. If those items were in her nightstand, what else did she have around?

Chapter 1

Opening the office door was not something I wanted to do today. In fact, I hadn't felt like doing it for weeks—not since my partner had been killed in a hit and run. I'd closed our last case a few days ago and was at a loose end. I'd seen a lot of death and loss, but this one really hit home. It was personal. They say life goes on, but it's not the same.

Simon and I had known each other for years during our service in the San Francisco Police Department. For different reasons we'd left the department. Later we'd teamed up as private investigators. We'd worked well together, he had tech skills, I was more comfortable with people, and together we'd built a solid reputation. Now, I wasn't sure what I wanted to do. My *Spidey* senses went off. Someone was behind me. I spun on my heel. I surprised her.

Startled, she jumped. "Mr. Lee?" she asked, letting the question hang, her expression a mixture of concern and determination.

Pushing open the door, I gestured her to enter. "No. I'm Hammett, Mr. Lee's partner. Do you have an appointment?"

She entered the comfortably sparse reception-waiting room and moved into our...*my* inner office. I took it all in. Our desks were so different. Simon's was pristine and untouched, while mine was its usual

1

confident mess. I observed her, she was slightly taller than average, looked fit, well put together, and dressed in what could be described as retro chic. It looked good on her. Age-wise she looked to be late thirties, maybe early forties. She carried an air of confidence that spelled survival of life's challenges and control.

She looked directly at me. "No. No appointment."

"Mr. Lee has passed away."

"I'm sorry to hear that. Please accept my condolences."

I looked at her more closely. No one said condolences anymore. It was "I'm sorry for your loss." We'd been taught that phrase in the police department. *Intriguing*.

"I'm Mas Hammett. Sorry. My partner's death has been difficult. How may I help you?"

"I'm Sophie Chandler. My sister, Suzanne Chandler, had an appointment with Mr. Lee, and I haven't heard from her in a couple of weeks. I'm worried about her. This is the longest we've been out of touch. Should I report her missing?"

"A couple of weeks? You waited a few *weeks* before checking on her?" *Some caring sister.*

"Our relationship is…complicated. Sometimes, we spoke daily. Others, not for several weeks. This was the latter."

"Do you know why she contacted us? I mean, Mr. Lee?" Sophie fiddled with her purse while I went to Simon's desk and looked at his day planner. It was open, as he'd left it. I saw the initials SC and 8:00 PM crossed out. 10:00 PM had been re-entered for the same night.

"No idea. She just said she had an appointment

with an investigator…Mr. S. Lee. I called several companies before I found you. Your secretary confirmed Mr. Lee was a partner here, but she wouldn't give out any other information."

"She wouldn't. Was your sister visiting or living here in San Francisco?"

"She's been living in the Bay area for about four years, working for a Silicon Valley company, and she enjoyed the San Francisco lifestyle."

I knew that could mean a multitude of things in this city. *She's hiding something, or at the very least, not telling me everything. Very interesting.*

"Well, someone with her initials had a meeting with Simon. Simply a time, not a place. I assume you've tried her cell? Landline? Social media?"

Sophie looked at me as if I was an idiot and gave me a curt "Of course."

Simon hadn't made that meeting. It had been the night he'd died.

"How about we just go visit her home and see what's what? You have the address?"

"Of course. What will you charge for this? Don't you need a contract or something?"

"No charge for driving you to and from. Call it a loss leader—a free introduction to San Francisco." Wanting out of the office, I was going to use her as an excuse. Besides, she was intriguing, and maybe it would take my mind off Simon's death.

"What if she's not there?"

"One step at a time. Don't go borrowing trouble. Let's go."

Chapter 2

I led Sophie out of the building into the chilly sunshine. She shivered, and I offered her my coat.

"No, thank you. I'm just tired from the flight."

"Where did you fly in from?"

"Philadelphia."

Everyone thinks San Francisco is hot because it's in California. I always kept a sweater or jacket in the car.

Mark Twain once said, "The coldest winter I ever spent was a summer in San Francisco." Well, I liked the weather. If others didn't they could leave, because the weather ain't changing.

I unlocked the SUV and waited until she'd settled before I started the engine. Pulling out into the North Beach traffic wasn't as bad as I'd expected. I always expect it to be bad.

Sophie was quiet on the ride, giving monosyllabic answers to my few questions.

Suzanne lived down on the Peninsula in San Carlos—not a hike. Exiting at the Holly and Brittan Streets exit, we entered a quiet neighborhood with suburban ranch-style houses nestled next to one another. After a few turns, Sophie pointed to a neat little house with a Mini parked out front. I pulled up and parked behind the small car. As I passed, I felt the hood—cold as sin. The car hadn't moved that day, and judging by the layer of dust, it hadn't moved in a while.

The area was still. No neighbors chatting amicably.

"Do you have a key?

She shook her head. "No, but Suzanne would have left a spare hidden somewhere."

We searched all the usual places. Nothing. Then, I realized it might be in, rather than under. The third one was our lucky break. Inside one ornament the key was clipped so it wouldn't rattle when it was moved.

The door swung open, then stopped, impeded by the pile of mail behind it. The house smelled stale, abandoned. I picked up all the mail. I looked carefully into the house, taking in the entire scene, then moved inside further, with Sophie calling her sister's name quietly at first, and then more stridently. Her anxiety showed.

I looked around, searching for anything that seemed out of place.

The house was a comfortable size for the area—two bedrooms, a master with an ensuite bathroom, an office, another bathroom, an open kitchen and dining room, and a sitting area with a large TV. Out back was a small, well-maintained yard that needed watering—another clue something wasn't right.

Once I'd surveyed the entire house, I systematically went through the premises, carefully starting in the office. Her laptop was closed on her desk. I opened it using a pen. The screen blazed to life. "Any idea on a password?"

"No, but it won't take me long to get in. Let me sit. You go sleuth elsewhere." She noticed me regard her. "I have a good idea what she'd use."

"Great. Let me know when you're in. Look for

anything in her e-mail for threats or anything travel related."

"Threats? You think something's happened to her, don't you?"

"Could be." I answered her with a look that said more than I intended. "We need to contact her employer and find out if she's traveling, or whatever. We'll also contact the police when we're done here. Covering bases."

Somberly, Sophie turned back to the laptop. I went into the bedroom, starting with the nightstand. Not much in the bottom drawer. The next was more interesting—several sex toys, dildos, a vibrator, and several types of lube. *No condoms. Solo show. To each his own.* The top drawer had several more items of interest—handcuffs, and good quality ones at that, leg cuffs all with keys attached, and two sets of nipple clamps. This was turning out to be a very interesting day. If those items were in her nightstand, what else did she have around?

Methodically, I went through her closet—business wear, or what went for business wear in Silicon Valley. I'd learned that a guy in the hoodie could be a drug dealer or a billionaire, and it wasn't always easy to tell which was which. I moved from right to left. Toward the end, I discovered several garment bags zipped closed. Laying them on the bed. I opened the first and revealed several leather outfits...more like harnesses...strips of leather held together with rings and locks. If Suzanne was roughly the same size as Sophie, these were hers. Closing the bag, I didn't want Sophie to see, in case she wasn't aware of Suzanne's proclivities.

The next garment bag held a bolero straight jacket in red leather and hanging off the same hanger, a black and red single glove. This girl was really into restriction and with the items I'd seen, this was not a solo occupation. Quickly, I closed the bag and did a quick look in the third bag. More of the same. I put the bags back as I'd found them.

I knelt to look at her shoeboxes and was about to remove the first lid when Sophie walked in.

"I do so love a man on his knees. Sorry. That one just slipped out."

"Uh, huh. Sure."

"Got into her computer." She laughed. "Surprisingly, Suzanne has improved her electronic security. Anyway, we're in. I have her e-mail account."

"When was the last sent an e-mail?"

Sophie looked worried. "The day she met Mr. Lee. The time stamp was six thirteen."

"She must've left just after to make an eight o'clock appointment."

"I thought you said the meeting was at ten, not eight?"

"True. I wonder who changed the time, Simon or your sister. I think Simon was hit on the way to meet her. The timeline fits with the police report."

Sophie nodded. "We still don't know why Suzie was meeting Mr. Lee."

"No, we don't. Do you have her work number?"

"Yes. Should we call her office?"

"Let's see who answers. Ask for Suzanne. We can go from there."

Sophie made the call. Someone answered on the first ring. She put her cell on speaker. "May I speak to

Suzanne Chandler, please?"

I heard the voice on the other end. "I'm sorry. She's out of the office. Who's calling?" I made a cutting motion across my throat so Sophie would end the call.

"I'll just call back. Thank you." She hung up. "What the hell?"

"We need to visit her office and ask some more questions. You can't read a face over the phone."

Sophie nodded. She pulled out a business card. It was Suzanne's, with all the required info.

I'd heard of the company, Rant Applications, but wasn't sure where it was located.

Sophie beat me to it and plugged the address into her phone.

We locked up, taking her laptop with us. I didn't mention what I'd found. I'd keep that for later.

Chapter 3

Back on Route 101 south, we made our way a few exits down the peninsula. "How do you want to proceed?"

She looked pensive, unsure of what to do.

"I have a suggestion. We can ask for her boss and say you haven't heard from her, that you're worried and looking for information. They probably won't give you much, if anything. If she isn't traveling on company business and they haven't heard from her, our next stop will be the police department to file a missing person report."

Sophie nodded.

The desk at the entrance of Rant Applications was glass, trimmed in expensive wood. Two women were behind the reception desk.

"What can I do for you?" the older lady asked.

"Could I please speak to Suzanne Chandler's manager?" The two women looked at each other. The older asked what it was in regard to. I told her it was a personal matter and handed her my card. She made a call, mentioned my name and occupation. "Please wait here. Mr. Howard will be down to see you shortly."

We waited in silence.

Soon, we were approached by a tall, sharply dressed man who introduced himself as Byron Howard, VP of Human Resources. "May I ask why you're interested in Suzanne?"

Sophie jumped in. "I'm her sister, and I haven't been able to contact her. It's not usual. In fact, it's never happened before. I've just come from her home, and it looks deserted. Could you please tell me if she's traveling on business?"

Byron looked us over. "May I see some ID? We don't typically release information about our employees."

Sophie was ready for the request and had her driver's license ready.

I caught a quick glimpse. It was a Pennsylvania license, but that was all I could confirm.

Byron looked it over carefully before handing it back to her. "Please understand, we have to be careful. There isn't much I can tell you, but we're also worried. Suzanne is well liked, and she's a huge asset to me, personally, and to the company, in general. We haven't seen or heard from her in quite a while. She is not traveling on business. She just stopped coming to work. At first, we thought she was sick, but she never called in. Since we didn't know of any other issues, we assumed she'd abandoned her job."

Sophie's voice took on an edge. "Don't you think it strange for someone so well liked to just abandon her job?"

Byron shrugged. "It happens. We had no valid emergency contact numbers. We tried the ones we had, but they'd been disconnected with no forwarding numbers. Not much else we could do."

Sophie jumped on the information. "Could I please see the numbers? One might be my old number. I updated it with her a while ago."

"I will have my assistant provide them to you. If you hear from her, let us know. Now, I have a meeting I can't miss. My assistant will be down shortly."

As he walked away, Sophie said, "Bullshit. Suzanne always followed processes and procedures precisely. We're very different in that respect. She followed the established route. Either he's lying, or she deliberately put in false numbers."

"Let's wait and see."

Shortly, a young woman approached and gave Sophie a folded sheet of paper. "I hope Suzanne is okay. Here's a photocopy of the page. I thought it would be better than just a couple of numbers."

"Thank you." As soon as she turned, Sophie opened the sheet and looked at the numbers in the emergency contact boxes. Tears welled up in her eyes.

I walked her out of the building and sat her on one of the smoker's benches. "You recognized the numbers. Whose are they?"

"One is our parents' old home number. They're deceased...have been for years. The other I don't recognize. It could be a friend's. She deliberately didn't update her file, and I don't know why she wouldn't have me on there."

"Hey, next the police department. You okay?"

"Not really. I think something bad has happened to her."

I touched her shoulder. "Once we report her missing, the police will do a hospital check with her description. She might've been in an accident. Let's go back to her place, pick up a photograph, and her tooth and hairbrushes for DNA samples. That will save some time."

Chapter 4

On the way back to Suzanne's house, I asked Sophie where she was staying.

"I booked into a hotel near your office and dropped off my suitcase before I came to meet Mr. Lee."

"Call him Simon. Everyone else did. He was immediately on good terms with everyone he met. A friendly sort, not like me."

She laughed. "Your bark is worse than your bite."

"You haven't seen me pissed off."

She snickered again. "But I have seen you on your knees."

That was the second time she'd mentioned it. Thinking about her sister, I began to wonder about her.

We pulled up to the curb outside Suzanne's house. It took no time at all to put the brushes in ziplock bags and for Sophie to print a recent photograph off Suzanne's social media account.

The police department was close. Showing my credentials when we entered, I said, "We need to report a missing person."

We were shown into an interview room. Then, an officer joined us and began taking down details, and he accepted the photograph but held off on Suzanne's brushes. He took Sophie's contact information in San Francisco, reading back her cell number, which I entered into my phone while pretending to check e-mail.

After we'd finished, Sophie felt at a loss. "What do we do now?"

"We wait and see what their report turns up and get you back to your hotel."

"Thank you for all you've done today. I know the police are investigating, but I want to do something, too. I want to hire you to look for my sister if you do missing persons?"

"I think I can handle it, but I want to be clear. I'll need all the background I can get on your sister. Everything. Fair enough?"

She nodded.

"We can stop off at the office and set you up with a contract, then go over the fee schedule and the per diem. Okay?"

"Sounds fine, Mr. Hammett."

"Please, call me Mas."

Pulling into the increasing traffic, I thought about what I'd discovered in Suzanne's bedroom. Did I approach the subject by asking about their childhood, what was Suzanne like, what she did for fun, education/work experience, etcetera? Perhaps. Working it that way seemed to ease Sophie into a chatty, more relaxed mood.

She described their childhood as full and happy…the usual stuff. Suzanne was two years younger than Sophie and was always trying to catch up, following her and hanging on her coattails. "Sometimes, it was a pain, having Suzanne around all the time, but it also gave me someone to boss about. If you haven't noticed, I'm a bit of a control freak. I like being in charge."

"Really? I hadn't noticed."

She threw her head back and laughed. "Is it really that obvious?"

"With you, pretty obvious. It's surprising the things you discover when you're observant." I let my comment linger. From the corner of my eye, I could see her looking at me.

She was silent. Finally, her voice took a defensive tone. "What did you find?"

Taking my time, I finally responded, "Let me make this very clear. I don't judge. I observe. I live in a glass house, so I don't throw stones." A moment later, I chose my words carefully. "I found multiple items strongly suggesting your sister is into BDSM. Too much for a test run or a fling. Several items suggested a partner. Did she have a boyfriend?"

Sophie fell quiet again, deep in thought, eyes fixed straight ahead. "When we sign the paperwork and you accept my fee, I'll feel better about talking about my sister's private life. It will all be confidential, right?"

"Yes, unless you plan on harming someone or yourself—" I chuckled. "—it will remain confidential until you give me permission otherwise. Good enough?"

"Good enough."

The drive back into the city was quiet and slow. I used all the alternative shortcuts I knew—*Thank God for Google*. We took a longer route, but it ended up being quicker.

I parked in the spot I rented full-time—the only sensible way to park in San Francisco.

Chapter 5

Opening the office door for the first time in a month with a purpose, I wanted answers. I felt something—nothing good, but something I could sink my teeth into. After seeing her house and the brief meeting with her boss, I was convinced. Call it cop sense, experience, a feeling—whatever—something bad had happened to Suzanne.

Besides, Sophie intrigued me with a connection I hadn't felt in a very long time. In no time, she'd signed the standard agreement, and I ran her credit card for the fee and a second swipe for the week's per diem advance. I hoped it wouldn't take a week to find Suzanne.

I should've remembered the old saying, "Be careful what you wish for, you might just get it."

After we'd completed the client agreement, I asked again. "All signed up. Now, please give me all the background you can about Suzanne."

"You mean her sex life?"

"No, I mean everything. Everything you know about her. It's all valuable. All the aspects of her life, everyone she knew, met, dealt with. Her work, social life, who she played with, boyfriends…everything." I threw in who she played with as a throw-away comment regarding her BDSM activities to see if I got a reaction. I did.

Without thinking, Sophie said, "I don't know who she was playing with. Wait. You set me up!"

"Not really. I figured you knew more about her BDSM life than you were letting on. I really do need to know everything. I assume, from the outfits I found, she was a submissive and into bondage. Correct?"

"Yes, but I don't know who she was involved with. She'd broken off her last relationship months ago. She was probably doing pick-up play with people she knew in the community. How do you know all this?"

"This is San Francisco, the home of 'The Folsom Street Fair.' As a SF inspector, I got to see and know lots of things." I stopped talking, lost in my own thoughts. I flashed back to how I'd met Simon and how, later, we'd both left the force for such different reasons.

Sophie's voice broke through. "Where were you just now? It sure as hell wasn't here. I guess you have some secrets. Want to share?"

Shyly, I declined. "Let's go get something to eat. I know a great French restaurant. The waiters all have attitudes, but the food makes up for it in spades."

Suspiciously, she looked at me, as if deciding whether a meal with me would be a dangerous event, but took the chance.

The restaurant was as advertised. A surly waiter showed us to a corner table, thinking he was being smart by shoving us into a corner.

For one, I appreciated the privacy it gave us.

Sophie was engrossed in perusing the menu, which gave me time to look at her. I already knew the menu by heart. She was attractive in a been-around-the-block way. Not used, but she had a tough layer on the outside, and I had the feeling she wouldn't let anyone inside her shell without good reason. Building her trust would take some time.

She looked up, catching me by surprise. "Like what you see?"

"Just curious."

"Yeah, well, curiosity killed the cat."

"True, but I'm more of a big dog."

"And all dogs should be kept on a leash."

"Depends on how well they're trained."

"Are you well trained?"

"I've had exceptional training, and I've exploited the training in real-life situations."

"Really? I'd like to see how well you're trained After all, dogs are trained to obey, aren't they?"

I had the feeling we were no longer talking about my professional training and that made me uncomfortable, another feeling I hadn't had in a long time.

"How about we order and talk about your sister? I still need all the background you can give me, and we need to go through her laptop. I'd like to hear everything you can tell me about her. Maybe we can do the computer tomorrow morning. Does that work?"

"That's called changing the subject." She looked at me sternly. "Okay. If that's the way you play, sure. Tomorrow will be fine to look at her computer."

The surly waiter took our order while Sophie talked about Suzanne. I took notes when I needed to, and Sophie repeated parts as I requested or expanded on them for clarification. As promised, the food was excellent, and the Chardonnay from Sonoma matched perfectly. The conversation stuttered and became sporadic as we plowed our way through the food.

"Coming from Philly, I'm pleasantly surprised how good the food is here. I don't think of San Francisco for French cuisine."

That gave me an opening. Expanding on my love of San Francisco, I told her about the influx of multiple cultures, including French. She was a good listener, rarely interjecting, but laughing in all the right places. I felt more comfortable with Sophie after her earlier pointed comments. She looked more relaxed…well, relaxed like a predator waiting for a slip or error. Then, she'd pounce.

I hadn't had a meal like this in a while and didn't want it to end so soon.

Sophie cocked her head at me. "Thank you for a delicious meal, but I need to get to the hotel. I'm three hours ahead of you, and not fond of flying. I'll see you tomorrow, yes?"

"Sorry, my fault. I should've realized you were on East Coast time. Sure. I'll pick you up. Or would you rather meet at the office?"

"Let's meet at the office. Eight AM? I'll be up early. Is that okay?"

"No problem. I'll be there, bright and early." I made a mental note to text our…*my* admin, Maria, to make sure the coffee was on. Neither of us were early birds, and since Simon died, it would be good to get back into a routine.

I escorted Sophie to her hotel and said goodnight. As I did, a feeling of foreboding hit me. I tried to shake it, but it was persistent.

Chapter 6

I could smell the coffee aroma seeping down the hall before I got to the office door, and I was sure we were the first folks in at this ungodly hour, this morning or any morning. Was I that smitten? I'd agreed to be in at 8:00 AM.

When I'd texted Maria, her immediate response had been, "Are you fucking crazy?" So much for employee respect. Mollified by my excuse it was for a client, she agreed to come in early.

When I opened the door, Maria looked up with a deep frown and a quick nod to my office. Sophie couldn't be here already. I was ten minutes early. I groaned inwardly. I needed my coffee. The one thing our office had all agreed on was to have good coffee. Right now, I just needed *any* coffee.

Sophie was seated at Simon's desk, working on her sister's laptop. She looked up when I walked in. "I hope you don't mind I set myself up here." Before I could answer, she continued. "I've skimmed over most of her e-mails. She had three accounts with Gmail—one for work, even though it wasn't her work computer, a social account, which is pretty general, and a private account." She looked away as she mentioned the last one.

I figured that one was for her BDSM lifestyle. My money was on a KinkInc account. KinkInc was not so much a dating site as a social meeting place for kinksters of all persuasions. I wanted to see where Sophie went with it, so I played dumb. "How private and exactly what did it cover?"

Sophie looked at me, her eyes questioning.

I looked directly back at her with a blank face.

"It's her kink account. It was how she communicated with others in the kink community, through a web site called KinkInc."

"Okay, okay. I know about KinkInc. I just wanted to know if you'd be open with me. Sorry. I'm cranky without coffee, and this is early for me. I should've told you 10:00 AM would've been better."

"Mas, don't be an asshole. I know you have secrets and so do I, but I want to trust you to find my sister. Finding her is really all I care about right now. Get your coffee and let's get to work."

She turned back to the laptop.

I left to get coffee. As I walked, a thought struck me. *That isn't her work computer. So where is it?*

Inhaling the aroma and feeling the heat from the coffee cup, I dove into the black abyss as the caffeine hit me, and I started to feel human again. When I returned, I pulled up a chair and sat next to Sophie so I could see the screen.

She pulled up Suzanne's KinkInc account. It looked like most other social media accounts—profile, photos, what groups she was a member of, events she was attending or considering.

Nothing stood out. Her profile was concise, well written, and better than a lot of the ones I'd seen. "What does her KinkInc mail look like? Anything raise a red flag to you?"

"Not really. I'll go through all her contacts and look at the profiles. She played at the Cauldron and Sorcerer's public play spaces. Apparently, they're both very well run. Do you know them?"

"Yes." I agreed with her.

"When do you think we'll hear back from the police about the missing person's report?"

"As soon as they hear anything. They'll also look at any Jane Does in the system."

"You mean the morgue?"

"Yes. The longer it takes, the less likely she'll turn up in the morgue. That's an easy check. Same with the hospitals. She could've decided to just disappear."

Sophie's head snapped around to me, her eyes fiery. "No. That's not her. She's in trouble. I need to find her."

"Okay. You know we may never find out what happened, right? A lot of missing persons end up permanently missing. Are you prepared for no resolution?"

"No. I might not like it, but I'll find an answer."

I admired her conviction. From my experience, sometimes, there were no answers, and if there were, she might regret looking.

We spent time going over Suzanne's accounts. Sophie knew her way around a computer. She was fast and efficient, much better than me or Simon, and he was pretty damn good. I didn't know what she did work-wise.

Not much came out of our efforts from a leads perspective. Although Suzanne lived on the peninsula, I didn't think it would hurt to run the information through one of my contacts in the SFPD. I made the call, and she agreed to look at the information, though no promises on a timeline.

Sophie uncovered a play party at the Cauldron that night. "I want to go. Maybe some of her friends there can shed some light on Suzanne's disappearance. I think it's worth a shot."

I'd bump into people I knew, which gave me pause.

Sophie smiled a secret smile. "Have you ever been to a play party?"

"Don't worry about me. I've been around the block a few times. Have you?" Hopefully…I'd dodged that bullet well. Since this was a case, I'd deal with whatever happened personally and spend the next few hours following up on items I'd ignored or let slip through the cracks.

Sophie showing up had gotten me going again. We broke for lunch. Maria brought in sandwiches from the deli around the corner and more coffee.

"I have my own work to catch up on. I think I'll go back to the hotel to freshen up for tonight's visit to the Cauldron."

Nodding, I waved as she headed to the door. "I'll pick you up at eight."

"Don't bother. I'll meet you there. I have the address. Don't be late."

Then she was gone, leaving me to wonder what game she was playing.

Chapter 7

The rest of the day I spent clearing up crap I'd ignored. It needed to be done. I sent Maria home. Her early start had her dragging by mid-afternoon, and I had lots to think about, including the upcoming event at the Cauldron.

Finally, I'd had enough. I couldn't concentrate. I was still confused about Sophie, concerned with the lack of information about Suzanne, and frustrated by my overall feelings about everything. I wasn't used to being so impressed by my clients, but something about Sophie pushed my buttons. Physically, she was attractive, not in an "oh, she's cute" way, but in a gut sensation, a more visceral way. Something between us connected. I just couldn't put a finger on it…at least, not yet.

At home, I showered and made myself something to eat. Puttering about my apartment, I was restless. I tried to compartmentalize the different issues, but they all seemed to merge into one big bowl of mental spaghetti. I'd think about one issue then another would creep in. I'd follow that train of thought and another would jump in. It was like a never-ending tangle. They were all interconnected, and I'd just have to deal with it. It wasn't the way I usually did things, but I had no choice.

I checked the clock. *Time to get ready*. Dressing

would be easy—black shirt, black jeans, black shoes, and to top it off, a black leather blazer. Done. Now, all I had to do was figure out how to handle tonight's event—business and pleasure.

Parking was always difficult, so I used a rideshare. I didn't have to wait long. Twelve minutes later, I was outside the Cauldron. The street was busy, but not bustling…at least not yet.

The door security nodded to me as I entered—a huge slab of a man I'd arrested when I was an inspector and later, helped to get the door job. He'd made some not-so-smart decisions in the past, but he was very capable and loyal to a fault. He'd turned his life around.

Walking up the stairs, I wondered how many times I'd done this over the years. Cat's Eyes was working the desk. She was wearing a long, Grecian-style dress in scarlet red chiffon. It draped over her body, clinging and floating at the same time. The neckline had deep, plunging Vs, back and front. Her unfettered breasts moved freely under the semi-sheer cloth. Her hair was piled on top of her head, emphasizing her long neck, surrounded by a narrow metal collar.

When she saw me, she waved and came at me with open arms. She waived the entrance fee, which I insisted on paying. After all, I was working.

"Mas, it's good to see you. It's been too long. We were all sorry to hear about Simon. Did you get our food basket? It's going to be a great night tonight. Lots of folks are here already. Oh, God. I'm going on, aren't I?"

I hugged her back and smiled. "Yes, you are. It's good to see you, too."

We both laughed.

I moved into the club as more people arrived at the desk. As BDSM clubs go, this one had space, was well known, and more upscale than some would expect. I chuckled. I wonder what people would think if they knew the average IQ of the BDSM community member was higher than the average Joe Public. I wasn't sure it meant anything, but it was an interesting statistic.

I went directly to the bar—a no alcohol bar—and ordered an orange juice with seltzer. Drink in hand, I did a tour of the club. Some attendees were already in scenes. Two of the Saint Andrew's crosses were in use and a steel cage was occupied by a naked man whose owner was negotiating a rental with another top. Having checked out the space and confirming Sophie hadn't yet arrived, I returned to the bar.

The bar had filled up and was busy, but not too crowded. Sipping my drink in a secluded corner I waited for Sophie to arrive. It looked to be an interesting evening. I hadn't realized how much I'd missed coming here.

Halfway through my drink, my mind was miles away when I noticed a pair of high heels, standing in front of me. I looked up sharply. It was Sophie, but not the one who'd entered my office. No, this was a very different version.

She stood with her hands on her hips. "A gentleman would offer a lady a seat and a drink."

Surprised, I stood. "Please, take my seat. What would you like to drink?"

Then a hot flush hit me. Now, I knew what had my guts churning. She was a top—a dominatrix—just as her sister was a submissive. I should've known—her always wanting to be in control and the loaded comments she'd made about me being on my knees. Well, now, she was in the open while I still had some secrets. I was planning on letting those out carefully, when I was ready, though I suspected she correctly pegged me as being on the submissive side of the coin.

She smiled. "Oh, anything reddish will do."

I went to the bar and ordered a cranberry and OJ with seltzer, wondering how I'd been so obtuse to miss the signs. As I walked back toward the table, I observed her.

She wasn't one of those stereotypical doms, all spikes and black leather. Sophie was a dominant because that was who she was. She wore a tight, body-hugging dress, made tighter with a waist corset. It nipped in her waist, emphasizing her boobs and hips. She was covered up, leaving much to the imagination, which revealed a lot about her. Her stocking encased legs were long and crossed, while the split in her dress fell open, giving a good view of her legs. She looked good and I wanted more of her.

What the fuck am I doing? We're here to work, not play. I can't allow myself to be distracted.

"I think you'll like this. If not, I can change it." Sophie reached for her glass and our hands touched. Mine tingled with pleasure.

"I'm sure I will. If not, I'll let it slide." She was playing with me.

"We'd better start asking questions before everyone gets too involved with their activities. I know a few people who've been in the scene for a long time. Sound good?"

"Your town. I'll follow your lead."

I nodded and gestured for her to follow. We went

26

back to the front desk, and I asked Cats' Eyes if she could take a break.

"Sure, Mas. What's up?"

"Cats' Eyes, this is—"

Sophie reached out her hand. "Hi. I'm Circe. I'm looking for my sister. She disappeared about two weeks ago, and I know she frequented here. Can you help us? Please?"

I was surprised she hadn't used her real name. She'd said she didn't know anyone out here. I looked at her with narrowed eyes. I had to find out why she'd used an alias.

Cats' Eyes looked at Sophie, as I knew her. "What name did she use? I'll help if I can."

Sophie looked relieved. "She usually went under her KinkInc name, Sub-lime. Here's a picture of her." She handed a photograph to Cats' Eyes.

I saw an immediate spark of recognition.

"Sure. I've seen her around. I didn't really know her. Actually, I've seen her more at Sorcerer's than here."

I showed her the list of Suzanne's friends we'd pulled from the computer who'd said they'd be attending and asked her if she knew any of them.

She looked over the short list and pointed out three names. "Only one is here right now. His name is Two-serve. He came in about ten minutes ago. He's really nice." She looked about and grabbed my arm. "There he is."

I followed her line of vision and we fell in behind her.

Cats' Eyes tapped Two-serve on his arm. He turned and caught Sophie's eye. His eyes grew wide. "Sub-lime?"

Sophie shook her head. "No. I'm her sister and I'm looking for her. You thought I was her?"

"In this light, you look a lot like her and without glasses my eyes aren't the best. Sorry. Where's she been? I haven't seen her for a while."

"I was hoping you could tell me. I haven't heard from her in over two weeks. We talk often, if only for a couple of minutes. I'm worried about her and was wondering if you could help."

"Sure, if I can, but I haven't seen her since the last play party, three Saturdays ago. She seemed fine and happy. Just having a good time."

"Do you remember who she was with?"

He looked to one side, trying to remember. "We played together with a Dom couple, Boss Bull and his wife, Bitchess. They should be here tonight. Oh, and later, I saw her talking with a man. I didn't recognize him. I don't think he's a regular here. He looked foreign. Sorry. That's the best I can do. If there's anything else, please let me know. You can contact me through KinkInc. I really like Sub-lime."

I could tell he was sincere. Cats' Eyes returned to her desk duties while Sophie and I made the rounds, watching various people play. One threesome caught both our attention. The lone female was dressed in a lace maid's dress, showing off her tits to best advantage. Her short skirt was fluffed out with multiple layers of tulle petticoats. She'd been strapped into a sling by the two males who escorted her, making sure her bare pussy was open and exposed. They were teasing and tormenting her swollen labia with tongues and toys they carried in utility belts, refusing to let her climax. She writhed against her restraints, to no avail.

Another threesome caught our attention. Two men had placed a woman on a spanking bench. They'd fixed her wrists and ankles to the solid bench and had secured her skirts up over her back so her ass was bare, ready for paddling. One of the men chose a paddle off his belt while the other stood in front of the woman, unzipped his pants, and pulled out his semi-hard cock. She automatically opened her mouth and started to suck his cock to fullness. She jerked as her ass took the first blow from the paddle. From her reaction, this wasn't the first time she'd been paddled while sucking a cock. After a dozen strikes, the men switched places. The new man preferred a flogger. It looked deceptively soft, but I knew better.

The woman worked the new cock deep into her mouth. The flogger fell with a practiced hand and she was soon moving her ass, aroused and rising to meet an orgasm. Before she could, the men switched places again. The spanker changed to a lighter paddle and was circumspect in placing his blows. The one in her mouth exploded, shoving his cock down her throat and squirting his load into her. She groaned and spluttered without spilling a drop. I could see her swallow while the frustration rose on her face. She wanted to orgasm.

I was beginning to envy her.

The men released her and, unsteadily, they moved her to the single bed in the corner. One man connected her wrist cuffs behind her while the other cleaned off the bench. She seemed dazed. The first man lay on the bed and told her to sit on his face. She descended onto his tongue and her expression told me she'd found the right place. The man worked on her pussy, holding her thighs down tight. The second man unbuttoned the shoulders of her dress and pulled it down, exposing her full, tight tits. Her nipples were like small pebbles and just as hard, her aureoles crinkled like discarded wrapping paper.

The man pulled a small rubber flogger off his belt and quickly struck her left tit, causing her to jerk up. The man under her reached up to steady her. She tried to move sideways, but this only made her tits swing. The flogger stung her tits and hard nipples. Again, she tried to rise. The flogging stopped and the man under her moved her down his body to his jutting cock. The woman lifted herself up and settled on his hard dick, moaning as she descended his length. He moved inside her as she pushed against him. The flogger started again, alternating tits with both hard and soft strikes.

The bottom man moaned and grabbed her tits, holding them for his partner. His moans became louder as he jerked up and, grunting loudly, shot his cum directly into her pussy. The woman was close to orgasm, still moving on his cock. He moved her off and laid her on her side, moaning in frustration. The two men cleaned themselves off and lay on each side of her, holding her gently, stroking her hair and body, and quietly whispering to her.

Sophie broke the moment with a nudge. "That should've been a two-woman, one-man sandwich. Let's move and see if the Dom couple has arrived."

I tried to tear myself away, but I was horny. The woman's reactions had gotten my juices flowing. I knew what it felt like to be in that moment and I wanted to feel it again. My engorged cock strained in my tight pants. Regretfully, I pulled myself back into reality and business.

The couple still hadn't arrived. The club had filled, and it was getting difficult to move around easily. We settled back in the bar with a view of the entrance and the play space. Sitting next to Sophie, I didn't have a view of her face, so I concentrated on her voice.

She was silent for a few moments. "You were there, weren't you? Right there."

I wasn't going to lie. I never did in this place. "Yes, I was right there." I stared straight ahead, concentrating on her voice and blocking out all other sounds.

"I understand, Mas. I know what it's like—the power and the release. You don't have to be afraid of me."

Where the hell does she come off thinking she knows me?

"You don't know me and I am not afraid of you. You're a client. I don't trust you yet. That's all."

"You have shadows, Mas. So do I. I'll never abuse this side of you. I don't expect you to trust me yet, I just want to find my sister. After that, who knows what will happen."

I laughed. She obviously didn't know me at all...or my history. "Sophie, don't play games. You've obviously done some digging on me. This is San Francisco. I'm more out than you think. As an ex-cop, I've certainly been there—done it and seen it. Most of it was crap. Piles of stinking crap, body parts, and week-old corpses...and all the nasty things people do to others. Damn right, I have shadows and secrets and ghosts and shit that creeps up on me in the middle of the night. I deal with it in my own way. So, don't play games. Clear?"

"Clear. I didn't mean to sound condescending. Of course, I did some checking up on you. Most of it was on Simon. I'm not stupid. I wanted to know who my sister was dealing with. It seems you had a raw deal with the police department."

How'd she know about that? The records had been sealed, and the PD definitely wasn't going to spill that can of beans. Maybe I needed to do some digging on her and get ahead of the curve, for once. I still knew a few folks who worked Cyber in the PD. I made a mental note to call in a favor. "Yeah, well, the past is past. Let's just get your sister home."

A couple entered the bar, followed by Two-serve. He caught my eye and nodded in the direction of the new couple.

Chapter 8

We approached the couple slowly, taking them in. They were of average height with good builds. The guy carried a few extra pounds. She was his height in her heels. She'd probably had a boob job, but she was well put together and dressed to impress, a mixture of leather and lace. He mirrored her with leather formalwear. Her tooled-leather corset in black and gold looked expensive. They were laughing at something the bar man had said.

Two-serve stood in front of them, made a comment, and looked at us.

Their smiles disappeared and both heads nodded in unison.

We stepped up to the threesome and introduced ourselves. I used my real name, Sophie her community name, and they responded with their KinkInc names. We moved to a corner where we could talk more privately.

"I'm looking for my sister." Sophie asked the questions, and I observed the responses, picking up on the non-verbal cues. "She's missing and we believe this is the last place she was seen. Do you remember playing with her?"

The man responded immediately. "Yes. Of course, we do. Sub-lime is a friend, and we've played together often. We'll help any way we can, right?" He looked at his wife, who nodded.

"The last time we saw her was here. We did a scene with her and Two-serve. We had a great time and no problems. She seemed fine. She'd parted from her Dom a while ago. Which is why she was free to play with us and had several times."

I watched them closely, but nothing jumped out as being untrue or suspicious. We continued talking, going over the night in as much detail as possible.

Boss Bull was mostly quiet, but something sparked his memory. "Toward the end of the night, I did see her talking with a man. He looked Japanese or Chinese. Certainly Asian."

"Can you describe him? Any and all details."

"Yeah, but it was last month, and I wasn't paying particular attention."

"Don't worry. Just go with the flow. Let the images and details come. We can sort them out later."

He closed his eyes took a deep breath. "He was taller than Sub-lime, but not by much, slim with very well-groomed hair. He wore a sharp suit. It had metal sheen to it. Silk, I guess. I got the impression he was foreign. By that, I mean he looked more formal, like a foreign executive. He never smiled, but it didn't look confrontational. They both looked relaxed."

Great. An Asian businessman in San Francisco. What a rarity.

"He was wearing high heels."

Sophie cocked her head. "You mean like women's heels?"

He shook his head. "No, stacked heels. Like cowboys wear on boots, but I don't think these were boots."

"Cuban heels, maybe?" I'd seen them before.

"Yes, that's it. They're more refined than cowboy boots, right?"

She knew what I was thinking. Tracking him would probably be impossible.

We thanked them for their time, and I gave them my card. "Give me a call if you think of anything." I'd said those same words thousands of times, but it couldn't hurt.

"Did that really get us anywhere?" The frustration seeped into Sophie's voice.

"Yes. One step at a time. We know she was here that Saturday night. The day after, she was due to meet Simon. That gives us a timeline. Now, we fill in the time between then and today. It's a long, slow, process." I was really hoping the missing person report would have something.

Sophie looked over to me. "Are you in a relationship of any sort?"

My answer was short. "No."

"What's your secret?"

I looked at her. "What do you mean?"

"You stay calm. I know you think something has happened to Suzanne, but you don't let it show. I jab you to get reactions, and you mostly let it bounce off."

"I have thick skin."

She looked at the table. "Was being a cop that bad?"

"No. It was the best thing about me, and I was very good at it. I felt I was making a difference and to a degree, I did."

"So, why'd you leave?"

My eyes bored into her. "You're the one with all

the answers. You were the one who brought up the secrets thing."

"I know some things, but not all. I'm curious what makes you tick. You're very competent, in control, but I see another side, a submissive side. Passive. Something you don't easily give into. You're complicated. I like complicated. It's interesting."

"It's probably best you stay out of my messy life. Besides, you're here for your sister."

My mind went back to that shitty time. Like picking a scab, it hurt, but I couldn't quite leave it alone. Simon had helped me get through the worst parts and now, he was gone. Life really was a crapshoot. She was right on one account. I did think something had happened to Suzanne.

"Do you want to stay here or leave? We probably won't get much more out of tonight."

"I want to stay for a while…see the local flora and fauna. I might like it here."

"Won't Philly miss you?"

She ignored the dig. "I can do what I do anywhere. Are you staying?"

"For a while. I want to catch up with friends. See you in the office tomorrow?"

"Yes, and not so early. I promise."

She wandered off while I sat thinking for a few moments. Maybe I should've told her what she wanted to know. Shaking off my thoughts, I moved to the front reception area, the one place in the Cauldron where phones were allowed. I sent a text, called in a favor, and chatted with a few of the attendees, catching up and accepting several sincere condolences. They were genuine and heartfelt. A bit of the black cloud lifted

This case was getting under my skin and so was Sophie. The blood was flowing through my veins, and my energy was slowly returning without the help of a lot of caffeine. It felt good.

Sophie wandered through the crowd, making connections. Leave her to it. I moved outside to wait for my ride home. I would play another night.

Oso, the door security guard, joined me, chatted about nothing, and filled some time. Out of the blue, he turned to me and gave me a bear hug. "Sorry to hear about your loss, man." That was it. He turned away, stone-faced, as usual.

I was astonished. It was the most emotion I'd ever seen from him. When he'd been in trouble or facing his own losses, he'd been stone faced. His action touched me.

The ride home was slow with evening traffic. I was in no hurry. The only thing waiting was my empty apartment and, hopefully, a good night's sleep.

Chapter 9

Shooting up in bed, and disoriented for a moment, I located the clock, noting it was just short of eight o'clock. I wasn't late, but I shook myself awake, that bad feeling I'd felt the night before was seeping into my subconscious. Showering and dressing quickly, I dreaded what the day would bring.

After a quick breakfast from the deli, I was entering the building when Sophie crossed the street. She waved, and I waited for her. She opened with "You look terrible, and you left way before I did. Anything productive?"

"So-so. How about you? I saw you making friends."

"San Fran is so much friendlier than the East Coast."

"Glad we meet your approval."

That brought a sharp look and a comment. "What's that all about?"

She shook her head. "I stayed and asked around about Suzanne, or Sub-lime. A couple of people remembered her, but nothing more. One of her friends showed up late, but he didn't offer more than we already had. He said she seemed fine and had enjoyed her two scenes that night. I asked about the Asian man, but he said he hadn't seen him."

"Sorry. I get snippy when I don't have coffee.

Come on up. I'm sure Maria will have coffee on."

Mollified, Sophie followed me up to the office.

My phone went off as we were walking down the corridor. It was Maria. "We're walking in right now."

Before I could say anything more, she interrupted me. "Bill needs to see you ASAP."

"Bill" was our code word for the police and from the tone of her voice and the ASAP, they were already in the office.

"What's wrong?" Sophie's brow crinkled.

"Nothing, as yet. The police are waiting."

"Is it about Suzanne?"

"I don't know. Maria just gave me a heads-up." I increased my pace and quickly reached the door, Sophie right on my heels. I recognized the two men waiting for me. I'd been the inspector in charge of a team that included Kenzo Otake.

The men stood as we entered. Kenzo greeted me. "Long time, Mas. Long time. Sorry about Simon. You know Inspector Jack Callen."

He looked sincere as he held his hand out.

I took it briefly. Same with Inspector Callen. "Sure. Good to see you. Maria, coffee for all, please." I showed them through to the inner office.

The two men looked at Sophie. If they asked her to wait outside, it was probably not related to her sister. If they included her, it probably was about her sister. They didn't object.

With Kenzo and inspector Callen seated around my desk, Sophie, looking apprehensive, took Simon's old chair.

Kenzo started by opening his notebook, a delaying technique. Then Maria brought in the coffee, and Kenzo visibly relaxed, helping himself to black with sugar. Everyone else reached to prepare their own while the air crackled with nervous electricity.

My office, my terms.

"So, Kenzo. This a social call?" I wasn't going to make this easy for him.

"No, Mas. Unfortunately, it's business. We understand you reported a missing person yesterday in San Carlos. Correct?"

I looked at him, trying to get a read. "Actually, it was Miss Chandler who did the reporting. She's retained me to find her sister, the subject of the report. Do you have information?"

"We may. We would like to ask Miss Chandler some questions."

I looked at her, and she shrugged.

Kenzo turned to her. "When was the last time you spoke to your sister?"

"A day or two before she went missing."

"You live in Philadelphia, correct?"

"Yes. What do you know about my sister?"

"We aren't sure of anything, yet. What do you do in Philadelphia?"

"I work in the tech field."

"Exactly what does that mean, Miss Chandler?"

"I consult and freelance on tech issues."

"Software? Cyber security?"

"Often." Sophie wasn't making it easy for them, and I wondered why. Typically, a relative of a missing person was as helpful as possible...unless there was something to hide.

I need that info on her, and quickly.

"And what did your sister do, here in California?"

"She worked for a tech company."

"Did you talk about work in your frequent conversations?"

"No. We were more about the social thing."

"I understand you offered some items to the officer in San Carlos, for identification purposes. Do you still have them available?"

I spoke up for the first time. "They can be made available." The detectives looked at me. I didn't like the look. They were holding something back, and I wasn't happy. "Are they required?"

"Mas, we would like to accept Ms. Chandler's offer to have them on hand. For efficiency. You understand."

I chose my words carefully, "You have a body and you need to identify or disqualify, right?"

Sophie's face registered what I'd said. She slumped into the chair, her hard shell cracking. Tears welled up in the corners of her eyes.

"I am not at liberty to say. We have some leads…several leads. We are following up."

Now, I was getting pissed. They were trying to play me.

"Cut the crap, Kenzo. Sophie has a right to know. I know how this is played. Do you have a body or not?"

"Mas, don't push on this one. Don't push."

"Push? Are you kidding me? My client has a right to know if you have a body that could be her sister. If you do, she can confirm or deny the identity."

"Please, if you do, I'll identify the body…*if* it's her." She seemed to have shrunk. She wasn't the brash, confident woman from last night.

Kenzo looked at me.

"Sophie, would you mind stepping out for a minute while I have a chat with my former colleagues?"

She looked at me sharply but didn't argue. She visibly paled as she walked from the office and closed the door behind her.

When I was sure she was out of earshot, I turned to Kenzo. "Stop the bullshit. You have a female body, it's a mess, and you need DNA to confirm or eliminate the vic, right?"

Kenzo sighed. "I wish it were that easy. If I confide in you, you have to keep it to yourself. She can't know, at least not yet. Is that clear?"

Inspector Callen chimed in. "Kenzo. You can't do that. This is an ongoing investigation."

"My decision, Jack. It's on me."

This was something out of the ordinary, and I was all in, especially if it had something to do with my client's case. "You have my word. Nothing from me, not even to Sophie."

He looked relieved. "We have eight bodies with the ME. They were found in the Bay."

I knew what that meant. The sea life had gotten to them, and they wouldn't be pretty. Even a few days in the bay could do some major damage. I stayed silent, waiting for him to continue.

"A father and his son were fishing off the docks, south of China Basin. The son was first to get his line out, and before his dad could throw his out, the kid snagged something. He said it was that quick. He yanked on the line and it came free, so he reeled it in.

The dad saw something on the hook, flat and white. That's when the dad realized it was an ear. A *human* ear. The guy tells the kid to hand him the rod and get back to the car. He calls 911 and tells them where they are and what they found. He keeps his kid in the car and stays with him until the patrol car arrives.

"They needed a dive team, thinking it was a suicide or an accident. But it was too dark then, and they had to wait until the next morning. They took statements, and the father and son were released to go home. They were told to stay quiet until we could make a public statement.

"Next day, the divers went down to investigate. Almost immediately, they found a cage with human remains. They sent up a marker buoy and called for a boat with a hoist. As they waited for the boat, the two divers expanded their search area, making sure they hadn't missed anything. That's when they found a second cage, the same as the first, loaded with bodies.

"Within minutes, they found two more cages, all with bodies. They weren't sure how many bodies they had, only that all four cages contained human remains. Lucky me, I caught the case. We have eight bodies and are treating this as a serial homicide." He stopped, taking a long drink of his now-cold coffee.

Probably a safe assumption. People don't usually commit suicide, then stuff themselves into cages. "Any IDs yet?"

"No, too soon. The medical examiner is taking her time, crossing all the T's and dotting all the I's on this one."

I remembered the ME. She was caustic to everyone. None better had served San Francisco, and her results could be relied on to stand in court. She had chewed up more than one defense attorney, much to the delight of the prosecutors. "You mean, the way she always does?"

Kenzo smiled. "I guess so. No arguments with her work. I wish she was faster. Her clients aren't going anywhere, but the perps could be. Still, I'll keep her."

"When do you expect the results?"

"Well, if we had some comparable DNA, it would be quicker."

Touché. Laughing, I opened my desk drawer and tossed him the hairbrush and toothbrush in their separate bags.

Kenzo caught them. "The SFPD appreciates your assistance in this matter."

I turned the conversation back to Suzanne. "If you identify Suzanne as one of your vics, I want in. Before you say no, you know I'll investigate anyway. I've taken her sister's money, and I *will* be involved. I can be an asset to you. I don't have the restrictions you do. Deal?"

"No deal. At least, not yet…and probably never. I'll have to run that can of worms up the chain. I'm sure as hell not making that decision."

Pete chuckled.

"I'll get back to you with the results as soon as I have them."

"How soon on the DNA?"

"With a comparison sample, forty-eight to seventy-two hours. This one will get bumped up to the top of the pile. We're still raking through the missing persons reports. Until we have a better timeline, we're going with the assumption the first bodies were dumped four to five months ago. That's just going off visuals of decomp.

"I'll be chasing you if I haven't heard from you in

forty-eight."

"Mas, it might take seventy-two."

"Then you'd better call me and tell me that. I'm serious. I want in on this."

"Okay, Mas. Understood, but consider my position. I'll book you if I need to. Got it?"

"Consider hers." I tipped my head in the direction of the door. With threats delivered, we both understood the lay of the land.

They stood, thanked me for the coffee, and left, nodding in Sophie's direction as they exited. As soon as they'd gone, Sophie and Maria followed me back into the inner office.

"What was that all about?"

Their eyes shone with anticipation, but I'd promised Kenzo I wouldn't divulge his information.

"They have some leads and are investigating several missing persons that may or may not be connected to Suzanne's disappearance. Other than that, I tried to convince them to let me join their investigation if—and it's a big if—it's connected to your sister. They didn't shoot me down completely and promised to get us any information as soon as they got it."

"Bullshit." Sophie shook her head.

I looked at Maria and nodded. She took the hint and left.

Chapter 10

Sitting on my desk, I stared at Sophie. I didn't know what she was going through—the stress of not knowing—but I'd seen and been through similar situations. I had to bring her back into focus.

"You don't trust me. Fair enough. I don't trust clients who don't tell me the truth. We can end this, here and now. I'll give you a full refund and call it quits, but I will say this. I'll work hard for you—put myself on the line for you, life and limb included. So, you want out or are we going to continue?"

Sophie eyed me suspiciously, trying to make up her mind. The internal struggle showed in her eyes. Finally, she threw up her arms.

"Okay, but from now on, you tell me everything. I'm not some fainting maiden. I can handle myself and we're going to have a come-to-Jesus talk right now or I'll walk. Got it?"

I smiled at her, which seemed to make her angrier.

"Don't be condescending, or I'll kick your ass." Well, she certainly had spirit…in spades.

"How many corpses have you seen?"

She looked surprised at the question. "Two—our parents at the funeral home."

"No." I wasn't going to make this easy for her. "Those were nice clean bodies, and prepped for you. I'm talking about a shooting vic with his brains all over the wall, or the suicide who hung themselves and the body wasn't discovered for a few days.

"How about the wreck where you can't tell the body parts from the tangled car wreckage, or the vic who's been in the bay for a few weeks, being chewed on by the marine life? Those are corpses. They're not pretty. Actually, they're pretty fucking ugly."

My voice rose, and the bad vibe returned. I was pretty damn sure the samples we'd supplied would match one of the bodies found in the bay. I didn't know why I felt so strongly, but I did.

Sophie's eyes went wide. "Mas, okay, calm down."

"Sorry, sometimes I get flashbacks, in all their sordid glory." I sat. "So, let's get to Jesus." I waited for her to start, with either questions or confessions, I didn't care which.

Sophie looked uncomfortable. She sipped her coffee, put it down, picked it up, and took another sip. She wouldn't meet my eyes. "What happened with the police department? I know some of the story, but not much. It's sealed. It looked like you left under a black cloud, though."

I thought she might start with that, so I deflected. "Fine, *if* you tell me what you're hiding. People with missing sisters are more forthcoming and helpful to the ones looking for them. Criminal record, maybe?"

"Not exactly."

I laughed. "That just means you haven't been caught. This isn't going to go well, is it?"

"All right. Let's just say with my work, the lines sometimes get fuzzy."

"I still don't know exactly what you do, although I am making some inquiries along those lines."

47

"You won't find much—innuendo and supposition, not much else." She smiled. "I'm as invisible as I can be in this digital age. Okay, I'll tell you about me, as long as it still falls under client confidentiality."

My interest was piqued. "Agreed. It's confidential."

Sophie relaxed. "Our father was a really boring accountant, but he was an early computer geek. He taught us how the hardware worked, then the programs, and finally, how to write code. Suzanne was better at coding than I was, but I worked harder. She got wrapped up in the coding itself, while I was more interested in what it could do...the applications. We diverged. She was the scientist, and I was the rebel. We basically grew up in the tech industry.

"Both of us have multiple degrees in computers and related fields, but she always followed the straight and narrow. I was, shall we say, more *adventurous*...off the beaten track. I've had my brushes with authority, but nothing was proven. To be honest, I've been known to bend the rules a bit."

I interrupted her. I knew enough through working with Simon that she was a hacker. "You mean you're a black hat hacker?"

She looked surprised. "No, not a black hat. More like medium gray. Where did you learn the terminology?"

"From Simon. Please, continue."

"Well, you're kinda right. I've been on both sides of the fence. I'm independent, pick which projects to take, and control my work life. I'm very good at what I do, so I can afford to work the way I choose. I make good money, and I'm mostly off the grid. I prefer being in the shadows. It gives me flexibility and control."

There was that word again. Control. "So, what exactly do you do?"

"Not an easy question. I protect clients and also search out those who attack my clients. Proving what they've done isn't always easy. Sometimes, it's a proactive hack to prevent one from happening."

"Who are your clients? I don't mean by name— just in general."

"Again, not an easy question. Individuals, corporations, businesses of all sizes. Anyone who has sensitive information or intellectual property is a target these days."

"That's a lot of vagueness. So, if you're so into the tech world, why aren't you here on the West Coast?

She bristled. "Don't have to be or want to be."

"I really don't know any more about you than I did before."

"You know more than most. You know more about my private life than anyone other than Suzanne and a few very close friends."

I wondered when she would bring that up. "You're not on KinkInc, then?" I already knew the answer, but she gave me a withering look.

"Are you kidding? I like to be in the shadows. It might be okay for Suzanne, but it sure as hell isn't for me. Now, it's your turn. You don't have to tell me everything. I'm most interested in your history with the police force."

Chapter 11

Figures. It was the biggest disaster in my life and I still held a grudge, though not with the SFPD. They'd been pretty stand-up about it, considering the circumstances. Falling silent, I gathered my thoughts.

"Ever since I was a kid, I wanted to be an SFPD inspector. See, other cities have detectives, but here in San Francisco, they're called inspectors. That sounded pretty cool. I joined as a high school grad, went through the academy, and put on the uniform, aiming to be an inspector. I did my time in the 'blues.' I studied, took all the exams, and got a degree in criminal justice at night school. I worked my ass off. I wanted to be out in the field, not a politico or paper pusher. I wanted to help people. Maybe I was naïve, but I felt I was making a difference...at least for a while." I stopped talking, lost in memories—good and bad.

Sophie realized I was lost in thought, and she let me drift.

"Getting my inspector's shield was the best day of my life and the proudest for me and my family. I worked all sorts of cases, mostly violent cases. My team had a pretty good closure rate. Then, I moved into serious crime and homicide cases. There were some pretty ugly scenes. You kinda get used them, but you pay the price. They leave scars. No one can see them, but they're there and they revisit in your dreams.

"Anyway, I was eventually put in charge of a team, and the four of us did some great work. The oldest member, Frank, got sick and died of cancer—diagnosed and dead in six weeks. That was a pretty shitty time. His replacement was a woman, Valerie.

"We had no gender issues on the team, and she seemed to fit in fine at first. Then, it became clear she was ambitious...at all costs. She'd always manage to twist the report to make her look good. I talked to her and tried to make her understand it was a team effort—team success was success for all of us.

"That was my undoing. She viewed me as a threat and made a play to take me out and to make herself look good in the process.

"Let me digress here for a moment. You assumed I was on the submissive side of the kink coin, you're right. I always have been. Being submissive, giving up control, became more important...like a release valve. The more crap I saw as a cop, the more I needed a release.

"Some people drink, gamble, or screw around. I needed to give up control, let someone else be responsible for a while. I played in private with like-minded folks. Finding a mistress was eye opening. She was...well...*is* a professor at Berkeley, and we entered into a D/s relationship. It worked well for both of us, at least until Valerie fucked it up." I took a deep breath.

"The other team members didn't like working with Valerie, and before I could resolve it through the proper channels, it all fell apart. She accused me of sexual harassment and trying to rape her. As you know, consent in the kink world is a baseline. There was no way I'd mess up like that, and I didn't find her that attractive. Of course, any time a female subordinate makes accusations, they're taken seriously. She fabricated a series of incidents where she claimed I'd made unwanted advances. She invented times and dates—all her word against mine. That would've been enough, but she over-played her hand with the rape charge.

"Of course, I denied the charges—didn't go with a union representative. I wanted someone outside the department. It wasn't that I didn't trust the union. I just wanted the best defense I could afford. Aside from being innocent, I had something else in my favor. Statements were taken—very detailed statements, especially from her—particularly about the rape charge. She claimed I'd been drinking and had actually penetrated her, but because I'd had a few drinks, she was able to push me off and escape. Bitch."

Even now, it rankled. The old anger built, still raw. I clenched the arm of the chair in a death grip.

Sophie broke the tension. "How'd you prove your innocence?"

I laughed. "It was easy. Like I said, I was in a D/s relationship with the professor. I was her sub, and she was into control…though nothing that would impact my job. She liked to control my orgasms—when and how—so she had me wear a locked metal chastity device. I couldn't have fucked anyone. I couldn't masturbate or even touch my own dick without her unlocking the cage. You know about them, right?"

Sophie nodded.

"Well, mine was very secure with a built-in lock. So it's almost impossible to open without a key. Internal Affairs questioned her, and she reiterated her story. My lawyer took an affidavit from my mistress—she was OCD when it came to details about her kink. She had the dates, times, and duration of my releases, down to the second, all on spreadsheets.

"I was concerned if it got out, it would affect her position at the university, but she said not to worry. She had tenure, and everyone already thought she was eccentric. She told my lawyer it was fine with her. So, Valerie and I took polygraph tests—mine came back fine, but hers was inconclusive. There are ways to beat a poly. We had an in-house hearing, facing a panel of senior officers. Valerie was very confident until my lawyer questioned her about the rape details. Then, she became uncomfortable. She hesitated in some of her answers, and that was when my lawyer went after her.

"He hit her with the proof I physically couldn't have raped her and because she hadn't reported it at the time, there was no physical evidence. The IA panel believed me and my mistress's testimony, but the police department didn't want any publicity, so she was allowed to resign. I was encouraged to resign, but I didn't want to. One of the senior officers said, 'If you'd been gay, no problem,' but they couldn't employ a 'pervert,' as they so subtly put it. My attorney was worth every penny, by the way. He negotiated my full pension as part of the deal. With my years served and previously spotless record, there was no opposition. After all, I *was* innocent. Still, it cost me the only job I'd ever wanted." I stopped, out of things to say.

Sophie looked at me with sympathy. "You survived, and you seem to be doing pretty well."

I grimaced. "Not the same. I like what I do now, but part of me died that day. It was Simon who kept me going."

"How's that?"

I figured since I was confessing, I might as well tell her the whole story. "Simon was really good with computers. He worked in the SFPD cyber division, tracking fraud and all sorts of online nasties. He also had a real skill for trapping online predators, particularly kiddy predators. He could really imitate the part of the child, both girls and boys. But Simon got burned out. He felt guilty about all those he couldn't help or find. We originally became acquainted meeting over dead children. When he heard I'd resigned, he reached out to me. We met for coffee, and he asked me what I planned to do. I told I didn't know.

"He surprised me when he suggested working together as PIs. He told me he wanted to work with me because I cared, and he was tired of working in a sewer. No matter what he did, the scumbags found a legal loophole to escape. He took early retirement, and we set up shop. I never realized how important he was to me or how much he meant to me. He kept me occupied and working so I didn't have time to worry or feel sorry for myself. By the time I sat back and thought about what had happened, we were working more hours than I had as an inspector." I laughed at the thought.

"That must have been hard for you."

"You're the first person to hear the story. It was…is…a lot more complicated than that."

"I'm sure it is. Thank you. You said you aren't in a relationship now. How come?"

"After all the nonsense with my case, Mistress and I agreed it was probably better if we didn't see each other for a while. We drifted apart and never reconnected; our relationship was another victim."

"I'm sorry. I know how difficult it can be to make that kind of connection. I never have...at least, not yet."

I looked up at her. There was a sadness that seemed to emanate from her like a grey cloud. This was getting way too maudlin for me. "Let's go get lunch, and I'll show you some of San Francisco."

Chapter 12

"You up for a walk? We're a few blocks from Chinatown. It's easier to walk than drive."

"Sure. Why not?"

Pleased at her response, I continued. "I need to know more about Suzanne's job and bounce some ideas off you. Okay?"

"No problem." As we strolled toward Chinatown, Sophie asked me what I'd thought of our visit to Suzanne's company.

Replaying the visit in my head, some things didn't seem quite right, but nothing stood out. "Nothing stands out. Why?" I wasn't going to play all my cards at once.

"I didn't expect you to pick up on it. I know my sister."

"Well, I did wonder why the VP came out to meet us in the lobby, rather than her direct manager. It was also odd they didn't take us into an office or conference room to speak privately. And why did they give up her contact information so easily? Fake contact information, I might add. Aside from that, what did I miss?"

"You saw it, as well, huh? Flim-flam. My sister could no more work in HR than I could fly. Did I mention I don't like flying?"

I couldn't resist smiling. "Not in control when you're on a plane, huh?"

She shot me a dirty look. "Funny man. Yes, that, too. Suzanne was awesome in the tech stuff, but interpersonal, not so much. Actually, she was horrible at it, unless she was being submissive. I guess we're both pretty screwed up."

"Don't worry about it. Everyone's screwed up, to varying degrees."

"Well, aren't you a ray of sunshine?"

I laughed. "Sorry. My cynical side occasionally shows through."

"Only occasionally?" She gave me a wry grin.

"Okay, you got me. Most of the time. Here we are. I hope you like spicy food."

"Yes, I do. I like a lot of things spicy." She let that hang.

I ignored it. We didn't have to wait. We were quickly shown to a bare table, with paper towels as napkins. Chopsticks wrapped in paper stood in an old mug and two small teacups had been placed at the end of the table, along with hot tea in a dented stainless-steel pot. I poured.

Sophie took a long look at the teapot then scanned the restaurant, noting the faded red velvet wallpaper and chipped waving cat. "You really know how to impress a girl. Do you always bring your clients to these luxurious establishments?"

"Only the ones I like."

She laughed aloud, making two other patrons look at us. Then, her face grew serious. "Do you think Suzanne's company is hiding something? I do."

I'd thought about the visit and I'd come to the same conclusion. "Yes, I do. With what you've said about your sister's work, I think they're hiding her true position. Do you think she could be a tester for their new products?"

"You mean a beta tester? See if they can break their own product before they release it? Maybe. She was very good, but here in Silicon Valley, she was in a big pond with a lot of smart sharks. If we knew what she did and what she was working on, it would give me a better idea. Let me see what I can come up with."

We looked over the menu, and I made some recommendations.

She insisted on picking one dish. She couldn't completely give up control, even in a restaurant. At least her choice was a good one—scallops in a spicy garlic, black bean sauce.

We continued our discussion as we ate. By the end of the meal, we were both perspiring and my mouth was sending emergency signals to my brain. It felt good.

After lunch, we strolled back to the office. We each had our tasks. I would look into the company and Sophie would start digging. I didn't ask how. Honestly, not wanting to know, at least not yet.

Sophie said she would like to work from my office, if that was okay with me.

I asked Marie to give her Simon's set of keys. I stayed at the office and logged on to get the Rant info, made some calls, and thought about Suzanne. She didn't seem high enough up in the company to put her in jeopardy…if she was one of the bodies in the bay.

Sophie worked for a while then said she was going back to her hotel.

Engrossed in my work, I absently waved a hand. "I'll let you know if I find or hear anything. I'll see you tomorrow."

My cell interrupted my search. It was my contact reporting back on Sophie. The conversation was short, but valuable. She'd been working in the cyber community. They knew her name. She'd also worked for the establishment. She was picky about her projects and had turned down several lucrative corporate contracts. There was nothing to indicate she'd been involved in any completely illegal projects. My contact said if Sophie was half as good as her reputation, she'd be an asset to me, and she might even know if someone had been making inquiries about her. She'd been hard to track, leaving very little trace, with only teeny tiny electronic footprints and mostly anecdotal information, rumor or inferred. Very few people had actually met her. Most of her interactions had been done computer to computer or by telephone. That made me wonder how people knew it was truly her.

Apparently, she insisted on payment up front for her work, and once she'd been hired, the project would be completed as per contract. If the originator wanted the project cancelled or stopped early, they would bear the loss. My client was secretive, smart, and driven. Something I'd have to be more aware of. I knew what it felt like to be driven. The best parts of me were two friends, persistence and stubborn. They had gotten me through difficult cases before.

I finished up the day, with some progress, but not enough to make me happy. There were far too many questions surrounding Rant Applications. Walking a circuitous route, I made my way home. It was bustling in North Beach, as usual. This area always made me feel more alive—the small, independent shops, the lively cafés, bars, and restaurants. The major reason I liked living here was the positive atmosphere. I needed to feed off that positive energy.

I made dinner while listening to the news on the television. There wasn't much to speak of—the usual traffic snarl-ups on the Bay Bridge and the major roads. Opting for a loud CD, I worked out in the second bedroom. At the end of the hour, I was drenched. I stripped off and enjoyed the stinging hot shower, relaxing in the heat and steam it created.

An old image popped into my head. Visiting the Cauldron and seeing all the people there in a safe, non-judgmental environment had made my memories surface. I missed that part of me. I'd pushed it away…submerged it.

Now, it was full frontal, and I didn't want to push it away again. Those feelings were part of me, and I wanted to be made whole again.

After drying off, I opened a dresser drawer I hadn't explored for some time. There it was—the black velvet bag.

The ambiguous shape inside that bag held many memories for me. My hand shook. I wanted to open the bag and revel in what it had meant to me. Would it be the same? Knowing I couldn't go back, I could only go forward on a new path or further down the old one. It didn't really matter. Taking a deep breath, I reached in and took the bag in one hand. The weight surprised me. I'd forgotten the density. I laid it on the top of the dresser, undoing the string closure with fumbling fingers. Finally, the opening came loose. I held the bag in one hand and tipped the contents into the other. It landed with a slight rattle. The light reflected off its polished surface, glinting…winking at me like an old friend.

The chastity cage was exactly as I'd remembered it, only this time, the two keys were with it. Carefully, I laid the bag down and put the cage on top of it. Sitting on the edge of the bed, I looked at the cold steel, feeling I'd missed out on something. The cage had been a part of me for a long time, only to be shunted into the dresser, ignored like an unpleasant relative. That was something I could rectify. This time would be different, at least until I found a partner or at least, a key holder.

Laughing out loud, I felt lighter. I returned to the bathroom. Since I'd stopped wearing the cage that had saved me from a false rape charge, I'd let my pubic hair grow back, an easy fix.

Running hot water into the sink, I found my trimming scissors and cut my pubic hair as close as I could. Even this got me hard. Thinking about what was going to happen next made me horny.

I stroked my dick, feeling it grow hard. It felt so good—thick, warm, and firm to the touch. I closed my eyes, concentrating on the warm, throbbing cock in my hand. The feeling almost brought me to tears. I hadn't felt like this in a long time. I slowed my strokes, then reached into the cupboard under the sink and found a bottle of lube. I smeared it all over my cock, relishing the slippery sensation. The scent of it wafted up, bringing back memories.

Stroking harder, faster. It wasn't long before my shooting cum lined the sink. I let out a loud groan of pleasure, as the first ejaculation exploded, followed by several more spasms. The release felt incredible, better than any in recent memory. Why the hell hadn't I done this before?

Recovering my breath with my cock deflating in the mirrors' reflection, I looked at my own face. I was flushed, and I looked better than I had in a long time. I sure as hell felt better. Time to finish what I'd started.

Running the hot water, I splashed it over the basin. Then, I took my shaving brush and lathered up, coating my entire pubic area in white. I put a new blade in my razor, carefully scraping away the white soap, leaving pink, bare flesh. Over and over, I pulled the razor until my pubic area was hairless again, my dick responding to the new sensations. I felt light-headed. Quickly, I washed away the remaining soap and slathered moisturizer over the freshly shaved area, partly to protect the skin and partly to make it easier to get the cage on my dick.

My cock filled at the thought of encasing it in steel, though I could release myself at any time. It was a feeling I remembered and relished. It was a start.

The two stainless-steel parts were spotless—the back ring containing the lock and the cage. I ran my fingers over the flat flange on top of the cage, which slotted into the lock. The chastity device was well designed to be worn under regular clothes.

Taking the back ring, I surrounded my cock and balls and clicked it into place. It was snug, but not uncomfortable. My cock was another matter. I ran the cold water, soaked a wash cloth, and wrapped it around my cock. That took care of the rising erection.

Sticking my cock in the cage, I used cotton buds to arrange myself comfortably. When I was satisfied, I connected the cage to the back ring, sliding the metal flange into the lock and clicking it shut. The only way out was with the key.

Immediately, I started to get an erection. It felt wonderful, but I couldn't touch myself or do anything about it unless I opened the cage, and that would defeat the purpose. Looking in the mirror, seeing my genitals trapped in shiny steel, made me harder. A random thought flashed through my mind. *I wonder if Sophie would enjoy being my key holder.* I tried to push the thought from my mind, but it wouldn't go away so I tried the fantasy on to see how it fit. It fit well, but it wasn't something I was going to bring up or even hope for. There were bigger issues at hand.

I slid into bed, hoping for sleep unmarred by the ragged dreams of past victims.

Chapter 13

The night wasn't kind. I slept well for a few hours then my mind took over, flitting from fact to supposition to assumptions. My cock reminded me of what I'd done. Maybe I should've waited until this case was resolved. Too late now. Except, I could release myself. If I did, I knew I'd regret it.

In the morning, I set my sights on uncovering all I could about Rant Applications. Rather than waste time going to the office, I would work from home. I let Maria know.

"I already have company." Sophie had already arrived and put coffee on. "Mas, this woman has a work ethic, and I'll be ordering more printing supplies. She's chewing through it like there's no tomorrow. She can get you on your cell or e-mail, yes?"

"Sure. I'm holing up today. No plans to go anywhere. If that changes, I'll let you know."

Maria sounded more cheerful than she had for some time. Maybe this case would have some positive benefits for both of us.

Digging around, I found all the superficial info I expected to find. I raked through the San Francisco Chronicle archives, finding interesting bits and pieces, but nothing that would help us with Suzanne—no takeover rumors or rumors of any kind, positive or negative—the usual Silicon Valley financials and prospectus.

Sitting at my desk, I was constantly reminded of the metal cage. Every time I went to the bathroom, I had to sit to pee. The visual reminder was always there. In some odd way, being locked up took my mind off other things. It cleared out the ran erratic thoughts and allowed me to focus on what I had to.

I called a couple of journalists I knew from my days as an inspector. They were crime beat rather than tech, but said they'd ask around for me when they could. I waited to hear from Kenzo, hoping Suzanne wasn't one of the bodies in the ME's enclave.

My phone rang, but it was Sophie.

"I haven't found much on Rant, but we were right. I managed to find some HR organizational charts, and the asshole we met gave us his real name. He's the VP of Research and Development, pretty near the top of the chain in Rant. I think Suzanne was testing something new. She reported directly to him. Whatever it is, it's a big deal, at least for the company. I haven't found out what it is yet. Still working my way around stuff."

"Any idea if it's purely internal? Do they have any outside investors? If so, where from?"

"No idea yet. I thought of that, and I'm looking for anything that would indicate foreign interest. This was a little more difficult than I expected, but now, I have some avenues to follow."

"Would India, Japan, China, or Korea be likely candidates?"

Sophie went silent, thinking. "My money would be Japan and China first. Possibly Korea, but probably not India. At least, not yet. Why?"

"Something I came across in the Chronicle

archives. Rant has had interest from overseas businessmen. Nothing out of the ordinary or enough to raise suspicions—they all seem to be kosher—but it makes me wonder about the Asian man Suzanne was last seen with. It's probably not connected, but still…"

Another pause. "I'll add that to my list of items to look for, especially from Japan or China. Do we have a timeline?"

"If it's related to Suzanne, maybe six months, then work from there. Probably no further back than nine months. Did you get a good look at her personal hard drive?"

No pause this time. "Of course. Nothing out of the ordinary. In fact, it was too clean, so I did a little digging and someone—could've been Suzanne—has deleted e-mails and files. I managed to resurrect some, but nothing of interest."

I sensed some reticence in her voice. "Any more info on her KinkInc account."

She replied quickly. "Was I that obvious?"

"You forget I'm very good at listening—unconscious vocal inflection and such. So, yes. It was obvious. And?"

"I pulled up several more profiles that were in her e-mail more than once. None seemed more than casual friends. I'll check into them further."

"Send me the profile names, and I'll investigate them. You concentrate on Rant, okay?"

"Yes. Makes sense. See you tomorrow?"

"Yes. I'll meet you at the office. Maria says you're an early bird."

"I can be, when I'm working. Maria is cool. She even went out and got me lunch without me asking.

She's a gem."

"Shit. She never does that for me. She must really like you."

Sophie laughed. "Is she gay?"

"Nope. Live-in boyfriend. Why? Do you think she's hitting on you?"

"Not really. It's been a while since I've had people do nice things for me without wanting something in return. Curious, that's all."

"Okay. See you tomorrow." I ended the call and tossed my phone on the sofa next to my desk.

I worked through the day until the dimming light told me it was time to call it a day. I was feeling isolated. It was rush hour, and I wanted to feel part of humanity again. I threw on a light jacket and went for a walk around Washington Square, picking up a pizza to bring home. I often felt more tired sitting in front of a computer than I did after a physical day. I hoped for a better night than the last one.

****

The early wake-up after a fitful sleep didn't start my day any better. Needing some progress, I decided to call Kenzo if I hadn't heard from him by lunchtime. I was anxious to confirm or eliminate Suzanne from the mess Kenzo had in his lap. Serials were a nightmare to deal with.

Stopping by the neighborhood deli, I grabbed some breakfast then headed to the office. As I expected, Sophie was already there, hunched over her computer, her fingers flying over the keys. She looked up, nodded, and resumed her work. Simon's computer was open and running, too. She was working on both computers at once. I couldn't see hers, and I wasn't sure I wanted to.

I was no longer in law enforcement, but after so many years, I preferred to stay on the right side of the law. I'd dented and bent a few rules over the years, but I'd never completely broken any. Sophie didn't have my reservations. That was something I'd struggle with another day.

Settling into my chair, I enjoyed my breakfast, along with the coffee Marie had brought me. She refilled Sophie's mug, as well. The sound of tapping keys was soothing. As I observed her working, she was oblivious to my gaze. Her hair was tied back in a loose ponytail. A few strands had escaped and hung down each side of her face. She was wearing a tight pink top which showed the outline of her bra, her nipples pointed and well defined in the office lighting. Her jeans were form fitting without being sprayed on and her heeled feet were crossed under her chair. A soft leather jacket hung carelessly over the back of her chair. I didn't know much about women's clothes, but for all the casualness of her outfit, it looked expensive.

My cock responded with a mind of its own.

My cell buzzed me out of my reverie. I didn't recognize the number, only that it was from San Francisco. I answered out of habit. "Hammett and Lee investigations. How can we be of service?" The voice, I did recognize. *Kenzo*. If he was calling so soon, it had to be bad news. "Hey, Kenzo. Thanks for getting back, as promised. What do you have?"

Sophie's eyes were glued to me.

Kenzo said he was on the way over with some new information. "Will you be in the office for the next hour?"

"Yes. Miss Chandler is also here."

That brought a pause. "Okay. See you then."

"Well? What did they say? Is it Suzanne? Tell me what they said."

Kenzo's voice had been even, and I couldn't be sure, but I'd gotten the sense it wasn't good news. I looked at Sophie. "He's on the way over. He didn't say much, only that there was new information."

"You think it's about Suzanne?"

"Probably. I couldn't get a good read on his voice. I don't think its good news."

She sat back in her chair, looking weary. The stress of not knowing would wear on anyone.

Twenty minutes later, we heard the main door open. Marie showed Kenzo and Pete directly into my office. They looked like crap, working more hours than they should. Marie offered coffee, but the offer was dismissed with a wave.

Kenzo addressed Sophie. "I'm sorry, Miss Chandler, but we have some difficult news for you. We've identified your sister's body. We are very sorry for your loss."

In a moment of clarity, I knew I would get the perpetrator for Sophie. I wasn't sure why, but I knew he was mine. I'd never had a feeling like this before—never been so certain. I'd had lots of feelings on previous cases—pissed off, angry, frustrated—but nothing like this calm. "A definite DNA match? No question?"

Pete nodded. "Solid result. No question about this one. Again, Miss Chandler, we are sorry for your loss. We'll do everything we can to resolve her death."

The word "death" seemed to bring her out of her fog. "You mean murder. Can I see her?"

I glanced at the two investigators.

Kenzo shook his head. "We can't allow that at this time, and I would advise against it. Remember her as she was."

"I want to see her. I need to say goodbye."

I had to chime in. "Sophie, let them do their job. We can talk about it and make a decision later."

Both Kenzo and Pete shot me looks of thanks.

I noted the looks. *It must be really bad.* I'd make sure she didn't see what I'd seen too many times.

Chapter 14

Kenzo and Pete left their cards on the desk, saying they'd be in touch with any further developments.

Sophie sat in shocked silence.

I walked the inspectors out. "Kenzo, I'm serious. I want in on this. Officially. I'm already involved, so use me. Don't shut me out."

He looked at Jack. "Sorry, Mas. I asked my up-line and he said he'd think about it. Nothing definite."

"Was that before you had a confirmed ID?"

"Yes. I passed on your request when I got back to the office, the same day."

I fixed my gaze on him. "Ask again, now that you've confirmed it's Suzanne. I'm not going away. I'll share any information I have, and anything else we find."

Kenzo looked at me sharply. "We? You haven't involved Miss Chandler's sister in this, have you?"

"Have you forgotten she came to me? *We* supplied the DNA sample for you to compare." I was getting mad. "Have you identified any of the other vics yet? No? Didn't think so. We've given you the best lead so far, so cut the official bullshit and get me in."

Kenzo and Pete exchanged looks. Pete shrugged. "Okay, Mas. I'll do what I can. I promise. If you get the okay, it will have to be unofficial."

"I don't care. I'm going to get this perp, whatever

it takes."

Both inspectors gave me the hard stare. Pete cocked an eyebrow at me. "Don't do something stupid and fuck up our case. *Our* case, not yours. Got it?"

"No worries. I have never FUBAR'd a case. Right, Kenzo?"

He smiled. "No, Mas. You've never messed up a case, so don't start now. Color inside the lines, or I'll find a way to arrest you. We're clear, right?"

"Crystal, but don't expect me to let up on this. I won't let this go. I don't have to follow the same rules you do."

"Mas. Don't cross us on this case. There will be a lot of pressure to get it solved. Don't get in our way."

"Then get me in, and I'll help you."

Kenzo responded. "If they let you in, you play by *our* rules, not yours. Otherwise, I'll make your life miserable. I promise you that."

When they left, Marie let out a long breath. "Well, that went well. Mas, you really know how to piss people off, especially your friends."

I smiled wryly. "It's a natural talent." I went back into my office.

Sophie was sitting silently, a serene look on her face. Maybe it was shock; a normal reaction to hearing her only close relative had been found dead and had probably been murdered.

I'd seen every reaction imaginable, but never the look of serenity I now saw on Sophie's face.

She turned to me. "I'm going to get this fucker. Will you still help me?"

I'd dealt with all sorts of criminals, thugs, crazies, gangsters, psychos, and various "normal" people, but

I'd never heard the absolute dispassion in Sophie's, not even in sociopaths. I felt a chill run down my back. "Yes, I'll still help you."

Her eyes drifted up to mine. Her smile was icy. "Thank you. I'm going for a walk."

"I'm not sure that's a great idea."

"Don't worry. I'm not going to do anything stupid. I need to think and…prioritize. I'll be back in a while."

I let it go and watched her take her leave. Soon after, Kenzo called and told me his captain wanted to see me. "I'm on my way."

It didn't take long to get to headquarters. I got my visitor's badge and told the guard I knew the way, but he insisted I wait for an escort. I recognized the person he sent. It was Jose, another old colleague. We hugged.

"Great to see you, Mas."

It seemed like he meant it, but it might've been for old times' sake. *Time will tell.* We caught up on life as we walked to the squad room—it hadn't changed much. The paint was more worn, and the atmosphere seemed a bit more chaotic. The bustle reminded me I was once part of this hive of activity. Being part of the team had always felt good—knowing we would die for each other. Then, the resentment rose like bile in my throat.

Jose took me directly to the captain's office. Along the way, a few people waved in recognition. I returned the waves, knowing I was an outsider, betwixt and between. As a PI, I lived between worlds—the protectors and the protected. I hadn't realized the only place I felt at home was in the kink community.

At least I have a home.

The captain waved me to a chair as he finished his phone call.

I sat in the hard, worn chair, looking at the clutter of files on his desk. Some things never changed. Too much to do and not enough manpower or time. Management by crisis. Kenzo's case—my case—would be at the top of the pile.

The captain looked wearily at me and continued talking. Finally, he cradled the phone. I knew what he was feeling.

"Mas, I put my ass on the line for you. We're short-handed, and you were a cop. Emphasis on 'were.'

"You'll be a consultant. No contract. No fee. Nada. We let you in on this and you fuck it up, I will personally reopen Alcatraz and lock you up forever. Got it?"

"Yes, Captain. I got it from Kenzo, and now, I've gotten it from you. I want this perp as much, if not more, than you do. One of the vics is my client's sister. I have skin in this game."

"You've been out of the department for some time now. Remember where the lines are, and don't cross them. As of now, you're allowed to *consult* with Kenzo's team and no one else. You'll have access to all their findings, and we expect you'll be forthcoming with anything you find. He's giving a briefing now, if you want to join him. Anything else?"

"No. All good."

As I got up to leave, he said, "The only reason you're in on this is your prior record, and some people think you got a raw deal."

His comment was a nice surprise, but it didn't change anything. I knew the briefing room, so I made my way there…without an escort. Kenzo was talking to the other members of his team. Pete and Jose, I knew, but I didn't recognize the woman who completed the team. All their attention was fixed on the board. Grisly pictures pinned in pairs on a board were marked with a large "F" or "M" next to them. Only one had an identity. *Suzanne*. I didn't enter. I leaned against the door jamb and listened to what Kenzo said.

"We need to identify seven vics ASAP. Then, determine how they're connected.

I spoke up. "Well, they're all dead. That's a connection." I knew I was putting my foot in it, but I couldn't resist.

Kenzo turned, not amused. "Very funny, Mas. Gallows humor already." Looking at the woman, he introduced me. "Josie Hernandez, this is Mas Hammett. He'll be assisting us on this case, running parallel. We'll share information and resources. Take a seat. We'll bring you up to speed."

I took the closest seat, next to Josie. She didn't look happy to see me.

Kenzo continued. "The bodies were found in close proximity to each other. Steel cages, each containing two bodies—one male and one female. The ME is still processing them. Preliminary findings show the first pair was dumped approximately four months ago. Hopefully, the autopsy will narrow the timeline. The second pair, probably dumped three months ago and the next pair, from the decomp of the bodies, roughly two months ago. The last pair…three weeks ago. Mas's client's sister was the last female. Ages run between late twenties to mid-fifties. Again, these are all estimates. At least two have been strangled. The hyoid bone was snapped. With the others, we may never know the cause of death.

"At least three are Asian—two males and one female. So far, there's no obvious pattern of type or age. It's unusual for a serial to go after both sexes. This perp must have some messed-up pathology. We need to corner him fast. If the ME is correct, and she usually is, they were all dumped about a month apart. We only have a week and half before the next set shows up. He might not know we have his dumping ground. If he does, we probably won't find the next vics, unless we get lucky."

A uniform poked her head around the door and waved a piece of paper at Kenzo. I took it from her and handed it over.

Kenzo looked at it. "Two more IDs came in—a woman, Delia Chung, reported missing ten weeks ago. The time fits for the second dump. The male, Troy Jasonides, is from the first dump. He was reported missing sixteen weeks ago. Again, the time fits. That first pair are the most decomposed. We'll need to fill in the bios quickly, probably from missing person's reports.

"My team will dig into the vics we've identified, except Suzanne. That one will remain with Mas. We'll allocate more vics to him as we ID them. Any connections need to be identified. We have several sets of eyes on this, and we need to close quickly. Okay, get out and do this. Safely."

"I'll send everything I have on Suzanne, Kenzo. Don't make too many assumptions. The only connection for now is they're all dead. You'll get pressure to solve this, but don't go too fast."

I wasn't sure if he'd agreed with me or just wanted me out of his hair. He looked exhausted but nodded.

I asked, "When will your team send over the info they have so far?"

"Soon."

Jose escorted me down and out of the HQ building. We said our goodbyes and promised to catch up on personal stuff when we had the chance. Neither of us would follow up, and we both knew it.

Making my way back to the office, I hoped Sophie was okay and that she'd returned before I did. We had a lot to go over and plenty of planning to do.

Marie nodded toward the inner office when I entered, indicating Sophie had returned. I made my way in. "How was your walk? Did you like what you saw of San Francisco?"

"To be honest, I don't remember where I went or what I saw. I was wandering and thinking."

"Any conclusions?"

"Yes. I need to find some long-term accommodations. I don't suppose you know of any?"

Ironically, I did—Simon's apartment.

When we'd started up our partnership, we'd taken out key-man insurance. Since neither of us had any family to speak of, we left our assets to each other, except for a few bequests. I hadn't gotten around to putting it on the market. I still hadn't finalized the insurance claim—something else I'd put off, even with the reminders from Marie. It made it all too final. "If you don't mind using Simon's place. I haven't cleared it out yet, and it's dusty."

"You don't mind?"

"No, I don't mind."

"Then I'll take you up on your offer."

"What else did you come up with on your walk?"

"Well, I'm not going anywhere until I've solved Suzanne's murder." Her voice broke as she said her sister's name. "I've closed out all my projects, active and prospective. Most understood when they heard the news. A couple pushed back, and I told them I wouldn't work with them again. They can go fuck themselves."

I smiled. "Why turn away future business?"

"I didn't like them much, anyway. I've always run my business my way. I have more projects than I can comfortably accommodate, so I can afford to be picky. Being good has its rewards."

"You could always expand…hire people who think like you. You'd be in control."

She shook her head. "Nice thought, but I like to work alone and to my capacity. I take the risks I want. It wouldn't be fair to put that on someone else, especially when lines get blurred."

I liked her even more. "So, what else did you decide?"

"Some technical stuff. I need more computing power, so I've reached out to some contacts. They'll help me get the hardware I need. We'll be getting deliveries in the next couple of days. Don't worry. It's all on me. You may see a spike in your electricity use. By the way, where were you? You weren't here when I got back, and Marie didn't know where you were."

"We have access to the investigation. We work with Kenzo's team only. I'm sure they'll keep information from me…us…but for the most part, they'll share. They need the manpower, and we have a head start on them. We'll keep the investigation on your sister, and they'll divvy up the other vics as they determine their IDs.

"I think we need to revisit Rant and follow up on Suzanne's kink friends. I don't think they're involved, but I do want to find the mysterious Asian man. He could be connected. I'll get everything they have so far by e-mail." I felt like an idiot, rambling on about process and what to do, insensitive to the fact she'd only been told hours before her sister had been murdered. "Sorry. That was thoughtless. Really sorry."

"Don't worry about me, Mas. I'm pretty tough. I'm pissed and angry and I want revenge…and I'm going to get it. I'll cry and grieve after I get him. Hopefully, it will be on his corpse." She said the last sentence with the same icy chill as earlier.

"Okay. If I step over the line, let me know."

She smirked and took a moment before she said anything. Then she asked, "Why did you suddenly decide to wear your chastity device?"

That took me by surprise. Mine wasn't noticeable under clothes, unless someone was looking and knew what to look for. I fought to keep my voice calm. "What makes you think I am?"

She guffawed. "Mas, I've been around the kink world for a long time. You're walking differently—and there's a difference in your crotch area. It's a bit fuller, which makes it more noticeable, if someone's looking. I look."

I wasn't giving in that easily. "I think your imagination is running wild."

"No. I think you're embarrassed to admit you're wearing one. Who's your key holder?"

Something must have reflected in my face.

"You don't have one, do you? You did this recently, and you still have access to the keys. Did you mail them to yourself? Or do you use a time-lock safe?"

Fess up time. She'd covered all the bases. "You asked me about confidentiality when we met. I gave you my commitment as a PI regarding anything and everything to do with the investigation. I am asking you to hold anything I say to you with the same confidentiality. I've already told you about my history with the police department. You're the only one, other than Simon, who knows most of the story." I let the silence hang, dropping my eyes to my feet.

"Trust me. I know how hard this life is. Whatever we talk about stays between us. I take that very seriously. I base my business on my reputation of keeping confidences. You don't have to tell me anything. I'm just curious. You intrigue me."

Oh, what the hell.

"Yes, I'm wearing a chastity device, and no, I don't have a key holder…yet."

Sophie fell silent for a long moment. "Thank you for your trust. I may not look it, but I'm not in a good place, and I need someone to trust and rely on. It looks like you volunteered to be that someone."

"I told you, you can confide in me. We'll get the bastard who killed your sister. I promise you."

"Why are you so sure?"

"I don't really know. It's a feeling I have. That doesn't mean it'll be easy. We'll need to be very careful. Serials are careful people. They're planners and typically, very smart. If they weren't, they'd get caught sooner."

Sophie changed the subject. "Have you received the file from your friends yet?"

I hadn't checked my computer since my return, and

my phone was on Do Not Disturb. I opened my computer to several new e-mails with .org tails.

Sophie almost pushed me out of the way as she sat in my chair and opened each one, sending it to her computer without reading it. "When we respond with our information on Suzanne, I'm going to add tags to the information we're sending to see who gets it and where it goes. You okay with that?"

"I guess so. Why?"

"You said they might not give you all the information we need. Well, when they open our e-mails, the tag will allow me to get into their computers and view what they have and what they aren't telling us."

"You mean…plant a virus?"

"Not really. It's not malicious, and it won't do any harm. They won't even know it's there. It's sort of an emergency door for us."

"Part of the blurred line?"

"Kinda. I don't trust people. Certainly, no government agency. I've had too many dealings with them. You aren't going to tell them, are you?"

"No. I'm not part of that club anymore. That was clear to me today. Being in that squad room made me realize it's a closed society. I'm an outsider. It was a crappy feeling in one sense, but liberating in another." I took a deep breath. "We'll dig and ask the awkward questions—stirring the pot—and hope someone remembers something. I need you to get anything and everything you can find on Rant. Something's there, and we need to find out what it is. After today, I don't really care how we do it, within reason. Fair enough?"

"Mas, I hope you know what you're doing. I'm

trusting you with my sister's murder."

That was an unusual twist. People usually said "life."

"First, we independently review all the info the PD sent. Make notes. Anything that triggers a thought put it down. We'll compare and see what we've missed, if anything. Don't scan. Read every word and try to get a feel for how it sounds."

We each retreated to our respective computers and dug in for the afternoon. I was used to reading police reports. God, were they dry, but the information was invaluable. The preliminary reports were just that—lots of holes to be filled in with new information

Marie put her head around the door and said goodnight.

Both Sophie and I absentmindedly responded and continued working. By 7:00 PM, I was done. I had a stack of notes. Most needed more information. I called it quits for the night. "We need sustenance. Leave everything as it is, and we'll start on each other's notes first thing."

"What exactly do you call 'first thing'?"

Ugh. I wasn't looking forward to this. "Let's say eight? Good enough?"

"If I can't sleep, I'll get here early and put the coffee on. Then you can play catch-up."

I didn't have much choice. "See you in the morning. We'll get you moved into Simon's place, later."

We left the office, and I immediately missed her presence. *Get a grip. She's a client.* I had my laptop with me, with all my notes on it, so she'd have to wait for me to start in the morning. I thought of her ass bent over in those tight jeans and her nipples pointing out of her tight top. I'd lay money she'd worn that top deliberately. My cock filled my cage.

I don't need this. At least, not yet.

Chapter 15

I hadn't exactly told Sophie the truth. I wasn't going to leave anything until the morning. Once home, I put on a pot of coffee and planned to work until the coffee was gone. I changed into sweat pants and a loose tee shirt, my cage reminding me of my condition. I contemplated removing it. *Nope*. I'd returned to the kinky track, and I wasn't going back. All the threads of my life now would be woven together…period.

I sat at my home desk and fired up the laptop, reviewed my notes, and rewrote some of them. I removed my police shorthand, expanding the explanations. The coffee pot slowly emptied and by the time it was drained, I felt exhausted—though I had made some progress.

A homicide investigation is like a jigsaw puzzle. Sometimes, you build a frame and work inward and sometimes you work inside out. In this case, it seemed it was both. Patience would be the key.

Looking at what we had, I could only see bits and pieces that would eventually form a picture. In order to get my teeth into the investigation, I needed the ID of the other vics, particularly the pair before Suzanne and her partner. I already had some leads to follow. I'd examined the cage photos from the police report and knew similar cages were used in BDSM dungeons. They were expensive pieces of equipment, almost a thousand dollars a pop, so the perp had financial resources.

I carefully rechecked the cage photos. They all looked identical to me. What use would one person have for four of them? An order for four would leave a trail, unless he'd purchased one and had fabricated the rest himself. If they were completely fabricated by the perp, they'd be almost impossible to trace. Anyone could buy the material, rent a welding rig, and assemble four cages, but that meant metalworking skills.

The combination of leaving both a male and a female in each cage was puzzling. A deliberate mislead? Who was the intended victim, the male or the female? Or both? Something bothered me. Was this a psychopath or simply someone pretending to be one?

God, this was frustrating. I needed more information. Hopefully, tomorrow would be more of an action day. I needed to get this case moving.

I shut the laptop down and went to bed.

****

My neighbor, hollering at her kids to get ready for school, along with a headache, woke me. I dragged myself into the shower to wake up. At least this way, I'd get to the office early.

The sun was coming up on one of those perfect San Franciscan days where I knew life was good whatever the day brought. I dressed for work and subconsciously chose a looser pair of pants, until I realized how loose they were. I returned them to the closet and picked out a tighter pair. *Screw it. I'm not ashamed of who I am.*

If Sophie liked to look at my caged cock today, she was in for a treat.

With these thoughts swirling in my head, my cock

85

started to fill, expanding in its metal prison. My erection rose. I wasn't sure how much of this I could take without releasing myself and enjoying a long, slow masturbation. I finished dressing and ran out the door.

Even though I was earlier than agreed, Sophie still beat me to the office. She was working on her computer when I walked in. She looked up and smiled.

"Good morning. Coffee is on. Being an East Coast girl, I was going to get bagels, but I wasn't sure where to go, so I hope this is okay."

I looked at the bag. To my surprise, it was from Liguria Bakery, known for their focaccia. How the hell had she known they had the best focaccia in San Francisco? "Who recommended Liguria? They're awesome."

She smiled. "I asked the desk at the hotel where to get good bagels. They looked at me like I was an alien. They said get some focaccia from Liguria and whoever it was for would thank me."

"Damn right." I ripped open the first bag. The fragrance was intoxicating.

Marie came in as I was pouring my coffee. I indicated the bag and her eyes widened. "What's the occasion? You rarely bring in breakfast."

"It wasn't me. Thank Sophie. It was her treat."

"How'd she find out about Liguria?"

"Hotel told her." I stuffed a piece into my mouth. This was turning out to be a great day.

We feasted on the wonderful Italian bread and washed it down with coffee. Now, I wanted to get going.

Sophie surprised me. "Mas, I went over your notes last night."

What the fuck? How'd she get my notes when I'd only done them last night? "All right. We need another come-to-Jesus moment. How'd you get my notes? I just finished them last night. Did you hack my computer?"

"No, I wouldn't do that. I allowed myself access so whenever you worked on it, I'd get the same info. You're very through and analytical. I'm impressed."

"Fuck that. You said you wanted to trust someone and I was it, but how do I trust you now? It's not how I work. You pull this shit again, and we're done. I'll still find out who killed your sister—I gave you my word and I'll keep it—but not with you anywhere near me. Got that? Screw your need for control. We do this together, or get the hell out now. Your choice." God, I was pissed!

My explosion seemed to take her off guard. "Sorry, Mas. I wanted to work on everything all at once. The sooner we get the information, the sooner we can catch him. I didn't think you'd be that upset."

Upset was an understatement. "What don't you get about working together? You don't need to pull this shit. You're paying me. I'm on your side."

She deflated. "I gave us time to refresh our minds. It's a process and I know the process. I guarantee you missed something because you were tired and hadn't had the chance to step back and look at the whole picture."

I was still fuming. "What's your answer? I want it now. Do we work by my rules, or are you gone?"

Subdued, she leaned back in her chair. "Your rules."

"Are you sure? Because there is no next time. I'll dump you as a client, and you'll be out of here."

She looked like she was about to cry. I didn't buy that, either. "Okay, Mas. Your rules, I promise. I don't break my word, once it's given."

I retreated a little. "Your notes. I want to see your notes."

Life flashed into her eyes. "They're in your inbox. I sent them earlier. Oh, and l like your tight jeans. You bulge in them well." She said it with a smile.

She's going to drive me completely crazy before we're done. "Thank you. Now, go back and review my notes, and make sure you read everything. If you need clarification, ask."

"Really? You think I missed something?"

"Well, we won't know until you've been through it all again. Will we?"

Sullen, Sophie went back to her laptop while I opened mine and brought up her file. It was well organized. I read through her comments. She'd been very thorough, analyzing in a logical progression. Her work felt detached, almost cold. I wondered if this was her way of distancing herself from the facts related to her sister. She didn't seem like a cold person to me. Only time would tell.

We had reached similar conclusions on much of the information. I still had the suspicion we were being played. People don't like change, and killers usually stick to one technique of killing, but the report said there were several methods. Troy, the male in the first couple, was too decomposed to identify how he'd been killed. His hyoid bone wasn't broken, so the chances of strangulation were slim to none.

Sophie hadn't realized the other body found with her sister was an Asian male. The ME postulated from the facial bone structure, he was likely Japanese. Was he the mystery man Suzanne had been seen with at the Cauldron? I hoped this wasn't related to the kink community. This case was hard enough without a serial killer targeting kinksters.

The perp was statistically male, for several reasons. It would be very hard for a female to manage those cages, especially with the dead weight of two bodies inside. Moving that much weight would be difficult for even a strong male. This had to be two perps? Maybe a couple? Maybe each perp had selected his or her own gender. Or maybe the opposite one. That could explain the vic's selection—couple on couple. A couple, each working on an individual would be even easier.

I made a mental note to either refine or discard that theory as we went along. I was a big believer in following the evidence wherever it took me.

Sophie had done a great job with her notes and analysis. *Must be her background.* As I finished her work, she said, "I don't think I missed anything. There are a lot of pieces and most aren't connecting. As I say in my world, need more data."

"I agree, for the most part. I suspect the male found with your sister was the Asian she was talking to at the Cauldron. Let's hope he's been reported missing so we get an ID and can work it from there."

"How did you come to that conclusion?"

"Only a theory. She was seen talking to an Asian man the night she disappeared then turns up dead with an Asian man next to her. Coincidence? Don't think so." As I was talking, an email arrived from Kenzo's team. I waved Sophie over and opened it.

Two more victims had been identified, Helga

Braun and Jack Mellon. They'd been the third dump. There wasn't much information attached—names and addresses, not much else. Kenzo assigned Jack to us because he was from the peninsula. They took Helga, a SF resident.

I noted the address in Redwood City. "Road trip. First, we'll move you from your hotel to Simon's place. Then, on to Redwood City and Jack's apartment. Last, we can annoy Mr. Lying VP at Rant."

Chapter 16

We headed to Sophie's hotel. Checking out didn't take long, then we went to Simon's apartment.

"Let's drop my stuff. I can unpack later."

I gave her Simon's set of keys. Thankfully, it was a quick visit, too quick for me to get maudlin.

The drive was the usual stop and start, though it could've been worse.

"Do you want to stop at your sister's house?" I'd give her the option.

"Not really much point is there?" she asked with a shrug. She changed her mind and said, "Actually, yes. On my own, okay?"

"Sure. No problem." I wondered what that was all about, especially after what I'd said about being open and trusting. Guess I'd have to trust her, and I wanted to trust her. I parked on the street outside Suzanne's place, staying in the car watching Sophie hesitantly opening the front door.

My mind wandered to what Suzanne might have been like—her laugh, what she liked to eat, her taste in music. I wanted to put a personality to the victim, it made working the case easier-sometimes.

When Sophie returned, she was carrying a sports bag in one hand. In the other, she waved a plastic baggie with what looked like a bunch of flash drives inside...if "bunch" was the correct term for multiple flash drives.

"What did you find?"

She turned toward me, her face flushed. She was clearly excited. "I haven't been thinking clearly since finding out she'd been murdered. But I know my sister. The deleted files didn't make sense. She was obsessive about details and kept immaculate records—had every tax return she'd ever done. I was missing something, so I poked around. Not in the obvious places. She was more creative than that."

"So, where'd you find them?"

"Laundry room. There were two open boxes of dryer sheets, the first one half empty and the second one was full. That didn't make sense. So I dug around in the fuller of the two. Nothing. But under the contents of the used one, I found a baggie containing these flash drives. I'd bet she has a safe deposit box somewhere too."

"What do you expect to find?"

"No idea. Guaranteed a lot of useless stuff, but we might find some answers." She examined the flash drives more closely. They were all labeled, some with work labels. She pulled out her laptop.

"Do you go anywhere without your computer?"

"The shower."

"Very funny."

Her fingers raced over the keyboard. "Seriously, when they make a waterproof one, I'll take it in there, too. My computer is my work...my lifeline to everything I do. Sorry. You'll just have to deal with it."

I concentrated on driving to Jack Mellon's apartment. It was basically the next town down the peninsula from Suzanne's. All the cities on the peninsula ran into each other. Only the city limit signs and the change in numbers on the businesses indicated one from another. Jack's apartment building wasn't in the best neighborhood, but it was more seedy than dangerous.

Sophie was so engrossed in her laptop, she didn't notice when I parked. Her head shot up as I closed my door. "Hey. Wait for me!" She did something on her computer, put it back in her bag, and tossed it over her shoulder. "What are we doing here? We don't have a key or warrant."

"You really want to wait here until a warrant arrives?"

"No, but are you okay with this? Won't we be breaking some law or something?"

"Yes, but like I said, I'm not in that club anymore." Thinking about her question for a split second, I said, "Fuck it. Let's go."

"How are we going to get in? We don't have a key."

"Not an official key, but it works."

Thankfully, Jack's apartment was partially hidden by an overgrown shrub on the far end of the building. I pulled out my key gun, examined the door and dead locks, then I noticed a more secure lock above the other two. Interesting. I wondered why this door had three locks, while the other doors had the standard two. This was going to be more challenging than I'd thought, but not impossible. "Keep an eye out and stand so you hide me."

She shielded my actions. "This is the first time I've physically broken into a place. It's exciting. What happens if we get caught?"

"Shut up and let me work." The deadbolt locks were easy to open. The third took longer than I planned. Just as the lock clicked and I swung the door open, Sophie whispered that someone was coming.

Together we almost fell into the apartment, closing the door quickly and quietly. We shrank behind it, holding our breath. Nothing. We released the breaths we'd been holding and took in our surroundings.

Sophie began to enter the apartment, but I put a hand on her arm to stop her. "Here. Put these on." I handed her a pair of latex gloves.

"Do you always carry gloves?"

"No, but I have them in the car, just in case. Always take a good look around before you do anything. Observe how things look. Taking a place in can tell you a lot about a person. It's info we can use. What do you see?"

Sophie stopped and scanned the apartment working the room in a logical manner. It was an open plan— living room, kitchen, small dining area that led to a small deck at the back. It was only one bedroom, with a bathroom leading off a small corridor to the right, enough for one person or a couple starting out. "What do you see?"

"It's really small. One person, obviously male, which we knew."

"How do you know it's only one person?"

"If there were two, he would've been reported missing. Plus, there are no photos of anyone, male or female. Almost no personal items at all. He wasn't going to be here for the long haul. The dining room has been set up as an office, so probably few, if any, friends. I'd say he was a loner. Even from here, I can see his computer set up is expensive and elaborate. He was no amateur. So, how'd I do, Mr. Detective?"

"It used to be inspector, not detective. Not bad. You missed that the place has been turned over. 'Thoroughly searched,' if you want an exact term."

"How can you tell?"

"Look at the furniture. There are marks indicating the pieces haven't been put back exactly in the same places. Everything I see indicates a left-handed person, but the TV remote is on the right. Plus, this place is too clean for someone who's been missing for two plus months. Someone has been in here since Jack went missing. Do you see a laptop anywhere?"

Sophie looked pissed. "How'd I miss all that?"

I laughed. "Easy. Experience. You still picked up on a lot of stuff, and I wouldn't have known about the computer system. I would've assumed he was a computer nerd or gamer."

"Oh, no. This is major equipment. No amateur hour here. He had to be experienced to put that together. This didn't come from any local box store. It wasn't as expensive as it used to be, but it was still a sizable investment."

After we'd looked over what we could see, we moved into the apartment.

Sophie went directly to the computer and switched on the power. Lots of little lights sparkled.

I left her to what she knew, and I looked around for...anything odd or out of place. Checking the kitchen, nothing of interest. In the fridge, some food had turned, confirmation that Jack hadn't been here for a while. Whoever broke in had been searching for something specific. It had been much too thorough and clean for a chance ransack. I'd bet no fingerprints would be found.

Nothing popped until I hit the bedroom. The bed was a sturdy, heavy, metal-framed affair with a vertical frame on the foot end of the bed. It had holes and eye bolts to attach things…or people. That got my attention. I made a methodical search of his bedside nightstand. Nothing of interest—a flashlight and a switchblade. The closet revealed a selection of jeans, some designer brands. *Interview jeans*? He also had a multitude of graphic T-shirts and a series of garment bags pushed against one end of the closet. They were all open. Searched? Probably.

They each contained a different outfit. He was quite the chameleon—staid, young, preppy businessman, sharp, Italian-suited entrepreneur, and more. Six in all.

I peeked under the bed and found a large, soft bag. It felt heavy. Slipping the zipper open. I was right. Most had been carefully placed in separate bags—butt plugs, cock rings, vibrators, and all sorts of kink toys. He had several paddles, and crops of different weights. Leather—ankle and wrist cuffs, and a stiff posture collar, all lockable. So, Jack was also into the sub side of the BDSM lifestyle. A connection or a coincidence?

I called out to Sophie. "Any chance you can get into his computer's hard drive?"

She came into the bedroom and saw what I had laid out. "Mas, you're so romantic, but now's not the time to play."

My look made her giggle, the first happy giggle I'd heard from her.

"Sorry. I needed to relieve the stress. I've never

done the breaking and entering thing before. Is this all Jack's stuff?"

"Well, it's not mine."

"Touché."

"So he was into BDSM. I don't think he was a top. What do you think?"

"Agreed. Back to your question about his computer. Whoever was here took his hard drive, and I can't find a backup anywhere. What do we do now?"

One thing I knew was that computer geeks always backed things up, usually in more than one way or place. "Let's look at this from his point of view. How would you back stuff up?"

"Probably the cloud or external hard drive, depending on what it was and how big it was. Maybe flash drives, too, though I didn't find any. Either he didn't use them or they've been taken."

"Hmm. Where would I hide things I didn't want people to know about?" I headed back to the dining room and scanned his desk. I went through all the drawers on the left and under his desk. Definitely a leftie. As I expected, no paper, not even a sticky pad. Jack was a child of Silicon Valley and he did everything electronically, even notes. "Do you notice anything unusual about the work station?"

She looked at it for several minutes. "No. What did I miss?"

"You didn't understand what you were looking at because it's not unusual. Any paper on his desk or in the drawers?"

"No. He worked electronically. Lots of us do. Some, exclusively. Why?"

"Then why would he have a mug full of pens next

to his desk?"

"No reason at all."

"Exactly. You expect to see pens on a desk, so when they're there, you don't notice them. I think we just found his flash drives."

Sophie lunged for the mug, taking out the first pen. It was a flash drive. The next pen was a real pen. She sorted through the pens discovering several flash drives with no identifying labels.

We put the pens back and high-fived each other. Someone had taken his laptop, phone, and hard drive, but they'd missed the flash drives. We were lucky.

I returned Jack's collection of equipment to where I'd found it. Being into BDSM, Jack was probably on KinkInc. We needed to uncover his online name.

The easiest, way was to look at all the subs and switches in Redwood City on KinkInc and compare the profile images with the vic's picture. Even if the faces were blurred out, the background in the image could tell us a lot about who Jack was online. If we discovered who his friends were, we could create more leads.

I considered this a successful visit. I'd pass on the BDSM info to Kenzo's team as a possible connection between the vics.

Chapter 17

The set of keys I found in the kitchen worked in the door. This would make it easier if we had to return. We climbed into the car, and I weighed whether we should put off the visit to Rant Applications until we'd reviewed the flash drives we'd found. They could have important information that would give us leverage, or point us in the right direction for our questions. "Sophie, how long do you need to get into all those flash drives?"

"Why the rush?"

I chose my words carefully. "They might have information that could give us an edge when we talk to Rant. If we go in knowing nothing, they'll sense it and blow us off. If we have hidden cards in our hand, that gives us an edge."

She nodded. "Makes sense. I can breeze through my sister's, even if she has them password protected. Jack's, on the other hand, could be an issue. It will depend on how good his skills are. I can do it, but it might take longer than you want. It's the best I can offer."

"Don't worry. It's a plan. Suzanne's drives first, then Jack's. I'll let Kenzo's team know about the BDSM connection and see if any others had KinkInc accounts. I'll figure out if Jack was on KinkInc and find his user name. That sound like a plan?"

"Yes. No problem. I'll start on Suzanne's as soon as we get back to the office."

I put in a call in to Kenzo. He was out, and I was transferred to Josie. I told her, "We're digging into the information you sent over. I have a call into Suzanne's work place. I'll follow up on that.

"Anything else?" It seemed like she wanted me off the phone as quickly as possible.

"Yes. Would you check to see if any the others had accounts on a site called KinkInc?"

"Uh, sure. I'll look into it." She disconnected with a click.

"Was that normal? She didn't sound happy to hear from you."

"She came after my time, so she doesn't know me. She probably resents that I—or we—are involved with the investigation. Not our problem. Besides, we have a back door, right?" I smiled and she laughed.

"Yes, we do." The drive back into the city was slow. She was silent, engrossed in her work. My mind wandered. I wondered what it would be like to be her submissive and how much control would she want or need, letting my imagination run free. I imagined being under her control and wondered how long she would keep my cock locked up. I didn't think she'd be quick in letting me out for a release. In fact, the thought of her being strict with me made my cock fill. The confinement wasn't uncomfortable, but I had to wriggle in my seat to ease the pinching.

It dawned on me how much I'd missed being involved with the kink community. Missing the release of being in a D/s relationship. My thoughts moved from my cock to Sophie. She was an attractive woman…smart and driven. I still didn't know much about her, but I wondered what she looked for in her kink relationships. It couldn't hurt to have that conversation. I'd just have to be careful about the timing.

As soon as I parked. Sophie was out the door and off to the office without a word

Marie looked up when I entered. "There are a bunch of boxes for Sophie. I signed for everything. I hope everything is okay. The delivery guys were a bit sketchy."

I'd forgotten to tell Marie about the stuff Sophie had ordered. "Yeah, I am sure it will be okay. If not, Sophie will take care of it. How much stuff was delivered?"

"Three different deliveries. One guy looked like he should be in San Q. The other two didn't look old enough to drive. They took everything into your office. They didn't want me to help. When I asked for the invoice, they said they had been e-mailed to Circe Cyber Security. Who's that?"

"I think that's Sophie's business back East."

I peeked into my office. Boxes without labels were piled up. Sophie was checking them and rearranging them to her liking.

"Need a hand?"

She waved me over. "Yes, but only your muscles to restack the boxes. I want to be sure it's all correct before I unpack everything."

For the next twenty minutes, Sophie instructed, and I rearranged the boxes. Finally satisfied, she said, "Now, I can unpack and put this lot together."

"Okay. I'm going to look for Jack's kink life

account." Retreating to my desk, I logged onto the KinkInc site, choosing Redwood City, the listings popped up in indiscriminate order. I hated that KinkInc didn't have filters.

Eliminating all female profiles, I scanned all the males, ignoring those outside the age range and all Doms. I opened each sub or switch profile, looking for Jack Mellon. Many profiles had images rather than photographs. I went into each profile, looking at all the pictures. Some had selfies and play-party photos. I groaned when I saw Redwood City had seventeen pages of twenty-four profiles each. A lot would be female, which would reduce the search number, but still left plenty to investigate.

Click, scan. Click, scan. I worked my way methodically down each page. As I worked, I became efficient at trolling the profiles, looking for clues.

Sophie was having a great time, ripping open boxes and unpacking. The office began to look like a tornado hit it. Occasionally, I'd hear a curse and a finger being sucked.

My attention refocused on scanning and clicking. I made it through eleven pages before I took a break. "Do you want anything?"

"No." The answer came from behind a tower of metal and wires. That was enough for me to go to the outer office.

Marie chuckled. "Sounds like she's building a monster in there."

"Close enough. I need to give my eyes a rest." I stretched and closed my eyes for a few minutes, then went back to the chore at hand.

Page thirteen. Bingo! The same bed frame and

nightstand I'd seen in Jack's apartment. I knew there was more than one bedframe like it, but in the same city? Doubtful.

I examined the photo. The person spread-eagled across the frame was a white male. His head was covered with a hood, so I couldn't determine hair color. His stature matched Jack's from the police report. I looked for anything I could us to identify him as Jack Mellon, but the image was too small to be certain.

Looking at other photos from the same session I found a closer shot of his back. Four moles in a line on his left shoulder. If it was Jack and the moles had survived the stay in the Bay, I'd have an identification. The profile name seemed to fit. Code Switch. His friends list was short. I scanned the profile names—a mix of subs, doms, and switches. Then I called Sophie over to get her take on what I'd found.

Grudgingly, she left what she was doing and looked at my screen. Her eyes lit up when she saw what I pointed out.

"That has to be Jack. Where does that get us?"

"I'm not sure yet. We talk to his friends. They may be able to help us figure out exactly when he disappeared and who he was in contact with at the time. How are you making out?"

She looked over to her growing electronic chaos. "It's going well. I haven't built anything for a while, so it's taking longer than I thought. When I have it running, I'll go through my sister's flash drives and have a go at Jack's. I'll need some decompression after that. There's a party at Sorcerer's tonight. Wanna go?"

Where'd that come from? Sophie seemed to be able to switch from one subject to another without a blink.

"I'll think about it."

"Scared to be seen in public with me? I won't bite…unless you ask me nicely."

Earlier, I'd resolved to get back into the community. Now, I had my chance to put up or shut up. "Okay. We'll go."

She gave me a pouty look. "Don't be so enthusiastic. I might get the idea you actually *want* to go."

"Sorry. You seem to change direction so easily. You catch me off guard."

"Well, here's another direction. Bring your cage keys."

I raised an eyebrow. "What are you up to?"

"Guess you'll have to wait and see…*if* you have the balls to bring them."

With that challenge, of course I would bring the keys. Although my anxiety level immediately rose. My dick filled the cage. God, how I wanted to come. As soon as the thought entered my head, I needed a release.

She must've read my mind. "Of course, you *could* spoil everything and jerk off before tonight's fun. Would you do that?"

Like an idiot, I said, "No. I wouldn't do that."

She laughed. "Let me get back to work so I can clear up Suzanne's stuff."

I wondered what I'd gotten myself into.

She was already back working on her computer construction. She pushed the boxes and packaging out of the way and flipped the switch. I heard buzzing, and lights flashed on and off. Sophie surprised me by asking for a bucket of water.

"What do you need that for? I didn't think water

and computers were compatible?"

"This is a water-cooled system. When I work for long spells, water keeps the system cool. I'll need to test everything and then I can start working efficiently."

Marie had overheard the conversation. "I'll get it," she hollered from the reception area.

I went back to screening Jack's online friends' profiles. They were all local to San Francisco or on the peninsula. The furthest was in San Jose, the closest in Redwood City. I pulled up Code Switch's friends. I followed the same process as before. Some had hundreds of images. *Don't these people have anything better to do?*

When my eyes started to hurt, I called the ME's office and left a message for her assistant to check for moles on Jack Mellon's back. That would confirm the profile.

Getting through all his friends' profiles without going blind, I didn't glean much from them. Most seemed to have been in the kink community for some time. There were lots of Folsom Street Fair photos, the San Francisco annual leather and kink festival. I told Sophie what I had and hadn't found, and that I was going home. "See you at Sorcerer's."

"Fine. Don't be late."

Chapter 18

The first thing I did when I got home was retrieve the keys to my chastity cage. I knew what they represented to my past, but I wasn't sure what they meant to my present or for my future. Was I ready to move into a kinky future? I'd thought so, until Sophie had caught me off guard with her request.

My cell phone interrupted my reverie. I recognized the strong voice as another of my contacts I'd asked to check on Sophie. "Thanks for getting back to me. Do you have anything?"

"Of course. Why'd ya think I am calling you?" Connie always had a sharp tongue. "I got to make this quick. Sophie Chandler is a careful person with a miniscule footprint. She has a good cyber reputation. She's worked with all sorts of people, including very official entities, all sorts of initials that probably don't officially exist, and with some not-so-official folks. But it's all rumor—nothing concrete. If the rumors are true, there have been a few downright dangerous people in the mix. Be careful, Mas. She has a reputation for being loyal to whoever is paying her, and she never betrays a contract. She's rumored to have done some major projects and become wealthy in the process. Again, nothing even close to being verifiable. Only crumbs on her personal life. She has an office in Philadelphia, but it's really a front—a plaque on a wall in a shared office.

No marriage license. Her driver's license address is the office. There were some suggestions, but no confirmation, that she's into kinky sex. She's got one small business account here in the States, based in Delaware. Conclusion is she mostly uses offshore accounts. Tax returns are a mystery. She lives off the grid as much as I've ever seen. Bottom line, Sophie Chandler is trustworthy and loyal to her own set of rules, dangerous to others. Hope that helps."

"Hey, Connie. I really appreciate this."

Her response was immediate. "I know Mas, and now we're even."

"Okay, Connie, we're even. But if you ever need anything, don't hesitate to call."

"Thanks." She disconnected.

Another bridge up in flames, and I didn't even know why. Everything she'd told me about Sophie matched what I'd observed. I was good at reading people, but Sophie was as difficult as anyone I'd seen. Tonight, I'd need to have a conversation with her…and a negotiation. Perhaps, she'd be less guarded in the kink environment.

I'd trust my intuition, which was to trust her, at least until her sister's murder was resolved.

Making dinner was an easy affair. It's called take-out. I ate, even though I didn't feel like it. I was thinking about Simon, and about moving Sophie into his old apartment, soon to be mine. It had reawakened memories.

Trying to push those conflicting thoughts to the back of my mind, I got ready for the night. I had no intention of playing at Sorcerer's, so I dressed in my usual dungeon black, head to toe. I picked up the chastity keys, weighed them in my hand, and put them in my pocket, but then thought better of it. Pulling them back out, I removed them from the plain ring. I rummaged through my office drawers and found what I'd been seeking—a key ring made from a bullet, one shot from my old PD weapon. It was the last tangible memento from that time. This would be a good use for it. I added the two keys and put it back in my pocket.

Sorcerer's was farther than the Cauldron, though still an easy location. I loved my city's activity. It was always buzzing at night. It reminded me of Europe, with its sidewalk cafes, people meeting and conversing, and laid-back energy. Moving through the crowd, listening to the laughter and the ebb and flow of chatting people. I liked the energy.

The front desk at Sorcerer's was covered by someone I didn't know. Paying the entrance fee, I entered the familiar layout. Nothing had changed since my last visit, and that felt comfortable. The interior was brightly lit in the social area, with subdued, cozy lighting in the play area. It was still early to be so busy. I had to wait for my drink. The bar-person recognized me and mouthed a hello as she made my drink. I responded in kind.

Most of the seating had been taken. The usual mixture of couples, threesomes, groups of friends, and individuals not attached to anyone floated from group to group. The play area was efficiently laid out, allowing multiple players to have scenes at the same time.

The dungeon monitor was someone I knew—also an ex-cop—a top known as Big-Boots. He used to be a motorcycle officer with knee-high black leather boots, which he always wore. He claimed they were "comfortable." He saw me and came over with arms wide open. He was a hugger and a gentle giant.

"How's it going, Mas? I heard about Simon. I'm sorry, he was good folks. Haven't seen you around for a while. Everything okay?"

Seeing him brought back memories of the first time I'd come to Sorcerer's—good memories.

"Yes, for the most part. Still working as a PI. Sort of coming around after Simon's death. It's been a slow process. You'd think it would be easier as we've pretty much seen it all, but it isn't."

"No shit, brother."

As we talked, I scanned the people in the play area. Belatedly, I realized Sophie was one of them. She'd been facing away from me when Big-Boots had come over. Now, she was looking straight at me. I stared back. She smiled and went back to paddling the ass of a willing supplicant. If Big-boots had been talking, I hadn't heard a word.

He nudged me. "She's a cutie. First time here, apparently. Got here early and put herself about. Certainly not a wallflower. In good shape, too. This is her second session. She sure knows what she is doing."

Where did she get her equipment? Then, I remembered the bag she'd taken from her sister's house.

Sophie was wearing a corset, different from the one I'd seen her wear at the Cauldron. This one was made in gold brocade. It looked almost too small for her, though it covered her tits. Her sister must've been a similar size, just a tad smaller in the boobage. Sophie's were in danger of spilling out. The fit enhanced her already-fine figure into an hourglass. Modestly, she wore loose, wide-legged black pants over the bottom half of the corset. They ended halfway down her lower leg. What I could see of her legs were encased in hose. I'd bet money they were stockings. Her feet were encased in high-heeled black patent pumps, a flexible shoe, easily used for business and pleasure.

She swung the paddle with a practiced hand— accurately and with superb control. I almost laughed aloud at that thought. *Of course she had control.* She played with the woman strapped to the spanking bench, elevating her anticipation with every slap of the flexible paddle. I was transfixed.

From across the room, I noted the tendrils that escaped her tied-back hair were stuck to her neck. She was working her own body, as well as the one in front of her.

The restrained woman's ass and thighs glowed a rosy pink, which deepened as I watched. As Sophie continued to work, the pink turned to red. The woman pulled against her restraints and cried out for permission to come.

Sophie denied her, using her time well, and backed the woman off, relaxing her frustration, then slowly building her back up, caressing her with the paddle, the instrument of torment and pleasure.

Within minutes, the woman was openly begging for release.

Sophie relented and brought the restrained woman to a shuddering orgasm with a flurry of light, stinging smacks. When the recipient was spent, Sophie released her and took a robe, handed to her by the woman's partner. Sophie helped her stand and steadied her, wrapping her snugly. She lightly kissed her on the forehead and released her into the arms of her partner, who thanked her.

Sophie thanked one of the dungeon servants for cleaning and sanitizing the bench and walked over to where I was waiting for her. She looked relaxed and euphoric. "I feel so much better now, and I still have one more scene to go…unless you'd like to volunteer as a fourth?"

"No, thank you," I said quietly.

"Oh, come on, Mas. Where's your sense of adventure? You won't know if you like it unless you try it."

"What makes you think I haven't tried it? And lots of *its*? You don't know me, yet."

"Yet. I like that. Bodes well for the future. I like yet. It's a positive."

"You seem to have warmed up. Would you like a drink?"

"Yes, I would. Whatever you brought me the other night would be nice. I'll walk with you. My next appointment is working a kitchen shift until ten, so we have some time to chat."

That she'd found three people and negotiated scenes with them in such a short time surprised me. Pick-up play was not usually that easy for an unknown such as Sophie/Circe.

Returning to the bar, I got her drink. Sophie found two seats, though not as private as I would've liked, but in this environment, there were few secrets.

I handed her the drink. "You never cease to surprise me. I must say, you look beautiful. I assume your equipment is from Suzanne's house?"

"Yes, and this corset. I brought minimal wardrobe with me. I didn't know how long I'd be staying. I knew the SF scene was more open than that on the East Coast and wanted to explore it while I had the chance."

"And now?"

She looked puzzled. "And now, what?"

"How long do you expect to stay?"

"I don't know. Certainly as long as it takes to find whoever killed my sister." Her tone had turned frigid; she could turn it on or off at will.

"Sorry. Didn't mean to bring up that subject tonight."

"It's okay, Mas. I compartmentalize well, disconcertingly so, at times. Tonight, I need to relax and recuperate...get my batteries recharged. I enjoy BDSM activity and need to do it."

"I understand that better than you realize."

She nodded. "Believe me, I do understand. I recognized something in you the minute I met you. You have an inner strength. It takes more courage and strength to be a submissive than a Dominant. I couldn't do it...wouldn't want to. Which leads us nicely into my next question."

I asked it for her. "Did I bring my keys?"

She smiled. "Your keys? No. Did you bring THE keys to the *chastity cage*?"

Now that the question was out in the open, my breath felt hot and my chest clenched. This was how I'd felt when I'd handed over the keys to my previous key holder.

"Yes, I brought the keys to the chastity cage." My cock responded to the predatory look on Sophie's face. *By bringing the keys, I'd subconsciously agreed to whatever she asked of me. Otherwise, why would I have brought them?*

Sophie grinned. "Well, that's a good start. Let's decide where we go from here."

I wasn't going to make this easy for her. "Bringing them doesn't mean I'll hand them over without negotiation and some safeguards."

"I would expect no less. After all, you're submissive, not stupid."

"Thank you. So…what's your offer?"

She laughed and snuggled up next to me. "Oh, it's not going to be that easy, Mas. You must ask me to be your key holder."

I looked at her sharply. She was serious. An excitement rose inside me, one I hadn't felt for a long time. I wanted to serve this woman—a woman I hardly knew. Intuition made me trust her with the kink side of my life. Feeling as if a weight had been lifted off me.

"Are you all right, Mas?"

I was more than all right. A feeling of euphoria swept over me. Getting the chastity keys out of my pocket, I knelt in front of her. "Sophie, would you be my key holder?"

I'd surprised her, and it showed on her face. Her brow furrowed, questioning my sincerity. She scanned my face, then accepted my request. "That is not the name I choose for this life. Forgetting that will negatively impact you."

"I understand, Circe. Please, would you be my key holder?"

She lifted me up from my knees and sat me back down beside her. "Your gesture was a surprise. I wasn't sure you were sincere. I believe you are, and for that, I thank you." She leaned over and kissed me.

Feeling her kiss burn, I trembled at what was to come. My cock was dripping pre-cum, and I was horny. Watching the night's activities and the result of my interactions with Sophie/Circe had me wound up, ready to come at the slightest provocation. I was an idiot not to have masturbated before coming here, and I regretted it.

She noticed the play of emotions on my face. "We have a lot to discuss before I accept your keys."

We spent the next forty minutes negotiating the terms of our new relationship—our responsibilities and the rules of engagement, as it were. We both agreed up-front this was a separate life from our work life, and it needed to remain so. The discussion went back and forth. We kept at it until we were both satisfied.

"Deal. You may kneel and formally ask Circe to be your key holder until further notice. I will send you an electronic copy of our agreement. After all, it will be a living document."

We both knew what that meant. She smiled an open, happy smile, and I liked the way it looked on her.

Kneeling in front of her, my eyes lowered, I took the keys in both hands, palms up. "Circe, I'm formally asking you if you would honor me by being my key holder, as agreed."

"Mas, I accept your keys as per our agreement. You may kiss my feet as a gesture of your acceptance."

I felt her lift the keys from my palms, which were now moist. They weighed next to nothing, but my hands suddenly felt lighter. Placing my hands flat on the floor, I leaned forward and kissed the tips of Circe's high-heeled pumps. A few of the other guests had heard the exchange and were applauding us. That brought me back to reality. I blushed.

The feeling was a release. I was home, and wherever Circe and I went it was right, and I knew it.

She had me sit next to her, and the next thing I saw were the keys to my cage, dangling from a chain around her neck. My eyes fixated on them, the keys just hanging there, down her cleavage, between her, pushed-up, corseted, overflowing tits.

I groaned.

That brought a full-throated laugh from her. "Too late to back out now. I'll be a good and caring key holder. Never fear. We'll have fun with this. Are you feeling horny, by any chance?"

"Yes, Circe. I already was, and promising you I wouldn't jerk off made it worse."

That brought more laughter. "I'm pleased you kept your word. That means a lot to me. You will get your rewards, at my choosing. After all, you know my need for control." Her face flashed serious, then cleared. "Time for my next whipping boy. Care to participate?"

"No. I'm good."

"Are you sure? One never knows how generous I might be after three go-rounds of physical exertion. I might need another form of relaxation."

I was torn between the promise of a maybe and the reality of having my ass paddled by someone I was working for. I was going to have to resolve this issue soon. "I'm sure."

"Your loss." She left to find her next willing ass.

I stayed in the bar, working through our agreement in my mind. I was both nervous and excited. My cock had filled the cage to bursting, and it felt good.

I made my way back to the play area, looking for Sophie. She was in the process of strapping a man down to the spanking bench. They were talking. I assumed they'd already negotiated the scene and were getting into their roles. Watching her was interesting. She worked quickly and efficiently, obviously experienced with dungeon equipment. Not many watched as the scene hadn't started yet, and there was plenty to occupy everyone's attention. I was sure she'd soon be the center of attention again.

As the scene developed, more curious guests started watching. Sophie had strapped him so that his knees supported him, pushing his ass out as an easy target, and allowing her access to his cock and balls, while keeping them away from the paddle. She played with the man, teasing his cock and warming his ass with strikes designed to get his attention, not to mark him up. She spread her blows across his exposed ass and thighs. His balls were tight and his cock filled to an erection, which Sophie kept in a state of rigidity. The physicality of landing her controlled paddle slaps had her breathing more heavily than before.

The man enjoyed every stinging blow. His ass and thighs rapidly changed color.

Intermittently, Sophie stopped and worked the man's cock like she was milking a cow, without release, then returning to heat up his ass with her paddle. When she was satisfied with the color of his flesh, she went back to milking him, stopping before his release. When he begged her for an orgasm, she leaned in and said something to him.

She exchanged her paddle for a crop. She landed her first blow heavily across the widest part of his rouged ass.

He jerked away.

She allowed each blow to register.

He cried out at each strike's stinging pain and begged her for a release.

After landing ten vicious blows that left welts across both ass cheeks, she stopped, lubed up her hand, and grasped his dick. She manipulated him, slowly at first, then picked up speed. He screamed for permission to come.

Sophie finally acquiesced. The man jerked forward as far as he could, shooting his cum onto the bench under him. The lines of cum made long, glossy, wet streaks on the vinyl bench. She continued to milk him until he begged her to stop.

Sophie released him from the bench, steadying him as he stood. He sank to his knees, thanking her. He shakily stood again, and his partner took him away. The dungeon servants quickly cleaned up the bench and sanitized it for the next occupant.

Sophie looked tired. I went over to her to congratulate her on a good scene. "Well done, but why didn't you go with them for aftercare? Everyone I know does it, and it's what's always happened to me."

She looked at me sadly. "You didn't do much pick-up play, did you?"

"No, not really. If I did, it was with someone I knew. Why?"

"If the person has a partner or close friend, it means more than with a stranger. I didn't know any of them before tonight. It makes more sense that someone they have a deeper relationship with cares for them. My relationship is, at best, a couple of hours old." She sounded mournful, something I hadn't heard before.

"Are you all right?"

She perked up. "Yes. I've just never found the right person for a committed relationship. While I really enjoy the pick-up play—it releases and relaxes me— I'm still looking for the relationship my sister had. She worked at it and usually found partners who meshed well with her. While most didn't last, a couple lasted a while, and her last one lasted almost four years. I've never made it that far. I think it's my fault. Maybe, I want too much control or I'm not willing to risk myself like she did. Look at me, rambling on. I think you're taking advantage of my weakened condition, Mas."

Smiling, I said, "I don't think you're ever in a weakened condition. Let's get you back to Simon's— your place." It was hard having her in Simon's house. Damn. Grieving was so hard. I guess that's what makes us human—the more we care, the more we hurt.

I flagged a cab and gave him the address. This had turned out to be an interesting evening…at least, my cock certainly thought so. I dropped Sophie off at Simon's, then went home to my empty apartment, slightly regretting not accepting Sophie's offer to play tonight. I just wasn't ready for that. Close, but not quite.

Chapter 19

The next day, I considered it a victory beating her into the office, though not by much. We chatted briefly, catching up on our separate tasks. I continued looking into Jack's friends while she dug into her sister's flash drives, which she'd put off to build her computer. Some flash drives were password protected, though that didn't seem to slow her down.

I hadn't really discovered anything new from Jack's friends. I'd have to start going to the events they had listed to try to meet them, hoping I'd find something to tie Jack and Suzanne together, unless we found another avenue to investigate.

The ME's office called and confirmed there were moles on the victim's back, which confirmed Jack's online profile as "Code Switch." At least that was progress.

Kenzo called and said they'd identified two more vics. The woman found with Troy Jasonides was an artist, Jamie Masters, and they were still digging into her background. Her body was in the most advanced stage of decomposition, which had delayed her identification.

The other victim's identity was an American-Vietnamese businessman. He was found with Delia Chung. He owned a chain of grocery stores on the peninsula and was thought to be in Vietnam on business, which had delayed reporting him missing. We now had seven of the eight bodies identified, but not much in the way of connecting them, and we were still lacking the identity of Suzanne's cage partner.

"So, what have you found?" Kenzo was hoping for more info.

"We've positively identified Jack Mellon. As soon as I know anything more, I'll call." I hung up and gave Sophie the updates. "I think we need to get into Jack's flash drives, and then pay our delayed visit to Rant."

"Agreed. I may have found a possible identity for our mystery man. Most of the data on her flash drives was run-of-the-mill stuff, but there were a few work items. She was working on a project called Dissolve. There wasn't much, only a couple of innocuous e-mails to Byron Howard, saying she'd hit some snags, but expected to resolve them with the designer. What I found interesting were a few e-mails related to a visit of a Japanese man she was going to meet. The e-mails were all sent from her home computer, so it might've been easier to use her personal computer at night."

I interrupted her train of thought. "Did she use a name?"

"Oh, yes. All messages started out 'Kasagawasan.' "

"I'd put money on business. That's a formal greeting. It must've been important. Japanese men generally don't like doing business with women, though that's changing. I assume you have an e-mail address for him?"

"Of course. Why?"

I smiled. "We—or rather, I—am going to send him an e-mail that will generate some interest if it's him and if not, even more interest."

"If it's him, he's dead and can't answer."

"Your perception is only eclipsed by your beauty." She deserved the response. "No, he won't answer, but someone will. Someone has access to his e-mail, probably his assistant. We'll hear back."

Sophie went back to her sister's flash drives as I composed my e-mail to Japan. I scrapped it several times. I knew about Japanese formalities from dealings here in Japan-town. I finally created an e-mail that satisfied my requirements—polite, short, and with enough mystery, a response would be mandatory. I hit send and sat back. With the time difference, it would be a while before I got a response, even with the insane hours Japanese businessmen worked.

My thoughts shifted to the best way to approach Rant's Byron Howard. Dropping the name "Dissolve" wouldn't work. He could brush that off as a failed project or deny it altogether. We needed more intel on Dissolve. I was toying with the idea of asking Sophie to get into Rant's systems, but I wasn't sure if I really wanted to know if she could or would. I wanted the information, but if we couldn't use it in court, would it be worth it. I wanted to nail this psycho the right way.

My thoughts were interrupted by Sophie's loud exclamation. "Mas. Mas! I think kink is a connection. Kasagawa was the Asian man seen with Suzanne at the Cauldron.

"I found e-mails mentioning their plans to meet the Saturday Suzanne disappeared. I did some digging on the e-mail address they used for their correspondence, but it wasn't his business email. The one you used for your message *was* business. We need to check

Suzanne's KinkInc account again. We weren't looking for ex-U.S. contacts." Her excitement was contagious.

"He must've listed a local address on KinkInc or we would've noticed a Japanese location. Leave that to me. I'm so cross-eyed looking at profiles, it can't hurt me. If you could check Jack's flash drives, that would be awesome."

She nodded. She headed back to her computer and inserted the first of Jack's drives.

I pulled up Suzanne's profile and reviewed all her male friends. Aside from one or two in Philadelphia, they were all local to the Bay area. Shit. Why didn't I notice it before? "Koi-man."

Nice play on words, it wouldn't have raised any flags without the new information. I clicked on the icon and it took me to Koi-man's profile. His profile fit— Japanese man, submissive, into high-tech and new frontiers, looking for play partners and a long-term partner. Blah, blah, blah. Actually, his profile was better than many locals.

I'd wait for a response to my e-mail before I told Kenzo's team of the victim's possible identity. The kink aspect was looking good. However, being a cynic and suspicious, I wasn't going to jump on it as the only reason for the deaths.

So far, three of the last four victims had been involved in the hi-tech industry and two connected to Rant. Too much of a coincidence for me, especially since Byron Howard had lied to us. I'd do my best to keep the Silicon Valley victims for us. Kenzo's team could take the rest, though I'd keep my promise and give them all the information we collected. I hadn't said how or when.

The rest of the day, I played around, looking at Kasagawa's friends—at least the ones in the Bay Area. It looked like he was a player—more private party than the public. So why did he meet Suzanne at a public play party? More questions. Lunch came and went, and by late afternoon, Sophie cursed.

"This son of a bitch was smart, but not as smart as me. I've cracked his passwords. Note the plural. Sneaky bastard used different passwords for each flash drive and they weren't 1-2-3-4-5-6 or his address. Now that I have all of them, I'll crank through them in no time. I'll have everything by the time you get in tomorrow."

"I was going to visit the Cauldron tonight to see if I could catch up with both Suzanne's friends and Kasagawa's. Want to join me?"

"Are you asking me on a date?" She looked at me coyly.

"Nope. All business."

Her head dropped to look at her screen. "Then screw you. I have work to do. If something looks important, I'll call you. Okay?"

There wasn't much I could say to that. "Okay."

"Don't have too much fun. Oh, but you can't, can you?" She pulled out the keys to my chastity cage from under her shirt and twirled them around her fingers.

Damn. I was starting to get hard in my cage.

She must've seen the change in my expression because she laughed. "Fleshing out the ironwork, as it were?"

I'd asked for this and now, I'd gotten it. I was in the place I wanted to be—torn between the pleasure of frustration and the frustration of pleasure. I left in a hurry and went home before I said something I'd regret.

It was a quiet night at the Cauldron. None of Jack's friends showed up...at least none I recognized. I went home and crashed.

Chapter 20

After a restless night, I got up, dressed, and left for the office, wanting to find out what Sophie had uncovered—if anything. She'd promised to call if she found anything significant but hadn't. I was sure there was something we'd be able to go on. I was also sure it couldn't be as simple as a psycho killing arbitrary people. There had to be a purpose. Psychos always have a purpose or agenda, however wacked out it was.

The office was quiet, lights were on, and I heard the hum of electricity. No Marie. I'd beaten her in. I regretted not carrying my weapon. I was authorized and permitted to do so, but I didn't make a habit of it, preferring less lethal means. Today, I wish I had. It was too quiet, and I knew Sophie wouldn't have left all the lights on when she'd left.

Cautiously, I made my way to the inner office. I gently pushed the door open. Nothing. I pushed it open wider and saw Sophie's legs tucked under her chair, unmoving, with no torso above. Quickly, I moved to Sophie's side and found her crashed on her computer, sleeping. She looked peaceful and as serene as her position would allow. Her hair was loose, spilling over the desk, and her make-up was smudged. She looked relaxed and vulnerable, and I felt an urge rising to protect her. Gently, I touched her shoulder.

Sophie exploded up from the chair. "Get away

from me, you bastard." Her arms rose to a defensive posture. Her hair flew about and her eyes were wild.

I jumped back at the ferocity of her reaction. "Sophie, it's me. You were sleeping."

She sagged like a rag doll. "Sorry about that." Her voice was soft and quiet.

"Are you all right?"

Bleary-eyed, she nodded. "Yes. You just surprised me. I must've been dreaming."

"More like a nightmare. Want to talk about it?"

"No. What I *do* need is coffee and breakfast. We have some interesting material to go over."

She looked a mess, but I wasn't going to let her off that easily. "You said you'd call if you found something interesting. So why didn't you call? Or have you done something on your own?"

"I'm sorry. I was going to call you. I just crashed out. Jack was sneaky with his work. It took longer than I thought it would, but I think I know what he was up to. If I'm right, it's linked to Rant and my sister."

I was all ears.

"I think Rant and Jack were working on a program for breaking encryption, big encryption—governmental stuff and financial institutions. The big boys—things that are almost hacker proof. Hackers usually get in due to human error, rather than through the system itself.

"Well, Jack and Rant were testing a set of programs that would break those encryptions—a universal cyber key. Nothing would be safe. I didn't think it possible, but that was what my sister was working on. Project Dissolve."

I stayed silent. If true, this one would stab Silicon Valley in the heart and would be a darn good reason for murder. Governments would kill, literally, for a key like that. Anyone in business, legal or otherwise, wouldn't think twice about killing for it. "This makes much more sense than the kink angle. We have to tell Kenzo about this."

Sophie smiled. "Can I get breakfast first?"

I'd forgotten she'd been here all night. "Sure. My treat." I hadn't eaten, either. We headed to the door where Marie intercepted us. She did a double take on Sophie, but said nothing.

As we hit the stairs, Sophie said, "There *is* one other thing." She stopped.

I looked back at her. "Yes?"

"The Japanese man's name is Yohji Kasagawa. He showed up in correspondence between Rant and Jack— full name and the same business e-mail you used. He was investing in Rant, so the project must've had some teeth to get his attention."

Three bodies connected to one location and a project. That finished it for me. This wasn't about killing for fun; it was about the oldest motive in the book, money.

"This isn't some psycho loose in the kink community."

"How can you be sure? They were all personally involved in kink, too. Even Kasagawa. All went to kink clubs, and my sister and Jack had played in public. If we're right, Kasagawa was the Asian man with Suzanne at the Cauldron. Did you ask Kenzo for info on the other victims' personal lives?"

"Yeah. I left a message with a team member. I'll follow up on that while we get breakfast. Were you able to get through all the drives?"

Sophie shook her head. "No. As I said, Jack was good, and there was a lot of information. I still have a couple to go through."

We sat down in the diner, both silent, processing the developments and enjoying the coffee. We both started to speak at once. She let me go first.

"We need to get to Byron at Rant. We need to shake that tree."

She laughed. "My thoughts exactly. Let's see if I can get more info on Dissolve. Maybe we can really shake him."

I didn't think Byron would fold that easily, although every one cracked with the right leverage.

We ordered our food and more coffee came. As I was drinking, I called Kenzo. "Kenzo, are we on speaker?"

"Yeah, why?"

I ignored the question. "Do any of the other vics have any ties to the kink community? I left Josie a message about it."

"Yes. All five had profiles."

"Possibly. I think we've identified the last victim, the male found with Miss Chandler. He's a Japanese businessman with residences here and Japan. His name is Yohji Kasagawa. He looks to be a tech investor type."

"How did you find out about him?"

"There was e-mail correspondence in Suzanne's archive." Not exactly a lie. "I've e-mailed his office to get confirmation. I'm sure his company will want a DNA confirmation. I'll let you know when they contact me. It would be better if that went through official channels. Agreed?"

"Agreed. You know how formal the Japanese can be. Connect them to my office, and we'll deal with it. How sure are you?"

"Pretty sure, but not a hundred percent." I wanted to red herring him until Sophie and I'd had the chance to talk to Byron. "Do you really think this is a psycho, or something else?"

"Mas, don't go conspiracy on me. So far, it looks like a psycho, targeting the aforementioned folks in pairs. We're looking through a lot of leads. I think we should meet up to go over everything we have. You said you'd share information, and I'm going to hold you to that. We need to get this wacko before he hits again."

"Sure. Later today. Right now, we're chasing a few things down. How about late this afternoon? We will come to you. Okay?"

"That works. And don't miss the meeting. Wouldn't be prudent."

I chuckled. "We wouldn't dream of standing you up." I hung up before he could say anything further.

"Aren't you pushing it a bit?" Sophie asked as our food arrived. "You didn't actually lie, but you were pretty close. What are you going to tell them about your theory?"

I pondered her question. I had to tread a fine line. I wouldn't actually lie, but I'd be careful what I shared and how I said it. "Depends on how we make out at Rant with Mr. Byron."

We finished our meal and left, feeling better with food and a plan. The walk back to the office was brisk and businesslike. As we approached my office, we saw dark shadows through the window. Three men in dark suits turned as we entered. They were Japanese.

Marie gestured with her head. "These gentlemen are from Japan and want to speak to you."

The men bowed, and I returned the bow, then pulled out my business card and handed it to the shortest one, who was standing slightly ahead of the others. They looked like bodyguards. The smaller man bowed and accepted my card with both hands. He examined it and carefully put it away in his card case. He returned the gesture by offering me his card.

I mimicked his gesture, taking it with both hands. Damn sure I want to examine this one. His name was Mr. S. Saito, Security, Ishiwara Investigations. His address and telephone numbers followed. Out of habit, I turned the card over. The reverse was in Japanese. I assumed it was the same information translated. "Saito-san, I apologize. I do not have my card in Japanese."

His English was excellent—accented, but clear. "Please, it is of no matter. I appreciate your courtesy. May we speak privately?" He didn't introduce the other men.

"Of course. Please, this way." I showed them into the inner office; only Saito-san sat. The other men stood behind and to one side of Saito.

Sophie followed and sat out of line of sight.

"How may we assist you, Saito-san?"

"Hammett-san, this is a delicate matter. We were surprised when our client received your e-mail. As soon as we realized you might have information about Kasagawa-san, I came here to see you. I assume I can count on your discretion?"

"You can rely on my discretion, Saito-san, and that of my partner, Ms. Chandler." Partner was a stretch, but I wanted a second pair of ears and Sophie was a partner on this case. She had plenty of coin in this game.

She chimed in. "Saito-san, I assure you of my discretion."

He acknowledged her with a slight nod. "That is gratifying to know. I understand you would like to speak with Kasagawa-san?"

Here we go. This was going to be an interesting conversation. I'd had dealings with the large Japanese community in San Francisco, but this was the real thing. *Patience.* If they wanted something from me, they'd have to give me something in exchange. "Would you care for some refreshments? Tea or coffee?" The offer seemed to surprise him.

"That is very kind. If you have tea, that would be most appreciated."

Touché. "Marie, would you please make us all some green tea?"

A small flinch. He didn't expect us to have green tea.

"Unless you would prefer Indian?"

"Thank you. No. Green tea is preferred."

We sat in silence until Marie returned with five cups of green tea. I was sure it wasn't up to his normal standard; this was San Francisco, not Tokyo.

He sipped it and nodded in appreciation.

"I apologize it's not up to your domestic quality. I hope it is acceptable."

Now, he smiled. "Tea is always refreshing after a long flight."

They'd come straight from the airport to my office. Good to know. Now, we could get down to it. "How may we help you?"

Saito stared at his cup before starting. "Again, I

must insist on confidentiality."

I bowed my head.

"Kasagawa-san has been missing for several weeks now. We did not realize he was in the United States. We assumed he was in Japan. He had no scheduled trips to the U.S. He seems to have disappeared, which is not something Japanese businessmen do." He left it open.

My turn. Do I play it out some more or drop our suspicions on him for a reaction? "Saito-san, I believe we have some bad news. We are convinced Kasagawa-san is deceased." I let that float, not mentioning murder.

No reaction. He must've had a suspicion something bad had happened.

"You don't seem surprised at our news."

"No, Hammett-san. When we could not locate him, we tried all his numbers, including his local residence, with no results. You say you believe he is deceased. Why do you say that?"

"A man's body was discovered in San Francisco Bay. A man resembling his description was seen with another victim, and they were found in the same location. She's been identified and working back through her contacts, we identified Kasagawa-san."

"You said victim. Do you mean he was a victim of an accident or of a crime?"

"We believe he was murdered."

"But he has not been confirmed as a victim?"

"No. We only made the connection yesterday. You acted very quickly to get here so soon."

"We try to be efficient. I assume the local police department is handling the matter?"

"A San Francisco special homicide team. I'll

introduce you to the inspector in charge. I do have some questions for you, if you can answer them."

Saito watched me carefully. "If I can."

"Thank you. I need background information, to help with a case of my own. Nothing confidential. Can you confirm Kasagawa-san was investing in hi-tech?"

"I can confirm that."

"Thank you. Were his sexual proclivities widely known?" I knew this was pushing it.

"And this relates to your case how?"

"He was last seen at a BDSM club here in San Francisco with another victim. They were both found together."

"I do not think I will answer any more questions."

"Saito-san, you have our word. We are discreet. His tastes are his business. We're not judging him. We just want to find out who killed them."

"What is your interest in this case?"

I looked over to Sophie, who nodded. "My partner's sister was the other victim found with Kasagawa-san. We have a personal interest in solving this crime."

He turned to look directly at Sophie and bowed. "You have my condolences. Losing a family member is always a great sadness." He turned back to me and continued. "Kasagawa-san was a particular man. He enjoyed pleasures not common to the rest of us. He was more circumspect in Japan."

"Thank you. I will call ahead to say you are coming." I wrote out the address of the police department. "If you could get a DNA sample, I'm sure the authorities would find it most helpful in making a positive identification. I could take you to his residence, if you'd like."

"Thank you, Hammett-san. I have a local contact downstairs. I would appreciate you calling, as I have your tea."

It had been worth a shot. Now, I'd have to go official to access Kasagawa's place. There was probably nothing there. If Jack's and Suzanne's places had been tossed, odds were Kasagawa's had been, too. *No stone left unturned.* Whoever had done the first two could've missed something.

I made the call to Kenzo. He was out, but Pete Callen was there, and he took the call. He thanked me and reminded me about the meeting later that day. I asked if there was anything further they could send over.

"We've already sent what we have. You should check your e-mail."

Screw you, too, Pete.

We said our goodbyes, exchanged offers of sympathy, and they left.

As soon as they'd cleared the door, Sophie said, "How long do you think it will take for Saito to get to the PD, do the interviews, then have the PD load it into their computer?"

"Don't know. Probably by the end of the day, maybe sooner."

Sophie grinned. "I've always liked back doors; ya never know when they'll come in handy."

I'd begun to like her back door into the PD. I tapped my watch. "How long to finish Jack's flash drives?"

Her response was curt. "Fucking slave driver."

I smirked. I wasn't the control freak.

"Couple of hours, max. Are you going to warn Byron we're coming?'

"Not sure yet. If we ask for an appointment, he'll be warned. If we just show up and he's not there, it's a waste of time. I think making the appointment is worth the risk. He doesn't know we know about Dissolve."

Sophie agreed.

I made the call, pretended we didn't really know his position in the company, and claimed we had some information. Byron asked if we could do it over the phone, but I declined, saying it was better done face to face. He reluctantly agreed. We set the time and ended the call.

Sophie buried her head in the flash drive contents while I looked over the bios the PD sent on the five other vics.

Chapter 21

The biographies of the vics were new to me. They'd filled out Jack's, and Kasagawa's was still too new. I figured we should start with the couple who were deemed to be the first victims, Jamie Masters and Troy Jasonides.

Troy Jasonides worked in San Francisco real estate, and from the financial statements, he was doing very nicely—healthy bank balances, well-funded investments. He had mortgages and stakes in several properties scattered across the city. He also had a KinkInc profile. I noted his profile name for later use. The only enemy, for want of a better word, was a Soren Sorenson. That conflict had been noted by several people the inspectors had interviewed. Most people in San Francisco had heard of Sorenson Construction, known for its ugly monster buildings. Personally, Soren was disliked for his dubious business practices and the number of lawsuits filed against him. I made a mental note to leave that one to the PD. Kenzo was welcome to him. I was convinced Suzanne, Jack, and Kasagawa were all connected, but I wasn't sure how those three connected to the rest. I was pretty sure all their KinkInc profiles were misdirections to put the hunters off the real trail.

Jamie Masters was an artist, blogger, and person about town. That she hadn't been blogging wasn't unusual. Apparently, when she was working on an exhibition, she'd often disappear for months at a time, then start up again right before the exhibition. She lived on the East Bay in her studio. She also had a KinkInc profile. I noted her kink profile name.

The inspectors had done a good job digging into her financials. She wasn't wealthy enough raise flags, but comfortable enough. Her social media was another story. She had followers and critics, some minor spats on social media, but nothing to kill over. Then again, I'd heard some weird reasons for killing.

Her nemesis seemed to be a Krista Jones, editor of a SF-based art and culture magazine, *The Left Coast.* She'd written scathing critiques of Jamie's last two exhibitions, which had publicly caused some bad blood between them. Jamie certainly had her fair share of fans. Some had even threatened Krista. There was nothing concrete to make me believe they were involved in the killings and nothing to connect them to each other or anyone else…yet.

Trying to keep an open mind, I put the bios down and went on to the next two victims, Delia Chung and Hoang Du. Delia owned two high-end retail stores. She was supposed to have been in Asia and Europe on a buying trip, so no one worried until three plus weeks had passed. One of her managers had tried to contact her with no response. The manager finally reported it to the police, who took the report. They checked the airports for her passport number and airlines, but no hits. She'd been in a relationship with Krista Jones that had ended acrimoniously, but the relationship had ended well over a year ago, and it looked like both had moved on. Delia had a KinkInc profile. I added her profile name to the others. I was missing something, but I couldn't put my finger on it.

Next up was Hoang Du, a Vietnamese son of boat people. He owned a string of small ethnic grocery stores on the peninsula. Hoang was a widower with two grown children. The sons were college educated and involved with running the family corporation. They all had clean records, aside from several speeding tickets on the older son. All had been paid with no further issues. His financials were clean. He sent money to relatives still in Vietnam, but there was nothing suspicious about the amounts or the frequency.

The only fly in the ointment was a run-in with a gangster named Phan Thanh Binh down on the peninsula. He'd been arrested, served a year in jail, and had been released two months before Hoang had disappeared. He'd been brought in for questioning but had an air-tight alibi. Still, he hadn't been eliminated. He could've ordered a hit, but if he had, why the second body? And a bigger why, why the first two? Neither made sense. From a gangster point of view, he'd want to take credit for the killing to intimidate others. Hoang also had a KinkInc profile. All these leads seemed to be headed nowhere.

The third couple was where Jack Mellon entered the picture. His death companion was Helga Braun. I quickly ran over Jack's bio—nothing new and nothing we hadn't already been over several times. Then, something in the police report caught my eye—a name we hadn't seen before. James McCarrigan. I knew that name, but I couldn't place it. I hoped it would come to me but knew there was no use forcing it.

Moving on to Helga Braun. She was a PhD

candidate at Berkeley, barely making ends meet with grant money and part-time jobs bartending and tutoring undergrads in physics. Even the title of her thesis was beyond me. The inspectors had discovered a series of sharp, contentious e-mails between her and a Professor Fong Yang, also at Berkeley. It looked like Helga was about to disprove one of the professor's well-published theories, and he wasn't happy about it. Helga was also on KinkInc. With her schedule, I wondered how she fit in any playtime at all. Still, she went on the list.

Was her dispute with an aging professor something to kill about? That brought me to Suzanne. Who did she have a beef with? We hadn't even found a hint of a disagreement. Kenzo's team was working on the psycho angle, and I had encouraged it a bit. I felt it was more about Suzanne and Rant, a feeling that wouldn't go away, though I still hadn't pinned down why. I needed a motive to tie everyone together.

Who would profit from the deaths? Rant certainly wouldn't benefit from Suzanne's. She'd been an asset. Kasagawa had stature and was already rich.

A competitor? Doubtful. Jack and Helga were the oddballs. They were young and didn't have much in the way of assets. How did anyone benefit from killing them? The business feuds and run-ins with all the others didn't make sense, either. They didn't move in the same social circles. There seemed to be no real connection between them, other than they all had KinkInc profiles.

I reviewed the list of eight KinkInc profiles and was about to start digging when Sophie yelled, "Eureka. I've found it!"

I raised an eyebrow. "What is *it*?"

"These flash drives were well protected. There wasn't much on the others, but these few are gold mines. They contain his working copy of the Dissolve program." She stopped looking puzzled.

"What's the problem? Is it connected to Suzanne?"

"Shhhhhhush." She ran back to her computer. Her fingers flew over the keys. "Son of a bitch. He's one clever bastard. This was a scam."

"How do you know?"

"I don't, which is why I'm sending the whole thing to *Fiend* back East."

"Don't you mean friend?"

Sophie laughed. "No. Fiend is a much more apt description. I use him when I'm crushed with work, on a deadline, or stuck."

I smirked.

"Yes, it happens."

"Is your fiend trustworthy?"

"I'm sending him this, aren't I?"

"Just checking. So, what do you think is going on? And what type of scam could he be playing on a company like Rant?"

"I can't be sure until I hear back from Fiend. I know this will pique his interest. I think Jack Mellon was a scam artist. He has some great code on here, and it will work on some encryption, but nothing like what would be needed to hit the big boys. A program like that would need lots and lots of flash drives, all bigger than these to hold the code. That's what tipped me off."

"How would Jack hook Rant and pull the wool over their eyes?"

"A good pitch. Don't forget, if this actually worked, it would be worth trillions of dollars to whoever owned it. Think of it like a hotel. Each room is a computer. The room key only works on one room/computer. This program would allow you to open any room/computer, at will…any room/computer in the world. He would've provided a small sample with the promise that as each module worked, he'd provide more parts of the program. In the process, he'd get access to Rant's systems and use them to funnel cash out of the project into his bank."

"We didn't find a bank, or any indication he had anything other than the stuff in his apartment."

"It's there somewhere. The people who searched his apartment took his laptop and the hard drive to his home set-up. We may never find it now."

"I wonder if the folks who turned his place over were looking for the program or the money."

Sophie frowned. "Or both. Let's go see Byron and push a few buttons."

I stopped for a minute. "I think Suzanne suspected something. She was going to meet Simon and ask him to investigate. He was a computer geek. Not to your or Suzanne's level, but he was a good investigator."

"Do you think he was killed because of this?"

"I don't think so. Simon's death was investigated thoroughly. It still looks like an unfortunate accident. Let's get to Rant so we have time to make it back for Kenzo's team meeting."

"Do we want to give him a heads-up? Make sure he's available to see us?"

"We have an appointment and now, we have something to get his attention. Dissolve should pry something loose. We also have a strong suspicion Jack was skimming cash out of the program. He'll have to decide on the spot what to tell us. I'm betting he'll want to know how much we know about Dissolve. If this is as good as you say, he'll be shitting bricks. If it's a scam, he'll want to know how much we know, and more importantly, he'll be motivated to keep it very quiet."

"Okay. That makes sense. I think Suzanne had uncovered Jack's skimming and hired Simon to confirm it."

I thought about that. "If so, then why was she killed? Jack was already dead. Let's see what gives at Rant."

Chapter 22

The drive to Rant was uneventful, and it gave us time to talk over the information we'd found on Jack's flash drives. Sophie didn't expect to hear back from Fiend in Philly regarding the Dissolve program for at least a day or two, if not longer. We weren't concerned. We had a copy. And we had information we could use as leverage.

We decided I'd open the meeting and, hopefully, get him off balance a little. Sophie would take the lead in the tech conversation, if it went in that direction. She had the technical ability to talk with him as an equal— or superior. I'd observe and look for evidence of lying.

My adrenaline flow increased as I pulled into the parking lot. We were now on the offensive.

The two women at the reception desk didn't remember us, at first.

"Mas Hammett and Sophie Chandler for Byron Howard, VP of HR. It's regarding Dissolve."

The older of the two seemed to recognize us and called in to Byron's office. His assistant responded by saying he was in a meeting and wouldn't be free to keep his appointment with us. I insisted she pass on the Dissolve message and let him decide.

Sophie and I retreated to the awful-colored chairs, making sure the receptionists saw us making ourselves comfortable. A few moments later, the elevator opened and Byron's assistant strode over to us.

Snippily, she said, "Mr. Howard will see you now. Please sign in and wear your guest badges where they can be seen."

"Thank you," Sophie and I said together.

We signed in, collected our badges, and followed Byron's assistant to the elevator. We rode up in silence.

I smiled to myself. I'd gotten part one right. I was curious to see how good Mr. Byron was and how worried we could make him.

We were shown into a conference room. I put my finger to my lips, and Sophie nodded. I pulled out my phone and texted her. —*Don't say anything. Assume everything we say will be recorded. Only use text, okay?*—

Sophie read my text and smiled.

We sat in silence. He was making us wait. *Great tactic.* I relaxed and closed my eyes. I knew I had more patience than Byron. After all, I was the one with the information.

Ten minutes grew to fifteen, then to twenty. Finally, the door opened with a flourish. Sleepily, I stood and offered my hand. Byron didn't take it.

All business today. Fair enough.

"Mr. Byron Howard, VP of HR and Director of Research. Thank you for seeing us." He flinched at the two titles. *Got him!*

"Yes, well I was hoping you had some information on Suzanne. We've heard nothing."

Not bad. Ignore my opening. "Oh, you won't be hearing from Suzanne. She was murdered several weeks ago."

A deep, worried frown creasing his forehead. "Are

144

you sure? How did this happen?"

"We aren't completely sure yet. The police are still investigating."

He sat in silence. He seemed surprised at the news. Either that or he was worried. The first probably meant he wasn't involved in her death…at least the actual murder, anyway. The second meant he knew and was involved.

"Mr. Howard, can you confirm Suzanne was working on a project named Dissolve?"

"I'm not saying anything further without counsel present." He made a call from the central tel-com and asked that Mr. Antonucci and Mr. Gilbert to join him immediately.

We waited in silence.

Mr. Antonucci arrived first and sat next to Byron.

"We can understand you have to be cautious, but this is a murder investigation. Perhaps you can answer this. Do you accept outside investments in specific projects?"

Mr. Antonucci nodded. "Sometimes. It depends on the project, who the investors are, and the timeline. Why do you want to know?"

Time for another jab. "Well, it could involve national security, and if the investor was a foreign national, it would raise some red flags."

Byron was regaining some of his composure. He looked at Mr. Antonucci, who again nodded. "We have a number of foreign investors, but all our projects are of a commercial nature."

Sophie responded. "I'm sure you do, and not all your commercial projects remain so, especially the one Suzanne and Jack Mellon were working on."

"Jack who?"

No flinch at the name, but too much of a delay in answering. He was lying, and we already knew it. Jab again. "Byron, did I forget to mention Jack Mellon is also dead?"

Byron was beginning to look uncomfortable.

Mr. Antonucci cleared his throat. "I don't think Mr. Howard has anything else to say."

The conversation was at a crossroad. He could either clam up or open up. I was hoping we could push him to open up. Just as I was about to open my mouth, the door opened, and a man walked in. He was of average height, slim and hard looking. This man was not an attorney.

Byron introduced him. "This is Mr. Gilbert. He is the head of our security department."

Mr. Gilbert nodded in our direction.

"Mr. Hammett is a private investigator, and Ms. Chandler is Suzanne's sister. They've just informed us Suzanne was murdered."

Mr. Gilbert looked at Sophie. "I am sorry for your loss. How can I be of assistance?"

I watched him closely. He said all the right things, but he was cold and impassionate. He had the look of ex-military, not a run-of-the-mill grunt. I knew this man would be very dangerous to anyone who crossed him. *Time to be very careful.*

"Mr. Gilbert, what is your specialty? Cyber security or the typical physical type?"

His response was vague. "All sorts. Whatever the company needs are at the time." He was off-hand and casual.

Now, I was sure he was ex-military…of the more

clandestine type. "We were hoping you could shed some light on Suzanne's disappearance."

His stare went right through me. He considered my request, and his answer was slow and deliberate. "I don't think we can help you. When Mr. Howard mentioned your previous visit to me, I did some checking. Suzanne was working on a highly sensitive project. Her work computer was always secured here on site. We accessed and reviewed her work. There was nothing untoward, all work related. We don't have any information on her personal life. She kept to herself. This may sound cold, but our first priority is to protect the company."

"That is your prerogative. Of course, we will take the information we have to the inspector running the murder investigation, including our information on Project Dissolve, Jack Mellon, and Suzanne. That will open an investigation into all your projects to ensure there are no national-security breaches. It could take months, and the publicity would be quite extensive."

Mr. Antonucci gave us a thin smile. "Threats will only earn you a court date."

I returned his smile. "Mr. Antonucci, I'm not threatening anyone, just laying out the process I'll have to follow to comply with the law. As you know, it is my duty to hand over any material information to the official investigators."

Gilbert responded. "Jack, however, is not an employee of Rant. Never has been."

"You know that, as Head of Security, right? We know he wasn't an employee. He came to Rant with a project you couldn't resist. Dissolve. He needed your resources but was willing to share because the payoff would be huge for everyone."

Howard took that bait. "You don't know what you are talking about. I think it's time you left."

"As you wish, but don't you find it coincidental he was murdered approximately a month before Suzanne? And Suzanne was found in similar circumstances as Jack? We know Suzanne was a beta tester and we know Jack developed the program, which all leads back to you in research, not HR, as well as Rant."

"All circumstantial." Mr. Antonucci leaned forward.

I'd deliberately left out Kasagawa. Something about Mr. Gilbert had me on edge. "Yes, but we have enough to have the police and DHS crawling all over you and Rant for a long, long time. We want to find out who killed them, not damage your business."

He seemed to think on that. He looked at Byron and Gilbert, who nodded. "What do you need to know?"

Sophie spoke up. "We think this is about Jack Mellon and Dissolve. We believe Jack was defrauding you…skimming cash from the project. You should have a forensic accountant go over the project financials. We believe he siphoned off a lot of cash."

Bryon feigned surprise. "I don't think so, but it's worth investigating. However, I won't tell you anything about Dissolve. It is proprietary, and very few know about it."

"Fair enough. Again, we'd strongly suggest you do the financial investigation." I watched their faces and reactions. Mr. Antonucci's face was blank, but Byron and Gilbert seemed relieved at our line of questioning. They were hiding something.

Byron spoke up again. "I think a financial review would be advisable to guarantee all is as it should be."

Mr. Gilbert agreed saying, "We will find any loopholes and close them."

"My sister must have suspected something, but before she could do anything, she was killed."

Neither Byron nor Mr. Gilbert responded, so I jumped back in. "The police are working on the theory they were killed by the same person, and it involved kinky sex. We aren't sure we agree. Jack and Suzanne were both employed here."

Antonucci interjected. "Jack was not an employee. He was a contractor."

"Rant is the only connection between any of the victims."

Mr. Gilbert's turn. "She was found in the bay?"

I thought I saw a hint of a smile cross his lips.

Antonucci looked surprised.

"Yes, she was found in the bay."

Gilbert's tone was clipped. "Do the police know who or why?"

I wasn't going to tell him more than I had to. "They have several lines of enquiry." That wasn't a lie.

He continued. "If there's nothing else, I think we've given you all we can. I assure you we will be looking into your financial accusations."

Sophie looked at me, and I shrugged. "Thank you for your time. If you think of anything further you can divulge, please don't hesitate to contact me." I handed them my business cards.

Howard just put it in his pocket. Antonucci slid it into his note pad, but Mr. Gilbert studied it carefully, as if memorizing the details.

As we were leaving, Mr. Antonucci said, "I do have a request."

Sophie and I looked at each other.

"Would you please keep all this as quiet as possible? If Jack Mellon was skimming, we'll fix it quickly and internally."

I shrugged again. "I have no issue with that, as long as you keep it quiet until we've caught the perpetrator. I'm convinced it has more to do with Jack's fraud and kink life than Rant. Both Suzanne and Jack have links to the kink community."

Gilbert grinned at that.

Howard looked serious. "It will take time to do a thorough review, and it will slow us down. It's not ideal, but it happens on projects. Please keep us informed on your progress, if you can."

"Sure thing."

As we left the conference room and were escorted back to reception by Byron's assistant, Sophie gave me a dirty look. We handed in our guest badges and signed out, noting the time. We would be cutting it close for Kenzo's meeting. We'd spent more time with Rant than I'd expected, but it had been worth it.

As soon as we climbed into the car, Sophie turned on me. "What the hell was that? You didn't even go after the Dissolve aspect. Money and kink? Are you kidding me?" Her face was red.

"Sophie, they know something, and they're working hard to hide it…at least Howard and Gilbert. I didn't want to overplay our hand. Let's wait and see what your friend Fiend comes up with. Right now, they think we think it's about fraud at Rant and kinky sex. I don't want to scare them off or make them think we're on to the scam. He likely knows there are problems with the program. Mr. Gilbert is the one who worries me."

"Mas, there are always problems with programs. It doesn't always mean they're scams. Okay. We'll wait until I hear back from Fiend. Why does Gilbert worry you?"

"There is something about him that bothers me. He's more than he seems. I'm positive he's ex-military. He has an edge to him that only comes from…very hard training."

We lapsed into our own silence, thinking about the visit and the upcoming meeting. The drive back was slow. The car's solid rumble went up through my groin, and my trapped cock appreciated the vibrations. I glanced at Sophie. *Oh, fuck.*

She was absentmindedly playing with the keys on the chain around her neck, twirling them around her fingers.

"Do you have to do that?"

"Do what?" She looked down, unaware of what she'd been doing. "Oh, this? Sorry." She laughed. "It helps me think."

"Well, it doesn't do anything for me or mine, thank you."

"I like teasing someone with a locked-up cock. It's fun. Besides, you love the frustration. If you didn't, you wouldn't have locked yourself up, and you certainly would *not* have given the keys to someone else."

Damn it, she was right. Just talking about it had gotten me hard.

She reached over and tapped my cage with her finger. "If you're good, maybe we can let you out, with conditions of course. Sound fair?"

"Depends on the conditions."

Sophie laughed. "Nothing too difficult. Nothing that will break our agreement."

My cock pulsed, thinking about its release, and I went back to driving and hoping I'd be unlocked soon.

Chapter 23

Parking wasn't a problem. I headed straight into a visitor's spot.

Sophie hung back, a bit anxious.

"Don't like official buildings?"

"Let's just say certain official buildings make me nervous. I like to remain in the shadows."

"Do you want to leave? I can do this on my own."

"No. I want to hear what developments they've come up with. We aren't going to tell them anything we don't have to, right?"

"Right. This is…was…my environment, so let me do the talking, unless it gets technical, computer-wise. Okay?"

"Sounds good. I'll play the grieving sister…helping out."

I looked at her, surprised.

"Don't worry. I won't fall apart. I'll grieve for Suzanne when I am ready, not before. Let's do this."

We signed in, told the desk who we were seeing, took the obligatory guest badges, and we waited for our escort. This time, it was Josie. She still wasn't happy to see us. I smiled at her. "Much progress?"

"Kenzo's meeting. Wait and see."

I smiled bigger. "How do you like working for Kenzo? He was great on my team."

That earned me a glare from Josie and an inquiring

look from Sophie.

We were ushered directly into one of the meeting rooms. We were the last to arrive, other than Kenzo. I introduced Sophie to Jose and Josie. They both nodded. She knew Pete from his visit to my office.

There was no conversation. They resented my involvement and they sure as hell didn't want Sophie involved. She was a civilian—a vic's relative, no less—and by now, they'd done a background check and hadn't found much on her, which wouldn't please them. *Oh, well. Life's a bitch.* I'd been stuck with my share of crap when I'd been an inspector. My mind drifted. All sorts of memories flooded back, now they didn't sting as much. Maybe I was finally moving on and coming out of the depression caused by Simon's death. Kenzo walked in, arm full of files. He didn't look happy. He'd been instructed, I was sure, to close this case quickly and quietly. So far, the media hadn't gotten wind of the bodies in the bay, but I could see the headline: *Bodies in the Bay Killer* or maybe *Bayside Serial Killer*. It would bring back memories of the Zodiac killer. To say the SFPD was sensitive about serial killers was an understatement.

The white board was covered with the eight victims—driver's license photos for the domestic vics and a grainy, blown-up passport photo of Kasagawa. Kenzo started it off.

"We had a visit from a company representing Mr. Kasagawa's interests. We'll be releasing his body to them once the ME has completed the autopsy. That will be later today or tomorrow, at the latest. All the vics have been identified, and background bios have been started. We're still waiting for info to come in from other jurisdictions. So far, the work has been thorough.

"We're going on the premise this is the act of probably a pair. We're creating a psychological profile. I don't want the feds involved in the day-to-day, but they're the best at profiling. They found this double killing interesting. The FBI will get back to us as soon as they can; they understand the urgency and have told us to expect more bodies. We're hoping he/they haven't been spooked about the dump site and have set up remote cameras covering all of the dock. Even if he comes in by boat, we'll get him on tape."

I raised my hand. "What if he's done? What if this isn't a serial killer in the normal sense?"

Pete chimed in. "What do you mean?"

I posed a theory, knowing it would likely be shot down. "What if the killings were done to cover up something else?"

Josie snorted, Jose shook his head, and Pete looked at me like I was nuts.

I expected their reaction, but I wasn't going to explain my thought process.

Kenzo took the lead. "Mas, who the hell kills seven people just to cover up the eighth? Regardless, there are too many victims. That's the way we're looking at this until we have proof of something different. Got it?"

I shrugged.

Kenzo continued. "We know all the vics were into kinky activities. Mas found that connection, so he's going to continue on that line while we dig into the other aspects of their lives. The only ones that seem to have known each other outside of the kink connection were Krista, Delia, and Jaime, all with diverse backgrounds, gender, ethnicities, financial status, and age. We've found that each vic, except for Suzanne Chandler, had at least one antagonistic dispute in the recent past—though none seem worth killing over. Nevertheless, we've all seen the slightest or imagined wrong end up with a killing."

Sophie gingerly raised her hand. Kenzo nodded. "You keep saying *he* and *him*. Is there any chance we're looking for a woman or a couple?"

Josie groaned, and Pete fidgeted.

Kenzo responded directly to Sophie. "Miss Chandler, let me say we appreciate your assistance. First, most serial killers are male. Statistically, it's highly unlikely this person is a woman. Second, killing the men would take a lot of strength. We believe two were strangled. Third, cramming two bodies into those cages then moving them wasn't easy; the dead weight of the bodies and cage together would be difficult for a strong man. Fourth, we think he disposed of the cage and bodies by boat, which means the person or persons had to maneuver the filled cage onto the boat, then into the bay.

"Marks were found on the cages that look like they came from some form of lifting or loading mechanism. The combined information makes us think the perp is male, more than likely a pair, both male. I hope that answers your question."

I chimed again. "What are the chances it could be a couple, primary and an acolyte? That could explain the couples as victims."

Kenzo noted my comment. "That's something the feds brought up, too, and they'll consider that when they build their profile.

I continued. "Have you been able to trace the

cages? From the looks of them, they were all custom. Only a few suppliers make that quality. Anyone ordering four at once would be unusual."

Pete responded. "We've contacted all the manufacturers we could find. We think the perp ordered one and duplicated it by using the first as a pattern. The steel tubing can be purchased at most building supply houses, as long as the person knows how to weld."

I processed that. "If he got one, what's to stop him from taking the measurements from that one and going to other fabrication shops to have others made? He could pay cash; no records. Then, he has four identical cages...or more. There's a fabrication shop on Folsom street that does nice work. I had some stuff made for my place. Can't hurt to ask. His name is Jim. Ask him for a list of other custom fabricators."

Pete noted the name and address. "Thanks, Mas. I'll follow up with this."

Kenzo cleared his throat. "Can we get back on track? One person is off the possible list. Professor Fong Yang has an airtight alibi for the time Helga went missing. Doesn't mean he couldn't have hired someone, though it's unlikely he had a motive for the other seven. Krista Jones is more interesting. She had a long-term relationship with Delia Chung and a not-so-pleasant split a year ago. She also had an ongoing spat with Jamie Masters, neither of which leads us to a great motive. Apparently, she's like that with everyone—a real bitch princess. We didn't find anyone who liked her. Jose has some updates, as well."

Jose flipped open his notebook. "First, we thought Phan Binh could be out for revenge on Hoang Du for testifying against him, but he's not stupid. He'd know, if anything happened to Hoang, he'd be the first one we'd finger, but he has an airtight alibi for the time of Hoang's disappearance. All of this seems to be irrelevant—a lot of misdirection and fluff. We're digging deeper, but so far, there's nothing to go on." Jose looked directly at me.

My turn. *What to give and what to keep to ourselves?* I thought I'd start with the kink aspect. That would keep them interested and off the main thrust of our investigation. "We'll be looking into all eight vics' kink background. All had KinkInc profiles and were identified as submissive or submissive-leaning switch. Kasagawa will be the most difficult to investigate. He had residences in both Japan and here. Some profiles go back numerous years, judging by the photos and images logged. I've recently filled in the profiles. So not much to tell yet, but I'll send a report on each as I complete it. Hopefully, they're connected. That would help us.

"Suzanne, it turns out, wasn't working in HR; she was a beta tester for Rant Applications. Her boss came clean when Sophie took him to task about her good tech skills and her not-so-good personal ones. Jack Mellon was a freelance computer geek who has worked for some of the Silicon Valley corporations, as well as some start-ups. We'll need a warrant to search his home."

Kenzo nodded and noted the request on his iPad.

"We had a visit from a Japanese security company; we passed him on to you."

Again, Kenzo nodded.

"Mr. Saito told us it was an unscheduled visit. I convinced Saito we weren't looking to out his boss, and he confirmed Kasagawa was on the kink side of the fence. We can confirm Suzanne and Kasagawa met at the Cauldron on the weekend they went missing."

Josie gave a derisory snort. "As if kinky folks are reliable."

"I think you protest too much. Touched a nerve, did I? Perhaps you're suppressing your inner desires. You know, hiding one's true feelings can cause all sorts of issues."

She snapped back. "You don't know anything about me."

"You don't know anything about the kink community. If you did, you'd keep your mouth shut and be thankful for the lead."

Kenzo jumped in. "Leave it alone, Josie. And Mas, get on with it."

I took a deep breath. "They were taken between midnight and one AM on the Sunday morning. Not sure who was the target, but Kasagawa was the wealthy one—venture capitalist. I think Suzanne was in the wrong place at the wrong time." I left it at that, hoping the inspectors would go with the inference that Kasagawa was the target.

Pete nodded. "Yeah, I think Kasagawa makes more sense."

Thanks, Pete. Glad you agree.

We continued for a while longer, pushing around ideas and the list of suspects. It was obvious one size didn't fit all. We went over who had beefs with the victims. Sorenson, real estate; Fong Yang, academic at Berkeley; Phan Thanh Binh, Vietnamese gangster; and Krista Jones, a magazine editor. I didn't mention James McCarrigan. I wanted to find out more about him before announcing anything to the team.

Kenzo wrapped things up. "Until we get a profile from the feds, we'll work on the assumption we're looking for one perp with the likelihood it's a pair, and they're psycho. There's a lot of pressure coming down to get this case solved. Whatever anyone needs, I'll make sure you get it." Looking at Sophie and me, he added, "I need you two to be team players. If you have anything, other than conspiracy theories, get it to the rest of us ASAP."

I nodded as we left. I was feeling a little guilty I hadn't been completely open with Kenzo, but he'd also made it clear I wasn't a member of the official team. I wanted to close this case as much—if not more—than he did, and that was what I was going to do, with Sophie's help. Pete escorted us to the exit. We handed in our guest badges and left the building.

Sophie visibly exhaled. "Well, that sucked."

I laughed. "Not your usual environment, huh?"

"That was uncomfortable. Not sure if it was because you were all talking about Suzanne in the abstract, because you weren't exactly forthcoming with what we have, or the fact they resented you being there."

"I didn't lie to them. I just let them make their own conclusions. I want to investigate James McCarrigan. Can you do your hacking thing and dig some more on them?"

"Oh, now my 'hacking thing' is okay?"

"I've had a revelation. I've always thought I was one of the good guys…and I still do. It's just now I have an advantage. I'm an independent good guy, so I'm not confined by the same rules as other good guys. Right now, goal one is to get the person responsible for your sister's death. Period."

Sophie smiled and took my arm in hers. I smiled back.

We made it back to the office in good time and headed to our own workstations. I dove into all the new KinkInc profiles. The good thing about San Francisco was it had a huge kink community, but that was also the bad thing; it was a lot of ground to cover. There were very few friends in common between the eight murder victims, and the ones who were, didn't seem to warrant further investigation. Kasagawa had few U.S. friends, and they were all over the Bay area. The others had friends throughout the Bay area, California, and the entire U.S. I knew we were missing something, but just what, I couldn't pinpoint. Was it possible eight people had been killed to cover up one select victim? That didn't seem logical. I let it go and focused on what we had. "Anything surface on McCarrigan?"

"Nothing bad. Tara Zosa is a connection between McCarrigan and Kasagawa. She's known in hi-tech and biotech circles as a networker and fixer…and for brokering deals. She speaks Japanese and Chinese fluently enough for business, has a degree from Stanford, a masters from Berkeley in international relations, and an MBA, to boot. She started in real estate, and then she moved into hi-tech, using her start-up genius husband's contacts in Silicon Valley. Looks like she was a natural. Recently divorced, though that seemed amicable. She's financially sound—comfortably off, even by SF standards. She still works, and her commission structure is pretty tasty. Damn. I'm undercharging for my services. She was contracted with Kasagawa's company until very recently. Ooohh, this doesn't look good." She went silent.

"What doesn't look good?"

"There was a parting of ways. Looks like Kasagawa ended the relationship…cut her off short. From these records, they had a business relationship going back years. I wonder what caused Kasagawa to end it. That would've cost her a lot of commission income."

"Could it be a conflict? Who else was she connected with?"

"I'm getting there. Leave me alone. I need to do some more searching. I'll get back to you."

My e-mail dinged to announce new mail from Inspector Pete Callen. They hadn't let the grass grow under their feet regarding cage manufacturers.

Jim on Folsom street has been helpful. He said he made a cage matching our dimensions about six months ago and another four months ago for different customers. The first was cash, but he had a name. The last one was sent off to be chromed, so it wasn't one of ours. He even volunteered to look at the cages personally.

The cages had been cleaned. There were no remains in evidence.

Apparently, every welder is different, kind of like fingerprints. Jim inspected the four cages. He didn't make any of them, and although he couldn't give me names, he said they were made by different people, one likely left-handed. He gave me a list of a few other fabricators in SF who do this type of work. We're following up on his list. Will keep you in the loop.

Maybe if found, one of the other fabricators would remember something useful. All the bits and pieces were waiting for us to put them together and solve the puzzle.

Sophie stopped clicking her keyboard.

I looked up and saw her staring at her screen. "What have you found?"

"Huh. Tosa really embedded herself in the businesses on the peninsula. Tara has a lot of contacts and many of them are highfliers. She's the real deal. She'd been working with Kasagawa for years and about a year ago, she hooked up with that name you wanted checked out—James McCarrigan. Tara was a broker for McCarrigan and a local start-up—something to do with information storage. Whatever it was, it took off, and the company was bought by one of the Silicon Valley monster companies. Then, about five months ago, they had some dealings—a flurry of e-mails—then nothing. It all stopped, or they decided to use a different form of an encoded communication like Kik. No trace on that channel. It could've been a deal that went south, but I don't get that feeling."

"You get feelings off e-mail?" It was kind of a smart-ass comment, but I was interested. To me, face to face was the way to read people. E-mail was information—no inflection or expressions.

Sophie pulled out my chastity cage keys and twirled them. "Be careful, smart mouth. I could temporarily lose these."

That wiped the smile off my face.

"Would I or wouldn't I?"

Immediately, I wanted out of my cage. I wanted to get laid or jerk off—some kind of release. I'd forgotten how good the teasing felt and how much I longed to come, knowing it was out of my hands.

"Mas, you read people. I read computers. There are subtleties in how each person writes and uses e-mail. I've been doing this a long time. Trust me. I get the feeling this was not the end of the contact."

"Sorry. I should know better by now. I think we need to talk to Tara Zosa. Exactly when did Kasagawa end his dealing with Zosa?"

Sophie went back to her screen, and I heard her tapping away. "Ah-ha! Looks like Kasagawa fired her—for want of a better word—nine months ago, before the Dissolve project was kicking off with Rant. Do you think she knew or told other investors about Dissolve?"

I thought about that. "It would make sense. If Tara represented Kasagawa, he'd have first refusal. Maybe Jack Mellon did some of his own promotion so others would hear about the project and would push Kasagawa into committing. Others likely wanted in, but Kasagawa shut them out. You said the program would be worth billions, right?"

"Mas, you couldn't write a check big enough. You could buy your own country, and a good-sized one, at that. The potential value would be literally incomprehensible."

"Worth killing for!"

She nodded. "This is the sort of thing governments would go after, and nothing would get in their way. Nothing and no one."

"If we're right, we're getting in over our heads. You said you thought this was a scam, but what if no one else knew it was? Byron suspects something now, but he isn't going to broadcast that Rant was scammed by a rogue programmer. I think we should give Tara

Zosa a call and see what shakes."

"Doesn't that defeat the purpose of keeping this to ourselves?"

I sighed. "Okay. We'll put that off, for now. We'll wait until we hear back from your contact in Philly. Any news?"

"Not yet, which means he's still tearing it apart. Do you want me to call him, or should we be patient?"

"He's your contact. Do what you think is best."

Sophie pondered the question then looked at her watch. "If I haven't heard from him by tomorrow afternoon our time, I'll reach out to him. The East Coast is three hours ahead, though that's not an issue. He lives in permanent twilight. I prefer he come to me with what he has. That okay with you?"

"Sure. Like I said, he's your resource."

Sophie's face shifted like a chameleon. She became more animated, as if she'd made up her mind about something. "I'm taking off. Going to take a long, hot bath and have a relaxing dinner. Would you like to visit for a nightcap and discuss some key items?" Her lips rose into a smirk.

I was thinking about Tara and had missed the inference. It sunk in a moment later, after I'd agreed to visit her.

Shit. What now?

Whatever it was, it was better than another evening alone.

Chapter 24

Heading home, I was thinking about what might happen later that night. I was excited and apprehensive. While I'd begun to trust Sophie, this would be uncharted waters for both of us. My cage filled at the thought of what she'd demand of me. How I wanted a release.

This felt good, in a contradictory way—wanting a liberating orgasm, yet trapped and not knowing when or if I'd get that reprieve. I'd never completely understood why or how my urge to give up control had come about, only that it was a core part of me—like breathing. It became more developed as I got deeper into the PD and needed a release from the all the crap. Being submissive didn't make me happy or sad; it was something deeper. A sunny day made me happy, and cold, rainy days made me sad. Submissiveness was in my DNA, in my soul. Without it, I wouldn't be Mas.

I took my time showering and shaving, taking extra care with my pubic area. I dabbed a fragrant salve on the freshly shaved area, then reheated last night's leftovers and plopped in front of the TV. I wanted to review some of the information on our case, but my mind kept wandering. I wondered what Simon would've thought of me letting Sophie stay in his apartment. He probably would've smiled and said, "Welcome. Make it yours."

I don't really know what I watched. One program blurred into the next. Nothing held my attention. I dressed casually, button-down shirt, light sweater, jeans, and comfortable walking slip-ons. I took a jacket and walked toward Simon's apartment, anxiously interested in whatever the night held.

The night air was damp. It was going to be a foggy one, a layer that would cocoon the city in its white shroud like a protective cover. For now, the lights still burned bright, not yet diffused by the coming fog.

It took fifteen minutes to make my way from my apartment to Simon's. I was hit by nostalgia and the overwhelming urge to grab the now with both hands. I reached into my pocket, retrieved my set of keys, took a deep breath, and put the key into the lock with shaking hands. I pushed the silent wrought-iron gate, carefully closing it behind me. I quietly climbed the stairs and opened the door to his living room.

"Sophie?" I turned to close the door and when I turned back around, I was surprised to see Sophie, standing there, looking stunning.

Her face was stern, her feet planted in a defensive posture. "When you come into my home, wherever it is, please ring the doorbell to announce yourself. My name is Circe. Tonight, you are lucky." With that, she showed me her hands. Her left hand contained a can of pepper spray; in her right was a taser. She was certainly not defenseless. "Understand?"

"Yes, Circe. I understand. I didn't think. I'm used to entering with my own keys."

"I assumed it was you but was prepared. A girl has to be careful, especially in a strange city."

I nodded, drinking her in.

Circe had let her luxurious blond hair cascade about her face, down onto her bare shoulders. She wore the same corset she'd worn to Sorcerer's. The gold brocade looked brighter and richer tonight, her tits overflowing the cups, threatening to escape at the slightest forward movement.

I almost moaned out loud.

Below her corset-trapped tits, I could see the tied bow of a long wrap skirt in a semi-sheer shimmering gold fabric. The leg that showed through was long and clad in a sheer black stocking. The garter clip holding the stocking showed at the apex of the skirt's slit. A gold-colored, high-heeled pump encased her foot. She looked like Circe, the witch from mythology, whose name she'd taken. She was a vision I hadn't expected, and my eyes were drawn to the keys that hung into her cleavage.

"Don't just stand there, come in. I guess you know where everything is, right?"

I nodded, unsure what I should say.

"Good. Then pour me a liqueur. A new bottle of Grand Marnier is on the counter in the kitchen. Bring me the drink so we can get on with the evening. Any questions?"

"Not now, Circe. Perhaps later."

"Excellent. Now, get to it."

I knew my way around Simon's apartment. I heard Sophie, or Circe, moving about and sensed she'd left the living room. Concentrating on getting the drink she ordered, I found a small glass that could be used for liqueur and carefully poured a good measure of the warm amber liquid. *Think! Don't just take her drink in by hand.* Simon had some trays around somewhere, so I rooted around until I found a small tray. I carefully folded a napkin along one edge, then placed the drink in the middle, like in the better SF hotels that I couldn't afford to frequent.

I returned to the living room with her drink and found her sitting in one of the armchairs, her back straight, legs crossed, her skirt slit open, and her leg exposed up to her hip. The black stocking was a stark contrast to the creamy thigh above it. The garter disappeared into the higher folds of the fabric. I was so focused on her, I didn't notice the four cuffs on the floor to one side.

She reached for her drink. "Thank you, Mas. Now, undress completely and put on the wrist and ankle cuffs."

This was getting real. "Circe, may I ask a question?"

"Of course."

"Thank you. We have not negotiated a scene or gone over rules, limits, or safe words. This is all very sudden and not the way I usually do things."

She smiled. "Mas, do you trust me?"

"I'm getting there. On the kink side, I'm not sure what to expect."

"Honesty. How refreshing. If you want, you can leave right now, though I hope you won't. I guarantee you will leave here unmarked, except perhaps from the cuffs. This is a getting-to-know-us session. You are bigger than me—and far stronger—so the cuffs are for my peace of mind. We will enjoy this evening, perhaps as the start of something more. Do you trust me that far?"

I stared at the sturdy cuffs, as well as the locks and

chains. Once they clicked closed, I'd be at her mercy. I wanted this. I *really* wanted this. I had missed this feeling. My gut said *go along.*

"Yes, Circe. I trust you that far."

She beamed. "Then undress and put on the cuffs." I took two steps toward the bathroom when she stopped me. "Oh, no, Mas. Strip here. I want to see you revealed, piece by piece. This is part of my pleasure. You do want to please me, right?"

My voice went quiet. "Yes, Circe. I do want to please you."

"Pardon? I didn't quite catch what you said."

I cleared my throat and tried to find my voice. "Yes, Circe. I want to please you."

"Good. That's what I thought. You need to speak clearly."

I hadn't stripped in front of anyone for a long time. Humiliation was part of the dominant's power. The naked person always felt more vulnerable in the presence of a clothed person. At least, I always did.

Starting with my shoes, I kicked them and my socks to one side. Then, I moved to my light sweater, followed by my shirt. She gasped when I turned. She saw, for the first time, the scars where I'd been stabbed—old, worn scars. I turned back to face her, knowing she wanted to see my discomfort. I loosened my belt and slid my zipper down. I heard her soft breathing and saw my keys, rising and falling in rhythm with her full breasts. My cock stirred. I eased my jeans down my legs.

Her eyes followed my jeans' descent, then widened as she noted the bullet scar in my left thigh.

Kicking off my jeans, I collected them and added

them to the rest of my clothes. All I had left was my tight underwear, my cage obvious through the fabric. I eased them down and added them to the pile. My cage stuck out in front of me, my cock erect in its prison, flesh pushing out through the slots in the cage.

Circe eased back in her chair, a satisfied smile gracing her face. "You have taken good care of yourself." She pointed to the cuffs.

The cuffs, another item from Suzanne's cache, were good quality—heavy, thick lined leather, metal D rings stitched and riveted on. I attached the wrist and ankle cuffs. The leather was soft with wear and felt comfortable. I looked up at Circe.

She nodded.

I lifted the chain. It was a hogtie—four lengths of chain attached to a central ring. I laid the ring on the floor with two pieces of chain on the bottom and two on the top. Squatting, I locked a piece of chain to each ankle ring, leaving two pieces free. Kneeling, I reached behind me, picked up a piece of chain, and locked it on my left cuff. Repeating the process with my right cuff. I was effectively at her mercy. Naked, with my limbs joined behind me, I lowered my head in supplication, waiting for her command. I was intoxicated with the feeling of helplessness. I didn't think my penis could get any harder. I could feel the heat rising off me. I was burning from the inside, and I was home. This was where I belonged—on my knees, bound, in front of a woman, wanting to serve.

Sophie seemed to anticipate my reaction. She lifted a glass of cold water to my lips.

I felt disoriented. When she spoke, it seemed to come from far away.

"Mas, I appreciate your trust in me. You will not be disappointed. I am going to ensure all the locks are securely closed. Then, I will be able to relax and have some fun." As she moved behind me and crouched down, my keys swung away from her, touching my back.

Their touch seared into me like hot iron. I groaned out loud which caused Circe to chuckle loudly.

"You did a nice job of binding yourself."

Music to my ears. The cold water had brought me back to reality. I refocused on her. She had returned to the chair.

She sat on the front edge, her legs splayed wide, and her skirt pulled open to her waist. Her garters led my eyes up to her cunt—open, wet, and inviting. Her labia were like petals on an exotic, intoxicating flower, ready to be devoured by the faithful. Her blond bush was neatly trimmed, framing her dripping pussy. "You can have this, if you can get here."

I struggled forward, sliding and shuffling my restrained body toward her glorious prize. My efforts drew laughter from Circe, who encouraged me to greater efforts. Slowly, I edged between her legs, settling as close to her wanting pussy as I could, but trapped by my bonds, my mouth couldn't reach her nirvana.

Circe reached down and pulled me forward, using my knees as pivot points.

I tipped forward, my face landing in her pussy, my tongue on her slit.

She let out a long moan, saying, "You know what to do." Her voice was breathy.

I needed no encouragement. I lapped at her

wetness, drinking her in like she was the fountain of youth. She tasted clean and fresh. I worked my way up and down her slit, teasing her clit. Using my tongue as a flat paddle, I lapped at her, changing to a hard point, focusing on her clit.

She shoved me back. I knew I was merely the tool of her pleasure, and I was enveloped by it. My trapped cock had filled to uncomfortable restriction. I was torn between satisfying Circe and focusing on my own predicament.

She controlled the level of intensity by pushing into me, then pulling away as she rose to climax, groaning in pleasure.

My face was wet from her juices. I tried to absorb as much as I could, but they dripped off my chin. I nuzzled her bush, twisting the soft hair with my tongue and pulling on her folds with my lips, causing her moans of pleasure to rise and fall.

Circe was always in control, until the erotic elevator rushed to an explosion. Sophie grabbed my head and rammed it into her, clamping down on the sides of my head with her legs. Even with my ears closed by her thighs, I heard her scream out her orgasm. It came in waves, and she humped my trapped face, trying to maximize her pleasure until slowly, she subsided. She fell back in her chair, her full breasts heaving.

I fell forward, following her spent pussy, my head resting between her legs on the soaked fabric of her skirt. I'd never felt like this, not even with Mistress. I knew this was something special, and I wallowed in the feeling. This was an experience I wanted to repeat again and again.

After what seemed like ages, Circe helped me move into a kneeling position. She tossed me a set of keys. "You may release yourself while I have a shower." She walked slowly out of the room, leaving me to struggle with the keys.

Releasing myself was not easy. It took several attempts to get the key into the lock, only to find it was the wrong key. Finally, I released my right hand. After that, it was much easier and soon, I was free. My knees were stiff and sore, but I felt content.

She returned, wearing a silk robe that draped seductively over her naked body. The fabric fell softly over the smooth curve of her breasts and her hardened nipples. She smiled. "I told you, you could trust me. Not a mark on you. We had fun, didn't we?"

I grinned back. "Yes, we did." Then, I noticed she wasn't wearing my keys.

She followed my gaze and chuckled. "No, Mas. Not tonight. Tonight was mine and only mine. You gave up your keys voluntarily. I'm not cruel, but I do like to tease. The keys are well hidden for tonight. You can get dressed, and I'll see you tomorrow at the office. Have a good night." She wiped her finger on the tip on my cage. It came away wet. She wiped her finger on my cheek then sat and watched me dress.

I was so horny, I could burst, my frustration level through the roof. It felt great. I wasn't in control of any aspect of this situation. A satisfaction settled over me, a balance of frustration and contentment. I raised her hand and kissed the back of it.

She laughed. "I think we're way beyond that." She kissed me deeply, and I responded with the tongue that had caused her such pleasure.

Not remembering the walk home, I collapsed onto my bed and went out like a light. I slept deeper than I had in a long time.

Chapter 25

Waking early, I felt more refreshed than I had in many moons. I jumped out of bed, showered, and dressed. I needed to get to the office and work on catching a killer. We had enough leads to start eliminating people and narrowing it down. Turning on the television as I dressed, a news item caught my ear. *Serial killer*. Shit was going to hit the fan. I knew Kenzo would blame me for the leak, so I called him. No answer. I left a message, then called Sophie's cell.

She picked up on the first ring. Before I could say anything, she said. "What the fuck? Who was the asshole who leaked? Yes, I saw it, and I'm pissed. They used my sister's name. Bastards! They're going to blame us, aren't they?"

"For sure. I already have a call into Kenzo. Hopefully, we can head off the shit storm. Even if he believes me, the rug will be pulled out from under him. We'd be the collateral damage."

"I'm not getting sidetracked by some shit media circus. That's why I don't like working through official channels. They have no idea about security. It's the stupid people they hire; they're the weak link. I guarantee it was someone trying to make points or get payback."

"Sophie, it doesn't matter. We're going to do our thing. In a way, this could be a good thing; we won't be the media's focus. Kenzo and his team will be up to their eyeballs. We'll be invisible. If they use your name, I'd say the leak's in Kenzo's backyard, and we have an in there."

"Our back door. It could work in our favor."

"Let's wait and see. Kenzo's calling. Talk at the office." I switched callers. "Hey. Who has the big mouth? I saw the news. It wasn't us. I just got off the phone with Sophie, and she's as pissed as I am. You've got a leak."

He took a long pause. "Doesn't matter where it came from. The brass says you're off the investigation. Sorry. I tried to talk to them, but they wouldn't listen."

"You're making a mistake. We won't leave this case alone. Not a chance. Looks like we're going in different directions anyway, so good luck on finding your psycho. Oh, just a thought. When you see your team, watch for who's the happiest to see us gone. Bet they're your leak. Cheers." I hung up.

As bad as this was, it could work in our favor. The SFPD were looking for an out-and-out psycho. I was convinced the crime was connected to Suzanne and Jack Mellon.

Next, I called a journalist I knew at the *Chronicle*. He picked up, and I asked him what he had on the serial killer.

"Not much. Just got an anonymous tip that bodies were found in the Bay. Headline will be 'Bayside Killer.' "

"And that's all you know?"

"Why? How are you related to this case?"

"Just interested since I live close."

"Well, the sister of one of the victims is here in SF.

177

Should be more coming out soon."

"Got a name?"

"Maybe, but not willing to release details, if I have any."

For me, that confirmed the leak was from Kenzo's team, but who was squealing? I changed gears and grabbed my cell. "Hi, Marie. Could you please grab a bite for all of us? I'm headed in now. Oh, and if anyone calls for Sophie, you've never heard of her, capisce?"

"Got it, boss."

"And if you see her before I do, tell her not to answer her phone unless it's me or a Philly number she knows. Same with e-mail." I was mad about the situation, but now, I had to control it and plan out what to do going forward.

When I got to the office, I found my door locked. *Hmm. That's odd.* I banged my way in, in case there was an intruder.

Marie and Sophie came running out of the inner office with what-the-hell-are-you-doing looks on their faces.

"The door was locked."

"You said be careful with phones and e-mail, so we were careful with the door, as well. You okay with that?"

I couldn't fault Maria's logic. *Good for her.* "Yeah, I'm good with that…and thank you for it."

She smiled, checked the door again, and went back to eating her breakfast.

Sophie grinned. "Good morning."

I answered without thinking. "What's good about it?" I mentally smacked myself in the head. "Sorry. It's BC."

"What?" She looked perplexed.

"BC. Before coffee. Before you say anything and before we get involved with the day, I want to thank you for last night, though I'm not sure I understand everything. I'm just getting back to where I need to be, and you were…are…a major catalyst. You don't need to say anything."

She turned to face me and wrapped me in a hug. "My pleasure."

I needed breakfast. The day had started badly and too quickly for me, and I didn't see much change ahead.

As we ate, Sophie's computer dinged. She reached over and flicked on the screen. "Looks like we got the results from Philly."

"And they are…?" I asked around a mouthful of breakfast sandwich.

She opened the file, her lips creeping into a smile. "I was right. The Dissolve program is a scam. Fiend took the whole thing apart. Let me read it and understand it first, and then I will explain. Okay?"

What else could I do but agree? While she was occupied, I checked out Tara Zosa. With the breaking news, we might be able to use it to our advantage. I found Tara's office number and noted it. I'd still have to work out a strategy with Sophie. I talked with Marie about my plan for protecting Sophie. Marie was as sweet, polite, and efficient as you could ask for in an office manager, but she was also a great gatekeeper. After explaining what I wanted and why, she was in pit-bull mode. We agreed keeping the front door locked would be our new protocol, for now.

With breakfast finished, Marie went back to her own desk in the front office, pulled out a set of keys, and pulled a single key off the set. The key was for the back entrance to the building, if and when we needed a more secluded exit.

Sophie looked up. "Okay. Ready for some enlightenment?"

Nodding, I hoped I'd understand what the scam was about, aside from money.

"Here goes. Jack was a smart cookie, which we knew. What he did was cobble together several existing encryption buster programs, basically pirating them and merging them into what looked like a new platform. He was good. He could write code, and he spliced the programs together. What he did wasn't easy. Makes me wonder why he didn't just work with some tech companies on the up and up. He would've made good money and if he'd gotten on with a successful start-up, he would've been made for life."

I chimed in. "Sometimes there is no rhyme or reason. Perhaps he'd been burned and wanted revenge? Or maybe he just wanted to do things his way, right or wrong."

Sophie pondered that. "Possibly, but this was a well-thought-out scam. It fooled a lot of smart people, my sister for one. I know she eventually caught on and look where that got her." Her voice broke slightly. Quickly recovering, she asked, "Will this help us?"

"I think so. I don't know the ins and outs of all the tech stuff, but if Jack fooled Rant and your sister for so long, how long do you think it would fool someone less tech savvy than them?"

"A long time. At least until they had a thorough analysis of the program, like we did, or tried to use it to break a tough encryption problem and it failed. Why?"

"So, no one knows it's a fake? If Rant knows, they aren't going to shout that from the rooftops. What if the person who searched Jack's place didn't find the Dissolve program, or didn't know it was a fake? They're still out there, looking. Think about it. Jack, the originator; your sister, who worked on it; and Kasagawa, who invested in it, all dead, the last killings. I think the first four were decoys. I think Jack was the real target and your sister, the primary tester, was starting to have concerns. I think Jack was skimming cash, and someone eliminated her to keep it covered up."

"What about Kasagawa? Why was he killed? He was an investor but didn't know everything about the project from the inside."

"I've been pondering that. I think he was in the wrong place at the wrong time. Aside from Jack and Suzanne, who were killed weeks apart, none of the other victims seemed to have any connections. Suzanne and Kasagawa did. Outside of kink, they were connected at Rant. Jack was also connected through Rant. The killer needed two bodies to dump and Kasagawa was a convenient, second body. I think the kink aspect is a deflection; it's an easy connect for the police to bite on. The BDSM community isn't as open as the gay community, and it's very misunderstood by the public. I think we have a killer who wants to get their hands on the Dissolve program."

I sat back. Now that I'd verbalized it, the hypothesis made even more sense to me. The hard part was proving it. I waited for Sophie to say something—to tell me I was crazy, or it was rubbish.

She pondered it for a long while before answering.

"I think it's crazy. Would someone really kill eight people for this piece of junk?"

"They would *if* they believed it was the real thing. They don't have it or can't get into it, so far. Whoever has it, hasn't discovered it's crap."

"Let's say you're right. People, including the killer, would still be searching for it, right? They know Rant has it, or a good amount of it, so why not break in and steal it?"

"Probably because security is too tight and they thought Jack would have it on his own hard drive, which is missing."

"Okay. They may have it on his hard drive, but they can't get at it, yet. I'm sure he protected it well. He'd wouldn't want anyone to access it."

"You cracked his flash drives easily enough. Whoever has his hard drive has had it for, what? Over a month? Could he be that good?"

"I had a head start, and flash drives are easier to crack than a hard drive. There are many ways to compartmentalize the program and protect each section. It can take a long time to break something down and rebuild it."

"Your friend in Philly did a breakdown in two days."

"Yeah, because he is a genius, and I sent him open files. Oh, I forgot to mention, it's not the complete program on the flash drives. Just enough to determine it's a scam."

"Okay, point taken. I want to keep you out of the limelight. I want you to keep a low profile for a while. No one knows who you are, at least not yet. If they find out you're the relative mentioned in the media, they won't know where you're living. You like being off the grid, right?"

"Yes, as long as you don't shut me out."

"No chance. I need your dubious skills to make this work. Where can I acquire some listening devices? And what do you need so you can monitor them remotely?"

"Listening devices? Who're you gonna bug? You can leave all that stuff to me. How many will you need?"

I was entering uncharted territory. All my previous surveillance had been signed off on by a judge. *Not this time*. Sophie'd be much more adept at determining what was required than I.

"Tara Zosa—bug her office, for sure, and her home, if possible. I'd also like to get as much info as possible on Howard and Gilbert. I don't think Howard or Gilbert are major players. It doesn't make sense for them to kill Jack or Suzanne, at least not with what we have so far. So, you decide on what I need and how to deploy it."

Sophie thought for a moment before answering. "How soon do we need this equipment? ASAP, I assume? I'll make some calls. I also think we should clone her phone. Do you know how to do that? I can show you, if you don't. How will you approach Tara?"

"ASAP would be good, and no, I don't know how to clone a phone. As for contacting Tara, I think I'll use Kasagawa. I don't want to expose you. I'd rather explore Kasagawa being a foreigner, leaving you and Rant out of it, for now. I can concentrate on the kink aspect and his wealth, the track the police are taking. I'll say her name came up in my inquiries, and I'm investigating all leads. I can play it dumb. I'm sure she'll check me out, and you know what she'll find."

"I'll stay in the shadows, as long as I'm involved. I really want to check out her building and home. Do we know where she lives? Then, we can make a plan before you meet her."

"No, but I am sure you can find a way."

She smirked. "Let me make a few calls. We should be able to get what we need pretty quickly. It will cost us, but it'll be worth it."

"Fine. I'm going to bill it to my client's account, anyway."

She laughed. "Maybe the client will be the one collecting."

I smiled. We seemed to be getting to a level of easy banter, something I'd had with Simon and had missed. I left her to make her calls. I went back to hunting for information on Tara Zosa. I knew her office was on Battery Street, close to the financial district while not actually being in it. Getting into the building wouldn't be a problem. Getting in to see her could be. I didn't look like her regular clients, not even in my best suit on my best day. I'd have to find attractive bait, so she'd invite me in to see her. Then, she'd feel in control. In her own environment she'd be as relaxed as she could get.

Sophie got up, grabbed her bag, and left. "Won't be long. Got some shopping to do."

Before I could ask if she wanted me to go with her, she was gone. Wasn't much I could do except wait, so I took Marie to lunch, which surprised her.

"I think Sophie is a good influence on you. Keep it up."

"Really? Am I that bad?"

"No. You're getting better, that's all."

We laughed and chatted. The conversation wandered all over the place, and it was good to catch up. The past month or so had been a miserable shroud. I hadn't even realized how bad it had been. Now, the fog was finally lifting. It was good to get back to life.

We made our way back to the office. Sophie was impatiently waiting for us. "What took you so long? I'll have everything ready by lunchtime tomorrow. I still need to download some software, but that won't take long. Where were you? I managed to find Tara's home address. God, the police system is a mess. Finding anything is like wading through sludge. Anyway, I had a thought on how we can maximize our time and efforts." She looked at us. "What?"

Both Marie and I chorused, "Just wondering when you'd come up for air."

"There's a lot to do, and I have to teach Mas how to join the twenty-first century."

Marie looked doubtful. "Do I even want to know?"

I answered that with "No, you don't. What you don't know can't hurt you."

Sophie spent the next couple of hours going over what she'd bought and explaining how it all worked in the simplest terms she knew. When I met with Tara, my job was to keep her talking and distracted. I was to plant at least two bugs. Sophie would instruct me how when they arrived. She'd purchased several burner phones and showed me how to clone a phone, though she hadn't downloaded the software yet to make them work. I'd be able to clone Tara's phone, as long as it was on.

"How can I check to see if it's on?"

"Easy. Marie will visit Tara, too, but she'll stay in the outer office. As soon as you go in, Marie will text me *My place,* and I'll call Tara's cell so—"

"But we don't have her cell number."

"I'll take care of that. By the way, do you have an extra key-gun thingie?"

Now, I was getting worried. She read my expression.

"You don't want to know. It'll be fine. We're finally making progress, and this is something where I can be useful."

I left it at that. I gave her my key gun and called Tara Zosa. She wasn't available, so I left a message. I made sure Mr. Kasagawa's name was prominently mentioned and was intriguingly vague, with a hint of a threat, then called it a day. Sophie waved as I left. "I'm gonna stay for a while longer. I'll see you tomorrow."

Chapter 26

The next day dragged by as we waited for Sophie's delivery and a call back from Tara's office. Sophie said, "Will you please go do something? You're making me crazy."

I considered going to the shooting range, but discarded the idea. I didn't want to miss Tara's call when it came. I'd dangled enough bait, so now I had to be patient. We were thinking about lunch when my phone rang. I snatched it off the desk. "Hammett and Lee Investigations. How may I help you?"

I heard a sharp voice with a clipped accent. "Mr. Hammett?"

"Speaking."

"Tara Zosa. My apologies for the delay. I'm rather busy, at the moment."

"Of course. Thank you for returning my call. I've been retained to investigate a disappearance."

"And this involves me how?" She wasn't happy.

"I came across a Mr. Kasagawa, and I believe you conducted business with him."

"Some time ago, yes. Nothing recently."

"I know one deal leads to another. Hi-tech is a small world. You have a high profile and a solid reputation. I was hoping you could fill me in on some details."

"I'm still not sure how this involves me."

"I'm sure it doesn't, but I have to do my due diligence. It probably has nothing to do with you or Mr. Kasagawa's investments in Silicon Valley." My statement was met with silence except for her sharp intake of breath.

Tara took several moments. "If you think I can help, you're welcome to come to my office, though I'd only be able to give you a few minutes. As I said, I'm very busy."

Got her. She wants to know what I know. "Miss Zosa, that's very generous of you. I appreciate your time. I'm out of the office today. How is your calendar tomorrow?"

Another few minutes of silence.

I heard her fingers, tapping away at her keyboard—a short e-mail. I wondered to whom she'd sent it. Hopefully, Sophie would be able to backtrack it when she gained access.

Tara sounded more relaxed. "I can squeeze you in at eleven fifteen for fifteen minutes. Will that do?"

"That will be fine. I doubt I'll need that much. As I said, dotting the I's and crossing the T's. It's really a formality. Thank you again. See you tomorrow."

She hung up as soon I spoke my last words.

With that set, we had a plan. Sophie and I went over how to clone a phone again. Tara had called me from her cell, not her office line, so we now knew that number. Sophie instructed me where to place the bugs, in order of preference. It seemed easy enough, in theory. Reality was usually more complicated. This was more in line with spying. It was clearly illegal and for the first time, I was okay with it. *My, how things change.* Now that we had our timeline, Sophie had plenty to do. "I don't want you under my feet."

"Have you figured out who leaked the info to the media?"

Her face became serious.

"Not Kenzo, I hope."

"No, not Kenzo. De la Cruz."

"Bitch. She wasn't happy about us being involved from day one. Can you prove it?"

"Oh, yeah. No problem there. The proof is on this thumb drive. I think it was intentional. What are you going to do?"

"What do you mean, it was deliberate?"

"She gave the victims' info to another team, which is where the leak originated. It could've been accidental, though I think it was deliberate. She's corrupt, stupid, or both."

"Payback's a bitch. I'm not personally going to do anything. Marie will visit an internet café and send the file to Kenzo with a message. If he doesn't do something about her and the source of the leak, their incompetence will be leaked to the media. The SFPD did nothing to maintain the confidentiality of the victims. If that doesn't get a reaction and a result, we'll post it on the internet. No one will ever trust them again—especially, victims. They'll be well and truly fucked, deservedly so."

"Whoa. Remind me never to piss you off."

"This isn't about me. For whatever reason, they jeopardized the investigation in multiple ways. That's incompetence, and they know it." I called Marie into the office and explained what I wanted her to do and why. "Be sure to avoid any cameras."

"I know what I'm doing. See you in a few." She

grinned at Sophie, took the thumb drive, and left.

With that accomplished, and Sophie working and waiting, I took off.

I was mad at both Josie and her conspirator. Investigators didn't do that shit. It was petty and stupid. I stopped by home and picked up my pistol. When I'd handed in my PD Sig, I'd wanted a change, and the HK 9mm had been my choice. At the gun range, I purchased a hundred rounds and was directed to an alley. Eyes and ears protected, I loaded the magazine and spares, pushed the target out to five yards, and emptied the first magazine.

Fire, wait three seconds, fire. Repeat until the magazine was empty. Remove magazine, pull back the slide, rest the weapon on the bench facing down range, take down the target, and replace with a new one.

I repeated the process, increasing the distance by five yards with each new magazine. It wasn't as bad as I expected. Rusty yes, but not bad. I asked if I could do rapid-fire practice when I purchased another hundred rounds. Since I was the only person on the range, they agreed unless another shooter showed up. Then I'd have to go back to regular fire. I thanked them for the courtesy.

Loading the magazines, I relaxed, took my stance, and let loose. I wasn't as accurate with rapid fire but made enough hits to keep from worrying about anything coming back at me in a live situation. I swept up my brass then scooped the casings into a large bucket. I reviewed each of my targets. I folded the targets and put them in the trash. I'd improved over the two hundred rounds. It was like riding a bike. I made a mental note to get back to the practice range more regularly.

Feeling relaxed and content with the afternoon's focus, my cock started to fill—even that frustration felt good—which brought me back to the memory of diving into Sophie's juicy pussy. *So good.* My cage strained against my underwear. Without any recent physical satisfaction, it sent shivers through my entire body. I wanted to repeat that feeling…and soon.

When I returned home, my first priority was to thoroughly clean my weapon, twice, and store it safely. I rarely felt the need to carry a gun—my investigations seldom led to violent confrontations. I was happier carrying a spring-loaded baton which usually discouraged even the most aggressive confrontations.

Covered in gunshot residue, I stripped off the GSR-covered clothes and dropped them in the dirty bin, showered, and then ordered pizza.

Later, at the table as I munched, I mulled over tomorrow's visit to Tara's. The plan was simple—there shouldn't be any issues—and with the timeline Tara set, not much time for it to crash. I went over every detail in my head. I needed little time to place the bugs. I had Sophie's list of preferred places memorized, and I'd perfected the cloning procedure.

My biggest concern was taking Marie with me. She'd be linked to me—I came up with a work-around to keep her anonymous and would talk to her in the morning. Satisfied I was ready, I went to bed horny as hell, but looking forward to the action the following day.

Chapter 27

The alarm hammered me awake. I stretched awake, yawned, and dressed for the day. I decided on my best suit—no need to look like the stereotypical gumshoe—finished off with a nice button-down shirt, appropriate tie, and shoes that were worn, but of good quality. I debated strapping on my weapon—it could lend credibility—but then again, it would probably be better if I gave the impression of a gullible, not-so-swift operator. After all, I was there to plant the devices and clone her phone. I'd stoop a little, look a little less fit than I actually was, and get into character. The thought of action juiced me up.

Being the first to arrive at the office, I put the coffee on, called in a breakfast order into the deli, and texted Marie it was paid for and to please pick it up on her way in. We had several hours until I met with Tara, and I didn't want to waste them.

I cranked up my computer. I had an e-mail from Kenzo, requesting a call. *Short, sweet, and to the point. Gee, I wonder what that's about.* I placed the call; he picked up on the first ring. "Kenzo, it's Mas. I hope you don't want my help. Not gonna happen."

"No, Mas. I think you've done enough helping."

"Fuck you. See you around." I started to hang up.

"Don't hang up. That was unfair. The media is hanging on my balls and I've got nothing."

"Pity. We're making good progress. What do you want?"

"To apologize."

That stopped me cold. "What?"

"You heard me. You were right. The media leak wasn't you and—"

"I told you that. Did you really think we were that stupid?"

"Mas, I was on your side. Anyway, we had an anonymous tip, claiming they had proof it was one of my team, and I remembered what you said—to look at who was most pleased you were gone. That person and another from a different team leaked the info."

I played dumb. "So, who was it? Or can't you say?"

"Let's say the person in question is off the team and out of serious crimes. She's lucky she still has a job. The other one, similar fate. If I didn't know you better, I'd think you had something to do with this. Now, I'm trying to get you back on the case. We're even more short-handed now and bringing in someone new would mean playing catch-up."

I felt a bit sorry for him. I'd been in the same situation—but that wasn't my problem now. "Sorry, Kenzo. They made it clear I'm not in the blue club anymore. Unfortunately, it's taken me longer to realize and accept. That's all. If we get anything, I'll pass it on, but my client's case is my priority."

I was tempted to say something about conspiracy theories, but that would only lead to a fishing expedition. No, when we closed this one, he could have it all—the collar, the kudos, the press. We'd know what we'd done and that would be enough.

"Sorry how this turned out, Mas. If you need me, I remember how you treated me when I came to your team. I don't forget obligations."

"Shit, Kenzo. Don't go all samurai on me. You were born here and raised in a Catholic school."

"I mean it, Mas."

"Okay. Thanks. Bye." I hung up, thinking back to his first day on my team—wet behind the ears, but smart. He'd worked hard at everything, and he deserved better than Josie and her accomplice. Marie's arrival broke my thoughts. I set aside the past and looked forward to the day. I'd have to be firing on all cylinders and a solid breakfast was a good start. As we were setting out breakfast, Sophie arrived, looking frazzled.

"Something wrong?"

"Logistics. The bugs are on their way, but they're stuck in traffic."

"Welcome to SF."

We sat down and went over the plan as we ate, much to the women's annoyance. They went along to appease me. I showed them my slight stoop and shuffle, which they applauded. Marie mussed up my hair for a more disheveled look.

A banging on the front door shut it all down. I motioned for the two women to stay put then went to the outer office, closing the inner door as I left. Cautiously, I opened the door to find a young man in a hoodie, holding a small package. "Is Ms. Circe available for a delivery? I have to hand it to her directly."

Sophie heard his request, and she raced out to grab the package. The young man turned to go, but Sophie grabbed him. "Wait until I check it."

He shrugged and waited.

Sophie had the package open in seconds. She grinned. "All good. Please tip him a twenty." She passed me on the way back to the inner office.

He held his hand out, I tipped him, and he was gone. I locked the door.

Sophie was laying out small ziplock baggies on her desk. Each one contained a small box, far more than I would need.

"Why so many?"

A sneaky smile crossed her face. "I have plans for the others. I'll be leaving before you do. I have another appointment. Marie, don't forget the text as soon as Mas is in with Zosa."

"I got this." Marie huffed.

I remembered my plan to distance myself from Marie and made a mental note. Now, to get to Tara's.

Chapter 28

Sophie left for her mysterious meeting before Marie and I departed. I rechecked the listening devices, which were surprisingly small. Three of them rattled in my jacket pocket. Two I was planting and a spare. Better safe than sorry.

Finally, the clock rounded our appointed time. Leaving first, I hailed a taxi at the corner of my street. Marie followed ten minutes later. I'd wait for her outside Tara's office building and as she arrived, check my watch to make it look like our simultaneous entrance was a coincidence.

The day was warmish, though the breeze blowing between the tall buildings added a chill to the air. Frequently checking my watch, I hoped I looked like someone early for a meeting or an interview.

After several minutes, Marie walked purposefully toward the building entrance. I checked my watch again. Approaching the entrance from the opposite direction, I opened the door and held it for Marie just as she got there. I followed her to the elevators just as another couple came through the other door.

We all waited as the elevator arrived and disgorged its passengers. I entered last. The guy with the woman pressed the button for the fourth floor, and Marie chose the sixth. I pressed seven. The couple got off, and I rode up to six with Marie.

"Why did you choose seven?"

"Can't be too careful. I'll go up a floor and walk back down."

When I did, we entered the reception area together. I identified myself to the assistant, and she told me Ms. Zosa would be with me directly. As she turned to speak with Marie, her buzzer chimed, and Tara asked if I'd arrived.

"Yes, ma'am." She hung up the phone and turned to Marie, saying, "Please wait a moment. Sir, please follow me."

I followed her down a thick, plush carpeted corridor to the last office. She knocked and showed me in. The office was elegant and expensively appointed with windows on one side of the office, letting in lots of light. The wall behind the desk held artwork with a mixture of awards and photographs of, I assumed, very rich people she'd worked with in the past. The third wall was dominated by a large original abstract painting, bordered on each side with crowded bookshelves.

Tara Zosa stood as I entered, held out her hand, and offered a firm, short handshake. "Please, take a seat. I'm not sure how I can help you, and as I said previously, I only have fifteen minutes." She looked more anxious than I'd expected but stood tall in her business suit, feminized with a frilled white silk shirt, jade earrings, and a jade broach on her lapel. The jade had an antique feel to it. *No soapstone for this lady*.

"Thank you for seeing me." I handed her my card.

She set it on her desk without looking at it.

"As I said, I'm following up on anything and everything. I understand you had a business relationship with Mr. Kasagawa."

"Yes, a very successful one. We worked well together."

Past tense. She was hiding something. "Are you still working with him?"

She hesitated, just for a moment. "Yes. We have an ongoing relationship. We usually work together on his Japanese projects and my U.S. endeavors."

I made her tell and knew she was lying. She reached up to fiddle with her right earring. I knew her relationship had ended. I'd be sure to push on that one.

The cell on her desk rang. She looked at it, frowned, and picked it.

I pulled out my burner phone, as if to check a message, and initiated the cloning process. Letting it do its work, I palmed one of the bugs and surreptitiously reached under my chair.

She ended the call and put the phone back down on her desk. "Sorry about that. I'm not sure where these people get my number. Where were we?"

"Your ongoing relationship with Mr. Kasagawa. Were you aware he was in the country a few weeks ago?"

"No. He mentioned he might be coming here on a social trip, but I heard nothing further. So, no. I didn't know he was in San Francisco."

I'd never mentioned San Francisco. "He's involved I understand, with a company in Silicon Valley, I believe. They aren't very forthcoming, so I'm not sure if his trip was social or business. Anyway, he's not the purpose of my investigation. His name just came up during my inquiries, which is how I came to you."

She tensed, though it was well covered, then

relaxed. "Really, I don't know of any project or business he'd have with Rant Applications."

I hadn't mentioned Rant Applications. I watched her twirl her earring; her ear was going to be sore. *She may not know exactly what project, but she knew he had something going on.* "What can you can tell me about his social life when he was in San Francisco? That's an area I'm interested in pursuing."

Tara's shoulders relaxed. "Not much. Just some dinners. In some ways, he was very Japanese, preferring male company over dinner. I know he had some ex-pat Japanese contacts living here who he met with socially. Oh, and I don't know if it's true, but I heard a rumor he had some, shall we say, *particular* tastes when it came to sex. Apparently, he visited San Francisco's kink clubs when he was here." She gave me a sly smile and a wink.

I feigned surprise. *She knew about his kink side. Nice how she dropped that into the mix as an afterthought.* "That *is* interesting. The police mentioned something about that in connection with another missing person. Have you any more information about Kasagawa?"

"No. Like I said, it's a rumor. I'm not even sure if it's true. Do you think it's pertinent?"

I stroked my chin with my hand and walked over to the windows. I shoved my hands in my pockets and peered down at the street, watching the bustling late-morning traffic and pedestrians, rushing about their business. "This could be a new avenue for me to follow for my client. A woman was seen with him on the Saturday he disappeared, but no one seems to know where they were or what they were doing."

She watched me intently. "Do you think this has anything to do with the bodies they found in the bay?"

"I don't know. Last I heard, they hadn't identified all the bodies. So, I don't think so. Guess you never know. This *is* San Francisco." I chuckled.

She smiled and rose from her chair. "I hope I was of some help. Our time is up."

I needed a distraction. "Yes, you were. Thank you. I must say, your paintings are superb."

Her eyes drifted to the large piece on the opposite wall.

I quickly put a bug on the end of the bookcase, hiding it behind the sheer drapes. "May I take a closer look?"

I saw a brief flash of annoyance cross her face.

"Of course." She joined me at the painting.

I smiled at her and leaned in to get a closer look. Pretending to stumble, I caught myself on the bookcase. With a quick flick of the wrist, I put the last bug in the stacked books. "That is a great piece, and it fits in perfectly with your office." I thought the piece was ugly junk, but it got me what I needed. We shook hands and I thanked her again for her time. "I'm sure I won't have to bother you again. You've given me a new lead to follow. Now, it's up to me."

She nodded as she showed me out the door, the most relaxed she'd been during my time there.

Her assistant escorted me to reception, I thanked her, and headed down the elevator, thinking about what she'd said. Tara had known Kasagawa was here and was dead. She also knew more about Rant. I could see it in her eyes. She was quick to bring up the kink aspect the police were so fixated on. But why would she bring up the bodies? Unless she didn't realize Kasagawa was one of the bodies. I hoped I'd done my job right and at least one of the devices would transmit information we could use.

I flagged a taxi to return to the office for a debriefing with Sophie. As I did, I noticed a man, walking on the opposite sidewalk, slightly behind me. I'd seen him earlier that morning while I was waiting to meet Tara. He saw me looking at him and turned the other way. I gave him one last look, then relayed the address to the cabbie.

I closed my eyes and tried to fix the image of his face and any other details I could remember. He walked with his hands out of his pockets, looking aware. Yes, that was it—aware of his surroundings. He'd had some training, but I'd caught him by surprise. I dialed Sophie's cell. "Don't say anything. I think I'm being followed. Stay aware. Do some double-backs when you return to the office. Okay?"

Her tone was short. "Okay." She hung up.

Good girl. The cabbie took no time in getting me back to the office. I didn't care if they followed back to the office. If they knew who I was, they'd know where my office was. Nothing lost there. But I would have to be more aware in the future.

Marie was already back in the office, and she'd locked the door, following our new protocol. *She's a gem.*

Researching the KinkInc profiles was next on the list, while I waited for Sophie to return. I didn't like her keeping secrets from me. I took out the burner phone from my pocket and put it on Sophie's desk.

Dumbass. I'd switched off the burner phone by

accident. I was hoping it wouldn't mess things up. I felt like an idiot.

Sophie showed up thirty minutes later, smiling like the cat that had stolen the cream.

"What are you so happy about?" I was still mad at myself for the phone.

"Well, aren't we snippy? Just a successful mission, that's all."

"Mission?"

"Yes, mission. We now have ears in both Tara's office and home."

"Home? You broke into her house?" I was stunned.

"Of course. How else did you expect me to bug it?"

"That was a crazy risk. If you'd been caught, you...*we* would be in the middle of a shit storm. I—"

"Mas, stop thinking like a cop. I knew she wouldn't be there. I checked out the house. No one saw us."

"*Us*? Who was with you? You don't know anyone in SF."

"Mas, please calm down. I know someone who knows someone. This is part of my world, Mas. Trust me."

I was surprised but not really shocked. I fell silent, just looking at her. I'd underestimated her...again.

"I take calculated risks. I usually work out the risk/reward to the nth degree. This involves my sister, so I'll take on some extra risks to get the bastard who's responsible."

"So, you figured that out?"

She cocked her head.

"The person responsible may not be the one who killed her...or any of them. I want to get the person *responsible* for their deaths."

She stared at me, silent. Her tone turned icy. "I want *everyone* involved. Every single one of them. I want them to pay for what they did, even if I go to prison for it."

"Well, let's hope it doesn't come to that. I have a vested interest in some keys and wouldn't want them in an evidence locker." That lightened the atmosphere.

Sophie laughed. "Agreed. That wouldn't be a good thing."

"Next steps for the bugs?"

"I'll initiate the recording process, though it's pretty much automatic. Voice activated and all that. Anything on the clone phone?"

"About that. I'm afraid I turned it off without realizing."

"Nothing lost. We'll have a log of the numbers coming in or out. No big deal."

"I expected you to rip me a new one. It was a dumb mistake."

She smiled. "No big deal. Like I said, we can trace the numbers and find out who they belong to. To be honest, that's all I expect to get. No one is going to confess to anything on an open line, especially not someone like Tara. Oh, did I mention I also piggybacked onto her router at home? If she logs on there, we'll also have her computer."

I raised my eyebrows and sat back, wondering if anything was safe from her. "You really get off on this stuff, don't you?"

She raised one eyebrow. "You bet your ass I do. I love it, and I'm good, too."

"I see that. As a favor, please let me keep some

secrets, will you?"

"Sure. Well, maybe. Depends." With that, she went to work, initiating and cross-referencing the bugs.

I went back to the KinkInc profiles. As fruitless as I expected it to be, you never knew where a pertinent piece of the puzzle would show up. We spent the rest of the day working. Sophie pored over the technical data her friend had sent her, and I put together a comprehensive map of the entire case—broad strokes and details. We still had too many holes to get a clear picture. Sick of the profiles, I stood and walked to the door.

Sophie didn't even look up. "Feel like coming over for a night cap?"

I did a double take. "Uh…yes."

"Deep thought about that one, huh? See you later. Looking forward to it. Same time as before?"

"Yes, same time." I left before I said anything I'd regret.

Chapter 29

Watching for signs of a tail on my way home, I couldn't identify anyone. *Maybe I'm just being paranoid.* I was anxious and excited to see Sophie again, this time, I was hoping for an orgasm.

Time dragged by. I puttered about aimlessly until it was time to leave, then rushed out the door and headed to Sophie's. As soon as I stepped out, I remembered my tail. I was cautious and took the long way around, but still didn't see anything untoward. This time, I rang the buzzer, then let myself in, calling out as I closed the door behind me.

Sophie was waiting. She wore the same silk robe as the other night, but tonight, I could see the outline of a bra under the silk and a thin line around her hips—panties or maybe a garter belt. I was sure I'd find out, in good time.

"Thank you for announcing yourself. I am pleased you are a fast learner. I really didn't want to Taser you as a reminder."

I bowed my head. "I don't want to experience that again, either."

"Again?"

"Yes. I've experienced both. I was pepper sprayed in police training and by a suspect who didn't want to be restrained. I got the Taser when I was hazed by other cops as a rookie."

"That's terrible. The hazing, I mean."

"Don't worry. Karma's a bitch."

"Good. Now, we can concentrate on me. Aren't you over dressed?"

I started stripping but heard a tut-tut from Sophie.

"Shouldn't you ask permission to disrobe?"

"Sorry, Circe. Please, may I disrobe for you?"

"You may."

I undressed slowly, carefully folding my clothes.

She sat and watched, legs crossed, the smooth silk sliding off her upper leg, which was stocking clad. A garter secured the stockings. The creamy smooth skin above the stocking top fixated me…until I heard her words. "When you are done looking, you may finish disrobing; then kiss my feet."

Her comment immediately broke my fixation. I crawled to where she was sitting, bowed, and kissed each shoe.

She gently placed her raised foot against my chest and pushed hard enough for me to lose my balance. She rose and straddled me. The hem of her gown dragging smoothly over my bare skin sent shivers directly to my dick, which automatically responded. She leaned forward, hands on hips, and her gown fell open.

I had a perfect view of her bra-enclosed tits, but what really caught my eye was the key, swinging from a long thin chain around her neck. My eyes followed the swinging key, back and forward.

She saw my eyes, following the movement, and laughed. "What big eyes you have. Do they see something they want?"

"Yes, Mistress." My eyes grew wider. I wasn't at the place to call her Mistress. Yet, it had slipped out. I shut my eyes tight. *What the fuck have I done?* We were silent, letting my two words hang there.

Sophie stood and stared at me. "That was a surprise. I don't think either of us expected that. Do you regret it?"

Think. My emotions were a mash up, but something inside me was glad I'd said it. "No, I don't regret it. It slipped out. I'm not sure why, but I can guess."

"I'm not sure we are in that place yet. I need a release, and this is how I release. I don't want the responsibility of owning a sub, especially with all that's going on with my sister. Ownership is not a trivial matter."

I sat quietly for a moment before answering. "I'd expect no less. I feel comfortable as a sub with you. I'm not sure I fully trust you in the vanilla world, but here, it feels right. Sorry for spoiling the evening."

"Who said anything about the evening being spoiled? I fully intend to enjoy myself. What happens to you is quite beside the point."

Relationship or not, Sophie would get her release the way she wanted, and I, for one, wouldn't object.

Sophie grabbed the arm and leg cuffs from the side table and tossed them to me. "Put them on. I'm still not one hundred percent sure how submissive you are."

I had no issues being naked and bound, if it made her feel more comfortable. I just wanted to come, and I hoped she'd allow it. I'd do whatever it took to get my fuck rod a release.

I easily cuffed my ankles, then started on my wrists.

"Wrists behind your back, please. Then, lie where

you are on the floor."

It was harder than I realized, but I finally managed to get both cuffs closed. I lay on the floor, wondering what she had in mind.

She produced two rolled towels. "Raise your head up." She slipped one towel under my neck. "Sit up, if you can."

I used my hands to leverage myself up. Then she slipped the second towel under my spine. I stared up at her and marveled at how tall and majestic she looked. The shimmering silk moved with the rise and fall of her tits. I could tell she was getting aroused. Apparently, she liked helpless, naked, bound men at her feet.

Watching me intently, like a snake ready to strike, she slowly loosened the tie around her waist. The robe fell open, momentarily hanging on her breasts before dropping away. She wasn't wearing panties. Only her garter belt and stockings framed her pussy .

Wanting so badly to be in there, my penis filled the chastity cage. I inhaled sharply as she eased the robe off her shoulders and let it drop to the floor.

She stood over me, straddling my body. With a wink, she slowly lowered herself on me, one knee on each side of my head, her firm ass resting on my chest.

Waiting. I wanted to taste her again. Her breathing was rapid but controlled. She was building anticipation for what was to come. She inched up my chest, and I had a perfect view of her bra-covered tits, those firm orbs and pointed nipples, making peaks in the fabric. She rose and moved over my head. Exhaling, she descended onto my waiting mouth. The last thing I heard, as her thighs gripped my head, was a long, low moan.

I went to work on her already-wet cunt, and sucked her clit like a little dick. I was in heaven. Using my tongue, I impaled her as deeply as I could before going back to licking and lapping her lips and slit.

In control, she moved on my face as she wished, sometimes lifting slightly off me to reposition herself, then heavily settling back.

Trapped, I couldn't move my body, only my tongue, so I made it count. My eyes drank her in as she touched herself, teasing her nipples through the bra and squeezing and circling the nipple with her fingernails.

I wanted to give her the orgasm she needed. She squashed my head as she continued to ride me as if I were a piece of furniture. I felt her juices running down my face, lubing it as she slid back and forth. Sensing she was getting close, I flicked my tongue faster.

Just before the point of no return, she lifted completely off me. She leaned forward, resting on her outstretched arms, gulping in deep breaths. She waited until her breathing slowed, then settled onto me again. Regaining a rhythm, Sophie picked up her pace. She became more frenetic...more desperate. She ground her pussy against my face and tongue.

Sucking at her labia, nipping her lips with my teeth, I felt her shudder go through me. Riding me back and forth, she began making circles, gyrating her hips across my face.

Feeling her weight and drinking her in kept me hard. My cock throbbed inside the cage. Adding to my frustration, she teased her boobs, kneading them while I watched, yet never quite allowing them out of her bra. This was driving me insane. I could do nothing but satisfy the woman grinding herself to satisfaction on my face.

Suddenly, she pulled herself off me with a groan and leaned forward, like before. This time she rested on her knees and put one of her hands between her legs, rubbing her own pink slit and fingering herself.

I was mesmerized watching as she fucked herself with one hand, while the fingers of the other hand alternately disappeared inside the bra covering her luscious tits.

She moved the hand inside her, searching until she found my mouth. I sucked her fingers, wrapping my tongue around each one, trying to remove every drop of her essence, before she returned her cunt to my mouth. When she did, again I drove my tongue deeply into her, which resulted in a flurry of grinding, rubbing, and gyrating on my face. This time, there was no holding back. Her breathing quickened, and I could hear her ragged breaths, my head clamped between her sweaty, lubricated thighs. She rode me with abandon as she rose to ecstasy while I thrust my hips into the air in frustration, knowing nothing I did would get me off. I felt pulses in her skin as she shuddered and ground out a heart-rending moan, yanking at her bra and nearly tearing it off her breasts.

In an instant, she exploded, shuddering against my face, wet and slippery with her juices. She moaned and moved against me until the last shudder subsided. Spent, she leaned forward, her legs on either side of my head, her head down. "That was nice. *Really* nice. I needed that. You make a nice toy."

I said nothing. Inside I was screaming, "Please, let me come!" With the recent lock-up, her scent, and her orgasm, I wasn't sure if the pleasure of frustration or the frustration of pleasure was the driving force. All I knew was I needed to come.

Sophie stood on shaky legs, collecting her robe as she did. Draped and covered once more in silk, I could see tendrils of hair stuck to her neck and a line of perspiration on her lip.

She still looks divine.

She withdrew the key from her robe and twirled it around her finger, first one way, then the other, then back again, thinking. As if deciding, she stopped the key mid-twirl, took the chain from her neck, and knelt beside me. "Would you like to get out of your cage?"

"Yes, please."

"Very polite. If I let you out, would you like to come?"

"Yes, please."

"If I let you out and let you come, it will be on my terms."

"I understand."

"Would you beg to be let out and allowed to come? They are not the same thing, are they?"

"I will beg if you wish, and no, they are not the same thing." I was almost in tears. She was pushing my buttons.

"Actually, I don't require begging…tonight. I had a very good release. Now, about letting you out. Hmmmmm."

"I will beg you to let me have an orgasm."

"That's nice, but no. You will be let out…" She paused, grinning at me. "You will also be allowed a squirting release tonight."

"Thank you. Thank you. Any way you wish, Ma'am."

She laughed. "I know. And the Ma'am is a nice touch. You may use that title until we decide otherwise...*if* we get to that point."

I couldn't wait to have my release—to siphon the python, as they said. I was still lying on my back. Would she let me jerk off? Would she do it? She could do what she wanted, as long as I came.

She picked up a cushion and knelt beside me. "While I am your cage key holder, you will never be released without being restrained in some way. Do you understand?"

I understood all too well. It meant I'd likely not be touching my own prick in the foreseeable future, not while she had my...or rather...*her* keys. "Yes, Ma'am."

"Good. Now, we can get on with giving you a cum shot."

Oh, my God. Get on with it. My cock was pulsing with frustration, expanding flesh out of the slots.

She casually removed the key chain from around her neck. She grinned again as she inserted the key into the lock. The pressure of my expanded cock made the lock pop open, which brought a chuckle from Sophie.

"I think someone is ready for release." She eased the cage off my prick. It sprang up, released from its prison and the weight of the cage. She clicked open the base ring and for the first time in a long while, I could feel the air directly on my cock. It felt incredible.

"You have a nice piece of equipment. Of course, we wouldn't want you to wear it out, so moderation is important." With that, she picked up a bottle of lube and applied a generous amount to my standing fuck rod. I moaned as her hand skimmed my skin, making my shaft slick. She avoided the head of my cock, but pulled the foreskin back, letting it sit tight around the top of my shaft.

I moved my hips up and down in anticipation of what I hoped would follow.

"Stay still. I am in control of this event, and your dick belongs to me. I will play with it how I wish."

I remained still, my entire focus on my liberated cock.

Sophie increased the pressure on my slippery shaft, circling my erect member with her thumb and forefinger, sliding the circle up and down, but not touching the head.

I was simultaneously in heaven and hell. My balls felt tight against my body. I was ready to come as soon as Sophie let me.

She varied the pressure on my cock and the speed with which she stroked me.

My senses were on overload, overwhelmed by the feeling of being bound and masturbated, everything out of my control. I was stunned I hadn't exploded under her teasing.

Sophie backed off, holding my erect prick. Slowly, with a sexy, naughty grin, she continued stroking, picking up the pace. She now included my foreskin over the sensitive head of my cock. She stopped just long enough to slather more lube on my throbbing member so her hand could easily slip up and down, twisting as she moved.

I felt the surge and knew I wouldn't be able to stop. "May I come? May I *please* come?" I held my breath, not daring to breathe.

"Yes."

I bucked my hips into the air as my entire body

contracted and tightened. I squirted a stream of cream straight into the air. It landed in a warm, wet line on my stomach. I humped the air several times, ejecting my entire store of cum. I shuddered as her hand left my now-deflating member. She didn't say a word. The next thing I knew, the shower was running. I lay still, luxuriating in the memory of the orgasm.

As I came down, I realized I was still bound and helpless. All I could do was wait for Sophie's return.

She returned, wearing a practical robe with her hair wrapped in a towel and carrying a box. She knelt next to me and removed several wipes, which she used to clean off my cock thoroughly. As she did, I realized she was locking me back up. She lubed my cock and quickly replaced the back ring then eased the cage back on. I was, once again, imprisoned. My predicament hit home as she left the room with the key.

On her return, she lifted my shoulders, undid one of the cuffs, and gave me the keys. "Now, you need to clean up your mess. If you are very, very good and I'm feeling generous, I may even want to feel you inside me. If I decide to use your equipment, it will still be on my terms, and if you come before me, you will be severely punished. Now, dress and leave me to get a good night's sleep."

I was both excited and dejected. "Thank you, Ma'am."

"Good toy. See you tomorrow."

I released the rest of the cuffs. Dressing much more rapidly than I'd undressed, I left. Sophie blew me a kiss.

****

Feeling the afterglow as I walked back home, I

dawdled, my mind adrift, not wanting the evening to end. Halfway home, I sensed someone behind me. In an instant, my head exploded. I staggered falling against the wall. My outside leg burst into pain. With blows raining down on me, I struggled to stay upright. I went into self-preservation mode, covering my head with my hands and arms and using my leg to protect my groin. Stars filled my head. Through the lights, I made out fists on gloved hands. I screamed out, knowing I couldn't defend myself. The next best thing was to attract attention. I kept on screaming, even when the blows had stopped, rolling into a fetal position I blacked out.

My eyes flickered open, and I was assaulted by a distinctive smell and bright lights. *Hospital.* My head and left leg were on fire, and everything else throbbed. I heard the curtain retract and a nurse entered with an intern and a cop.

The intern spoke first. "Sir, how do you feel?"

I answered him through a spilt lip. "Like a champ. Ready for another round."

He smiled. "You were lucky. Nothing's broken. You have a concussion, badly bruised ribs, and an extensive hematoma on your leg, and some lesser ones on your arms. The nurse will give you some mild pain meds, and we'll keep you overnight for observation, just to be safe. The concussion is my biggest concern. Everything will heal painfully. The police are here to ask you some questions. Are you able to talk to them?"

I had little choice. "Sure."

The cop was young and, if not a rookie, pretty close. He withdrew his notebook. "Mr. Hammett, do you know who attacked you?"

I shook my head. "No idea. I was walking home and got coldcocked."

"Any idea why someone would attack you?

"I'm a PI, but I haven't pissed anyone off that I know of—at least not recently."

"We don't think you were robbed. We have your belongings. Would you check to make sure everything is there?" He handed me a plastic bag with my phone, wallet, watch, money clip, and keyring.

My hands were sore and abraded, but they didn't feel as bad as my forearms. Gingerly, I opened the bag and tipped the contents on the bed. My watch was fine. Same with my wallet—PI ID, my few credit cards. As I examined it, I realized I was seeing with only one eye. I raised my hand to the other eye, palpating the swelling. *No cuts.* My phone had survived with only a cracked case. *Thank God.* A folded piece of paper I didn't recognize. All it said was, *LEAVE IT ALONE,* printed in block letters. *Not very subtle.*

Setting the paper aside, I fingered through the keys and the money clip. I didn't remember how much I had, but it didn't matter. It would be all there or all gone. I'd never known a mugger who only took what he needed and left the rest. "It's all mine, and nothing is missing. Who called it in?"

The cop smiled. "Someone is looking after you. Four guys coming back from a fishing trip were driving by and saw it happen. They scared off the two men slugging you, called it in. How do you feel?"

"Better than being shot or stabbed." This wasn't random. I should have been more alert. My fun that night had cost me. "Do you have a description of the assailants?" He cocked his head at my cop speak. "I was an inspector...a while ago."

"Right. Uh, not much. One a little bigger than average. One a definite Caucasian. Both wore dark clothes, hats, and hoodies, and they ran off like they were in good shape."

That made me think. Muggers go for the gold. I wasn't the usual target—too big and not well enough dressed. And I'd been given a note. That put a different light on it.

The cop asked a few more questions as a matter of form and finished up by saying he'd file his report. "Personally, I think you were a target and not a random mugging victim. You may want to watch your back."

His comment reinforced what I already knew. A wave of nausea swept over me, and I suddenly felt very weary. *Concussion, for sure.* I rang for the nurse. "I want to sleep and not be disturbed."

"Please, be patient. We're completing your intake and will move you to a room as soon as possible." She grinned. She'd been there when they'd taken my clothes off to examine me and to do the x-rays. Oh, well. If they hadn't seen my cage undressing me, it would sure as shit show up on the x-rays. I didn't care. I was sore, hurting, and trying to think. That wasn't happening so easily.

She dimmed the lights and I dozed, though there was too much commotion in the ER to go out completely. They finally came and took me to a room.

The ER nurse had obviously spoken to the room nurse who said with a smile, "You are as safe with us as we are with you." She left, and I went out like a light.

Chapter 30

My aching limbs and massive headache made me recognize I was still alive, knowing the worst was yet to come. My head hurt like the cheap booze hangover. I buzzed for the nurse, who was far perkier than I could bear. I groaned. "I need coffee and my phone, in that order."

Her smile fell, replaced by attitude. "You can have your phone after the doctor has seen you and no coffee for you. I'll get you fresh water."

In another situation, I might've thought she was cute—I liked nurse uniforms, especially on well-endowed nurses—but I had to get a message to Sophie and Marie.

A few minutes later, she returned, clearly irritated. "Your phone wouldn't stop, so here it is. Please, be quick. The doctor will be in shortly."

Ha. Shortly was medical talk for wait an hour and maybe they'll show up to ask, "How are feeling today?" I harrumphed, then called Marie at the office and told her where I was. When I asked her to come get me and to let Sophie know I was running late, I heard her voice in the background.

"Bullshit. I'm coming with Marie."

I hung up. I couldn't deal with a loud voice right now.

Surprisingly, the doctor showed up soon after I'd

hung up. He asked all the usual questions.

"When can I get out of here?"

He made a show of looking at my chart, then sighed. "Anytime you want. This will likely fall on deaf ears, but take it easy for a few days. You were lucky. Your injuries could have been much worse, including your concussion."

"Okay, Doc. I get it. No promises, but I'll try to take it easy."

He smiled, nodded, and left, expecting me to do something stupid. I made a resolution to take it easy, at least until the headache eased. Then, I'd work out again to help speed up the recovery.

Marie and Sophie came in, looking stunned. Sophie seemed more shocked than Marie, who had seen me the worse for wear before. I hadn't seen myself yet.

"What happened?" Sophie's eyes were huge.

"I was mugged." I couldn't help but smile at the disbelief on both their faces. "I was set up and targeted."

"By who?" Sophie looked suspicious.

"We've stepped on some toes...regarding your sister. If it's okay with Marie, I'd like for you to stay with her for a couple of nights, at least."

"Oh, no. You're not going to push me aside like that. I can take care of myself."

"Sophie, I know you can. What they planned for me was much worse than what I got. I was lucky. I'll be more prepared next time."

Marie chimed in. "Of course, she can stay with me."

Sophie started to say something, but I cut her off. "Either you stay with Marie, or you stay at my place…or I stay at yours, which I actually own, anyway. We've stirred up something. I should've been more prepared."

Marie said, "It would be better if you stayed with Sophie at Simon's place. It's got two functional bedrooms."

I nodded.

Sophie didn't have a choice, but she was going to get her digs in. "You look like you were hit by a truck, so I'll be the one looking after you."

She always had to have the last word? My headache roared on. I wanted out of the hospital. Sophie went to take care of the paperwork, and Marie handed me a bag with some clothes I kept at the office. "After I get my underwear on, help me with my pants and shirt?"

"I know all about your cage thingy."

I went white. "What?"

"I'm not blind, Mas. This is San Francisco. I've been around the block a few times myself, you know. Sophie just confirmed it, that's all."

"Fine. Then help me get dressed."

"Glad to assist. Do I get to see it?"

So much for the boss getting respect. I was too tired and sore to argue. I pulled the covers back and eased myself slowly toward the edge. I turned so my legs were dangling over the side of the bed, my cage exposed.

Marie stared, more out of interest than embarrassment. She knelt in front of me and held my pants open as I tried to put one leg into each pant leg. "Okay, stop. This isn't working. Pick one leg up and put it in."

I did as I was told.

"Now, put the other one in." She bent over to pull up my pants, getting a great view of my chastity cage as she did so. If I hadn't been in so much pain, I know I would've gotten hard, exposed as I was.

"You have no pubic hair. You shave it off?"

"Yes. It's easier to keep clean."

"That makes sense. It's kinda cute, being bald there. I may have to experiment with Chung." Oh, great. Now she was going to pick on her partner to shave his pubes. *As long as he doesn't blame me.* Marie pulled up my pants and buttoned them.

Thankfully, the shirt was a button-down. My shoes were the only things wearable from the previous night. I slipped them on. My ribs ached with the exertion.

Finally, I was ready to leave. Marie picked up the plastic bag with all my belongings, and Sophie had taken care of most of the paperwork, so all I had to do was sign. Of course, the hospital staff insisted on wheeling me to the curb. Marie went to get the car, and Sophie walked with me as we waited. We were quiet for a long time.

"This is my fault, isn't it?"

I contemplated that before I answered. "Hear me out before you say anything. Promise?"

"Yes."

"Yes and no. Yes, it's your fault because I'm positive it's related to your sister's murder. No, it's not your fault, because I should've been more aware. I was distracted."

"You were distracted because of what happened at my place?"

"Maybe. Probably. That's an excuse. I should've

known better. We need to be more vigilant. We can't underestimate whoever did this."

Marie rolled up with my SUV. The orderlies helped me up and out of the wheelchair. I made it look more of a struggle than it was, in case we were being observed. I wasn't taking any chances. I made it into the front seat, and we drove off, with Sophie unhappily in the back seat.

We stopped off at my apartment to gather a bag of clothing. Making sure I wasn't observed, I also retrieved my sidearm and spring-loaded baton. I didn't want to raise any questions, and I wanted to be ready for anything. *No more surprises.* With my clothing in tow, we made our way to Sophie's place. The two of them fussed over me, and I played it up until Marie went back to the office to finish up some of the day-to-day items.

"Be sure the door is always locked, and vary your route to and from work. If you can, get Chung to drop you off and pick you up. Okay?"

"Got it, boss."

"I'm serious. Do it."

"Mas, I know you are. I'll be careful. I promise."

Exhaustion hit me. I hadn't eaten anything since the night before, so we decided on Chinese takeout. Sophie called for delivery from Simon's favorite place and as soon as it arrived, the smell got my juices going. We ate in silence as I wolfed it down. The doctor had warned I might feel nauseous from the concussion, but clearly, my stomach hadn't gotten the message. Sated, I took some muscle relaxants and headed to bed.

It was dark when I woke. As my head cleared, I saw Sophie, sitting in the chair, looking at me. "How are you feeling?"

"Hurting, but better. Anything happen while I was out?"

"Oh, not much. Just put your clothes away."

Damn. She'd found the pistol. "Thank you."

"Mas, thank you doesn't cut it. Why did you bring a gun?"

"Why do you think? What we've stepped into is getting dangerous. People get hurt in the real world. This is for our protection. If we don't need it, great. If we do, I'll have it. It's completely legal."

"This is a bit out of my realm. I always made sure I was insulated from the real world. Many of the people I've worked with, including the official agencies, aren't always nice, but I never asked, and they don't tell. Maybe I've been a bit naïve."

"A bit?"

"I deal in ones and zeroes. They can't hurt anyone."

"How do you know? You really don't know how what you do affects the downstream. You get information, pass it on, someone loses their job, or worse, gets killed because of those ones and zeroes. You're more fucking dangerous than I realized, not only to yourself, but to others."

"You can't know that."

"I deal in information, too. How do you think we solve our cases? Magic wands? Information. I've seen the effect information can have—CIs, snitches, criminal competition…Information is power. You said yourself this gizmo, if it had worked, would've given access to any information. So yeah, I know your information can be dangerous."

"You might be right. I keep myself isolated and insulated; I like it that way. I've never really thought about where it goes or how it's used. The work itself was the challenge. Sorry. I need to think on this."

Sophie got up and left the room.

I heard her shut her bedroom door. *Well, looks like I screwed that up nicely.* Nevertheless, it had to be said. We were getting to the point if they—whoever *they* were—were going to come after us. I wanted to be ready.

Chapter 31

Crashing early, I slept through the night. Medications are wonderful things under the right circumstances. I woke with the sun coming in through the blinds. I was still sore—second day sore. From now on, the soreness would gradually subside. The fragrance of coffee wafted in from the kitchen.

"I'm going to take a quick shower," I hollered out.

"Okay," Sophie called back. Standing under the hot, drenching water felt good. It made my abrasions sting. That felt good, too. I carefully moved my limbs in all directions. *Nothing too bad.* Thankfully, no ribs were cracked or broken. Bending and stretching hurt, so I couldn't shower the way I usually did. I gingerly dried and dressed then went into the kitchen for coffee.

Sophie was sitting in the chair facing the window. When she heard me enter, she turned. "How are you feeling today?"

"Sore. Really sore, but this should be the worst day. How are you? You look terrible. I need to apologize. I shouldn't have gone after you the way I did. Sorry."

"Yes, you should. I deserved it. I've kept myself detached from the effects my work could have. I've been living in a bubble of my own making, and it took you to make me realize I've been living on the black side of it all. I'm not going to apologize for it, but I need to make amends somehow. I just don't know how, yet. I'll think more on it and start by going back over my files, reviewing all the jobs I've done. I have to try to figure out what the negative effects were."

"All your contracts?"

"No, not all. I'll discount the ones where I was proactive in protecting companies from cyber-attacks and will concentrate on the others. It's not as many as you think. I was picky, and I was well paid."

"Well, as far as I can see, sorting out your sister's murder would be a good first step. Yes?"

Her head dropped and with it, her voice. "Yes."

I wanted to break the mood. "Any chance of breakfast?"

She smiled wanly. "Yes. It's called a 'diner.' Let's go, invalid. My treat."

I checked my pistol—safety on and a round chambered—and slid it into my waist holster. I covered it with a jacket. If anyone tried anything, I was ready to give it back. Better prepared, we left for the diner. Watching for anyone too interested in us, especially the guy I'd seen in front of Tara's office.

We made it to the diner without mishap. If Sophie had noticed the bulge in the small of my back, she said nothing. She looked drawn; maybe it was all finally getting to her. "Are you sure you're okay?"

The waitress automatically dropped off two cups of coffee, asking if we were ready to order. We ordered and sat silently until the waitress left.

"Yes. I didn't sleep last night. I kept thinking about what you'd said and how I might be responsible. I honestly don't know if I've been responsible for anyone's death, though I'm sure some unpleasant things have happened because of me."

"Beat yourself up later. Breakfast first, and we can review any data from the bugs. Then we work it from there and worry about salvation *after* we get Suzanne's killer or killers. Can you compartmentalize that?"

"Yes. I've already started going over the results from the bugs, nothing very interesting. Lots of wheeling-and-dealing business from the office. Tara sounds smart and well connected. I've gotten even less from the house. She came home, puttered about, watched some television, and went to bed. That was it."

I thought how long I'd sat on stakeouts before anything useful happened. "Don't worry. Something will give. It's not like the movies; patience will pay off today, tomorrow…sometime."

"How sure are you that Tara is connected?"

"I'm not sure she's directly connected, but I do think she knows someone who is."

"James McCarrigan?" It came out as almost a whisper.

"Yup."

Our meals arrived. We ate in silence, lost in our own thoughts. Fueled up, I was ready to get going, at least as fast as I could. Sophie paid, and we left for the slow walk to the office. I called ahead and warned Marie we were coming, and I'd use my keys to get in. The walk took longer than I'd thought, though it felt good to be mobile. The sun felt warm on my face. With my black eye and bruises starting to come out and color, we drew some odd looks. I entered the office and collapsed into the chair. The walk had taken more out of me than I realized. *So much for being fit.* I was pissed, and I wanted payback from the sneaky bastards who'd sandbagged me.

Sophie switched on her computers and donned some headphones, continuing to review the data.

I sat, thinking what might have set someone off on me. I stared at the note. *LEAVE IT ALONE.* There was nothing to be gained by reporting it. They'd worn gloves. The note paper was common enough, and the words had been printed to disguise the handwriting.

My guess was the person who'd written it was right-handed, but that still didn't do us any good. It just confirmed we were on the right track.

Assaulting me had been a mistake. The perp who'd taken out eight people couldn't take me out with an accomplice? Something was missing. My assumption was that Tara was circumstantially involved—maybe project Dissolve—but not in the murders. That was a different level of psychosis.

It all came back to James McCarrigan. No one else had the motive or the resources or any combination thereof, except for McCarrigan. Sorenson, the real estate guy, had the resources, but no connection to tech, and this had to be about Dissolve.

We needed more pieces of the puzzle to be sure. *Back to patience.* There wasn't much I could do. Bored, I asked Sophie for a headset and the office recordings. Couldn't hurt to have a second set of ears.

"You're really that desperate?"

I gave her the finger.

She laughed, tossed me a headset, plugged me in, and ran the recordings from when I'd left Tara's office. She was right. There was nothing of substance, though they were interesting in an observational way. I closed my eyes and listened to the quality of her voice. On one, her voice caught my interest. She seemed stressed at the other person's response, and she'd repeated their words. *Leave it alone?* Coincidence? No way in hell. And no way to know who was on the other end of that call. Damn. Why couldn't that call have been on the cell we'd cloned?

I snatched the headset off and waved to get Sophie's attention. I relayed my thoughts and conclusions.

"Mas, lots of people use that phrase."

"I know, but it's too much of a coincidence for me. Even an innocuous phrase can mean something to the right ears. My attackers left a warning note, then the day after, this call. I'm positive it's connected. I just don't know who else is involved."

"Even if you're right, we need more. Keep listening and hope she uses her cell."

Tara did use her cell. A lot. Mostly for social calls and events. She was always brief, at least during the working day.

We spent the next two days and nights listening and reviewing the recordings. Nada. Zilch. Zero. I was beginning to think maybe I'd been wrong about Tara's involvement.

Coming into work on the fourth day, I was greeted by a smiling Marie, who'd been assisting with the listening devices. "They found the bugs you put in Tara's office, though she and her partners don't know you've cloned her phone or bugged her home. Listen to the conversations. Coffee's on, and I brought in some focaccia, Sophie's request."

I hadn't seen Marie this excited for a long time. It was good to see. "Yes to coffee and the focaccia."

"Okay. Let's get to the conversations."

Sophie started them at the relevant sections Marie had marked and put them on speaker. Marie was right; we now had information to connect Tara to McCarrigan. It still wasn't proof of murder, but it was a good link and one to follow.

The conversation started on her cell at home. They chatted about business—first the Dissolve project and then, McCarrigan said his team was having trouble with the encryption. It was when Tara mentioned I'd visited her office the other day that McCarrigan went silent. He asked her where she was, and she answered.

"Good. Don't say anything in your office until I get a security guy in there tomorrow. I bet he bugged you. He's a PI and nosing into my affairs. Has he been to your home?"

"No."

"Good. I think I'll send him another message." He ended the call.

"Is that it?"

She rolled her eyes. "No. Not at all. It gets way better. Listen. They had a guy come in, and he found all three bugs."

"Which, by the way, you did a good job of planting."

"They found them?"

"I would've found them, too. If I'd planted them, they would still have been found. Shhhh. Listen. They're going to use them to try to set us up."

Again, I listened. The conversation turned to using the bugs to feed us misinformation. McCarrigan told Tara what to say and when, including some dropped hints about the Dissolve project. She was to call a number he gave her and make some arrangements for a couple who said they wanted to take advantage of SF's kink nightlife and visit the Cauldron. Tara asked why. McCarrigan sounded exasperated, and he told her to just do it. It made sense to use the Cauldron; kink was the common link between all the victims and the police were looking for a kinky serial killer. He would've had us checked out and would know we'd gone there. Not a bad plan, except we knew about it and would be prepared. This time, his message would be rebuffed in spades.

I had a feeling McCarrigan would be much more thorough than last time; he'd sent just two thugs to do me. This time, he'd send at least three to take on the two of us, if not more. They'd be expecting me and a woman and would prepare a surprise attack. We'd prepare as well.

Sophie interrupted my train of thought. "Well, what are we going to do?"

"Has Tara made the call yet? Setting the trap?"

"No. I'm continually monitoring the office bugs."

"Don't worry about that; we know the call will be made. We can pick it up later. We have to work out our plan. Nothing will happen at the Cauldron. They want us relaxed and taken by surprise. It will happen when we leave and are outside. We'll be easier to spot. It'll be late, with few people around. I have a plan, if you're up for it."

"Are you kidding me? Hell, yes, I'm up for it."

"You haven't heard my plan yet. How good are you with your pepper spray and a Taser?"

"You want references? There are people in Philly who regret messing with me. Good enough?"

"I'm serious. Our survival will depend on you doing your part. They'll likely send a minimum of three people, probably four. They know I'm still injured. They also know you're a woman and not as trained as I am."

"But I—"

"I know. Just looking at it through their eyes. They also think they have the element of surprise. Halfway down the block from the Cauldron is a small side street. It's dark and not well traveled. We'll lead them down that street. If there are three, they'll likely have one follow us to relay our location to the other two. If they bring four, they'll have two behind and two in front. This could also be a snatch to see how much we know. I'll come up with contingency plans, but in a nutshell, that's the plan. Oh, and no guns. I want them disabled and hurt, not dead."

Sophie looked pensive. "You're trusting me, aren't you?"

"Yup. I can handle two on my own, so three is no problem. But if they send four, we really need help. We can even the odds with the element of surprise. Are you okay with this? We *will* get hurt; no one gets out unscathed in a situation like this. The only question is who, and how badly."

"I'm in. All the way. I want to send a message back to them."

"You know, this will escalate the stakes and get more dangerous for us, right?"

"I understand. Where can I get more pepper spray?"

I laughed. "I'll pick some up when I run some errands later today."

She cocked an eyebrow but left the question unasked.

I had some calls to make and a couple of favors to call in. The calls were easy, then I turned my attention to the favors. My first stop was for pepper spray, picking up two new canisters with good expiration dates. Heading back to the office, I frequently checked over my shoulder. They knew we'd at the Cauldron the following night, so maybe they didn't want to waste manpower.

Opening the office door, I was met with smiling faces. "What's with the smiles?"

Sophie winked. "Just chatting."

I was pretty sure I didn't want further details. I tossed the two canisters to Sophie, who adeptly caught them. I suggested she keep her old one as a backup and put both the new ones in her bag.

"Thanks, Mas."

The rest of the day was quiet. *The quiet before the storm.*

Sophie and I monitored the recordings. Nothing off the home bugs. As expected, Tara was in her office, and her cell was quiet most of the day. She was busy, well-connected, and driven. Becoming successful in a male-dominated business took energy, brains, and determination. It would be interesting to see how deeply she was involved with McCarrigan. I figured he would keep her out of the messy parts. The fewer people who knew, the better.

We traded shifts every hour. She worked late into the evening. Later when her staff had left, she made the call we were expecting. She did a good job. It didn't sound particularly scripted, even though we had advance knowledge of the content. She dropped enough hints about a secret project to pique our interest. Then, she left for home.

Sophie and I called it a day. Their trap had been set and so had ours. Now, all we had to do was execute.

Chapter 32

The dawn dragged across the bay. It was foggy and grey, one of those San Franciscan days where you just don't want to get out of bed. I knew the day would drag, but I was looking forward to the night. We were playing with an advantage, and I wanted to make the most of it.

I showered and left for the office, still maintaining my heightened awareness. The lights were on in the office, and the door was locked. *Well done. Following protocol.* I used my key and relocked the door.

"Good morning. Sophie's already in." She paused, as if deciding. "Can I ask you something?"

"Sure." It must be semi-serious. Normally, she'd just ask.

"It's kinda delicate."

Oh, shit. She's going to quit on me.

"Mas, have you thought about what you're going to do when you finish this case? I mean…with Sophie. I *really* like her…and you need a partner. You're good together. Sorry. Just thinking."

Wow…Where did that come from? I had to admit, I hadn't thought much past the next day or what was going on with the case. It did raise an interesting point, both personally and professionally. "I honestly don't know. I haven't thought that far ahead. You'll be the first to know. Besides, Sophie already has a thriving business in Philly. She may not want to move here. Let's just survive this case first, okay?"

"Okay, but promise me you'll think about it."

I smiled. "I promise."

Sophie didn't even look up when I entered. The computer's glow highlighted her face. "Hi. Nothing interesting on the recordings except that Tara likes to scream when she does herself with a dildo. Sounded like she was being attacked. I almost called emergency services."

I had to chuckle. Thoughts of emergency service guys breaking down the door to find her naked on the bed, doing herself with a big dong, flashed through my head. I felt the anticipation of the coming night, creeping up on me. My feet began to itch. I had to do something, deciding to review all the information we had on the bodies in the bay again.

The most detailed information concerned Suzanne, Kasagawa, and Jack Mellon. If McCarrigan was behind killing all the victims, for whatever reason, how could we prove it? He wasn't going to confess. If anything, he'd probably try to kill us. We needed leverage and outside backup, but not the SFPD, though playing them might be useful. I made some notes and put down a few ideas. I'd have to cover everyone's ass, or we'd all go down. I looked across the room. Sophie was still playing with her computer. "I'm going to lunch."

"I was just checking on the police investigation through our back door. They're still going after the serial killer angle from a kink perspective, but they're not getting anywhere. No surprise there. Is there any way we can use the police to help?"

"I was just thinking about that myself. I'm not sure,

but I think there might be a way. When I put it all together, I'll run it by you. What do you want for lunch?"

"Anything. I'm not that hungry. I think I'm nervous about tonight."

"Second thoughts?"

"None. I just want it over. I hate the waiting."

I laughed out loud. "Me, too. Trust me. It will happen soon enough, and the nerves will disappear." I left her to do whatever she was doing and went for a walk, still watching for a tail. This time, I saw him.

I stopped at the deli, grabbed lunch, and went the long way back to the office, stopping to chat with folks I knew in the area—storekeepers and locals—just being normal. I hoped tonight's assailants would include the two that had coldcocked me the other night. I wanted payback.

Lunch was a quiet affair, each with our own thoughts. The afternoon dragged, and I went home early. Sophie and I agreed to meet at her place and to travel together to the Cauldron.

Marie waved goodbye. "Be careful. I'll see you later."

"Bit late for that isn't it?"

She play-punched me. "Well, because of you, I added 911 to my speed dial."

When I got home, I ran on the treadmill for thirty minutes, just to get my blood pumping. After showering, I dressed for the evening—black, loose-fitting pants with a wide belt, a skin-tight workout top under a black fitted shirt—less to grab hold of—black Doc Martens, and thin, black leather gloves. A black beanie finished it off.

I wound duct tape around the paper wrapper on a roll of quarters to be sure they didn't break—the extra weight added impact to a punch—and shoved them into my pocket. The spring-loaded baton was illegal. I'd worry about that when the time came. As I hooked it to my belt, I pocketed my driver's license, my PI ID, and folded some cash into a zip pocket. I rechecked everything once more, then snatched the baton and snapped it out, compressing the baton until I heard it click home in the handle. I still had the touch.

Calling Sophie from the rideshare, I gave her an ETA. She must've been watching for me, because she came out and was in the car in seconds. We were silent on the way to the Cauldron, each lost in our own thoughts. She had dressed all in black, close-fitting clothes under a tight black leather jacket. Her purse fell across her body—both hands free. We looked ready for a metal concert, a kinky night out, or a robbery—take your pick.

The entrance to the Cauldron was busy. I nodded to Oso, manning the door. He nodded in return. Even this early, the place was buzzing with energy. We heard screams as we made our way to the bar; someone was getting off early tonight. *Lucky them.* We weren't here to play. Our only disadvantage was not knowing the couple who'd be setting us up…if they showed up at all. Perhaps, it had all been a ruse, just to get us to a place where we could be spotted and taken care of.

As the evening progressed, I became more convinced the plan was just to get us to a known place, so I decided to enjoy myself. I socialized and introduced Sophie as Circe, always keeping an eye out for the "couple," just in case. We observed several scenes, and I made sure I noted which ones interested Sophie the most. Predictably, she noticed the ones where the woman was the dominant, regardless of the other players. She was fixated on the action like a predator waiting to pounce.

By midnight, I was convinced we'd been set up just to get us to the Cauldron; if we disappeared, the Cauldron would be last place we'd been seen, and we fitted the male/female couple pattern. "Time we got this show on the road. You ready?"

"Yes." Anticipation filled her eyes.

We said our goodbyes and left the club, walking slowly. We walked arm in arm down the block. At the corner of the side street, I took a surreptitious look back and noted two men, also walking down the block. They were too aware for just a stroll. My adrenaline rose. "Do you remember the go word?"

"Of course, I do."

"Good. Don't turn around. We have two behind us. Be ready, but wait for my word. Got it?

Sophie's voice was clipped. "I got it. Don't worry about me. Let's get these bastards." Her voice was level but full of determination. We turned down the narrow side street. It ran the length of the block, with no other side roads to duck down, just as I wanted it. The city noise drowned out any footsteps behind us. We walked slowly, as if in no hurry, just going home. We were about halfway down the block when a van came into the bottom of the street, blocking us off.

Two men got out of the sliding door.

This was going to be a capture, not a kill encounter. *Even better*.

The two men walked quickly up the middle of the

road.

I glanced at Sophie. "Here we go. Whatever happens, don't quit until I say so."

"Got it." There was an edge to her voice.

The two men, nondescript in dress and appearance, moved over to the sidewalk and purposely walked toward us. We stopped, and they stopped directly in front of us. *First mistake. They're too close.*

The taller one smiled confidently. "You were told to leave it alone. Now, come with us."

I stood tall, sizing them up; they were relaxed and overconfident. I sensed two behind us. "And if we don't go with you?"

"Then we'll take you, one way or another."

I saw his eyes flick up; the ones behind us must be on the move. Second mistake—no coordination. "Okay…"

Sophie exploded into action. She whipped out her pepper spray and blasted the shorter one in the face, followed by a powerful kick to his groin, which cut off the start of a scream.

He pulled his hands to his face.

The man facing me, automatically distracted by the noise, looked to see what was happening.

Too late. I flicked open the baton and struck the man on his left collarbone. With a satisfying snap, the bone cracked. I quickly swung the baton out to my right, twisting and dropping my arm, smashing the baton into his left knee. With a sick thud, his knee buckled under the damage. As I recovered the swing, I hooked his leg, forcing him off balance. As he tumbled to his left, I raised the baton and brought it down on his right collarbone with a backhand blow. I heard another clear crunch. He crumpled to the ground, moaning and writhing on his wrecked knee.

Mine down.

As I turned, I saw Sophie drop next to her assailant and jab the Taser into the side of his uncovered throat. He shuddered and twisted in a St. Vitus dance, completely disabled. One of the two men following slammed face-first into the brick wall.

Oso had returned a favor. He picked the man up like a rag doll, took a long look, and dropped him into the gutter. With a last look, he turned and walked away.

Three down.

The last man had been distracted by what was happening to his partner, which gave me just enough time to get behind him and choke him out. As he went down, the van peeled away in a screech of rubber, I assumed to report the failure.

I inhaled sharply. These guys hadn't been their A-team—too many mistakes. It shouldn't have been this easy. I heard a guttural growl.

Sophie was kicking her downed man as hard as she could.

I pulled her away. "Enough. We're done here. I think they got the message."

Her chest heaved, and her body shook. Her adrenaline rush was in full flood. She briefly tried to fight me, then registered it was me. She collapsed into me, still shaking.

"Are you all right?

She tried hard to control her breathing. "Yes, I think so. To be honest, it happened so fast, I'm not even sure."

"It was too easy, even with the element of surprise.

They were clowns—rent-a-thugs, at best."

"What happened to the guys behind us?"

"Oso took care of one. I did the other."

"That was easy? Why didn't you tell me what you had planned?" As I explained, I sent a prewritten text to Marie.

"I didn't want to distract you. You did your part. I didn't want you thinking about anything else. We were lucky."

"I can't stop shaking."

"Don't worry. It's the adrenaline and the emotions—everything that's happened since you got to SF. Like I said, we were lucky. They underestimated us, and they paid the price. Help me get up sleeping beauty. We'll take him with us."

Sophie bent down, and we lifted the barely conscious man into a semi-standing position. She glanced at me. "Mas, I need to know why we came out unscathed. You warned me we'd be hurt. I was prepared. It's almost a disappointment."

I had to laugh. Just as I was about to respond, my SUV came flying around the corner with Marie behind the wheel. I opened the rear passenger door and pulled out a bag with a set of handcuffs. I snapped them onto the now-recovering man and put a bag over his head. With Sophie's help, we tossed him into the cargo space, warning him not to struggle.

Sophie got in beside Marie, and I climbed in behind her. As we drove off, I called 9-1-1 on one of our burner phones and reported a fight where people had been injured. I gave them the location and hung up. "Take us to the arranged location."

She nodded and wove her way through the night

traffic.

We soon pulled up in front of an abandoned warehouse in the Dog Patch. Another favor from Oso. The area was deserted. Marie drove through the gate and around to the back entrance. I raised the roller gate, and Marie backed the SUV into the open door. Once the gate was closed, I switched on the lights and opened the rear hatch. Roughly, Sophie and I rolled the man out. He was fully awake. I could tell by the way he flinched when we touched him. We marched him over to a sturdy chair and sat him down.

I tossed Sophie a roll of duct tape. "Tape his ankles to the legs of the chair." I took another roll and taped the chain joining his cuffs to the bar under the chair. He was secured and vulnerable, without a clue where he was. *Good. You should be scared, you bastard.* I rapped on his forehead. "Nod if you can hear me."

He nodded.

"Good. I'm going to ask some questions, and you're going to answer me. You won't like what happens if you don't. Got it?"

An emphatic nod.

"Excellent. Who hired you?"

Nothing.

"You *do* understand not answering is not cooperating. I think we need the blowtorch. Spread his legs and fire it up."

His voice turned soprano. "No. God, no. I don't know who hired us. It was just a pretend kidnap—part of the kinky fun the couple liked. We were to follow a couple coming out from the kink club, ambush them, bag their heads, then bundle them into the van that would deliver them to a group of friends. They said to be rough but cause no real damage. This isn't what I signed on for. I was just out to make a few bucks. I don't know anything else. I swear." His voice cracked.

I believed he was scared, but I wasn't sure about the rest. "Give me all the details. Names, places…everything from the moment you were contacted."

"Okay, okay. Just don't hurt me. I'll tell you anything you want to know. This isn't on me. Please."

I questioned him, and he answered with no hesitation or second thoughts. He convinced me he was telling the truth, as he knew it. Unfortunately, it didn't do us much good. He knew little and nothing that could be traced back to McCarrigan or Tara. It seemed the van driver was the connection between the grabbers and the destination. We had no license plate, and I was sure he'd given a false name to all involved.

I almost felt sorry for the schmuck. He'd been conned into doing a job he wasn't cut out for, and it had all gone very wrong. I cut the tape, freeing him from the chair. We loaded him back into the SUV and drove around for ten minutes, stopped, uncuffed him, and left him on a corner, still hooded and frightened. *Not our problem.* When we drove away, I noticed Marie's eyes were like saucers.

"Mas, were you really going to torture him?"

I laughed. "No. I knew he was the hired help and wouldn't know much, if anything. I just had to convince him I'd do it. He sensed there were others but had no idea who."

"Did you actually have a blowtorch?"

"Hell no.

Sophie chuckled. "You were going to tell me how

we got away without a scratch?"

I was quiet for a moment. We'd been incredibly lucky. "Well, we were already primed; we knew something was going to happen, so they had no element of surprise. In fact, we had it; they just didn't know it. They were set up, I assume by McCarrigan or one of his staff. They guy verified it was for kinky fun and not a serious kidnap. They made too many mistakes. They underestimated us. No offense, but you're just a woman and I'm a has-been cop. Easy pickings.

"They were just rent-a-thugs, probably out of a bar, who were offered quick cash for some fun with a couple of perverts. Easy. Now, they have some medical bills. Well…three of them do."

Sophie looked thoughtful. "Remind me to thank your friend. I guess we *were* lucky. That won't happen again, will it?"

"No, it won't. The opposition has now been warned. If there's a next time, it will be the A-team."

Marie's voice wavered. "Will there be a next time?"

"Unless we can get a permanent resolution—yes."

"I still need to find out who killed my sister. If it was McCarrigan, I want him taken care of."

"You know, if it *is* him, he ordered it but didn't actually do it himself. He wouldn't get his hands dirty. We don't have any proof he ordered anything."

"I know, but I am pretty sure it's him. He's involved with Dissolve, and everything revolves around that."

"Let's just go home and get some sleep. Tomorrow is another day, and I'm sure something will shake loose from tonight's fiasco."

Chapter 33

After the previous night's events, I was even more vigilant, constantly checking my surroundings. I made it to the office in good time and was the first to arrive. I had just started the coffee when Marie came in, followed by Sophie, who looked the worse for wear. "How are you? Not the best night?"

Subdued, she walked past me into the inner office.

I followed. "What's bothering you?"

She sat down heavily. "I couldn't sleep. I kept thinking about all sorts of stuff, mainly about what you said about us being lucky. It didn't hit me until I tried to sleep. We *were* lucky, and I scared myself. I completely lost control. If you hadn't pulled me off that guy, I could've killed him."

"It's called adrenaline. Don't worry about it. Hopefully, you'll never be in that situation again."

She looked at me. "That's wishful thinking. We're in trouble, aren't we?"

I'd been thinking long and hard about that. "No. We *are* in jeopardy, mainly because we don't have a clear picture of everything, but I think if we're careful, we'll be fine. We need to re-evaluate the info we have and rethink some of our assumptions."

That piqued her interest. She was about to speak when Marie brought in coffee for all of us.

Sophie wasn't done. "What do you mean?"

"We already have a lot of information, and we've been looking for who has the most to gain, but what about who has the most to lose? We're assuming McCarrigan is the one behind it all, but what if there are several players?"

Sophie looked puzzled. "Shit, this is complicated. Okay. Start from the beginning."

"Exactly what I was hoping you would say. We agree the first murders were a distraction to hide Jack Mellon's murder, so why was he killed, and who benefits from it?"

Sophie jumped in. "Rant benefits. He was skimming cash, which I'm sure pissed them off, and his program's a scam. They wouldn't want any of that getting out."

"Agreed, but enough to kill six people? And then your sister and Kasagawa? Your sister was onto something. I'm not sure if it was the program scam or the fraud, but she would've been an asset to Rant, not a liability. Kasagawa was a major player. Killing him would attract attention, unless the police were convinced it was part of a kink crime, like all the others. McCarrigan's involved somehow. I think he's the one who stole Jack's hard drive, and he hasn't been able to break it. Tara is involved because of McCarrigan, and I believe he's responsible for the attack on me and our attempted kidnap last night."

"Why do you think it was him and not Rant?"

I paused, taking a long drink of coffee before I answered. "Because it was sloppy. The hired help was untrained and made too many mistakes. If it had been Rant, Mr. Gilbert would've organized it and with his military background, he'd use skilled folk who wouldn't make mistakes, and we wouldn't be talking about it right now."

"So, are we back to liking McCarrigan for the killings?"

"I don't think so. If he had access to the people Mr. Gilbert does, he would've used them. The first attack on me was a warning, and last night was supposed to be a kidnap. Both were sloppy. He's in the information and money business. He already has what he wants—or what he thinks he wants—but he just can't access it. Killing people doesn't seem logical for him. Where's the benefit? Jack is the man with the golden key, and your sister's murder makes no sense. Or Kasagawa's. In fact, beating Kasagawa in business would've been much better than killing him. No. We're missing something."

Marie, who had been sitting quietly, spoke up. "Could there actually be a psycho out there, just killing for the fun of it? Sorry, Sophie. I didn't mean it like that."

"It's okay, Marie. I think Mas is right. There is a maniac killer out there, but it's all connected to Dissolve, the killings, and probably Rant. I think it's just business to him...or them. If they were prepared to kill eight people, it's something worth hiding and protecting. If the program Jack designed had worked, it would *literally* be priceless. Big bucks are involved."

"But it doesn't work, does it?" Marie looked at Sophie.

"Right. It's junk, but not everyone knows that, which adds another layer of complication."

The phone rang. The sound seemed too loud in the silence. Marie snatched it up. "Good morning. Hammett and Chandler Investigations. Yes. I will see if he will take your call, Mr. McCarrigan."

That took us all by surprise.

I nodded to Marie. "Put him on speaker. Good morning, Mr. McCarrigan. How are you and your handymen?"

His laugh held no mirth. "As well as can be expected after meeting you last night."

"That sounds like an admission of guilt."

"Not at all. Just a slight misunderstanding, that's all. I think we've gotten off on the wrong foot, and I'd like to make it up to you. How about we meet to discuss something to our mutual advantage? You pick the time and the place."

"How about police headquarters?"

He laughed aloud. "I love a man with a sense of humor. However, I'll decline that particular location."

Places ran through my mind. "Boudin Bakery, the outside deck. It's public and crowded, but we'll still be able to chat."

"I agree. Say…midday? Lunch will be on me."

"Ms. Chandler will be accompanying me. You may bring someone, if you wish."

"I'd expect her to be there. So kind of you to allow a companion for me. See you promptly at noon. Goodbye." He hung up.

We sat there, stunned. I never expected him to call. It gave me food for thought. "So, what do you make of that?"

Sophie answered first. "He's playing us. Probably pissed his goons didn't get us. I'm glad you picked a public place. I don't trust him."

"I don't trust him, either. This is going to be an

interesting lunch. This doesn't change my thinking. I can't see the value in McCarrigan doing the killings, and if we play it smart, we may get some answers."

Marie asked, "So where does that leave us?"

"Making progress. We'll know more after lunch. Marie, I want you to go with us separately and keep an eye on us. If you see anything out of whack, give us a heads-up. I don't think he'll play games. He wants something from us."

Sophie looked skeptical. She busied herself with her computer screen.

Keeping myself busy, I stuck to what I knew best—hard facts and people info.

Something buzzed around the periphery of my consciousness, but I couldn't quite grasp it. Until I figured out what it was, it would be a distraction. Instead, I focused on the important elements. Plotting out timelines and motives helped me focus on all the different lines we had going. Every crime has several components—motive and opportunity, and variations within. This one had lots of everything.

One thing was certain—these killings had been planned and planned well in advance. San Francisco's kink community was one of the largest in the world, and it made a good distraction for the SFPD. But if the killings were planned that far out, was the end game already completed or still to be finished? *Not finished.* Finding the bodies had been an accident, so we still had time to find out what was going on. I kept looping back. As soon as I thought I had a good grasp of something, it would fail to fit the puzzle. The biggest piece was who gained the most from all the deaths and chaos.

Sophie broke my train of thought. "Mas, Marie

says we have to leave to make the lunch with McCarrigan."

"What? Oh, yeah. Be right with you. Quick question. When you found the org chart for Rant, did you only find Byron's or did you get the org charts for the whole company?"

"I found lots, but I was only looking for Byron. Why?"

"Just thinking it might be a good idea if we looked up Mr. Gilbert. After all, Byron lied about his position."

"Okay. I'll do it as soon as we get back from lunch. It won't take long."

With that, we left for Boudin. I was getting hungry at the thought of that awesome sourdough bread. It made my mouth water. We took two cabs, just in case.

McCarrigan was waiting for us.

We ordered and waited. Sophie went to find a table. It wasn't busy yet, thankfully. It wasn't tourist season. I carried the tray for Sophie and I. McCarrigan carried his own. I was surprised he'd come alone. "Chose to go solo today, huh?"

"My driver is about somewhere. I have nothing to fear from you. I underestimated you, for sure, but I don't fear you, so please, let's have a nice lunch and chat."

He had a point. As long as he wasn't responsible for the killings, he didn't have anything to worry about.

"Good point, but do we have a reason to fear you?"

"I don't think so. I hope we can resolve that completely over lunch."

"Why don't you start? For the sake of honesty, we aren't recording this."

He smiled. "Doesn't matter. I have a jammer

running in my pocket. Shall I continue?"

I nodded. "Please do."

"As I said, I think we got off on the wrong foot. I'm not particularly sympathetic in business. I want what I want, and I don't like losing to anyone. I'll go to many lengths to get what I want. Admittedly, I've bent the rules, here and there—even broken some—but I draw the line at murder. That *is* what you suspect me of, correct?" He looked directly at Sophie.

She kept her gaze on him, unblinking. "Yes. I believe you're responsible for my sister's murder, and if I can prove it to my satisfaction, I'll finish you." It was a statement of fact, icy and expressionless.

McCarrigan looked back at her, uncomfortable at her tone. We were all silent for a moment. "I can assure you, Ms. Chandler, I am many things, but I'm not a killer. I guarantee you neither I, nor anyone who works for me, had anything to do with your sister's death. That is why I wanted to meet with you. I believe your sister discovered something at Rant way over her paygrade."

"Dissolve."

McCarrigan looked at her then me. "Yes, Dissolve. What do you know about it?"

Sophie again answered. "Probably more than you do. You stole Jack Mellon's hard drive from his home computer, but you can't break his encryption, so you don't know what you have, or in this case, don't have."

McCarrigan's voice grew cold. "What do you mean, 'don't have'?"

"You think you have another winner program, one that will unlock any computer in the world. No encryption would be safe from you. It's a once-in-alifetime deal. Everyone would want it—governments, criminals, corporations, everybody. Right?"

Suspiciously and with some concern, he nodded. "How do you know all this? And where are you going with this? You want in? I've already told you, I don't play well with others."

Sophie sneered. "You really don't know, do you? This is priceless. You haven't been able to access his hard drive. You're so smart, yet you missed the shortcut. I did, until Mas brought it to my attention. Whoever you used to steal the hard drive missed something—all the flash drives on his desk were—"

"What flash drives? There was nothing else on his desk."

My turn. "Yes, there was. A mug full of pens on a desk with no paper. The pens disguised the flash drives. Sophie opened them, and we discovered quite a lot about Dissolve."

McCarrigan's composure cracked. "So, you're ahead of me? You're correct. We haven't been able to break into the hard drive, yet. Seems Jack was good at protecting himself. Do you actually have the program?"

Sophie was back in control. "No, not all of it—it's too big to fit on a few flash drives—but enough to get the idea of where he was going with it." We'd decided beforehand he'd have to pry each piece of info out of us, and we'd keep our cards close to our chests.

McCarrigan looked pensive. "I want that program. What will it take for you to hand over what you have? I will pay very, very well for it. I will even give you a share—a minor share—of the business when it goes commercial. Of course, I would require contracts and confidentiality agreements. It will make all of us immensely wealthy. Well, what do you say?"

We smiled at each other, which McCarrigan mistook as agreement. Sophie quickly dispelled his assumption. "I don't want your money. Give me my sister's killer, and you can have everything we have on Dissolve. An even exchange."

"Doesn't Mr. Hammett have a say in this?"

"No. I've employed him to find my sister's killer, and the information was uncovered due to my expertise. It's my decision."

I nodded.

"Ms. Chandler, I wish I knew. I'd hand over that person for no charge. Why would I kill anyone related to Dissolve? It's not to my advantage. I *wish* Jack Mellon was alive. Then, I'd have a chance at his hard drive. I wish I'd listened to him when he approached me before he hooked up with Rant, but I had other projects I was working on at the time, and his program seemed too farfetched to be real, much like the holy grail of computing. Rant has some serious foreign investors with deep pockets." He stopped.

I was starting to believe him. He was right. There was no upside for him to kill anyone involved with Dissolve. "When did you appropriate the hard drive?"

He laughed at my discretion. "Call it what it is, Mr. Hammett. I had the hard drive stolen two days after he disappeared. Only, we didn't know he had disappeared. My people figured he was working at Rant or out of town. They'd been following him, but they lost him. So, they took the opportunity when they had it. Once I had the drive, they didn't bother following up on him. Why would they?"

"That makes sense. Did you follow anyone else

involved with Dissolve or Rant?"

"No. There was no need. We had what we wanted. I didn't connect any of this to the bodies in the bay until you started asking Tara about Kasagawa. The police hadn't released the names of the victims. I was surprised when I found out Kasagawa was one of them. I knew of him. We'd met. We were competitors.

"I started to keep my distance from him. I'd heard through the grapevine he was in the Japanese mafia. You know, the Yakuza. Though, I don't think it's true. I think they used him as a middleman. Clean hands, and all that. Rumor was he cleaned their money for them by investing in international businesses. I can't prove any of that, but the info came from reliable sources.

"I'd say whoever is responsible for killing him is in a lot of trouble, if they ever find them. I damn sure wouldn't be here talking to you if I was responsible."

He was right. If—and that was a big if—Kasagawa was connected to the Yakuza, it would explain how Saito had shown up so quickly and why he was so leery of any assistance from us or the police. I also agreed whoever was responsible was in a world of hurt. Maybe they didn't realize he was Yakuza. He presented, from all accounts, like any other Japanese businessman and was, in fact, a legitimate player. Everything seemed to lead back to Rant.

"Do you think there's any chance it's a serial killer?"

I answered quickly. "The person *is* a serial killer, but not a psychopath. All the killings were designed to hide at least one murder—Jack Mellon, for sure. I think you could be right about Suzanne. She was digging into something at Rant. From what we've uncovered, it looks like fraud. Jack was siphoning off cash from the project."

"Cheap little shit. I didn't like him. He reminded me of a used car salesman. Stupid, too. If the project works, he would've been able to buy his own city. Hell, he could've bought his own country. Shyster mentality. You have to think big."

I just smiled at him.

"What are you not telling me?"

"Let's put it this way. When we've found Suzanne's killer, it might be worth your time to have another conversation with Sophie, if you're smart."

"And I suggest you look at Rant, paying attention to those who have a lot to lose. That's just as powerful a motive as gain. Tara did a lot of business with Kasagawa and they parted ways, partly because I'd started to build a relationship with her. Someone from Rant had a direct connection to him. I don't know who, but my money would be on Byron Howard. Do you know him?"

We nodded.

"I *would* like to have another conversation, particularly about the information you have and how I can obtain it. Hopefully, soon?" He stood. "I'm sorry for your loss. I hope I have convinced you I'm not responsible. I wish you success in your quest."

Quest? That was a bit much. He wasn't some romantic figure, and neither were we. This was a case, and that was becoming clearer. I still had some work to do to fit all the pieces together, using Sophie's expertise to solve some of the issues that were still nagging at me. I was glad we hadn't told McCarrigan the Dissolve program was junk, at least not yet.

Sophie nudged me to get my attention.

"Sorry. I was miles away. I'm convinced he wasn't responsible for any of the killings. I think Jack was supposed to be the last one, but your sister discovered something, which made her a liability. It all leads back to Rant; everything else is a distraction—all the bodies, the kink aspect, McCarrigan. We need to dig into Rant. I found out as much as I could about them through my channels. Now, I need your skills.

"First, we need to dig deeper into Byron and Mr. Gilbert, but carefully. We don't know who we're dealing with or how endemic it is within Rant. Someone there is responsible for all this...or knows who is."

Sophie was more subdued than I expected.

"Why so quiet?"

"Because you were right about McCarrigan. He's a nasty asshole, but not a killer. I don't think he had anything to do with the killings. He had too much to lose and nothing to gain. Damn. I was so sure he was involved. I guess I have a lot to learn about murder investigations."

"Don't worry. Let's just move forward. McCarrigan is out of the picture. The police can do whatever they wish. Kink is out of the picture, too. That leaves Rant, so that's where we'll concentrate. Can you hack them without being discovered or leaving a trail? We're dealing with someone who kills for diversion, and they won't think twice about killing us if they think we're getting too close. This won't be like dealing with McCarrigan's goons. We won't see them coming until it's too late."

"Trying to scare me?"

"Yes. I'm scared, too."

"You are?"

"Yes. Those original killings took planning and were executed with no discernable evidence. Nothing definitive has come back on the cages. No one remembers seeing any of the victims on their last nights, except Suzanne and Kasagawa, and no one saw them after the Cauldron. People don't just disappear.

"They were targeted and taken cleanly. That takes discipline and planning. The bodies probably should've been dumped farther out, but even so, they were only found by accident. Had that father/son fishing trip not happened, the bodies wouldn't have been found for a very long time, if ever.

"There has to be more than one person involved. The weight of the cages and the bodies is substantial, even with a boat and a winch. It all smacks of a command chain—a head planner with others following the orders. This takes training, likely military training. If we go up against a military-trained unit, even if they're now civilians, we'll be outmatched. We have to be smarter, and we need reinforcements."

"Now, you're scaring me." She paused. "You know, I'm not stopping. I won't stop until I get those responsible, even if I die trying."

"I'm hoping it won't come to that. You have a set of keys I really want to keep around." That broke the tension.

"Then you'd better make sure you look after me."

"Trust me, I am and will, and not only because of the keys." *Why'd you say that, you idiot?* I wanted to unring the bell, but I couldn't. Fortunately, it hadn't registered with her.

"Where can we get help? Neither of us trusts the police. We can't rely on Oso to watch our backs. He shouldn't be pulled into this. And Marie would be in jeopardy, too. Right?"

"Yes. Anyone associated with us would be in danger."

"So, who do we ask for help?"

I had some ideas on that. I just needed additional info to crystalize a tentative plan. "I have some ideas, but they will depend on you doing what you say you can do."

"What do you mean?"

"Can you hack Rant without being caught?"

"Yes."

"You're sure? This is critical."

"Mas, I told you. I've worked for some very shady people. I'm still alive, not in jail, never been arrested, or charged with anything. I'm very good at what I do."

"Okay. Don't forget, my ass is on the line, too. I'm out of my depth with all this cyber stuff. Remember, you'll be going up against a Silicon Valley outfit."

"Mas, I haven't told you a lot about my business, partly because it's none of your business and I keep confidences. You'd be surprised at who my client list includes. Trust me, I can do this."

"And I don't want to know, correct?"

"Correct. Give me a detailed brief on everything that you need and want. The more you give me, the better I can perform." The transformation from being scared to a task-oriented professional was amazing.

"I still have to work some details myself. As soon as I get it sorted out, I'll get it to you."

"Good. Let's grab Marie and get back to the office.

You have work to do."

We filled Marie in as we made our way back to the office. Until I sorted out my thoughts, Sophie had little to do. So, they took the afternoon off—Marie playing tour guide—spending the day doing all the things tourists in San Francisco are known for. In a way, I was glad. It would give me time to think and organize myself.

"By the way, I think I'm going to check out the Cauldron tonight, if you want to come along."

I hadn't even realized what she'd said until the door closed, and it was too late to comment. I shook my head. I didn't want any distractions right now. I put my notes down on paper, organized them into a final copy, and shredded the rest. Then, I made the calls I'd been neglecting and left messages as needed. Finally, I leaned back in my chair.

I'd done all I could do. The plan should work, as long as Sophie could deliver on her end.

Sophie's comment about the Cauldron crept back into my head. I hadn't played in public for a long time, until Sophie-Circe. Maybe it would do me some good. The Cauldron was safe. The dungeon monitors kept it safe for everyone, and I trusted Circe's kink persona.

Deep in thought about what it would be like to be Sophie's submissive, I almost didn't hear the phone ring. I automatically answered, "Hammett and Lee Investigations."

"Hi, Mas." It was Kenzo.

"Hi, yourself. I'm busy."

"Take it easy. I'm not calling for anything in particular. I just wanted to see how you were doing."

"Really? Out of the goodness of your heart? Come

on, Kenzo. You want to know where we are on Sophie's sister. You got nada on the kink aspect, and you got screwed by two of your own. You've got nothing, and you want to pick my brain cuz the brass is busting your balls to get it solved. Did I miss anything?"

"Yes, you did, but you're right. I don't have anything new on the victims. No one saw anything, anywhere. A complete wash. Whoever did these killings is smart and very careful. But I meant what I said last time we met. I do have your back, and I still owe you. Anyway, we've concluded these killings are not about the kink community. We have other foreign avenues opening up, but nothing I can talk about. Promising leads, but you know how that goes. They can fizzle out fast, and something inconsequential can mean a break. Mas, be careful on this one. I'm a call away."

"Sure. You're still in my phone."

Wondering why he'd called and especially, why the warning. He knew something. He wouldn't have said it unless he was sure of some danger. *Shit.* I replayed the call in my head. Foreign. *Has to be Kasagawa.* Even when they'd been hung up on the kink, they thought Kasagawa was the target and not Suzanne. We thought Suzanne and not Kasagawa. My opinion hadn't changed. Kasagawa had been at the wrong place, at the wrong time. If he was involved with the Yakuza, whoever killed him either knew it and didn't care—which showed unbelievable arrogance—or they didn't know. That would be a mistake that could come back and bite them.

I was sure it was a "them," not one person.

Maybe I should go to the Cauldron for some down

time. Couldn't hurt, I could decide later if I was up for play. Who was I kidding? If I went, I'd play, if the opportunity arose.

Chapter 34

Decision made, I'd take the plunge. I felt at home at the Cauldron. If I were honest, it was the only place I felt truly comfortable. Eating a light dinner, I let the anticipation build, knowing if I showed up before ten, it would be a sparse crowd, at best.

Time ticked by. I had to get out and move. Deciding to walk the neighborhood before heading off to the Cauldron, I couldn't miss how North Beach was hopping and popping. I soaked up the energy and strolled past the cool, one-off boutiques, bars, and shops. As I passed a men's clothing store, I noticed a pair of pointy-toed black ankle boots in the window. They had stacked heels and sort of a throwback Cuban feel. I tried to remember what they were called. *Winkle pickers. That was it*. A row of black glass buttons up the outside of the boot finished them off. I had to have them.

The assistant was helpful, in a cool, off-hand, SF way. I had to go up a half size, but I was surprised how comfortable they felt. They were expensive but worth every penny. I'd probably regret choosing to wear them and carry my old shoes, but I looked good. Damn, it felt good to feel good again.

After I dropped off my old shoes at my apartment, I grabbed a cab and made my way to the Cauldron. Oso was standing in his usual spot. I marched right up to him and gave him a hug.

He looked at me like I was crazy. "You're embarrassing me, man."

I laughed. "I owe you. Just a thank you for the other night. We couldn't have done it without you."

He smiled. "Weren't nothing, man. They was rubbish. No cojones."

"Well, we still owe you."

"Nah. What you done for me was bigger. I don't forget. You need anything you call me. Huh?"

"Okay, Oso. Stay safe."

"Always, man." He turned back to watching the street traffic, and I went upstairs.

The club was filling and I could hear some action on the main floor, but I chose the bar; there would be plenty of time to view the players later.

Two-Serve was bartending. He smiled when he saw me and raised a glass.

I nodded, and by the time I made it to the bar, he had my usual drink ready for me. "Good memory."

"All part of good service." His face became serious. "Besides, I wanted to ask if you had any more info on Sub-lime."

I couldn't tell him what was going on, so I said the usual. "Not really. We're looking into a lot of different things. The only common thread was that every victim was involved with kink, to a greater or lesser degree. The police are following the kink serial-killer theory."

"And you don't think it's true?"

I didn't want to lie, but I couldn't tell him the truth, either. "I think there's a kink aspect to it, but I'm not sure that's the whole story, and to be honest, we've got nothing concrete yet. It's a long process."

Two-Serve's face fell. "I really miss her. She was a good friend. Her sister's here, and she reminds me of her. I wish I could be of more help, but that night was just another night at the Cauldron."

"Don't worry. The police are on it, and something will break, eventually."

He didn't look convinced. "Just like the Zodiac Killer." He turned to serve another customer.

My heart sank. The Zodiac Killer had never been caught. I wished I could tell him more, but I had to keep what we were doing under the radar. I took my drink and looked for anyone I knew. This was supposed to be a fun night, but so far, not so much.

I saw some players I knew and joined them; they welcomed me with hugs and kisses. Sitting and chatting, I felt more relaxed. I hadn't realized how tense I'd been. Suddenly, I felt hands on my shoulders. I startled and turned. "Circe. You surprised me."

Her soft, warm hands kneaded the tension out of my muscles. She bent down to my ear. "I was hoping you'd be adventurous and show up. Now, you have a decision to make. To play or not to play, that is the question?"

Feeling her hands on my shoulders, inhaling her perfume, and hearing her tempting voice, my cock reacted with a will of its own. I wondered if she was wearing my keys. I shifted in my seat, which brought a chuckle from her, followed by a rustle. A long chain dropped in front of me—the keys I knew so well.

She continued talking to me in low tones. "Yes, the keys are here. Does that excite you? You don't know if you will get lucky or not. I may have other plans for you. Are you willing to take a chance? How brave are you, Mas?"

My senses were in overdrive, my trapped dick straining against its metal prison. I was in heaven. "Yes, Ms. Circe. I'm willing to take a chance."

She took my hand and stood me up, looking directly into my eyes. "Mas, are you *really* willing to take a chance?"

"Yes, Ms. Circe. I'm willing to take a chance on you. I'll serve you as you wish."

"I want you to assist me tonight. You will be my service sub. This is a test. You will not be my primary focus. I have two scenes arranged. How you perform will determine how we go forward. Do you understand?"

"I understand, Ms. Circe. Will I need a safe word?"

"No, not tonight. I will allow you to socialize until I am ready for you. Then, I will give you further instructions. Clear?"

"Yes, Ms. Circe. Clear."

"Thank you for your trust." Circe turned and walked away.

I sat back, dazed. My companions teased me about subbing again after such a long absence—it was all good-natured and supportive—but now, I was getting apprehensive. What was she going to have me do? It couldn't be that difficult if I didn't need a safe word, but I'd forgotten there was more than one way to make things difficult for a sub.

Before long, I saw Ms. Circe approaching. She was wearing the gold-colored corset she'd gotten from her sister; she looked good in it. Her tits still threatening to spill out. *I can only hope.* Her lower half was covered in the smallest, tightest pair of black leather shorts I'd ever had the pleasure of seeing. They looked sprayed on, with an obvious camel toe protruding from her crotch. Her garters stretched down under the shorts, holding up black stockings. Her feet were shod in black patent pumps with a pointed toe and a nasty-looking steel heel. She was also wearing soft leather gloves, tight on her fingers and loose around her wrists. The leather looked as soft as silk. Her long, blond hair was piled high on her head in a ponytail. She looked ready for her workout.

My eyes drank her in. I wanted…no, needed…to submit to this woman. My gaze stopped on the keys, still swinging from the long chain around her neck.

As she approached, she smiled, took the keys, and tucked them into her gorgeous cleavage.

They were hidden, but I knew they were there. My dick, still semi-hard, returned to full firmness.

She stopped in front of me. Without thinking, I knelt in front of her, eyes down.

"Nicely done. You may rise. Keep your eyes downcast."

I did as I was told. It was then I saw her hands. She was carrying a leash.

"Strip."

I was stunned. That usually happened in another part of the club. Here I was, in full view of everyone, in a nonplay area. I undressed, now the center of attention. My face burned with humiliation, and my cage filled to bursting. *Oh, how this turns me on.* I could feel their eyes on me. I tried not to hurry, but I wanted it to be over. Soon, I stood naked, with my metal cage glinting in the light.

Circe circled me, ensuring I would meet her needs

and standards. She smiled and nodded. "You will do, for now." She clipped the leash to my cage. "You are not collared by me, so it would not be appropriate to use a collar. This will suffice to let everyone know you are mine. Follow me, eyes down."

"Yes, Ms. Circe." Picking up my clothes, I followed her like a lamb to the slaughter. She took the long way around the club, showing off her property, occasionally tugging on the leash to make sure she impressed on me who was in charge and to tease my throbbing, trapped cock.

I could still feel the burning in my face. I knew I was being ogled and viewed as a prize animal. It was humiliating and exhilarating, all at the same time. It always felt more vulnerable when I was undressed in the presence of clothed people. Since I wasn't serving, only being exposed, all my senses were focused on the embarrassment. If I'd been given a task, I could've focused on that instead. This was sweet torture, with Circe pushing my buttons.

Finally, we entered the main play area. A woman on a Saint Andrew's cross was screaming out in pleasure, asking for permission to come, which was denied. I had other things to think about, and I tried to block her out.

Circe dropped the leash, and it hit the floor, but not before tugging my cage downward.

I was fully erect in the cage; I could feel the blood pulse in my cock. The cage moved with every heartbeat, and I groaned aloud as my cage bounced back.

"You are my assistant tonight. Do exactly what I tell you and when. I expect you to perform to the highest of standards. You will remain silent unless otherwise instructed. Do you understand?"

I nodded.

"Good. Your first task is to clean, sanitize, and prepare the spanking bench. I will be watching you closely. You may start."

Putting down my clothes, I went to the cleaning station. It took me no time to get what I needed and prepare the bench. She sat and intently watched me as I worked. I could feel the drag of the leash on my genitals, pulling the cage down. It was a different pressure and a constant reminder of my condition. I was careful not to step on or yank the leash. I hoped if I pleased Circe, I'd get a release later.

After I finished preparing the bench, a man led a woman, wearing only a hood, up to Circe. Her tits swung as she tentatively followed him, her arms bound behind her. They spoke briefly, and he handed the leash to Circe, who signaled to me.

I moved to her and stood, eyes looking down, waiting for her instructions.

"Mas, fix her securely to the bench. Do not remove her hood. When she is secured, finger her and get her aroused, but do not take too long. This is for my pleasure, not yours. You will stay by me and hand me any implement I request."

Speaking quietly to the woman, I told her what was going to happen. She was already wearing wrist and ankle cuffs. Her wrists were joined with a spring clip. I moved her over to the bench, telling her to lift her leg and feel forward with her knee. She found the ledge and mounted the bench. I moved her forward and told her to squat. She was compliant and did as instructed. Finding the "D" rings on her ankle cuffs, I fixed them to the bench with spring clips. Instructing her to lean forward, I guided her down until her tits were squashed against the padded leather top, her leash dangling down in front of her.

Unfastening her wrists, I attached them to the bench. Then, I used the bench straps to secure her legs. I repeated the process with her arms. I checked to be sure she was firmly secured. Her ass hung off the end of the padded top, exposed and vulnerable.

I was horny and aroused, seeing her so compliant. I knew Circe was using and testing me. I wanted to fuck her and change places with her…to be under Circe's control. Slowly, I massaged her ass, moving in circles, ever closer to her lips. I could see they were moist, wet with her own juices.

She moaned, trying to writhe under my hands.

My cock stood out from me, even with the added weight of the dangling leash. I was powerfully erect. This was torture. I slid my fingers into her. There was no resistance.

She moaned louder, trying to push back onto my hand.

"Stop. That's enough. Hand me the first paddle."

Immediately withdrawing my fingers, the woman released a whimpering groan. I handed Circe the paddle handle first. She looped the rope lanyard over her wrist and gave the paddle a few practice swings. I moved out of the way and stood, hands behind my back, watching her, ready for her next instruction.

I heard the first blow over the festive music. The woman jolted, followed by a loud exhalation. The paddle was a blur. She jolted and subsided with each blow, tensing her ass muscles as the sensation traveled through her body. Soon, she was crying.

Circe was in her zone, oblivious to everything except what she was doing. Her blows were consistent, placed with an exactness I found fascinating, and I imagined what it would feel like to be on the receiving end of Circe's swats.

A bead of sweat appeared on Circe's lip from her effort.

The woman was openly sobbing, and the blows all melded together.

Suddenly, Circe held her arm out.

I took the rope off her wrist, holding the paddle by the rope at my side.

"Riding whip."

Snatching it from the table, I placed it in her open hand butt first.

At the first strike, the woman let out a scream. An angry line appeared on the widest part of her ass.

I turned to the cleaning table and cleaned the paddle, wiping it down with the woman sobbing screams in my ears.

Circe slowed, placing the blows with precision. She noticed I had finished cleaning the paddle. "Stand in front of her and play with her nipples, rolling and pinching."

Quickly, I stood in front of the bench. The flesh of my penis squeezed out the slots of the cage and the touch of the cage to the woman's hood sent shock waves to the root of my dick. I eased her tits out to each side, her nipples hard and set in crinkly aureoles. My touch brought a quick reaction from her and a swift slash from Circe. I did as instructed, rolling and pinching her nipples.

The woman struggled against her restraints. She tensed and relaxed in rhythm with Circe's varied blows.

Circe nodded to me, so I continued as she pulled a suede flogger off the implement rack. She placed the riding whip handle between the woman's ass cheeks and slowly inserted it, causing pleasurable torment. The woman tried to move against it, without avail. Her ass glowed red from the paddle, striped with welts from the riding whip and now, Circe flogged her over her back and ass.

I heard muffled moans coming from under the woman's hood. "May I please come?"

I looked up at Circe, who shook her head. "No."

The woman moaned and pleaded.

Circe continued to flog the begging woman while I played with her nipples, which had to be sore by now. A heavier blow landed, and she screamed for a release, and then shuddered when none came. Circe continued while the woman grew more desperate. She was clearly on the edge. Finally, Circe nodded, and I gave the woman the answer she so desired. Circe pulled the riding whip out of the woman's cunt.

The woman grunted and convulsed, the tension flowing from her body. She moaned and humped the bench, sucking in deep breaths then letting them go with long, low moans. She went on until she had no breath left.

Circe handed me the whip, told me to get her a bottle of water, and to release the woman.

Moving quickly to retrieve the water, I opened the bottle for her, cleaned the riding whip, and returned it to its place. Carefully, I released the woman. She remained motionless, unaware of what I was doing.

Once she was freed, her partner came over to her and stroked her back and talked to her through the hood. After a few minutes, he helped her rise and moved her off the bench. She was unsteady, so he hugged her and wrapped her in a light blanket. They left the play area so he could give her the aftercare she needed.

The whole event had me aroused and now, I was Circe's janitor, cleaning up after her. She was talking with another couple to one side. I concentrated on doing my work to please Circe. The Cauldron house slaves typically did such clean up, but I assumed Circe had requested I do it, instead. When I'd finished, I stepped aside, naked, ignored, and exposed.

Circe finished her conversation and returned to me. "Mas, so far, you've performed very well. I'm taking a break until my next scene. You will remain here, facing away from the play area, with your legs slightly apart, your hands behind your back, and your eyes down. Understand?"

"Yes, Ms. Circe."

"Good."

She moved off, and I stood as instructed. I hated and loved being humiliated this way. Exposed to all and I, of course, heard their comments as they looked at me or just passed by. I was serving, and that was my satisfaction. If this was what it took, I would pay the price. I knew Circe was testing me now and probably would again. I wanted to serve her.

My thoughts went back to what Marie had said. I wanted Sophie to stay in San Francisco, and I wanted to be with her and her alter ego, Circe. Soon, my mind wandered. In my own world, I remained a flesh statue, no longer aware of the crowd, their looks, or their comments. It was one of those Zen moments where I was at peace with everything. Another feeling I hadn't had in a long time.

I had no idea how much time passed. I vaguely heard my name, but I didn't want to leave my paradise. Then, it became more insistent. I shook it off and saw Circe, standing in front of me, looking concerned.

"Mas? Where were you?"

My voice came out as barely a whisper. "Drifting."

"Are you okay?"

"I'm fine. Thank you for asking. How may I serve you, Ms. Circe?"

"Were you in your own universe?"

"No, Ms. Circe. Just drifting." I felt peaceful…energized. All my senses were finely tuned. I cringed at the loud music. I shook my head and came back to reality.

Circe looked at me with genuine concern.

"I'm fine and ready to serve you, Ms. Circe."

With that, she snapped back into being my dominant. "Good. My next scene is getting ready. You will be assisting both me and his partner."

As she spoke, a couple joined us. I didn't recognize either of them. The man, wearing a tight black shirt and black kilt, stood stock still, expressionless, while his partner undressed him with a practiced hand. He was a big man, several inches taller than I was, and well built. He'd obviously spent considerable time on his physique.

In contrast, his partner was a petite Asian woman, perhaps Japanese, from her bone structure and dress.

She wore a transparent blue kimono. I could see she had small, pert breasts with dark aureoles and pointed nipples. The kimono's sleeves were held back with a twist of red silk. At her waist, she wore a wide obi-like belt tied into a huge bow. Below that, she wore sheer, navy, wide-leg pants tied in at the knee.

Ms. Circe said, "Prepare the Saint Andrew's cross and the spanking bench." I did as I was told and readied the equipment, standing aside, ready for my next instruction.

Naked except for high-laced black boots, the man stood, compliant.

Circe led him to the vacant Saint Andrew's cross. He towered above it. She secured his wrists while his partner fastened his ankles using the D-rings sewn into his boots.

I stood nearby, waiting and noticed a number of white dots on the right side of his immense back and a thin white line over one shoulder. They definitely looked like scars, and not from BDSM play.

Circe motioned me forward. "Fetch two pairs of floggers—the purple ones for Mistress Sumi-e and the red suede ones for me."

I picked up the required floggers, handed them off, and stepped out of the way.

The two dominants took turns on his back. Circe concentrated on his upper back, while Mistress Sumi-e swinging the floggers with an easy, practiced hand, addressed his ass and legs. His back warmed, changing color under the floggers. He started to squirm, and I could hear his breathing change to sharp intakes of breath and long exhalations.

The two mistresses in unison, four floggers with no

respite in sight. Instead, they increased their force.

The man strained against his cuffed wrists. I thought I saw the eyebolt in the cross bend when his muscles tensed. The veins popped out from his arms while the white marks on his back became more pronounced against the burn of the surrounding flesh.

Both women perspired from their efforts and the stuffy air of the now-packed Cauldron. They were the center of attention. Everyone was focused on the huge man being flogged by two different dominant females. They eased their blows down to nothing.

Circe waved me over. "Release him and move him to the spanking bench, restrain him securely and put these bells in his piercing. Make sure his ass is hanging off the end of the bench." She handed me a small bunch of bells on a chain with a clip at the top. I hadn't noticed a piercing when he had moved over to the cross. Now, I'd be sure to look for it.

First, I released his ankles, then his wrists. Meekly, he followed me. I scanned his dick for a piercing. He had a Prince Albert piercing—a closed ring through the head of his penis. He mounted the bench, placing himself as needed. I adjusted him, just a little, making sure his ass was over the end of the bench, and strapped him down as I'd done with the woman.

Once he was secure, I reached under him and felt his dick. *This is a first.* I'd never touched another man's equipment before. Ever. The heat rose in my face, and I did as I was instructed. Carefully, I found his hardening cock. Not sure if it was from the situation or from my touch. Wanting it to be over as quickly as possible, I found the ring and attached the bunch of bells, making sure they were securely attached. If they fell off, I would be in trouble and, worse, have to reattach them.

Ms. Circe and Mistress Sumi-e looked him over. Circe turned to me. "Fetch two riding whips."

I retrieved them and handed them to the mistresses, handle first.

They tested them by slicing them through the air.

The man was immobile, waiting for the first slashing blow to impact his jutting ass.

Mistress Sumi-e stood on his left side, Ms. Circe to his right, holding the whip in her left hand; she was a switch hitter. Her blow fell hard and fast, and he tried to lurch away, but the restraints held tight. Mistress Sumi-e and Circe alternated blows. Circe could hit hard left and right. The two synchronized their strikes. It was intense. The bells attached to his Prince Albert piercing rang out. His limited movement made the ringing more impressive.

As the blows intensified, Ms. Circe swung her arm and her left tit popped out. She was oblivious, focused on her efforts.

I drank in the sight of her tit swinging and bouncing with her efforts. My erection intensified; I was fixated on her. I knew the slightest touch on my trapped dick would have had me squirting, though I feared that wouldn't happen.

Slowly, they eased the frequency and ferocity of their blows until they stopped, breathing heavily. They tossed the two whips to me.

I nearly missed one. I assumed they wanted them cleaned and put away.

Ms. Circe called me over, her boob still out.

I couldn't take my eyes off her, but she seemed oblivious.

"Mas, you will help us get ready for the next round." She handed me a black leather harness and a dildo.

I immediately knelt in front of her, buckling the straps in place, making sure they were snug, but not restricting. After I inserted the dildo, Ms. Circe tested the fit and smiled at me. I melted. *A big old tough ex-cop. Me, on my knees, melting from a woman's look, one tit out and wearing a fake cock.* I wished it was going into me, though I'd never been a big fan of pegging. Now, whatever she wanted, I wanted. I was completely smitten. *What the hell is wrong with me*? I'd never felt like this before. Jolted out of my reverie with a slap. It wasn't hard, but my face stung.

"What are you waiting for? Mistress Sumi-e is waiting. Then, come back and lube up my dick."

I crawled over to Mistress Sumi-e as quickly as I could and repeated the process, adorning her with a harness and dildo. The dildo seemed enormous compared to her petite stature. I bowed and crawled away, returning to Ms. Circe.

Mistress Sumi-e stood in front of her submissive. She held the dong in front of him, entered his mouth, and began to hump his face.

Knowing what it felt like to have a fake cock stuffed in my ass, I dripped the lube on Circe's dong, making sure it was fully covered.

She grabbed the bottle of lube and moved behind the broad ass. Squirting lube on his ass crack, she spread it about with the tip of her cock, teasing and taunting him.

I could hear the man's muffled grunts as he deep-throated Mistress Sumi-e's cock.

Circe tossed me the lube and spread his ass cheeks with her hands, placing the tip of her cock on the puckered entrance in front of her. She gently pushed the head of her cock inside him, and he visibly relaxed. Slowly and consistently, Ms. Circe pushed against him, going deeper with every thrust.

Impaled from both ends, the man tried to move against each invading spike, knowing he was only the instrument for their pleasure.

Ms. Circe signaled for the lube again. "Lube up his ass. I want a smooth ride." I was about to stand so I could reach more easily. Ms. Circe said "No, from your knees."

It wasn't easy, but I managed to get the lube in the right place. My eyes were level with her cock, sliding in and out of his hole. She was driving me beyond frustration. I'd been out of a dominant/submissive relationship for so long, I'd forgotten this frustration, but everything flooded back. I not only wanted this, I needed it. My head swam. I sat back on my heels, trying to absorb the sights and feelings.

"We're done. Remove Mistress Sumi-e's dick, then release her submissive from the bench. She will take care of her property. Then, remove my cock and clean it up. I'll wait for you in the bar. Do not be too long. You may stand."

"Yes, Ms. Circe. At once." I kneeled in front of Mistress Sumi-e and removed her dong and harness, setting it to one side. I quickly released her property so she could attend to him.

The giant man's eyes were glazed. His back was red from the flogging, his ass striped with welts. Drool and lube ran from both ends. Mistress Sumi-e whispered in his ear, gently stoking his face. He tried to rise, but collapsed back against the bench. His second effort moved him to his knees. He rested against the bench for a moment then struggled to his feet with Mistress Sumi-e's help. It was an incongruous sight, her petite frame assisting a monster of a man. They stumbled off toward the rest area so she could care for him.

Ms. Circe stood, waiting for me. I removed her dildo and harness. She stepped clear and walked off, leaving me on my knees. I was still in service mode. I cleaned and sanitized everything they'd used, wielded, or touched. I worked quickly and efficiently, knowing others wanted to scene. I packed each item in its appropriate receptacle, keeping Mistress Sumi-e's separate from Ms. Circe's. I gave Mistress Sumi-e's play bag to one of the house slaves. Then I packed up Ms. Circe's, leaving it in the changing area before joining her in the bar.

I was shaky, on emotional overload. Feelings had been released after being suppressed for too long. Joy flooded through me, and I almost laughed aloud. Something deep inside of me rejoiced. This is where I was meant to be.

Ms. Circe sat in the corner, chatting with a couple. She had adjusted her tit back into the corset. She nodded to me, pointing to the floor at her side. I silently knelt and she placed her hand on my head, ruffling my hair. She continued with her conversation.

I listened silently. The couple wasn't introduced to me, and I didn't acknowledge them. After several minutes, they left.

Ms. Circe looked at me. "That was an interesting

conversation. They came over to compliment me on the last scene and wondered if you were available to be loaned out or rented when they had a private play party."

My head reeled. We hadn't progressed to that point.

"I explained our situation and they understood, but asked if we ever get to that point, to keep them in mind. You impressed them with your compliance. Don't worry. I take care of my property...once it's my property." She laughed a sweet, tinkling laugh. "Let's get out of here. I think I need some oral relief. This was a fun evening, wasn't it?"

"If you say so, Ms. Circe."

"Oh, come on, Mas. Your prick was squeezing out through its cage all night. You're horny as hell, and that turns me on. I like seeing you naked, well mostly, and your trapped cock, getting wood so quickly and keeping it. I bet it wouldn't take much to get you to shoot your load, would it? Could you do it with your cage on?"

"I don't know. I've never tried it." Even the thought of a trapped orgasm made me want to try. It would be better than no release at all.

"Perhaps we should try it after I've been satisfied, of course. If I'm not too tired. You can get dressed."

I picked up her play bag, and we left. After what had happened with McCarrigan, I scanned the area, just in case. We hailed a cab and rode in silence back to Circe's place.

We made good time. I followed Circe up the stairs, making sure the gate and doors were shut and locked behind us.

Circe directed me to put the bag in the spare

bedroom, then ordered me to undress. When I returned to the living room, I found her, legs crossed and hands resting lightly on her thigh, waiting for me. "Well? I am waiting."

I quickly stripped until I once again stood in front of her, naked and uncomfortable.

She looked me over, as if seeing me nude for the first time. Her eyes came to rest on my cage.

I glanced up at her; she wasn't wearing my key. My heart sank. No release tonight, or at least no freedom. Maybe she'd been serious about making me orgasm in my cage.

Her voice grew quiet. "Kneel." She opened her legs. Her pussy was glistening with moisture.

I licked my lips. I couldn't believe I was soon going to dive in there. I moved across the floor on my knees, stopping in front of her.

"No restraints tonight, yet." She let that hang for a moment then, leaning forward, she grabbed my head and plunged me into her cunt, grinding on my face. It felt primal.

I savored every movement. My face was for her pleasure, and she was using it well.

Guttural moans rose from her throat. "When I was flogging and whipping and fucking him, I wanted it to be you. I wanted you to be in front of me. I wanted to make you feel what he was feeling." She flushed, reliving the night, then came in a rush, bucking up and down on my buried face. Gripping my hair, she pulled me into her. With one final spasm, she jerked then went still, exhaling a long breath. She remained that way for a while, my head between her legs, my face soaked. Slowly, she gently pushed me away and smiled. "Don't move."

I was still in a daze from the speed and intensity of her orgasm. The thud of heavy cuffs hitting the floor brought me back.

"Put these on—just wrist and ankle—then follow me into the spare bedroom."

I did as instructed. The weight of the cuffs felt good. I trailed behind her.

"Lie on the bed, face up, arms to each head post, feet together."

She anchored my arms to the bedposts. Joining the ankle cuffs, she attached them under the end of the bed, added a strap around my knees, and spread me out like a flat crucifix.

"Now, our little experiment. I know you get hard in the chastity cage." *I already was.* "I wonder how much teasing it would take to get you to come, if you can. You've been titillated all night, and I think we can make it happen. Will you take that bet?"

I shook my head. I didn't know if I could or not, but I wasn't taking any chances.

She laughed. "Where's your sense of adventure? Tell you what. If you come, I get to keep you in chastity for a while longer. If you don't—" She stopped, grinning, before proceeding. "I'll let you out and you fuck me. How's that for a deal?"

I couldn't believe my ears, and it showed on my face.

"It's a deal." She looked as if she'd just made the best bet ever.

Growing concerned, I didn't want to be caged for a while longer. I *did* want to come. I wanted to fuck her, but I knew I would come if she teased me enough. It was a bet she couldn't lose.

"So, let's begin. You're pretty hard, but I think you can get harder." She fingered my trapped dick, making it ooze out of the slots. "See? I told you it could get harder. I just love the way your meat squeezes out of the slots in your cage." She ran her fingernails over the sensitive skin straining out of the cage.

I felt like I'd explode. The tickling sensations went straight from my cock to my soul. I could feel every heartbeat in my imprisoned prick. I willed myself not to shoot my wad. The sensations stopped, and I opened my eyes. She was gone. My prick pulsed my frustration.

Circe returned with something in her hand. She stooped to plug it in and I heard a faint buzzing. She held the vibrator in front of me, then gently lifted my encased cock and laid the vibrator between my legs. Carefully, she put my metal chastity cage on top of the vibrating head of the wand.

I felt the vibrations surge through me.

She turned up the intensity.

I tried to move, but I couldn't. I tried to think of something—anything—to not come, but it wasn't working.

"If you want something to take your mind off what's going on, you should look at me.

I slowly turned my head.

She was sitting in a chair, legs apart, spread wide. "This is what you want, isn't it? Don't forget. You only get to put your...I mean, *my* cock in here if you can hold out." She trailed her fingers over her slit, pulling her lips apart.

I could clearly see her pink, open, inviting pussy. I

tried to look away, but I couldn't move. I was transfixed. The vibrations and the sight of her openness, her fingers playing with her clit and pleasuring herself, made me want to scream.

One hand moved up to her corset-covered breasts, removing her left tit. She switched hands. Her right hand now played with her moist mound while the other released her right breast. She played with herself, alternating tits and her wet pussy.

I was in torture heaven. I didn't care how I got a release. I just needed it. Suddenly, I felt my balls tighten, and before I could ask for permission, the draining feeling surged, and my load came out through the end of the cage. This wasn't like any orgasm I'd ever had. It was a release, rather than a climax. I felt the sensation again, and more cum oozed out, this time, with less power. The cum spilled out of my cage, down the vibrating wand, and on to my legs.

Ms. Circe clapped her hands and laughed. "You came. You can come in your cage. That was fun. Next time, you need to ask permission, but I'll forgive you this first time."

This was a completely different release, and now that Ms. Circe knew she could make it happen, why let me out? Almost in tears, I knew there would be a next time. The only speck of comfort was that I'd pleased Ms. Circe. I was becoming more and more hers, but I wanted to be hers completely…and that scared me.

I lay quietly, not knowing what to say. She leaned over and kissed me deeply, her tongue invading my mouth. I responded with all my soul. Her tits grazed my chest, sending shivers through my core.

She pulled away. "Clean up time."

I assumed she'd release me to cleanse myself. After all, I'd made the mess.

"I'll take care of this clean up. Gotta keep my caged-up property clean. Can't have you thinking you'll be free every time."

"I will always follow your instructions."

"It's not that I don't trust you, but you are a man, so I don't trust you…yet. You could easily overpower me, and that would ruin our potential relationship."

Relationship? She's thinking along those lines? A peaceful shroud fell over me. Was it possible I could get the relationship I'd been seeking? I heard my lock release.

Ms. Circe removed my cage and put everything to one side. She wiped me down with tissues and cleaned off my sticky seed. Leaving a pile of used tissues on my shaved pubic area, she left me. She returned with a bowl of hot water. She placed the cage in hot water and swirled it around

She removed the vibrator and knee strap. All her actions were deliberate and precise. Sitting on the edge of the bed, she wiped me down with cleansing wipes. She chuckled when she felt me respond to her touch. Once she was satisfied, she dried my chastity cage and added a few drops of oil into the lock.

I wondered how she was going to get the cage back on, now that I was hard again. She'd obviously thought about that, as well.

Circe reached down to the side of the bed and placed something on my genitals.

As the freezing cold sensation hit my pubic area, I bucked. She'd wrapped a bag of ice around my genitals. I deflated immediately.

She smirked. "This isn't my first rodeo." She removed the bag and quickly dried my cock and lubed it for the cage. It slid on easily. She adjusted it with Q-tips, then closed the two parts with a resounding click.

I was, once again, a prisoner.

Ms. Circe released me from the bed. "You may dress and leave now. I'm tired. See you tomorrow."

With that, I dressed quickly and bowed to her as I left, making sure the doors and her gate were shut and locked. On my way home, even with my mind in turmoil from the night's events, I stayed aware of my surroundings, keeping a vigilant eye on everyone and everything. As a benefit, it kept my mind off the events and feelings I needed to process.

Chapter 35

My eyes flickered. The night before, I'd walked in the door, stripped, and crashed. Mentally and physically exhausted, I'd gone out like a light. Now, the sun shredded the shadows cast by my window blinds.

Loving the way the sun played with my room, I lay in bed, at peace, watching the dust sparkle like diamonds in the rays and the shadows come and go as the breeze shifted the blinds. The moments felt like a meditation. Then the fucking phone spoiled my mood.

I didn't recognize the number. Pissed, I snatched it up. "Mas Hammett.

"Just listen, grumpy. Follow the money and keep looking. It's all about the money."

Now, I was fully awake. "Who is this?" The voice sounded vaguely familiar, even if the voice itself was disguised. It was the language used and the repetition of the key word, money. I knew the pattern. I just couldn't place it.

"It's the money. Find and follow the money."

Short, sharp, and to the point. No way to trace that call. Anyway, I'd bet money the phone was a burner that had already found a new home in a public trashcan. Whoever it was had some skin in the game. McCarrigan? Doubtful. He had the program, even though he didn't know it was crap. *No money there, only embarrassment for Rant*. The police? Doubtful.

They were still fixated on the serial-killer aspect. Still, the caller had triggered something in the back of my mind. *Shit.* I'd let it come when it came.

My peaceful mood ruined, I showered. Feeling the hot water on my caged dick made me hard. That, and thinking about last night's adventures. I hoped Sophie/Circe was serious about a relationship. I was up for it. At least, I thought I was.

I called Marie and asked if Sophie was in yet.

"Not yet, boss."

I was surprised. I called her cell. No answer. Now, I was starting to worry. She was always in early and missing a call was almost a phobia; she always answered. I was about to redial when her number popped up.

"I was in the shower and didn't get to it in time. What's up? Business or pleasure?"

"All business. Meet me at the office ASAP. Just got an interesting call. Will explain when I see you." I hung up. I knew she'd be there quickly. Even if we couldn't trace the call, it might be possible to trace the phone's owner, a big maybe.

I briefly stopped for coffee, even though I knew Marie would have a pot on. I needed a caffeine rush. As soon as I took the first slug, I felt the warmth hit me; it felt life affirming. Sophie arrived a few minutes after me, looking much better than I felt. She was bright and fresh…not reflecting anything from the night before. "Good morning. What was so important you couldn't tell me over the phone?"

"Too complicated. I need you to do something." I explained the call I'd received and what I wanted her to do.

"Mas, I doubt if we can trace the call. I can try to reverse directory the number and search for the location that sold it. Maybe, we can look at the security cameras, if they had any." She was as offhanded as if she were asking for coffee.

"Do what you gotta do. I think this confirms we're doing something right."

"You do think we are on the right track?"

"Could be a diversion. I just can't think of anyone who'd really profit from giving us this info."

"Do you think it is a diversion?"

"No. I'm convinced Rant Applications is at the center of this mess, but I'm not sure who all the players are. Byron and Gilbert must be connected. I don't see Byron capable of murder, at least not directly. Gilbert is certainly capable, but he'd employ others to do the dirty work. The caller said to follow the money and keep looking, which suggests it won't be easy to find. Are you ready to do some digging?"

"Yes, I am. I'll take care of the phone call first; that's going to be a fast win or lose. Diving into Rant will take some time. They'll have some dense firewalls. I'm hoping I can use some of Suzanne's directories for navigation."

"Won't they know it's you if you use anything from Suzanne?"

"No. I won't use her passwords or anything that can be traced back to her. The directories are too generic. I'll only use them as a guide. I have your list. I'll make some adjustments to it, taking into consideration this morning's call."

"Okay. How much time will you need?"

She gave me a withering look. "As much as I need.

You'll be the first to know when I have something. Now, leave me alone to get on with it."

I shrugged and headed back to the front office, pondering why I felt I knew the caller. It bothered me I couldn't ID him. Sophie was hunched over her monster computer, typing away, so I told Marie I was going to the shooting range and to call me if anything happened.

She looked at me with disdain. "Really, Mas. You had to say that? Who else would I call?"

Damn it. I was surrounded by bossy women with no respect for my position of authority. I laughed at myself, thankful for them.

I picked up my pistol and went to the range; it was empty. I asked for permission to do some rapid fire and, as usual, was given the okay so long as no one else was on the line. I banged away, clip after clip. I was getting my groove back, but I wasn't quite there. I was still better with slow fire than rapid fire. Making my way back to my apartment, I performed my gun cleaning ritual, prepping it for the next time. I stripped and dropped my clothing into the hamper. Turning, I looked at myself in the mirror. It brought back memories and feelings from the previous night. Even on my own, my cock hardened at the thoughts. The humiliation of being brought off by a vibrator in my cage and having Sophie as Circe the tormentor and witness, made it better and worse.

I checked my phone as soon as I got out of the shower. Nothing. *Patience*. I didn't know how long it took to hack a company, but I guessed it wasn't like on TV where it only took a couple of key strokes. Sophie would let me know when she had what I'd asked for. Still, I had to do something.

Kenzo had been explicit—we were off the case as far as the PD was concerned. That didn't exclude me from asking the ME some questions regarding my case, Suzanne, and the other body, Kasagawa. I made the call and asked only one question. Did Kasagawa have any distinguishing marks or tattoos? I got a good result.

"Nothing other than an old surgical scar on his right knee and a tattoo on his left shoulder. A detailed multi-colored dragon. It's been there a while."

"What's his DOB?"

"August 18, 1976."

Doing the calculation in my head. It made sense. He was born in the year of the dragon. With no other tattoos, he was obviously not a full member of any Yakuza clan, but that didn't mean he was clean. As McCarrigan had said, he was a middleman—the clean face of investment money. I was sure he'd been in the wrong place at the wrong time. Suzanne had to be the target, and whoever took them didn't know Kasagawa or his Yakuza connection. How careful had Kasagawa been regarding his ties? Rant, and anyone doing business with him, would've done background checks. Time to pick McCarrigan's brain and to bother Tara Zosa for the same reason, though she probably wouldn't be pleased to hear from me. *Oh, well. She'll get over it.*

McCarrigan took my call and was as helpful as he could be, giving me another extension number in his company, asking me to give him time to brief that person, and requesting I call back in an hour. Tara didn't take my call but promised to call me back by the end of the day. *More effing waiting.*

Needing to do something, I went down to the

industrial dock where the bodies had been dumped. They had to have been dumped by boat—no other way of getting them that far out—so why so close to the dock? Why not take them farther out where there was less chance of them being discovered? I wondered what the view was like from the bay.

I pulled out a map from the glove compartment and laid it out on the hood of the SUV. I found my location and looked at the lines of sight. Looking behind me, it all made sense. The bodies had been dumped close enough to shore to be hidden by the location and height of the industrial buildings. If the dumpsite had been farther out, it would've been visible to the residential properties behind the industrial area. If they had gone even farther, they might've been seen by other boaters, commercial traffic, or official patrols, a bigger risk than dumping close into shore.

That answered one question. It also meant whoever had dumped the bodies knew the area or had been instructed to use it as a dumpsite by someone who was familiar with the area. More questions for Sophie to investigate. Who at Rant was a local or had been here a long time? I texted her the questions I had and asked her to add them to the list. No response, though I hadn't really expected one. I then called McCarrigan's office again. I was immediately transferred.

The woman didn't ask my name.

A different woman answered. "Is this Mas Hammett?"

"Yes."

"I'm not sure how much help I can be. Mr. McCarrigan instructed me to help you, as long as I didn't divulge any proprietary information."

"I appreciate Mr. McCarrigan's help. I'm looking for background on Mr. Kasagawa. I know he was a competitor."

"Oh, I will tell you what I can." Her voice warmed. "He was Japanese. He had a reputation in the U.S. as a fierce competitor, but nothing negative. No underhanded actions that we're aware of. He and his company did a lot of business in the tech start-up area. We were never able to pinpoint his source of funds, though we knew the money came from Japan. We had a few leads, but they dead-ended into banks or shell corporations. Some of the banks seemed too small to be investing large amounts overseas. There were rumors he was connected to the Yakuza, but we never found confirmation."

"Did McCarriggan ever beat him in any deals?"

She took a long pause. "Yes, we did. Only a couple of small ones. Nothing to write home about. Kasagawa beat us recently, but you already know that. He briefed me."

"Yes, he mentioned that. Is there anything else you can think of?"

"Not really. If Kasagawa needed to get financing in a hurry, it was always there. If he needed extra cash to sweeten a deal, he was able to get it, even with very short notice."

"Thank you…uh, I didn't get your name."

"Correct. Goodbye, Mr. Hammett." She hung up.

Smiling, I didn't really need her name. I just wanted to needle her. *Objective achieved.* Now, to wait patiently for Tara Zosa to call me. It was still too early for that, and there was nothing I could do at the office except get in the way, so I went home and worked out, feeling almost back to normal.

All the bruising was fading. Although I hated running, I knew it was the best way to get back into shape. The sweat ran off me, and it felt great sweating out the toxins and the frustrations of the case. Letting my mind wander, I heard the voice, telling me to follow the money.

The way he spoke…

It was so close, but I just couldn't grasp it.

Stepping off the treadmill, I took a long, hot shower, toweling off when my phone rang.

It was Sophie. "Hi. What's up?"

"You called me."

"Checking in. I'm making headway with Rant. I have some new directions. I got your text and added those questions to your list. Good ones. Logical and to the point. I hope to have some answers for you by late today or early tomorrow, but we're going to have to piece the answers together."

"Great. Whatever you get will help fill in the blank spots."

"Any news on getting reinforcements?"

"No, not yet. I have some calls out. Still waiting for responses."

"And you aren't going to tell me about them?" I could hear the accusation in her voice.

"Not yet. When I have something to tell, you'll know. Promise."

"I'd better be. I have a key you'd like kept safe."

That comment went straight to my dick. "Not just a key."

Sophie chuckled. "You say the nicest things. Let me know if anything breaks."

"Got it. That's a promise." She hung up, and I was left holding a silent phone. Sophie had really gotten under my skin. Suddenly, I felt lonely. I needed company, so I dressed and walked the neighborhood. It usually lifted my spirits. But today, not so much. It was Sophie I wanted to be with.

Puttering about my apartment with nothing to act on, I cleaned my sidearm again, checked it over, and reloaded it, keeping one in the chamber. I put it back where I could quickly access it. I threw in a load of wash and waited.

Tara's call came in early.

"Mas Hammett speaking."

"Mr. Hammett, I do not like being set up or spied upon. I'm only calling you as a favor to Mr. McCarrigan. What do you want?"

"Ms. Zosa, I'm investigating several murders, one in particular, so I'll do whatever it takes to accomplish that." Silence. I heard office sounds in the background.

"I still don't like being spied on. Again, what do you need?"

"Ms. Zosa, I know you had a business relationship with Mr. Kasagawa. I need anything you can tell me— contacts here in the U.S., his habits, anything about his business that won't break confidences or boundaries, anyone you can think of in Japan I could contact." She was quiet again. I could almost hear her think.

"I liked Mr. Kasagawa. He was never a friend, but he was a very good business partner. He was always open with me, and he was smart. He made some good deals, with my help. Some, I originated, but mostly, he started them and used me to work with him. He was courteous, charming, and generous."

I felt she was leaving something out. "And dangerous?"

"Why do you say that?" Her response had come too quickly.

"Because I believe he was a front for the Yakuza—a clean front for laundering money from Japan through banks into U.S. companies."

"What makes you think that?"

Now, I was getting annoyed. "Come on, Ms. Zosa. I'm not stupid. His easy access to financing. McCarrigan has his suspicions. You worked more closely with Kasagawa than anyone in the U.S. You must've had your suspicions, as well. Kasagawa didn't cut you loose. You decided it was too dangerous to continue. Correct?" I was fishing.

Her voice grew quiet. "Yes. I ended the relationship. It was a business decision. A third party—I don't know who—sent me some information, warning me there would be an investigation into his business dealings here in the U.S."

That caught my attention. "Do you know who was doing the investigating?"

"No. I don't even know if an investigation was ever started. I cut my ties with him as quickly as I could."

It could be another diversion, but she sounded worried. I knew she believed whoever had given her the information was warning her. "Was this before or after Kasagawa became involved with Rant Applications?"

"Before. Otherwise, I would've been involved with that deal, too. I know few details about that deal, but it seemed too good to be true. I couldn't find out much about this Jack Mellon, and what I did find wasn't great. I know Mr. Kasagawa put a lot of capital into the deal."

"What do you call 'a lot' of capital?"

That brought a low laugh from Tara. "Millions. Dollars, not yen. And no, I don't know how much, for sure. Like I said, I was warned off him. I can't afford a scandal. Do you know how hard it is for women in this business, especially in Silicon Valley? The old-boy network, looking down on me because I'm a woman. Well, I'm successful, and I intend to continue my success. If I was you, Mr. Hammett, I'd follow the money. It's *always* about the money. You needn't call me again. I won't take your call. Goodbye."

I was about to thank her, but she'd already hung up. That was the second time today I'd been told to follow the money. I sighed. There was nothing I could do now. It was all in Sophie's capable hands.

Chapter 36

The insistent sound of my phone going off woke me with a jolt. Sluggishly, I reached for it. Damn. I was sore from yesterday's workout. I'd slept like the dead, so that was a positive. "Hello." My voice came out as a croak.

A very excited Sophie on the other end shattered what was left of my peaceful night. "Get your lazy ass in here ASAP. Don't even stop for coffee…or anything else, for that matter. See you in ten minutes!" The line went dead.

Springing out of bed, I splashed my face, and brushed my teeth. I grabbed whatever clothes were handy, dressed quickly, then staggered out of the apartment, taking my life in my hands as I crossed the street against the light. Curses peppered the air, but I didn't look back. I made it to the office in under fifteen minutes—a record I didn't want to beat—and still got disapproving looks when I unlocked the door.

Marie stood with her arms crossed, and Sophie tapped her watch.

"So? Where's the fire?"

Marie left to get me coffee.

"First, we were right about the phone. It's a burner. They must've turned it off, so there's no chance of tracking it. I used the number and searched it, thanks to our back door into the SFPD. It was a convenience store in the Mission District."

I nodded. The Mission was not the most salubrious area of SF. "No surveillance footage, huh?"

"Well, yes and no. They do have active surveillance, but the data is wiped weekly. They still use tapes, and they reuse them over and over. That phone, along with five others, was purchased a couple of months ago."

"Six? That's a lot of phones. Sounds like an organized group."

"You mean, like the people who killed my sister?"

"They're organized, but I don't think they'd be telling us to follow the money. I think there's another player in the game, now I'm sure it's not McCarrigan or Tara. Oh, by the way, I spoke to both yesterday. Tara also told me to follow the money. She didn't specify it was tied to Rant, but she did say it's always about the money. She said Kasagawa's investment in the Dissolve project was millions of dollars. Does that make sense?"

"It could. It would mean he was convinced Dissolve was the real thing. Anyway, more good news. I'm into Rant Applications. Just started poking around. I'm looking at HR first to get as much as I can on Mr. Howard and Mr. Gilbert...org charts, reporting lines, etcetera. Then, I'll nose around in the financials, including their personal accounts. I'd bet big bucks they have offshore accounts. I do and would expect them to, as well."

"So, what do you want me to do?"

"Nothing. I just wanted to let you know where I was. We should have all the info soon, hopefully today. I'll print out anything of interest, so be prepared for a hefty ink bill."

"And none of this can be traced back to you?" I was concerned. So far, the body count was eight; I didn't want it to climb any higher.

"Mas, I appreciate the concern, but I do this for a living. We'll be okay, as long as I'm careful. And I'm very careful. Trust me."

There was nothing more I could say. I *had* to trust her. What was I supposed to do now? "So, now I'm like a spare dick at a party?"

She laughed. "For now, but I might need some decompression later, if you're up for it. Oh, but don't you need keys for that?" She winked at me. "See you later. I'll call when I have enough for us to review...datawise, I mean." She grinned.

I didn't like leaving her and Marie alone in the office, but right now, I'd just be a hindrance. I had to trust she knew what she was doing. Then, a thought struck me. I headed out of the office without even saying goodbye.

I went home, picked up my gun and camera, and walked down to my SUV. Plotting a different course than the way I'd come, I revved up the engine and turned left, looking for a parking spot with a clear view of my office building's front door. *Not too close, not too far.*

I hadn't been on a stakeout for a while. It was as tedious and boring as I'd remembered. Scrutinizing the people, the pedestrians, and the cars, I looked for repeat people or cars that drove by too many times. At first, I was vigilant, recording each tiny detail to memory, but after a while, I grew tired. It was boring as hell, but at least it was something I could do. I didn't anticipate anything, but if something happened, it would most likely happen from the front; easier access for people who didn't know the building.

Thankfully, it was one of those San Francisco days—sunny, but cooler than expected. I rolled the window down and flipped up a newspaper, pretending to read. I enjoyed people watching. The trick was to keep my eyes moving so I didn't miss anything important.

My stomach rumbled. *Lunch time*. I hoped Sophie and Marie would lunch together. A few moments later, I watched them leave, arm in arm. *Perfect. They should be safe in public*. I took the opportunity to get a sandwich and use the bathroom. Stakeouts could be disastrous on one's bladder, and I wasn't as young as I once was.

Stretching my legs, I walked up and down the block a few times. And came back to the SUV, refreshed.

The two women returned, laughing. I saw a car I'd seen earlier that morning, slow as it approached them. I couldn't see the driver well, but I could tell it was a man. The car stopped. I couldn't see either Sophie or Marie. The driver nodded, then drove off. Sophie and Marie continued to walk to the front door.

I called Marie's cell. "What was that all about?"

"What was what all about?"

"Why did that car stop?"

"He wanted directions. He'd been driving around all morning and couldn't find an address. Why are you following us?"

"What was he looking for?"

"Mas, don't be so suspicious. He was looking for

Jake's, okay?"

That explained it. Jake's was a sought-after custom tailor, tucked away in a back alley. If you didn't know where it was, it was an SOB to find. Panic over.

Then Sophie got on the phone. "Mas, are you playing silly buggers?"

"No. I'm useless in the office, so I staked out my own place. It can't hurt. Consider yourself lucky. I'm bored to death. I do want to look over whatever you find, okay?"

She laughed at my overprotectiveness. "Okay. I'll call you." She hung up as they walked into the building.

The rest of the day went by quietly. At five, Marie left the office. I was going stir crazy. I hoped Sophie wouldn't be doing a late night or worse, an all-nighter.

Thankfully, she called a half hour later. "I'm fried. I need a drink and a decent meal. Can we do dinner?"

"Of course! What sounds good? Fancy eating? Italian? Something else?"

"Any good seafood places close?"

"One of the best. It's close. Seafood is the specialty. This early, we should be able to get in without a reservation. I'm still across the street. See you in a few." I watched as she came out, carrying her laptop. I waved and she ran over to me.

She was excited. She set her computer bag on the floor of the car. "This doesn't leave our sight, got it? I have some flash drives, and all the data printouts. It's all in this bag. Mas, we hit the mother lode. I'll tell you about it at dinner."

I opened my mouth to interject, but she started again.

"Screw it. When I got into Rant, I was surprised

how sloppy they are for a tech company. Very little compartmentalization, so I wandered about easily. I hit a few bumps, but nothing too difficult. Then, it occurred to me it was *too* easy, even for sloppy. I dug some more. They've been sneaky, but I caught them."

She took a breath, so I jumped in. "Is it what we need?"

"Yes and no. I'm still digging, but we're on the right track. There's a lot of weird stuff that doesn't make sense. I'm sure Rant has offshore accounts, but I'm not sure yet if Howard and Gilbert do. The org charts were interesting. Howard has more responsibility and authority than we thought. Gilbert is what he said, Head of Security. I found a copy of his resume in one of the HR files. You were right; he's ex-military, but looks like he left under a cloud, reading between the lines. I think he did clandestine work, probably for units that don't officially exist. I've done some business with those folks. Anyway, he knows enough about cyber security to be dangerous, but not necessarily effective.

"I only had time to review the Dissolve financials superficially. There's been a lot of cash thrown at it— different SOWs and POAs—a lot of movement. Pretty sure there's been skimming, and probably outright fraud. Howard has to be involved with that. He has access and the authority to move and hide stuff."

"We've arrived. Let's see if we can get a table. We may have to continue this conversation after dinner. You never know who might be listening."

"Okay…Are you always this paranoid?"

"Only when I'm dealing with potential killers." Crap. "I'm so sorry. That was a dumb thing to say. I'm concerned what we may be up against."

She held my hand and said quietly, "At least I know you care. That means a lot. You make me feel safe."

I smiled at her, still feeling stupid. We left the car with the valet and entered the restaurant.

Paolo, the owner, was at the hostess desk. When he looked up, his eyes widened, and his face split into a big, toothy smile. He was tall and slim for a chef, with a big, joyous laugh and a shock of full white hair. "So, now you decide to come back to my humble kitchen, huh? How many months has it been? I've missed you. You have good taste." He grinned at Sophie. "Introduce me to your companion, or I may have to seduce her away from you." He laughed at his own joke. His laughter was infectious.

I joined in. "And your wife won't mind you seducing the customers?"

"How else am I going to get them to come back? Me or the food, what a choice?" He led us directly back to a table near the kitchen—his table—where he and his family ate. It was empty but looked as if it was ready for dinner.

I stopped him. "Paolo, we can't crash your family dinner."

He looked at me, puzzled. Again, he bellowed out a laugh. "No, no! My wife and family are visiting relatives in the old country. I'd love the company. Eating alone is a crime. Food is family and is meant to be shared. We will eat."

We sat down on each side of Paolo.

"I will order for us. I know the best dishes. After all, I created them." His laugh made heads turn.

The server approached with water and filled the

glasses while Paolo rattled off instructions in rapid Italian. The server nodded and left.

I introduced Sophie, who seemed completely lost under Paolo's effusive charm. We briefly told him the bare bones of the situation.

He took her hand in his. "Losing a family member is tragic. If there's anything I can do, you call me. Mas is a friend of mine so now, you are a friend, also." He was almost in tears, his sincerity obvious.

"Thank you, Paolo."

Then, it was back to food and smiles. "Now, we celebrate life and new friends."

The food came, calamari, shellfish, whole fish, and salads with olives of all colors and cures. We were served both red and white wines from Tuscany, while Paolo regaled us with stories of the restaurant business and made self-deprecating jokes.

Sophie asked him about the wine. "Aren't we supposed to drink white with fish and seafood?"

"You drink what's good. Some fish dishes have strong flavors and need a red to complement the dish; a white would be lost. Now, it's time for dessert."

We both begged off. He looked so sad, we agreed to split a gelato and a glass of his homemade limoncello, which packed quite a punch. Sated, we chatted over our espresso. It was the best meal I'd eaten in a long time and most of the joy came from being with Sophie and Paolo.

When we were done, he wouldn't let us pay. "The company of a good friend and a beautiful woman is payment enough."

We said our goodbyes, promising to come back soon. Waiting for my car, I said, "I still want to go over what you found tonight. Are you okay with that or would you rather do it tomorrow?"

"No, tonight is fine. I want to move forward. That was a nice distraction, and Paolo is a gem."

I loved her attitude and work ethic. "Good. Let's go to your place."

The traffic was light for that time of night, and we made good time. Even with the extended meal, it was still early. I hoped we wouldn't be hampered by the amount of wine we'd drunk. I had been more circumspect than Sophie, but still, more than I should have. I was driving. I parked as close as I could to Sophie's apartment, checking the area before getting out. All seemed clear.

Sophie unlocked her door and unloaded her laptop. She handed me a pile of e-mail chain printouts and other documents. They'd been sorted into Howard, Gilbert, a few from Jack Mellon, and financials. The financials were the thinnest.

Wanting to start at the beginning, I worked my way through the Howard pile. He was smart and good at making the trails and chains complicated, but not so complicated that we couldn't follow where everything went.

We had to retrace our steps several times to be sure we had a complete understanding of what had been done. We would get a better picture when Sophie pulled all the financials. We just knew we were on the right track. Mr. Gilbert was another matter. I agreed with Sophie's assessment about him being on the dark side of the military, and yes, he had some experience with cyber security, but it looked like he was more comfortable with the physical side of things. Everything we saw pointed to Howard being the top dog in this mess, with Gilbert by his side to cover it all up. Maybe even partners.

"Did you get through all of Suzanne's flash drives?"

"No. I stopped when we decided Rant was more important. Why?"

"I was thinking—"

She smiled. "You were actually thinking? Sorry. I couldn't resist."

"Sure." I rolled my eyes. "Anyway, I was thinking it would be nice if we knew what Suzanne had discovered and was going to talk to Simon about. She would've documented it somewhere, right?"

"Yes, she probably did. I have the flash drives hidden here. Hold on. I'll get them." She disappeared, retuning quickly with the bag of flash drives. "I've marked all the ones I've already reviewed. There's nothing relevant on them."

"Are you sure? She wouldn't have said, 'Rant is corrupt, and here's the proof.' She would've hidden it, right?"

"Yes, but I haven't found anything so far."

"Are they in chronological order?"

"Kinda. They're numbered, but it looks like she used different drives for different things, so I have to go into each one. I'm looking at the date range for entries and keeping it to our time frame."

"Sounds like a logical plan."

Sophie scanned the drives and reread the hard copies, in case she'd missed anything.

I got the feeling there was more we hadn't found. Everything we had was circumstantial, not enough for a solid case. "I'm going home. Don't work too late. It's another day tomorrow, and you'll have more to do."

She waved me away and said goodnight.

I made sure the doors were closed and securely locked behind me, then drove the short distance to my apartment. I secured my gun and went to bed, wondering what motive could cause the deaths of so many people. They had to be insane, but then again, money did that to people. The more money involved, the greater the insanity. *This must be a shit-load of money.*

Chapter 37

The hammering alarm made me jump. I rolled out of bed, a quick shower, and left for the office. I had things to do, namely, bugging Sophie about the financials.

The lights were on when I got to the office front door, and I was pretty sure it wasn't Marie. *Not this early*. I opened the door as quietly as I could, listening for anything unusual. Nothing. Just the clack of a keyboard. I opened the inner door but couldn't see anyone at Sophie's work area. Mine was hidden by the door. I moved back and looked through the hinge crack in the door. It was Sophie.

"It's okay. It's me." I moved into the room. "You can put the pepper spray down."

She wasn't happy. "What the hell are you doing, creeping around like that?"

"I wasn't creeping around. I was coming into my office. Anyway, what are you doing here so early? And how did you get here? I hope you were careful."

"Of course, I was careful. Your paranoia is rubbing off on me. And I ride-shared, door to door. As for getting here early, I have work to do, remember? I need this computer for the job. And how did you know I had pepper spray?"

"Saw you through the gap in the door. Fine. So long as you're careful. Have you eaten?"

"No. You?"

"No, but I see you made coffee. Thanks. I'll call Marie and get her to pick something up on the way in. To change the subject, I think we need to update Mr. Howard. After all, he wanted to be kept in the loop and it's the least we can do."

The look on Sophie's face said it all. "Are you nuts or are you being sarcastic?"

"Kinda both. I'm convinced Howard and Gilbert are responsible for the killings, but we can't prove it yet. So, we lay a false trail. We tell them no leads have panned out so far. Tell them the police are looking at a serial killer, and we're assisting them. That should give you more time to dig around."

"That's a good idea. I finished going through Suzanne's flash drives. There wasn't much, but there were references to Dissolve. She was sure Dissolve funds were being moved around, and there seemed to be chunks disappearing. She was suspicious of Jack Mellon, but I don't think she realized it was much bigger and higher up the chain. Before you call them, let me see what I can dig up today. I'm concentrating on Howard and Gilbert's personal financials and their company spend authorizations. Basically, anything that doesn't seem kosher."

"Okay. Sounds good. We'll hold off until tomorrow. I'm going to review all the docs you printed yesterday and piece them together, so we have a better idea of where the gaps are."

"Makes sense. So, when are you going to call Marie? I'm hungry."

I made the call. Marie, bless her, said no problem. We ate in silence, and the coffee pot was on constant refill.

"Ha. Mas, we're making progress. Howard and Gilbert both have offshore accounts, and there's something else. There are payments to a security company, and the dates closely bracket the dates of the killings."

That certainly got my attention. "How close? All four sets of dates?"

"Yes. There are payments on each side of the dates the victims disappeared. Almost like a deposit up front, then a balance."

"Of the murders? Do you know who the payees were and the amounts of each payment? And a total amount?"

"The payments were to a security corporation, a company called Shield Protection Inc. It was set up with Gilbert as the president, and it only has only two employees—consultants on retainer to Rant security. I have the names and I'm checking them through our SFPD back door. The payments were fifty K up front and fifty K after, so a total of four hundred thousand for eight murders. Does that sound right?"

I thought about it. It was a lot more than the usual hit for hire. The stakes must be very high. "It's more than I'd expect. We'll know more when you get the info back on the two consultants, if there is any. If they're ex-military, they could be off the radar."

"I am kinda out of my depth here. All my previous contracts were about cyber security. Mostly abstract information and data. I'm not used to the information being so physical."

"Yeah. I work from the other end; my information is physical, not abstract. I have a question for you. You don't have to answer now, or at all, if you don't want to."

"Ask away."

"If we can't get enough hard evidence to take this to court, or even if we do, how do you feel about getting justice for all eight victims?"

Sophie looked at me. The cold glint in her eyes had returned. When she spoke, her voice was equally icy. "I really don't care how it goes down, as long as the person—or people—who killed Suzanne get theirs."

"It could get dangerous…and legally iffy."

Her laugh was like ice shattering. "I don't care about any of the niceties. I want payback, and I want it to be permanent."

"Okay. Just checking. Keep digging." She'd given me a lot of food for thought. I didn't think we'd get enough evidence to get legal satisfaction, at least not against the people who were truly responsible. I had some thoughts on how to move forward, depending on what other info Sophie managed to find and the information obtained from the calls I'd made. "Sophie, while you're at it, see if you can find anyone at Rant who has a boat registered to them. If so, find out what kind and where it's docked."

"I'll add it to the list."

When Sophie came through, I was sure we could solve the killings, at least to *our* satisfaction. We now had the autopsy reports on all the victims via our back door. I went over them carefully. Eight victims. Two had been manually strangled, one had been garroted and had deep marks in the neck; the marine life had attacked the bruise line. One had a snapped neck with lots of tendon and ligament damage, along with a severed spinal cord. That took good technique and practice, not necessarily strength. One definite and one possible drowning. Kasagawa was blunt force trauma to the side of the head. They'd crushed his skull over the temple and had probably struck him from behind. One of the first victims' cause of death was still undetermined; the body had been too far decomposed to have an exact cause of death.

Eight victims with various causes of death. Serial killers didn't vary much. They might evolve over time, but rarely that much. All the methods were bloodless, other than Kasagawa, and his blood loss would've been minimal. The report stated he suffered a significant blow and would've been dead before he hit the ground. Again, technique, rather than strength. Bloodless killing methods meant less clean-up and less evidence to leave for forensics. They'd been methodical, planned, and careful. Back to Mr. Gilbert and the two Shield Protection employees.

As usual, the medical examiner had been slower than the PD wanted, but she'd done a thorough job on the autopsies, as Kenzo had said she would. *Shit. Kenzo!* A lightbulb went off in my head. The message about how I should follow the money. It had been from Kenzo. It was his grammar pattern I'd subconsciously recognized. Why would he give me that tip unless he knew he couldn't follow up? And why was he using a burner phone? SFPD didn't need to do that.

I had to talk to Kenzo off the record. I remembered his lunch habits. I told Sophie I was going out for a while.

She grunted and without looking up, waved at me.

I walked quickly to the parking lot. If Kenzo still

followed his old routine, I had time. If not, it didn't matter. I was betting on his Japanese heritage of order and discipline.

I peeled out of the parking space and made good time to the complex, two blocks from the SFPD headquarters. I parked as far away from the entrance as I could. I knew where Kenzo was headed, so I had to sidetrack him. I went into the karate dojo; it was almost empty. A black belt was at the front desk and a few early attendees were warming up. I didn't recognize the attendant. *Good. He won't know me, either*. He was tall for a Japanese man, his belt worn and frayed at the knot. He'd obviously been training for a while. He looked me over, either as a prospective client or an adversary.

I smiled. "Has Otake-san arrived yet?" I think he was surprised I asked using the honorific san.

"Not yet. May I help you?"

Good. I wrote "coffee" on the back of one of my business cards. "Would you mind giving him my card?"

He looked at it. "Sure. No problem. He's isn't teaching today."

I bowed slightly, saying, *"Domo arigatou, gozaimasu."*

He looked up and returned my bow. "Not at all. My pleasure." Sometimes, the formality of Japanese culture was very reassuring.

I left as quickly as I could. I didn't want anyone seeing me. I worked my way across the main floor and entered the café in the corner. Thankfully, the owner was behind the counter. I nodded, and he smiled back. I looked up to the second floor and cocked my head in that direction.

He nodded the okay.

I went through the employees-only door and went up the stairs to a small room with tables and chairs. Two tables were set up with Go game boards—a Japanese hangout. I didn't disturb anything. I just sat, waiting. I heard footsteps.

It was the owner, Wanatabe. He knocked on the door frame before entering, holding coffee and dumplings on a tray. He smiled again. "Long time no see, Hammett-san. You still like good coffee, yes?"

"Always, Wanatabe-san. Thank you." I knew better than to thank him in Japanese. I tried that a long time ago, and he had reprimanded me.

"This is America. We speak English at work. At home, I speak Japanese. We keep both languages alive." He grinned that I had remembered.

"I am hoping Otake-san will join me."

"Very well. I will send him up. It is good to see you again."

Otake and I had helped him years ago, and he hadn't forgotten. I wasn't surprised. I heard footsteps, quick and light, coming up the stairs.

Kenzo appeared in the doorway. "I wasn't sure what sort of welcome I'd get after our last conversation…"

At least he's smiling. I stood and bowed. "I owe you an apology. I was out of line. I shouldn't have taken it out on you."

"Agreed, you shouldn't have, but I understand why. Done deal. Let's move on. Why all the secrecy?"

"Because I got your message."

"My message?"

"Yes, your cryptic call. 'Follow the money.' "

"Not me. Why would I call you?"

"Kenzo, I—"

Wanatabe arrived with tea and more dumplings for both of us. He quietly bowed and left.

"Kenzo, I know it was you. It took me a while— you disguised your voice—but you couldn't change your speech pattern. I recognized it but couldn't place it until something else triggered the memory. I know it was you. Thank you. So, why the warning and tip on the money?"

"Mas, I'll deny everything outside these walls. This is completely off the record, agreed?"

"Yes. Just between you and me, period. I'll keep you out of it, I promise. So, what gives?"

"You *were* a bit sneaky, sending us on the wild kink chase while you had a better theory."

I shrugged. "The department shut me out because of Josie and her buddy. I don't have much luck with female police officers, apparently."

"No, but you survived. The bitch that set you up isn't even in California. Last I heard, she got a job in butt-fuck Texas as a security guard. And Josie is busted. No one will ever trust her again. No one wants to be her partner. Somehow, word got out. What a bummer. Anyway, you didn't do cloak and dagger to talk about old times."

"In the beginning, we thought Rant was connected, but not sure how, so we followed every lead. We got sidetracked, but it kept coming back to Rant. At one point, it seemed as if it was about Kasagawa...the money aspect. We believe Suzanne was the last target, not Kasagawa. She'd discovered fraud, but she didn't realize how high it went, and it cost her, her life.

Kasagawa was in the wrong place at the wrong time. When did you figure it out, and why the secret message?"

Kenzo was silent, gathering his thoughts. He took a deep breath. "As soon as Kasagawa's name came up as a victim, we were shut down by a government agency with letters for a name. They're after Kasagawa. Apparently, he was Yakuza, and they're after his money pipeline. They knew about his Rant connection. We were warned off—just follow the serial killer theory and leave Rant alone. Orders came from a very high level. We picked up on bits and pieces—like the Yakuza—through the grapevine. We weren't told shit, just *leave it alone*."

"Been there, done that. Don't miss it. It pisses me off how politics fuck up real police work." I could sympathize with Kenzo on this one.

"None of us are happy about it. We knew we were on the right track. Eight people wiped out? What about their lives? And the lives of all the people they knew?"

"Is that why you called me?"

"Yeah. No one else knows. I didn't even tell Pete or Jose."

"Where did you get the burner phone? I didn't think the SFPD used them."

"Lots of things have changed. I snatched the burner from an undercover operation that went south. They won't miss it."

"Kenzo, I'm about to trust you more than I ever have. We think we know who's responsible for the killings. We can't prove it yet—might never be able to—but if we need you to do arrests, can we count on you and your team? It will be about the killers, not the

Yakuza money trail."

"No problem, Mas. If we can nail the killers, we'll be happy. Just make sure you get the proof. Do I want to know what you're doing?"

I smiled and shook my head.

"Okay. Tell me what you can, and we'll wait on you. This stays between you and me, right?"

"Yes, just between you and me, for now." It was an easy truce, and I was glad we were back on level terms. We shook hands, and he left.

I sat down to finish eating and thought about the case, but my thoughts turned to the conundrum with Sophie. I liked her more than anyone in a long time, and not just because she was a Domme. I felt connected to her in other ways. Was it selfish if I wanted her to move to SF?

The dumplings had been delicious. I finished the last of my coffee, stood, and paid the bill. I thanked Wanatabe-san, and then added a mental note to bring Sophie here when this was over.

My need to shake things up beat the need for patience. Perhaps Sophie had dug up the information we needed while I was gone. Time was running out. Forcing the urgency from my mind as I drove, I was slightly more relaxed by the time I unlocked the office door.

As soon as I shut and relocked it, Sophie pounced. "I found the motherlode. We've got them. All the digging paid off, all the way down to your boat request, though it's mostly circumstantial. I can prove Howard and Gilbert were stealing millions from the project. I accessed their accounts."

Stunned, I grew cautiously optimistic. "How'd you

do that?"

"Don't ask. I have access to both Howard's and Gilbert's offshore accounts, and I can drain them anytime I want. There's a boat registered to Rant Applications that's used by the higher-ups for meetings and schmoozing prospective investors. It's been in and out of the dock, confirmed by surveillance cameras, and after tracking the two Shield Protection goons—who are ex-military, by the way—we found information. John Smith—yes, that's his real name—was dishonorably discharged for mistreating prisoners in Iraq. The other one was more difficult, but we found him. Pieter van der Haas. He's South African military—special services regiment—here legally on a visa, organized by our friends at Shield Protection. Not much else on either—no police records. They keep their noses clean, single…never married, and pay their taxes. That's it, personalwise."

"But—"

"They showed up on the dock's surveillance video. It's a very good system. Small cameras, all digital. The records go back almost nine months. Awesome records. Anyway, the dates they used the boat closely match the dates the people disappeared, by a day or two. I'm surprised they didn't notice the cameras or that Mr. Gilbert didn't tell them. Maybe he was keeping that information in his back pocket to deflect blame off him, if it became necessary."

I jumped in before she could start again. "Or they don't think anyone will be able to trace them. You can physically prove the fraud and the money trail? No question?"

Sophie smiled the biggest smile I'd seen. "Oh, yes.

No question they were clever, but I'm better. The money trail is convoluted, but I have it top to bottom. Proof positive it was them. And I can drain them with just a few keystrokes. Transfer all their money wherever I want, and they wouldn't be able to do a thing about it. Or trace it."

"You can do that?" I was curious but also a little worried.

"I can. Now that I'm in, they're the ones who aren't safe." Her smile dropped. "But this doesn't prove they were behind the killings, does it? Only that they're corrupt thieves, which these days, amounts to a fine and slap on the wrist."

"I'm afraid you're right. Dig deeper into Smith and Haas's e-mails."

"I am doing that. Jesus, Mas. Give me some credit. Nothing so far, though they do communicate a lot. Do you think they're gay?"

"Maybe, but I doubt it. We would've found something more obvious than e-mails. In this city, they'd be living together."

"Makes sense. So, what now?"

"We have solid proof Gilbert is behind Shield Protection, and the only two employees are circumstantially connected to all the killings. They were careful with the methods they used. We need to get actual evidence. We need them to roll on Gilbert. Did you copy the video of them using the boat?"

Sophie rolled her eyes. "No. I figured I'd just let them erase it." She scowled at me. "Of course, I copied all relevant data. Saved one set here and copied a friend, just in case something happens. Besides, I can always go back in and get the data again. I doubt they'll wipe it, because no one knows I've been in their records. Anything else you want me to check on?"

"Yes. I want the home addresses of John Smith…are you sure that's his real name? And Pieter. We need to check them out, first electronically and maybe in-person."

"Yes, it's his real name. Someone has to be named John Smith. I already have both addresses. I didn't do anything else—I waited to see how you wanted to proceed—but I'll start on them now, if you want."

"I want. Please, be careful. These goons would have no problem killing anyone who got in their way. I think it's time we broke the bad news to Mr. Howard."

Chapter 38

Byron Howard took my call as expected, and he would record the conversation. Opening carefully, I kept my voice subdued. "Mr. Howard. I'm sorry it's been so long. You asked us to keep you in the loop. Well, we've faced challenges with the leads. They've amounted to nothing. Have you remembered anything new since we last spoke?" I could almost see him smile.

His voice was as calm as the Dead Sea. "No. Sorry. Nothing. Have the police discovered anything you're aware of?"

"Well, we've diverged in our theories. As far as I know, they're still working on the serial-killer theory, since the victims were into kink activities. That's about all I know on their end. We could really use your help. If you think of anything, please contact me. You still have my number?"

"Yes, Mr. Hammett. I have your card. I don't think I'll be of any more assistance to you, though."

I was pretty sure he wouldn't be of any assistance at all. "We appreciate that, Mr. Howard. Thank you for your time. If anything changes, we'll be in touch." I hung up, hoping I'd sounded appropriately frustrated and discouraged.

Sophie asked, "How did it go?"

"I sounded pathetic and frustrated enough to make him thing we're stuck. Hopefully, that will reassure both of them that they're clear."

"What's wrong? You seem bothered by something. Is it Howard and Gilbert, or Shield Protection?"

"Neither. Like I said. We need reinforcements and not the SFPD. I made some calls, but I haven't heard back. I thought I would've by now."

"Who'd you call?"

"I can't tell you yet. I still need you to trust me on this one."

Questions filled her eyes. "You mean I don't want to know your methods like you don't want to know mine?"

"Kinda. I'll tell you as soon as I can."

"Is it critical?"

"Yes, I think so. At least for this to work out as planned...for everyone."

"You're being very cryptic. Do you want to know what I found on Smith and Haas?"

"Yes, of course."

"Nothing. They're clean as a whistle. Nothing suspicious about them at all, which is suspicious in and of itself. They don't spend more than their income. They live modestly. They belong to a gym that does a lot of martial arts training. Both have cars leased to Shield Protection. Both have offshore accounts. I haven't been able to get into them, so far. I'll need to get into their computers for that."

"No. Don't do anymore with them, other than reviewing their emails. We might be able to use those. I don't want them to suspect they're being surveilled or investigated. I want the element of surprise."

"Okay. So, now what?"

"First, I'm going to ask a favor of someone I know.

She's a forensic investigator. I want her to go over the boat and get evidence, anything that would tie Smith and Haas to the bodies."

"Shit, Mas. How many people have been on that boat before, during, and since? That could be a lot of work for nothing."

"Yeah, but it's worth a shot. If we get anything, it will be processed at a private lab, not the SFPD. It will stand up as an independent chain of evidence."

"How will your investigator get on board? If it's without permission, whatever she finds with be inadmissible."

"I didn't say it would stand up in court."

"Okay, I hope you know what you're doing."

"Me, too. Keep digging into Howard and Gilbert?"

"Sure. Anything in particular?"

"Yes. Travel plans, especially to counties with no extradition treaties."

"Good idea."

I left her to work in peace and made the call to my forensic contact. She agreed to do the job to repay a favor, once I'd told her what I was looking for and why. She said she'd have done it anyway, regardless. *Now she tells me.* Favors were too valuable to waste, though I didn't consider this a waste. Her only request had been for me to get hair or DNA samples for comparison. The victims wouldn't be a problem; I could get them from Kenzo. I'd have to get Smith's and Haas's from their apartments when they weren't home. Not something I wanted to do, but it was the only sure way to get what we needed. I'd need Sophie's help for that one.

My plan to go to the gun range to blow off steam

was interrupted by a phone call from an unknown number. "Hello. Mas Hammett speaking."

A click followed a moment of silence, and then, though I didn't recognize the voice that answered, the accent sounded familiar. It was the call I'd been waiting for. Now, all I had to do was persuade him to help. "Are you in the country?"

"Yes."

Good. "May we meet? I have some information you'll find interesting. Something you can use to assist in resolving an ongoing issue? Seven tonight. Text me. I'll be there."

One step closer. This was one meeting I was looking forward to. I continued home, picked up my pistol, and proceeded to the range.

The practice was paying off. Feeling better on seeing the results. Feeling accomplished, I returned home to my gun cleaning ritual. I wouldn't need it for tonight, though I would have to be on top of my game. Adrenaline rushed through my veins, and I laughed aloud. We *would* get these guys.

As usual, I was early, waiting in the bar at one of the better downtown hotels until it was time to meet. I used the house phone and was instructed to come up.

The elevator was packed, but the crowd thinned as we ascended the tower. I was the sole occupant when it hit the top floor. I lightly tapped on the door, noticing a shadow in the peephole.

The door opened immediately. The man waved me in, closing the door quickly and quietly behind me. A second man stood in front of me. He nodded to have me searched. Of course, I was clean. The man in front then waved an electronic wand over me. Very thorough. *No weapons, wires, or recording devices would get past that search.* Satisfied, the front man turned and walked into the main area of the suite.

I followed.

Two women occupied the room. They were dressed in American clothing but carried themselves like Japanese. One sat on one side and behind Saito. The other stood by the entrance to the kitchen area.

I bowed in front of Saito-san.

Surprisingly, he stood and bowed in return. "I appreciated your generosity and courtesy when we visited your office. Now, I can repay that hospitality. Please, sit. Would you care for tea? Or something a little stronger? I have a very good Japanese whisky."

"Tea would be wonderful. Thank you." I was sure the tea would be excellent.

"How are you feeling? I hear you were attacked."

I was surprised he knew, but I kept it off my face. "Yes, I was. It wasn't serious. Just superficial cuts and bruises. Some passersby stopped the attack and called the police."

While the tea was prepared, we talked about everything except the real purpose of our meeting.

The tea arrived on a lacquer tray. Saito insisted I drink first, but I declined, suggesting he should. As host, he insisted. I bowed and lifted the cup, placing it on the flat of my left hand and holding it with my right. As the cup approached my mouth, I inhaled the fragrance. It smelled like a fresh spring day. The cup itself had been handmade, each one unique and special. The tea was the best green tea I'd ever tasted. It made the tea I'd served look like pond scum in comparison. "Saito-san, I must apologize for the tea I served you."

"Not at all, Hammett-san. You do not have the resources I do. Your gesture was appreciated."

"Thank you. I think we're lucky, here in San Francisco. We have access to many different cultures, both the good and dark sides of them."

"It is easy to judge another culture from the outside by not understanding the nuances of that culture."

"True, but there are universal commonalities, like not murdering innocents. Business may be war, but the combatants aren't usually killed, at least not here in the U.S."

"Business is business, and business is war. Actions have consequences, ending in both physical and non-physical casualties."

I changed the subject. "How long will you be staying in San Francisco? I am sure you miss Tokyo."

"As long as it takes to finish my tasks here."

"Well, if there is anything I can do, I would be more than pleased to assist."

"Everything will work out, in time. I have just a small issue to resolve."

"I also have an issue to resolve. I have found that two people who have a single goal often find it mutually beneficial to assist one another to achieve a resolution."

Saito looked at me closely, his face giving away nothing.

"I wish to solve the murder of my client's sister and, by extension, the murder of seven additional people. That is *all* I'm interested in." I added emphasis to let him know I had no interest in the Yakuza…or anything else.

"That is interesting, Hammett-san. My issue, as

you suspected, is the death of Kasagawa-san. Perhaps, it would be in both our interests to accomplish a mutually satisfying resolution."

"I am sure the police are doing everything they can. I am only a private investigator. Perhaps, you wish to work with them; they have greater resources than I."

"Yes. I am sure they are doing everything they are told to do. However, I prefer to use what works best for me, and I find independent agents are frequently superior. They have information sources not always available through official channels." A slight smile touched his lips, though it failed to reach his eyes. It was as blunt as a Japanese man would get, and it was good enough for me.

"Information *is* a valuable resource, and sometimes there is no price." I didn't want him to think I expected payment.

That brought a bigger smile. "I am pleased you are not as obvious as I have been led to believe all Americans are."

I bristled. "Some of us even use chopsticks."

His smile faded. "I apologize. I did not mean to offend you."

"And I apologize for being rude after accepting your hospitality. Perhaps we should discuss some details to see if there is a mutual advantage. Do you agree?"

"Agreed. I have been hampered by your officials in my investigation of Kasagawa's death."

"That does not surprise me. If I may reiterate, I am *only* interested getting justice for my client, in any way feasible. Nothing else."

"That is an interesting perspective for an ex-police

officer."

"It's a long story, and I have found perspectives change with time and experience."

"They can. Many things change over time, both good and bad."

"If I may, Saito-san; let me be blunt. We believe we know who killed the victims in the bay." That caught him by surprise.

"That is interesting news. How have you managed to accomplish that, while your entire police department has not?"

"I have a secret weapon—my partner. She is also an investigator…of sorts." Not quite a lie. "Between us, we have figured it out, with a few assists, here and there."

"My principals and I would be very interested in assisting you in bringing this person to, as you say, justice."

"I'd hoped you would be willing to assist. It could be somewhat difficult."

"Difficulties are what I am paid to prevent and resolve."

"We have a good deal of circumstantial evidence, but almost no hard proof. We are working on that. I wished to gauge your interest, so please bear with me and I will tell you what we know, and perhaps require. May I have your word this conversation stays in this room?"

"Hammett-san, you have my word. I will reveal nothing unless it is absolutely necessary, and only to my principals. I pledge my assistance in any way…*if* I can. Is that satisfactory?"

"Saito-san, completely satisfactory. We believe the

first six murders were all that were originally planned. Their purpose was to cover Jack Mellon's murder. He was working with Rant Applications on a project called Dissolve. Kasagawa-san had invested heavily in the project. Millions of dollars, as I'm sure you're aware."

He nodded.

"The Dissolve project is a scam, created by Jack Mellon. He was caught skimming from the project. What he didn't know was that two other people at Rant were doing the same thing, only on a much larger scale. We have proof, and I believe we can recover most, if not all, of the diverted funds.

"Rant had Jack Mellon killed. We believe that was always the plan. We also believe they knew the project was a scam, and that at some point, Project Dissolve would crash and burn. Suzanne and Kasagawa-san were not part of the original plan. Suzanne found out about the fraud and the skimming and mistakenly thought it was only Jack, unaware her boss was also involved. As a result, she had to go. Of course, they had to kill a man with her to maintain the fictional serial killer's MO. Kasagawa-san was in the wrong place, at the wrong time. The killers didn't know who he was. If they had, they likely wouldn't have killed him."

Saito was impassive, taking it all in and waiting for me to continue.

"We have some evidence against the two killers, but again, no substantial proof yet. I would like to ask you a question."

He nodded.

"Are you more interested in the two who performed the killing or those who ordered it?"

"Why do you ask?"

"Because I think there's a way we can all get what we want."

"My principals feel, and I believe, the ones who give the orders are always most responsible. They should face the consequences of their actions."

I bowed my head in acknowledgement. "Thank you. Do you feel anything I have told you is incorrect or inaccurate?"

"No. What you have told me makes sense. It all fits with what little we have managed to uncover. You have made some assumptions regarding Kasagawa-san and they may or may not be correct. Regardless, I ask you to keep this conversation confidential from your side, as well."

"I have a legal way to make it entirely confidential." I pulled out a client contract I had pre-filled and signed. All I needed was a signature and a deposit. He'd then be a client, with all the legal privileges that went with it.

He lifted his hand and the woman who'd been sitting behind him brought an expensive-looking briefcase. She opened it and handed him a checkbook and a Montblanc pen.

"How much would be appropriate?"

"To ensure there are no questions, use my usual rates. Predate the check to two day ago." I told him my rates, and he calculated the deposit then added an additional weekly rate.

"Hammett-san, you work too cheaply." He handed me the check.

"Thank you. Perhaps for Tokyo. Now you are a client. Do you have any other associates here in the U.S., aside from the two who accompany you?"

"I have access to as many as we need. I simply need an hour or so notice. You will keep me updated with your plans?"

"Yes. I will keep you fully informed and will confirm all details as soon as I can. Is that acceptable?"

"Yes, acceptable. I will make suggestions, if I feel them necessary. Agreed?"

"Absolutely."

We spent the next thirty minutes going over what I'd planned. Saito was astute and made several suggestions, which I accepted. They were solid suggestions. We agreed not to meet again until our plan was put into action. We exchanged cell numbers, including Sophie's number.

How we moved forward would depend on the forensics and the information Sophie uncovered. It had been a good meeting. If everything worked out, we'd all get what we wanted.

I felt more relieved than I'd expected. Now that we had the reinforcements we needed, I realized how stressed I'd been about the danger Smith and Haas represented. If we couldn't get a fair trial in the courts, justice would be served, one way or another.

Chapter 39

Sophie was the first one into the office the next morning. She was itching to tell me what she'd discovered.

My meeting with Saito had been cathartic. It had focused me and had crystalized what needed to be done. Now, how to do it.

We had Kenzo inside the SFPD, the dubious resources of Saito, my forensic contacts, and last, but not least, Sophie. All the planning would be easier.

Sophie was surprised I'd come in earlier than expected. "What's the occasion? Someone's birthday?"

I chuckled. "No birthday, but I'm hoping you have good stuff for me; I have planning to do, and I need all the info I can get about Smith and Haas, and anything else you've managed to uncover."

"Jesus, I think I liked you better grumpy and late. All this energy is disconcerting. Let me get some more coffee, and I'll explain everything I have. Deal?"

"Warm up your computer. I'll get the coffee."

"Oh, God. It's going to be one of those days."

I poured a cup for me and refilled hers, then sat down at my desk. "Give it up."

"Nothing new on Howard or Gilbert. I'm tracking their credit card use. Haven't found any tickets to places without extradition. No tickets at all, for that matter. Nothing on e-mail that shouldn't be, so we're good with them. Smith and Haas are where things get interesting. I told you before we had them using the boat on the right dates, but nothing to connect them directly with the bodies, right?"

"Yes."

"Until now. I went through their email accounts— they aren't very tech savvy—and I managed to pull some conversations. They don't mention the cages directly, but they do mention having some custom metalwork done and the dumbasses talk about four different fabricators. They also mentioned the cash cost. That *is* a direct link to the bodies." Her voice shook. "Those bastards killed my sister!" I could see her fighting back the tears. "We *will* get these guys, right?"

I looked directly into her eyes. "Yes, one way or another."

"What do you mean by that? Do you actually have a plan?"

"I'm working on it. This new information helps. Any more where that came from?"

"Bits and pieces. Nothing as big as the cages. What are you going to do with it?"

"Do we have photos of them?"

"Digital, not hard copy. I'll print them up."

I waited. I'd take them to the fabricators and hopefully they would identify Smith and Haas. The prints popped out of the printer. "These are DMV photos. How'd you get these? No, don't tell me."

"They're the best photos I could find. The others are too surveillance-like and the ones from the boat dock are good, but dark." She cocked a brow. "A thank-you would be nice."

"Thank you."

"You're welcome."

I grabbed the photos and pocketed the name and addresses of the fabricators. I left as Marie was coming in.

Once in the car, I started with the fabricator farthest away and would work my way back. Traffic sucked. The first fabricators' yard was busy.

Proceeding to the office. The owner's wife was manning the counter. I identified myself and asked if she would look at a couple of photographs.

She picked out Smith immediately, saying she thought it was suspicious he'd paid in cash. "Even kinky people use credit cards. We've made several custom pieces that just had to be for kinky sex—but I don't really care. Money is money, and they're typically polite. This guy was different. He was nice enough, I guess, but he had an edge that made me uncomfortable. Nothing I could put my finger on, but I didn't like him."

"Did you deliver it?"

"No. He didn't give me a number or address. He called us to see if it was done. I checked the bills and they were legit, so I didn't ask for details."

"Thank you for your help." Things were finally coming together.

The next fabricator was a little tougher to crack. "I don't want to get in the middle of anything."

"You're not in any trouble. I just need to know if you recognize this man."

"Yeah, I've seen him. He ordered a cage and paid cash. The dude talked weird. Had some foreign accent, but I've never heard one like it before. Sounded almost German, but not. You know?"

"Did he ask you to deliver?"

"No. He paid in cash and picked it up himself in a van."

I smiled. Haas's accent was South African, not German. I didn't educate him. "Thanks for your time. You've been a big help."

Two down, two to go. Sophie had hit another jackpot. The third fabricator was reticent, too. I tried to put him at ease. "I just need to know if you've seen either of these men and if they ordered a dungeon cage made with specific dimensions. I won't involve you in any other way."

He narrowed his eyes, deciding. "I never look at people closely. Privacy and all. This guy does look a bit familiar, though. Don't remember a name. I can see if it's on the order."

I followed him into the office.

His partner looked up as we entered. "Everything okay?" he asked.

"Yes. I just need to know if you recognize either of these men." He checked my credentials, then bent over the photo. "I remember this guy." He placed his finger on Smiths' photo. "Name's 'Mr. Brown,' if you believe that." He chuckled. He moved to the filing cabinet, pulled the order, and made me a copy. "Paid in cash. I tried the number, but it was disconnected."

That all sounded about right. I looked at the receipt. The requested dimensions had been notated on the order—another confirming piece of information

"Does that help you any?"

"Absolutely. Thanks for your help."

Feeling triumphant, I made my way to the last fabricator, but when I turned into the drive, it felt odd.

Looking closer, I realized they were closed. *That's strange*. I read the telephone number off the window and called. No answer. Machine kicked on after the third ring. "We're sorry, but the office is closed for a personal emergency. We will reopen soon. Please check back." *Well, nothing I can do here*. I made a note to check back, if I needed to.

I now knew where they'd purchased the cages, but I still didn't know how or why they'd chosen their victims, aside from Jack Mellon and Suzanne Chandler, who'd clearly been targeted. How'd they know all were kinksters? They must've gotten the information from somewhere. I couldn't see them parking outside the Cauldron and Sorcerer's, waiting for easy targets. Gilbert was security for Rant Applications, and I was sure they'd have run background checks on Suzanne and Mellon, but I highly doubted their kink lifestyle had been a source of interest. Besides, it wasn't like they would've listed it on their resume or application. Those proclivities were well hidden.

Surveillance was the only way they would've learned about their hidden life. Suzanne would've been first, when she'd been assigned to the more sensitive projects, and Jack would've been checked when Dissolve had come about. When it had come time to dispose of Jack, someone probably suggested the idea of killing several couples to disguise who they really wanted. My money was on Gilbert, Smith and Haas only being the muscle. Not a bad plan; throw suspicion on a serial killer in a marginalized community. The discovery of the bodies was just bad luck. Then, Sophie and I came along. Hopefully, I'd played the dumb gumshoe well enough to allay any suspicions about our ability or our progress. All I needed now was a few more days. Legally or not, they were going down...all of them.

I realized my grip on the wheel was so tight it hurt. I slammed on my brakes to keep from running a red light. *Calm down. Breathe. Relax.* For the rest of the drive, I concentrated on the road.

Sophie accosted me the moment I walked in the door. "Well? What did they say? Did they identify them?"

"I saw three of the four fabricators. They identified our two perps. Two recognized Smith, one recognized Haas, and I suspect the fourth would've picked Haas. They split the orders between the two of them. All three cages were ordered within a short time frame and they paid cash. One even had the cage specs written on the order form. They gave me a copy. It matches those pulled out of the bay. We can double check with the police reports. I'd bet the last cage was ordered at a later date."

"You mean, they planned to stop after Jack, but Suzanne stuck her nose in where it wasn't wanted?"

"Pretty much."

"So, this means we have proof of their involvement, right?"

"It's still all circumstantial, and there are no ties to Howard and Gilbert. We need those two. They're the masterminds."

"But how?" She sounded almost plaintive.

"I'm working on that. If I needed to get an e-mail to Smith and Haas, but wanted it to look like it came from Gilbert, could you do that?"

"Of course. I can make an e-mail seem like it came

from God."

"From Gilbert will be fine. Any idea what sort of office space Shield Protection has? And the address?"

"Yes. They have a small single unit in an industrial park. Here's the address."

Another piece of the puzzle had just fallen into place. The location was close to the waterfront, and it would be quiet at night. I'd put money that was where the bodies had been stored. They would've put the bodies in the cages and loaded them onto the boat, covering the cage so it looked like a large crate. Nothing exceptional, at least not in San Francisco.

So, the last piece was how they grabbed their targets. I'd been mulling that one over for a while. They would, I assume, use a van with a side door. One would drive and the other would blitz attack, throw the victim into the van, and off they went, over in seconds. They could've used a Taser, or maybe they just manhandled them into the van. A little chloroform and it would be lights out. Suzanne and Kasagawa had been the last two, and they'd probably been taken together. Kasagawa had a head wound, which would've taken him out, leaving trace evidence in the process. Suzanne wouldn't have stood a chance against either Smith or Haas on her own. My next step was to try to find the vehicle, if it hadn't already been dumped. Okay, so first stop…the head office of Shield Protection. So long as Smith and Haas were otherwise engaged. Marie was up for that job.

Before we left, I put in a call to the friend who had examined the boat for evidence. "Hi, Cathy. Any news?"

"Hi, Mas. Did I call you or leave a message? No?

So, no. Nothing yet."

"Okay. Sorry. No need to be snippy. This is kinda time sensitive."

"Isn't everything time sensitive? That's just a euphemism for hurry the fuck up. Well, science can't be hurried. It takes the time it takes. You'll hear from me when I have something for you, good or bad."

"Got it. You got on the boat? Any problems?"

"You mean was I arrested for trespassing? The answer is no. We got on and off clean. Lots and lots of samples. Interesting stuff. Biologicals. Bodily fluids. Looks like it's a bit of a floating love shack. The good news for you is they don't clean very thoroughly, although she is a well-maintained boat."

"Don't forget we're even. Thank you."

"Mas, this one's on me, so long as you get the bastards. I'll let you know when any results come in. Oh, and thank you for the DNA comparison data. How'd you get your sticky hands on that? Isn't that police evidence?"

"You really don't want to know. Trust me. Safer, too."

"Okay. Whatever you say. I'm just glad I'm in the private sector now. Tomorrow is the earliest we can expect results. Don't call me. I'll call you. Bye, Mas. Be safe."

Visiting the Shield Protection location was next on the list, when we confirmed Smith and Haas were out of the way. We went in two cars, mine and a rental we picked up for Marie, and Sophie disabled the rental's GPS. I parked down the street from the Shield Protection unit.

Marie went in on her own, with her phone on an

open call to us so we could hear everything that went on. She gave a running commentary. Trying the door and knocking loudly. Nothing. She tried the roll-up door—locked. She looked through the small window in the roll-up door. "It's deserted. It doesn't look like anyone has been here for several days. There is a van."

"Okay. Get in the car and park where you can keep an eye out. Let us know if anyone shows up. We'll take it from here."

We drove in and parked in front of the door. It was a risk, but one I thought worth it. We had gloves and sample baggies, in case we found anything.

For a security company, their own security was absent. No cameras. Not even an alarm on the building. They may as well have left the front door unlocked, for all the time it took me to open the door. It obviously wasn't a long-term location for them. The furniture was probably left from the previous tenant. We scanned the room before moving inside. We quickly went through the desk drawers. Nada. The filing cabinet was locked, but that didn't slow us down. I popped it easily. The contents were more surprising. The top drawer held nine-millimeter ammunition and some loaded spare magazines. In the next one down, we found thin steel cable, still on a roll, along with a pair of cutters.

"How kind of them to leave the cable and cutters. Now we get a sample to hopefully match to a victim."

"Weren't they too decomposed for that?" She looked uncomfortable. Her sister had been one of the victims.

Using the cutters, I took a sample of the cable.

"Probably, but it's still another piece. The evidence is piling up, bit by bit, piece by piece. Every little thing helps."

The remaining drawers contained paperwork that was irrelevant, except for a receipt for boat fuel where the Rant boat was moored. I moved into the back room. Nothing interesting, other than a very nice compression pattern in the cheap rug, neat squares just like a welded cage would leave. I photographed the pattern and the room with my cell and checked the quality. Clear as a bell.

Next, the garage. The van was a minivan without windows, an older commercial version. I snapped a pic of the VIN number. *Probably fake, but you never know.* The van was locked. My police training came in handy again. I jimmied the driver's side door and looked over the space. The van had been cleaned, and they'd done a pretty good job. I used the interior buttons to open the other doors. Walking around to the passenger side, I slid open the side door, hoping for forensic evidence or a signed confession, though I didn't think I was going to find either of the those.

My phone went off like a fire alarm. Sophie looked up, questioningly. I jumped and answered it.

"A car is coming, but the driver doesn't look like the men in the photographs…"

We waited with baited breath.

"All clear. They went the other way."

We let out the collective breaths we'd been holding.

I turned to Sophie. "Anything in the paperwork?"

"Just the fuel receipt. The date matches the timeframe for Suzanne and Kasagawa. Other than that. Nothing. Just regular docs and utility bills."

"Okay, let's get the van examined and hope we

find something. If not, we may have to get Cathy out here, and I'd rather not do that."

"What are we looking for?"

"Anything human—hair, blood that will look dark brown, bits of fingernails, skin."

She turned her nose up at that but opened the rear hatch. We scoured the floor and sides but found nothing. Smith and Haas had done a good job at protecting the interior and cleaning out whatever had been left.

Suddenly, Sophie inhaled sharply. "Hah. Found a couple of hairs. Too long for Smith or Haas." She took photos of where she'd found them then put them in a baggie.

Fast learner. "I think we should get out of here. No use pushing our luck."

"I agree."

We put everything back as we'd found it, locking the van and file cabinet drawers. We locked the front door behind us.

Driving off, I felt a sense of relief. I wasn't afraid of confrontation—verbal or physical—but Smith and Haas were in a different league of dangerous. They had nothing to lose, not after eight killings.

We didn't see any other vehicles on our way out. Sophie called Marie and told her to go back to the office. We wanted to drop off the sample we'd found at the lab Cathy had used for her samples.

Getting to the lab took longer than expected, but it was worth it. We added our samples to the ones already in process. I suggested we take the rest of the day off and do some R and R. We could check in with Marie, and Sophie had her trusty laptop to be sure our suspects were where they were supposed to be.

Sophie reluctantly agreed.

I had an ulterior motive. This case was going to resolve sooner, rather than later, and I wanted to know where Sophie stood regarding San Francisco and our situation. I wanted her to stay. I'd fallen hard for her and not just because she wanted to whoop my ass. It was her...the whole package. She'd said she could work from anywhere. I wondered if San Francisco was among the anywhere. The weather was better than Philly year-round and while it was more expensive than almost anywhere else in the continental U.S. Nowhere was perfect. To me, San Francisco was about as close as it came. *Shit.* I was more anxious about broaching this than I'd been as a cop about telling my first family their child had been killed. Big, tough me.

Sophie buried her head in her laptop as I drove. I'd suggested lunch in Sausalito. It wouldn't be too busy on a weekday at this time of year. We could sit and eat, looking over the bay toward San Francisco. It was a good view and might provide a suitable opening for the subject.

The ride was quiet. I took a shortcut after we crossed the Golden Gate Bridge. The day was beautiful, and the traffic was light, just as I'd hoped.

As we entered the main street, Sophie looked up. "Wow. Why haven't we been here before? This is beautiful!"

"We've been kinda busy." I sounded snippier than I intended.

Sophie looked across at me but said nothing.

The valet parked the SUV, and we entered the restaurant. We were seated immediately. I asked for a deck table, and we were shown to one with a great view of the city. We ordered drinks and when they arrived, I sat, nursing it.

Sophie broke the silence. "Okay, Mas. I know you well enough by now. What's on your mind?"

"I don't know. Sort of confused."

"Come on, Mas. Spit it out. I'm a big girl. If you have a problem with me, tell me."

I laughed. "Oh, it's you, all right, but I'm the problem."

"What the hell is that supposed to mean?"

"I don't want you to leave when this is all done. I want you to stay in San Francisco. We make a good team, in and out of the office. You already have somewhere to live, so it won't cost you anything. You've said you can work from anywhere. This is a great place. And...I love you." It just slipped out. I hadn't intended on saying that, at least not yet.

She sat back in her chair, shocked. "Well, Mas, you certainly know how to surprise a girl. How long have you been thinking on those lines?"

"A while."

"That's a lot to think about. Funny, I've been thinking about staying on in San Fran when Suzanne's killers are caught. We do make a good team, in and out of the office." A grin blessed her face. "Somewhere to stay is not a problem. I've done very well financially. I don't spend much and maintain a low overhead. You're right. I can work from anywhere. I've gotten closer to you than anyone, ever. That kinda bothers me. It's not normal...for me. I've always envied Suzanne's relationships. So yes, I want to give it a go with you. I figure, if I can't make it with you, I might as well give up."

"I think there's a compliment in there somewhere."

We laughed, an intimate laugh shared by lovers, though we weren't really lovers yet. It felt good. Something between us had changed. We were more open, intimate...relaxed.

The rest of the lunch was a blur. I know we talked and laughed. It was like being back in high school with a first date. I was walking on air. Nothing had been settled, but the potential was there, and the possibilities were open ended.

Driving back over the Golden Gate Bridge, life seemed better than it had in a long time. We held hands from the parking lot until we entered the office.

Marie looked up as we entered. "Finally. Did you have some lunchtime delight?"

Sophie and I laughed. "Is that any way to talk to your boss?"

Marie smiled. "Cut the crap, Mas. It's about time. I've been waiting for you to get up the courage to say something. Sophie, you're just as bad. Remember the conversations we had a while ago? Oh, I shouldn't have said that, should I?"

I looked at Sophie. Sheepishly, she shrugged and looked like a shy teenager.

"Oh? And what did those conversations cover?"

Marie jumped in. "None of your business. It was girl talk, but you came out looking good. I'm happy for you both."

The rest of the day dragged, even when I was looking at Sophie, who was oblivious to my gaze. She was incredibly focused when she was working. She calculated the dimensions of the cages from the pictures

I'd taken of the pattern left in the rug and used a computer program to compare them to the ones on the fabrication order form I'd obtained that morning. They matched almost perfectly.

We really had a good case for the killings. This was enough for the SFPD to go to town on them. Still, it didn't connect Smith and Haas to Howard and Gilbert. They were the ones I really wanted. Even with a confession from Smith and Haas, it would be their word against established corporate executives.

That was the next part of the plan.

Chapter 40

Another good night's sleep. I wasn't sure if it was due to the conversation I'd had with Sophie over lunch or because the case was nearing a resolution and we were out in front for a change. If I didn't get a call from Cathy with the lab results, I was going to go stir crazy. These lab results would determine the direction of the plan. As soon as Sophie came in, I cornered her. "Any problem moving the money out of Howard's and Gilbert's accounts as soon as I give the word?"

"No. None. What are you thinking?"

"A timing thing. You can do it anytime? Even when the banks are closed?"

"Sure. Now that I have access, it will literally take a few minutes. I'll just stash the balances somewhere safe. Why?"

"Once I have everything in place, I'll tell you the plan. One more thing. I'll need you to be available at the drop of a text. As soon as I give you the word, move all their money. Okay?"

"Sure. No problem. You're being very mysterious. Should I be worried?"

"Not if it all works out. If it doesn't, call Kenzo and get out of town because Smith and Haas will be after you."

"Mas, you're scaring me."

"Good. If you don't hear from me when all this is

set up, run. Do as I told you."

"Okay, but I am not leaving this alone. I'll get what I want out of this, one way or the other."

"I believe you, and your part will be a key in getting your justice. It will be the whole package."

Hoping for the best, I made a call to Saito, asking him to call me at his earliest convenience. Two minutes later, he called back. Our conversation was brief and to the point. He said he needed time to get approval for my request, and he'd get back to me quickly. I twiddled my thumbs, waiting. Good to his word, forty minutes later, he called back with approval and a surprise offering.

As I pondered his gesture, Sophie's head popped up from behind her screen.

"Mas, we've got a problem."

"What is it?"

"I set up an alert for new activity on the Howard and Gilbert accounts. More money has dropped into them. It's more than just Kasagawa's investment. They must be scamming someone else, as well. They're getting greedy."

"Can you track where the money came from?"

"Maybe. Probably, from the Rant end, but it could take some time."

"And no one will know you've been in there?"

"Well, there's a chance, if anyone else was poking around or even just doing a routine security check, I could be flagged. Do you want me to keep looking?"

"No. Stay under the radar so you can clean out the accounts without raising suspicions. We can worry about where the other stuff came from after this is all over."

"Okay. Your call. Can you tell me anything?"

"Yes. I have the information for where to transfer the Kasagawa money, but take ten percent from each account and put it somewhere we can get at it."

"Why?"

"Saito said his principals are very pleased with our work and didn't expect to recover any of their investment. They insist we have a finder's fee, if we can deliver on our promise. Oh, by the way, he's now a client."

"Really?"

"Yes. It's also a way of not obligating him to us. Of course, if we can't deliver, they may come after us for the money, but it's a risk I thought worth taking."

"No fucking pressure, Mas. Shit. I wish you'd told me."

I looked closely at her. "Would it have made a difference?"

She smiled. "No, not at all. So, I simply have to transfer on your go-ahead. Let me see the details." I handed her my phone, and she sent the text to hers. "I hope you know what you're doing."

"Me, too. So, what do we do about all the new money? Can you separate it from Kasagawa's?"

"Close enough. A hundred thousand here, a hundred thousand there. Besides, it's not ours to worry about."

I was about to ask where when my phone went off. It was Cathy. *The forensics results. Yes.*

"Hi, Cathy. You're on speaker."

"Okay. Who's there with you?"

"Just Sophie and me. Marie's at her desk. Good news?"

"Christ, Mas. Calm down. We ran tests on all the samples we collected, and those you dropped off. First, the bad news. None of the samples matched any of the male DNA results you supplied. We *did* match hair and some skin cells from the boat to two of the female samples you supplied."

I hoped it wasn't Suzanne.

"The names are Helga Braun and Delia Chung. Like I said, whoever was responsible for cleaning the boat wasn't particularly thorough. We had a lot of body fluids, male and female, but only the hair and skin cells matched. I guess they changed the sheets more often. Now, the hairs from the van matched two different people. Helga Braun and Suzanne Chandler. They were almost a perfect match to both."

"Nothing to match the earliest victim? Jamie Masters?"

"No. If she was the first victim, however poorly they cleaned the boat, whatever trace was left would've been wiped out by now. I think it's probable, and this is just supposition since as there were no male matches, the perps raped the women victims."

Sophie blanched and gripped my arm.

I wanted to clear this one up fast. "Did you find any trace of Suzanne Chandler or Kasagawa on the boat?"

"No, nothing matched those samples. Either they weren't on the boat or the perps were more careful. They would've loaded them into the cages prior to loading them on the boat. It was easier logistically. The only reason the other two left traces was the perp or perps wanted to have their fun. Then, they put their bodies in the cages post mortem, before dumping them into the bay. From the reports you provided, I'd say the last two victims were more of a kill and dump, cleaner and quicker than the others. While the first bodies were decomposed, I'd expect the perps to stick with the same pattern...unless something made them change."

"Any comments or insights about the way they were killed?"

Cathy was quiet for a moment. "I agree with the reports, up close and personal. Seven of the eight were bloodless. They likely expected the boat to be cleaned more thoroughly than it was. This isn't the work of a solo serial killer. In my opinion, these killings were staged to look like a serial. There were at least two perps, considering the weight of the cage and two adult bodies. It would be almost impossible for one person to handle the weight. We didn't find any damage to the boat's woodwork, which means the cage was lifted onto the end deck before being sent into the water. This is just my opinion, but the test results will stand up in any court. Does that help?"

This was better than I could've hoped for. "Cathy, this is perfect. Please, send the actual results over ASAP. You've just brought us so much closer."

"Mas, you *are* going to get the police involved, aren't you?"

"Of course, I'll contact Kenzo. As I promised?"

"Yes. Good man. You sure? You agreed too easily." She sounded skeptical.

"I promise. Kenzo will handle the arrests." It wasn't quite the whole truth, though the part about Kenzo was. I needed him.

We said our goodbyes, and I hung up.

Sophie looked up slowly. "At least she wasn't

raped…and it was quick. I don't want it to be so quick when we get these bastards."

"If all goes as planned, it won't."

With the forensic results, we had enough to nail Smith and Haas, but we still had nothing on Howard and Gilbert. Our only chance was to turn Smith and Haas, which was the next part of the plan. So long as Saito came through.

I made the call, and we agreed I'd text Saito the time and place. He agreed to supply everything I requested, while I'd confirmed the plan.

Now, it was Sophie's turn.

"We need to get Smith and Haas to meet with Gilbert at Shield Protection tonight. Can you organize that? After regular hours, once it's dark, but not too late. Can you access Gilbert's calendar to see where he is tonight?"

"One day, you'll learn not to ask stupid questions. Already done. If he stays on plan, he'll be at some tech shindig on the peninsula. I'll look at his language patterns and work something out. How soon do you need it confirmed?"

I lifted an eyebrow.

"ASAP. Got it."

I left her alone to deal with the e-mail and went out to Marie. "Would you mind keeping Sophie company tonight? It could be a long one?"

"Sure, Mas. Chung is off on a business trip. A nice quiet evening will keep me out of trouble." She laughed at the look on my face. "Don't worry, Mas. I'll take care of her."

I thought of all the things that could go wrong, and I didn't like the results. *This has to go off without a hitch...and nothing ever goes off without a hitch. Shit, one step at a time.* First, get Smith and Haas to agree to the meeting at Shield. Then, notify Saito. After that, we'd be committed.

I was beginning to annoy both Sophie and Marie with my pacing. I hated waiting. Just because I'd learned patience, didn't mean I liked it.

"Hah."

I went to Sophie's side and looked over her shoulder.

"Confirmed. Both Smith and Haas will be at the meeting tonight. I also created an intercept for Gilbert's e-mails, in case one of them decides to contact him. No one will even notice. If either Smith or Haas does contact him, I'll intercept and answer for him. Gilbert will never know it happened."

"Jesus. Is there anything you can't do? All this access makes me nervous."

"Don't worry. I've already installed better protection on all your devices. It won't stop a determined attack, but it will delay them and make them think twice."

"You were going to tell me when? To be honest, I was more worried about you hacking me."

"Too late. I was going to tell you when we had a few minutes. So, what's the plan?"

"I go and meet with Smith and Haas. Saito will be there and so will some of his *associates*, for protection. I'll get there early and will be waiting inside with several of Saito's men. There will be more outside who will cover, once Smith and Haas are inside."

"Mas, are you sure? It sounds risky."

"We have to make them turn on Howard and

Gilbert. I'll need printouts of all the evidence we have on them and the video of them using the boat. The whole package."

"What happens if they push back and say it's all circumstantial?"

"Don't forget, I used to do this for a living. I was good at it. I'll lay it on thick, and they'll know exactly what I'll do with the evidence if they don't cooperate. The first one to talk gets the best deal. They either confess to the killings on behalf of their bosses or take the rap themselves, and I hand them over to the Yakuza."

"That still doesn't get us Howard and Gilbert."

"Not legally, but one of the options I'll offer is to confess and go through the U.S. justice system or leave with Saito and explain to his Japanese associates how they murdered one of their senior U.S. assets."

"But they didn't know who Kasagawa was."

"Do you really think that will matter to the Yakuza? Smith and Haas were the ones who killed him. Someone has to pay."

"So how does that get us Howard and Gilbert?"

"There's no way to legally get the people responsible for your sister's murder with the evidence we have. They've insulated themselves from the actual events. All we can prove is they're guilty of fraud and as you've pointed out, that gets them a slap on the wrist and a fine. You and I know they're responsible and Saito does, too. After tonight, Saito's principals won't want Smith and Haas. They'll want Howard and Gilbert. You won't ever get justice from the U.S. system, but you *can* get justice if we give the men responsible for Suzanne's death to Saito and his cohorts. Can you live with that?"

Sophie's eyes simmered. I could see she was struggling with her thoughts. This was all ending, and I wasn't sure what she would say. She'd told me she'd worked in grey areas, but this was decidedly black and off the books. Finally, she said, "I can live with that. I have one demand. I want to see them face to face before they go. Make sure Saito understands, or they will never find their money. I'll hold it ransom in exchange for the meeting. In fact, I'll show Howard and Gilbert the transfer. Agreed?"

"I don't think that will be a problem. You *do* realize we're condemning these two to death. I need you to be sure. There's no going back, once I leave."

"Mas, I've never been so sure of anything in my life. Suzanne and the others didn't deserve what happened to them. I hope Howard and Gilbert suffer. A lot. Those bastards are getting what they deserve. What do you need from me?"

"When I text you, I need you to block, stop, or cancel their credit cards. Next, text me their exact locations. Saito's men will pick them up. I'll send you a text to meet us at Shield Protection when it's done. Okay?"

"Yes, but be careful. Promise? I don't want to lose you."

That came as a surprise. Sophie wasn't the most demonstrative person. Her words sounded from the heart, and I loved it. "When this is all settled, maybe we can celebrate at the Cauldron...or at your place, wherever you decide. After all, you have the keys to my heart...or something."

That surprised her. She smiled coyly and shrugged.

Talk about a chameleon. I envied her ability to change in a split second. At least now, she was smiling.

Not sure what to expect tonight, other than it would be tense and potentially dangerous—fatally so—I knew Smith and Haas would be armed. The stock of 9mm ammo proved that. My body armor would come in handy, after all. I'd thought Simon was crazy for insisting on us getting body armor, but now, I was thankful.

All the hard copies went into a file, and I organized it so each piece would build on the previous one. Everything was circumstantial, but the city prosecutors had gotten convictions with less. Hopefully Kenzo would be good to his word, because although he didn't know it, he was a critical part of the plan.

Taking one of the burner phones Sophie had obtained, I slipped it into my pocket. I considered carrying my weapon but decided against it. Saito's men would have enough firepower for everyone. Time to make the call.

Saito picked up on the first ring. He said he'd pick me up, and we agreed on the place. He also confirmed enough associates to persuade Smith and Haas that a confrontation would be pointless...and fatal.

I said my goodbyes to Sophie and Marie. They'd be on duty until it was time for Sophie to face Howard and Gilbert. I felt my anticipation rise. *Good.* I'd be sharp for the confrontation.

When I arrived home, I immediately found my body armor still fresh in its package. Simon's face flashed through my mind as I opened it. What would he think of the current events? Stripping off my shirt, I put on the vest, then put my shirt on over it as I'd done thousands of times. This time the routine felt strange—strange but comforting.

No weapon? My decision turned to my baton. It wasn't much use in a gunfight, but I was comfortable using it in close quarters. Knowing I'd drive myself nuts if I stayed at home any longer, I left for my rendezvous with Saito.

I was content sitting, drinking coffee, and people watching. *God, I love San Francisco.* The variety of people just walking by the café amazed me. It wasn't a perfect city—not even close—but it was my home and I embraced it, warts and all. Looking out at the sidewalk, I twirled my empty cup around with my index finger. Saito pulled up in an enormous multi-person vehicle. The rear passenger door opened in invitation. I threw some cash on the table and moved quickly to climb in.

Saito sat in the front passenger seat. "Welcome, Hammett-san. Thank you for being prompt."

"The least I could do." I wasn't introduced to any of the men in the vehicle, but I counted two beside me and three more behind me. That made eight, including the driver and Saito himself.

He saw my look. "Do not worry, Hammett-san. Another car will meet us at the location. In fact, they should already be there, waiting for us. The office will be open?"

"It will be for me." I had my lock gun with me.

He nodded and faced forward.

The driver maneuvered the large vehicle through the traffic with practiced ease, while I sat back and ran the plan for the upcoming meeting over and over through my mind. Nothing stood out as a problem I hadn't considered or an eventuality I hadn't covered.

Now, it was down to how Smith and Haas responded. I hoped they wouldn't do anything stupid since they were clearly outnumbered and outgunned. They had been professionally trained, so I felt confident they'd play this smart.

The industrial park was quiet. The workers had all left for the night, to enjoy their evening routines with friends and family, unaware of the events unfolding in their day world.

The vehicle stopped outside Shield Protection.

I stretched the latex gloves over my fingers and exited with my lock gun in hand. Shielded by the open door, I sprang to the front door, and in seconds, we were in.

Two of the men quietly followed me. Guns drawn, they brushed past me and searched the building. When they returned, Saito entered with the remaining men.

I popped the file cabinet to check that the ammo was still there. It was, along with a nine-mil pistol. I checked it. It was loaded with one in the chamber. Unloading the clip and clearing the chamber, I returned it to the drawer and relocked it. The men had seen what I'd done, and they nodded. A silent crew. *Maybe they don't speak English.* I didn't know and didn't care. Saito would've briefed them.

After I locked the front office door, we moved into the back room. We had twenty minutes until the meeting time. It would be a long twenty minutes. My mind drifted to other stake outs and traps I'd been involved with. They had, for the most part, been successful, without any fatalities.

Where were Saito's other men, I wondered? The room was silent, except for the slow, regular breathing of the other occupants. Then a sound alerted me that Saito had received a text…Smith and Haas had arrived.

The door unlocked with a click, and a voice complained about the time. Another man spoke, and the main light flashed brightly. I ripped the door open and rushed into the main office. "Stay where you are." The Japanese followed, all fully armed.

The surprise showed on Smith's and Haas's faces, and before they could react, the rest of Saito's men arrived and took up stations behind them. They saw the weapons pointed at them. Seeing they were fully covered, they relaxed.

So far, so good. I looked carefully at the two men. They seemed so ordinary I would've passed them on the street without a second glance. "Good evening, Mr. Smith. Mr. Haas. If you're carrying, please divulge that now. You'll be frisked."

Smith looked the more uncomfortable of the two. "We have nothing of value in here. You're wasting your time."

I'd start with him. He was the weaker link. "On the contrary, Mr. Smith. There is something of great value here."

He looked puzzled.

"Are you carrying any concealed weapons?"

They both nodded.

Two of Saito's men frisked them from behind and found a nine-millimeter on each, plus an ankle 9mm compact on Haas and two knives on Smith.

"Anything else?" I knew the Japanese had done a good search, but I wanted to keep the advantage and lead them verbally.

Both shook their heads.

"Good. Now, we can get on with tonight's little chat. Please, sit."

They sat opposite me, across the desk.

"None of us"—I indicated Saito, his men, and myself—"want either of you. We're interested in the ones responsible for eight deaths. I'm sure, by now, you're aware someone is in deep shit."

One by one, the Japanese men accompanying Saito removed their shirts, revealing tattooed torsos. That got their attention. They knew what the tattoos meant. For the first time, they fidgeted uncomfortably.

I placed the first item of evidence before them and let it sink in. I set another piece down, and then another. I said nothing, but built the case, piece by piece, until all the evidence was laid out in front of them. The room was oppressively silent. I waited.

Finally, Smith spoke. "What do you want?"

"It doesn't matter what I want. I'm here on behalf of Sophie Chandler. She and Saito-san would like you to explain why you killed eight people, particularly Suzanne and Kasagawa and, of course, who instructed you to take that action."

Smith answered again. "Are you crazy? Do you know who we work for?"

I stared at him with disdain. "Do you recognize the men in this room, and who they work for?"

"This is America. They have nothing to do with us."

"Wrong. You killed one of their senior associates, Kasagawa-san. They have everything to do with you and this."

Haas finally chimed in. "What happens to us if we give you what you want?"

I slowly walked around him, pretending to contemplate his question. "Well…Saito-san and Ms. Chandler have no use for you *if* you give up your bosses and the complete story."

Haas spoke again. "All this evidence is circumstantial. What if we decide to take our chances?"

I smiled at him thinly. "Oh, you misunderstand. Either you give up your bosses and everything we need to get them, or you get a free trip to Japan, courtesy of Saito-san and his companions. And while I hear Japan is lovely, I don't think that trip would be good for your health."

They glanced at each other, knowing that would be a death sentence.

Haas shrugged, and Smith slumped and dropped his head. When he lifted his eyes, he said, "Okay, okay. What do you want to know?"

I had expected more resistance. "Everything you can tell us. Names, dates, actions, places. Oh, and I need you to write it down. I want to know who gave you the kill instructions. And as you write, no talking. I want to compare your notes and be forewarned, your stories had better be very close but not rehearsed." I put a note pad at each end of the desk and told them to begin. *This was too easy.* For a long while, the only sound was the scratching of pens on paper. "Be sure to sign and date them."

Once finished, I collected their notes. "Now, I want to hear your stories out loud."

Smith started first. "It was Gilbert. He told us our instructions and who to eliminate. He didn't care who the first four were. He just wanted them to be chosen from either the Cauldron or Sorcerer's clubs. One male and one female. He gave us the dimensions of the cages and where to get them made."

Haas joined in. His Afrikaans accent seemed to get thicker under stress. "Howard was with Gilbert. He was the one who told us to pick Jack Mellon and Suzanne Chandler. Again, they didn't care who the other victims were, as long as they came from the kink clubs. He gave us photos of Mellon and Chandler to make sure we got the right people. Chandler was an afterthought, quite a bit later." He looked at Saito. "We are sorry about your friend. He was with Chandler when she left the club, so we grabbed them both. He wasn't specifically chosen."

Saito, his face impassive, spoke for the first time. "Then his death is even more wasteful."

I had to ask.

"Did you kill Simon Lee?"

They looked puzzled, not recognizing the name.

"He was a private investigator Suzanne was going to meet."

Still nothing. Then, recognition flashed in Hass's eyes. "He was the PI. A hit and run, right? That wasn't us. We had nothing to do with it. You can't pin that on us."

I watched them closely for any sign of deception. Finding none, I texted Sophie and gave her the go ahead to send the physical locations of Howard and Gilbert to Saito's phone. I told her to get ready to join the meeting, and I'd text her again when it was time.

Soon after I sent the text, Saito's phone pinged. He checked it, smiled, and then quickly forwarded it.

I heard a car start and drive off.

So did Smith and Haas. Their eyes shifted to each

other, acknowledging their odds had just gotten slightly better. It was still eight to two—six to two, if you discounted Saito and me—which wasn't great, but they might be desperate enough to try it.

Haas looked at me, his chin jutting out. "So, what are you going to do with our coerced statements?"

The hint of a smile touched my lips. "I didn't coerce anything. You were given options, and you took the one you thought best."

"That doesn't answer my question."

"No, it doesn't. I think, since Howard and Gilbert will be taking the trip to Japan in your stead, it's only fair the SFPD get a shot at you. You know, for multiple murders. It gives the city a bad name if perps aren't brought to justice."

They both stiffened. "You said neither the Japanese nor Chandler wanted us."

"Correct."

"So why give us up to the cops?"

"Because your existence offends me. An average prosecutor will be able to nail your hides to the wall on multiple counts of murder. You'll never see the light of day again."

Smith dropped his head, but Haas still looked determined. "In that case, I want to add to my statement."

"Go ahead." *Here it comes. They'll try to play us, thinking they've lulled us into complacency.*

Haas stood slowly. "Pen's dead. There are some in the file cabinet." He inched over to the desk with his back to us.

I heard the cabinet open. My hand slipped to the hilt of my baton, and my finger found the release button.

Almost simultaneously, Smith and Haas exploded. Haas hit the man closest to him across the eyes with the gun from the cabinet drawer, then turned to me, looking to put me down. He squeezed the trigger but was only rewarded with a dry click as my baton came down hard on his wrist.

I heard a satisfying crack. At least one—probably both—bones broken. The realization that they'd been duped filled his eyes. He crashed to his knees and dropped the useless gun in the process.

Smith lunged, snatching a knife from his belt buckle. "I'm never going to jail."

I didn't see where the opposing blade came from, but it cleanly sliced Smith across his wrist, severing his hand. Blood gushed from the wound, spraying those in front of him. The shock registered on his face seconds before he screamed and crashed to the floor, splashing blood all over the office. It looked like a set from a horror movie.

Saito was the first to speak. He ordered something in Japanese, and the man dropped to his knees and bowed, responding quietly. Saito nodded and spoke to all the Japanese men. Two of them restrained Smith. Another applied a tourniquet. A third left and returned with a first-aid kit. He bandaged the man's arm and applied a pressure bandage to stop the bleeding.

Smith was going into shock. Lying on the floor, still clutching the knife, was his useless hand.

Saito turned to me. "It might be better if we meet Ms. Chandler and our other guests outside. I hope my man's action does not complicate your plan too much."

"No, it was a natural reaction. We have their

statements, and the evidence is in plain view. No search warrant will be needed." It would stand up in court, but it was a bit messier than I would've liked.

Haas overheard me. "This was all Smith, and I'm a foreign national. I'll demand extradition."

Saito looked at me.

"With the evidence pointing at both equally, a prosecutor should be able to make the case and get him incarcerated here. He's blowing smoke."

Saito looked at me quizzically, and I explained, "He has false hope. He's trying to bullshit us."

He smiled broadly. "I know bullshit. Very good. Let him 'blow smoke.' "

"Saito-san, when do you expect to hear back from your other men?"

"Already have, Hammett-san. They are on their way back with both parties secured. Perhaps, you would like to inform Ms. Chandler it is time to join us? We will also need a medical team to take care of Mr. Smith. I would very much like him to survive."

"Yes, Saito-san. I also would like that very much." I sent a text to Marie, asking her to bring Sophie to the Shield Protection office and to make sure she brought her computer. The instructions would annoy Sophie, but I wanted to take her mind off what was about to take place.

It worked. I received a snotty response from her before Marie had the chance to reply.

They'd be here in five minutes.

It had all come together quickly. Closure was rapidly coming. I was thankful but wondered how Sophie would feel facing the ones responsible for her sister's death. I vowed to be right by her side, in case she did something we'd all regret.

With a crunch of tires and dimmed headlights, Saito's men arrived. Howard was the first to climb out. He moved with difficulty with his hands cuffed behind him. As soon as he saw me, he started with the threats.

"Hammett. I'll crush you and that bitch. This is kidnapping. You'll regret you ever crossed me."

I shrugged. I had nothing to say to him, at least not at this point.

A second car arrived a few minutes later. In contrast, Gilbert was silent and very aware of his surroundings. Rather than speak, he observed the situation in what seemed like silent amusement. I figured he'd wait and look for an opportunity to escape and take it, if he saw it.

Saito had put Haas in the van in the garage to avoid contact with either of the pair of men.

Good to her word, Marie pulled up in my SUV.

Sophie hopped out as soon as the vehicle came to a halt. She walked right up to Howard's face. "Payback's a bitch, and I'm the bitch who will make you poor." She put her laptop on the hood of Saito's SUV so Howard and Gilbert could see what she was doing.

Howard exploded the instant he recognized his offshore bank's logo. "You can't do that. That's my *personal* account."

Sophie turned to him with a grin. "I know and now, I'm going show you what's *not* in it. Oh, dear. Look. Your account is empty, and I'm the only one who knows where all those pretty dollars are. Oh, and I've canceled all your credit cards." She looked over to Saito. "Saito-san, please confirm the account where you'd like the funds to be deposited."

Saito bowed and handed her a slip of paper.

Sophie looked at it and turned to her keyboard. She showed Saito the transfer amount, less our finder's fee.

He smiled and nodded.

Sophie turned to Gilbert. "You don't need me to show you how broke you are, too, do you?"

Gilbert gave a wan smile and shook his head.

Howard stared at him with disbelief. "Gilbert, do something. Get your men. Fix this."

"Shut up, Howard. This is as fixed as it's going to get for us."

Sophie then showed Saito the amount transferred from Gilbert's account.

Once again, he nodded.

Transfers complete, Sophie closed her computer slowly and carefully. She turned to face Howard.

I was ready, but I wasn't fast enough.

Before anyone could move, she withdrew her Taser and jammed it into Howard's groin. He screamed and dropped to the blacktop in agony.

I pulled her away screaming at both men. When I looked up, Saito's men were smiling. It was the first change in their expression all night.

Confined, Sophie tried to pull away. "You bastards killed my sister for a few bucks. Stupid, low-life, common fucking thieves. I hope to hell you suffer for what you did." She turned and hugged me tightly. Sobbing she whispered in my ear, "Thank you."

I held her for several moments, then told her to go sit in my car and not to get out, though she'd still be able to hear what was said.

Saito's men revived Howard, who climbed unsteadily to his feet.

His voice was groggy. "What are you going to do?"

Saito leveled his gaze on him. "Nothing…yet. You will be taking a one-way trip to Japan. There, you will explain why you had one of our most valued associates killed."

His eyes widened. "I didn't. It was all Gilbert. Him and his men. They did it all. I did nothing wrong."

I chuckled. "Well, not quite nothing. You *were* the brains behind the scam, and you *did* skim millions from Kasagawa's investment. Oh, and you had eight people killed."

"That wasn't me. It was Gilbert and his men. Ask them. They'll tell you it was Gilbert." He was getting desperate, his situation finally sinking in.

"We actually had a very nice conversation with Smith and Haas. Would you like to see them?"

That got Gilbert's attention. He looked surprised as he and Gilbert were ushered into the office.

Howard turned back in horror and threw up.

"Are Smith and Haas alive?" Gilbert's voice trembled

"Yes, they are. They have an imminent appointment with the SFPD, but I believe you two will escape the U.S. justice system, just like you planned. Somehow, I think you'll face another kind of justice. Goodbye Mr. Howard. Mr. Gilbert."

Saito's men escorted them back into the front office. In the headlights, I could see wicked-looking tanto knives and Howard cowering away from the men holding them. The men sliced down the expensive clothing until the men stood naked, except for their shoes and socks.

Howard was soft and pasty, while Gilbert was in much better shape, obviously, a holdover from his military background. I really didn't care what happened to them. I just didn't want to know.

Sophie, however, relished every moment. I could see the smile playing on her lips as the two naked men were bundled into the back of the SUV.

I walked over to my car.

Marie looked uncomfortable.

"Marie, if you want to leave, you can. You've done more than I should've asked."

"Forget it, Mas. I'm not going anywhere. Are you sure they're the ones responsible?"

Before I could respond Sophie said, "Yes, they are."

Marie looked over to me.

"Yes, Smith and Haas admitted to the killings, but they acted on the direction of those two." I pointed at Howard and Gilbert.

"What will happen to them?"

"I don't know. I *do* know we won't ever see them again, and they'll get what they deserve. Eight families will finally get some justice." I heard the door slam and watched the Japanese contingent leave. The parking lot went dark. "Marie, please take Sophie home."

"What made Howard throw up?"

"There was an incident, and Smith was injured."

"Can I see him? I want to see the men who actually killed my sister."

"Not a good idea, Sophie. You'll see them on TV, and we can go to court, if you want. Go. I'll get Kenzo up to speed and meet you at your place. Marie, would you mind staying until I get there?"

371

"Stupid question, Mas. We're family, or as good as any I have. Please, text me when you're on the way. Yes?"

What the hell had I done to deserve a friend like Marie? "Yes, I'll text you."

With that, Marie drove off with Sophie. The night surrounded me with the disappearing headlights. Only the diffused light from the office illuminated the porch. I walked back into the office. The smell of blood invaded my nostrils. Taking out the burner, I called Kenzo's personal line. He answered immediately, even though he wouldn't recognize the burner phone's number.

I spoke quietly. "You need to visit Shield Protection. Just you and a medical unit."

"Mas? Are you all right?"

"Yes, I'm fine. You just need to get here ASAP. You'll understand why you need the med crew when you get here."

"All right, Mas. I'm on my way."

"Good. Don't call this phone again. I'm pitching it. See you in a few."

I wiped the phone down. I had to be careful. One more use, and I could destroy it. I waited, just in case Kenzo decided not to come alone. The front door to Shield was visible. I could skip out through a hole in the fence around the back of the park but hoped I wouldn't have to do that. It was cold outside, but better than staying with Smith and Haas.

As instructed, Kenzo showed up alone within minutes.

I waited in case he had others coming in different vehicles, but the cold was getting to me and I had to trust someone.

Kenzo stayed outside, his back to the wall.

I approached, and he held up his hand in greeting. I responded likewise. "Thanks for coming alone. I appreciate it."

He looked suspicious. "What's going on, Mas? Are you in trouble?"

I shook my head. "No, but there's a bit of a mess in there. This isn't what I planned, but plans go astray. Got an injury in there. One of the two killers needs emergency surgery. The other is taped up and locked in a van in the garage. Warn the EMTs he has a broken wrist. I'll leave you soon. You have signed confession statements from both killers. John Smith…"

He looked at me in disbelief.

"It's his real name. The other one is a South African named Haas. He's a harder case and will try for extradition. Just warning you."

"You said there's an injury?"

"Yes. They tried to take us, and Smith lost his hand in the process. It was self-defense. It's messy, but nothing you haven't seen before."

"Us? Who did you—? You didn't bring Chandler's sister, did you?"

"Kenzo, do you think I'm that stupid?"

"No. So who was it, McCarrigan?"

That surprised me. He must have figured it out through the Kasagawa investigation. "Let's just say it was someone with mutual interests."

"Okay. Let's go in and see what we have."

We both were careful where stepped. I was more aware of the lay of the room, so I moved around more easily.

Kenzo recognized the way the hand had been severed at the wrist. "Shit, Mas! You climbed in bed with the Yakuza? Are you really that dumb? And now, you've dropped me in it. We were warned off investigating Rant cause of the feds."

"This is a separate business, which just happens to be owned by the VP of Security at Rant. The proof will be provided anonymously, along with lots of evidence that Smith and Haas were the killers, but they were given orders. It's all in the confessions. I doubt you'll be able to prove anything against the top guns...*if* you can find them. I'd suggest you not look too hard. Just be satisfied you've got the ones who actually did the killing."

"Mas, why get in bed with them?"

"I didn't. It really was mutual interests, and we had some leverage. Certain people owe us—a debt of honor—that will rankle them until it's paid off."

"That's a dangerous game to play."

"Not really. Not in this case." I heard the distant wail of the EMT sirens

"So, how do you want me to play this drama out?"

"You got a tip—anonymously, of course—you investigated it yourself so you didn't waste team resources. You found a file on the desk with evidence, linking all the killings. Have forensics go over the Rant boat for trace and the van in the garage needs to be torn apart. We've supplied some trace evidence, but I'm sure there's more if you really look for it. You might be able to add rape charges to the list. It looks like Smith and Haas had their fun with the female vics...except Suzanne. That one was done in a hurry. Not much of a blessing."

"Does Sophie know about the rape theory?"

"Yes. She may have thought of it herself and pushed it away. She also knows Suzanne's death was quick."

"Mas, if I can, I want you to share the credit for this. Wouldn't hurt your business."

I chuckled. Kenzo wasn't a headline grabber. He felt shared glory made everyone look good. "Thanks, Kenzo, but that would create lots of difficult-to-answer questions and could get us into seriously deep shit."

"You're probably right. I don't want to know. We good now, Mas?"

I thought about that for a second. I wasn't in the blue club anymore, but Kenzo was different. "Yes, we're good, Kenzo."

"Then, piss off, civilian. Let me do my job." He grinned.

The sirens were getting closer. I turned and left. As I walked away, I texted him the "tip" that had brought him to Shield Protection. He'd have to work out the timeline himself.

It had been a good night. I wanted to go home, but I couldn't, not until I checked on Sophie. Once I was a safe distance from the industrial park and on the main drag, I called a rideshare from my personal phone. As I waited, I wiped down the burner phone, dropped it, and stomped on it, kicking the parts under a parked trucks wheel. It took a while for the pickup.

I texted Marie as promised.

Aside from Smith losing his hand, the night had gone as I'd planned. I certainly wasn't going to argue with the result. I was grateful to be headed to Sophie's place in one piece. Funny, I viewed it as hers, not

Simon's anymore. I hoped she'd stay in San Francisco.

The night was cold, and the air coming through the rolled-down window felt good. Now that we were out of danger, my adrenaline dropped, and the exhaustion took over.

Chapter 41

The lights were on in Sophie's window. The warm glow was inviting. I climbed the steps and rang the bell before entering.

Marie was sitting in one of the living room chairs. She looked concerned. She put a finger to her lips as I entered.

I frowned. "Where's Sophie?" I whispered.

Marie put both her hands to one side of her head, indicating Sophie was sleeping. She nodded toward the bedroom.

"Go home. Thank you for doing this. I owe you." I hugged her, and she responded to my hug.

"No thanks required. I really like her, Mas, and you deserve a break. See you tomorrow. Oh, I won't be in early."

I chuckled.

Marie left quietly, closing the door without a sound.

Tired, but not sleepy, I took Marie's place in the chair. As soon as Marie left, the bedroom door opened. I looked up in surprise.

Sophie walked out, her hair a mess, her face tear-streaked.

"I thought you were sleeping."

She walked over to me with arms open.

Pulling her in tight, she sobbed against my chest,

like a long, slow heartbeat. I stroked her hair in silence, holding her and letting her cry.

As her sobbing subsided, she gently pushed away from me. She looked up, red-eyed. "Will you stay with me tonight?"

"Of course. Whatever you need."

"I want you to stay as Mas. Your key is in the bathroom. I want Mas, my friend, to stay, not the PI. Not the sub. Just my friend."

That was a surprise. "Are you absolutely sure?" I whispered in her ear.

You're not a rebound, Mas." She hugged me again. "Yes, I want you to stay with me. I need to grieve for my sister. I miss her so much. Even when we were apart, we were still sisters…she was my baby sister. You understand loss. And I'm staying in San Francisco."

That was an even bigger surprise.

She hushed me. "Don't say anything. There's plenty of time. Trust me on that."

"I do trust you. Come to bed. I don't want to sleep without you near me."

She stood and walked into the bedroom.

I made a stop at the bathroom. My key nestled in a small white dish, the chain piled around it. The stark contrast of the black key and gold chain against the whiteness was almost blinding. I wasn't sure what any of this meant for the future. I'd just take it for what it was. Right now, the woman I loved needed me. I stripped and removed my chastity cage, leaving it on the dish with the key in the lock.

Turning off the lights, I made my way into the bedroom, by way of the moonlight coming through the sheers. I could barely make out her shape under the covers when I slipped in beside her. She shivered at my touch and nestled back into me. She was soft and warm.

Strangely, I was wide awake. Occasionally, I'd feel her shake as she let out a sob. Slowly, the sobs subsided and low, even breathing took their place. I eventually drifted off.

When I came to, the sun was shining. Sophie wasn't next to me. I startled and started to jump out of bed until I heard her in the kitchen. It sounded like she was making breakfast. I followed the smell into the kitchen. She was wearing a tee shirt, her hair dripping down her back. I couldn't believe I'd slept through it.

"You were out, and I didn't have the heart to wake you." She looked pale but better than she had last night.

"How are you?"

Her eyes welled with tears. "Does it always hurt so badly?"

I thought about my own losses, and those of victims' families I'd seen as an inspector. "Pretty much. It changes over time, but you never forget. Everyone deals with it in their own way. It takes time, and it doesn't hurt to seek professional help."

"You mean therapy?"

"Yup. Remember it was mandatory…and for good reason."

"Did you ever do it?"

"Like I said, mandatory…any loss, getting shot, or shooting someone. First time, I fought it. I still had to do it, and by the end, I saw the value. It doesn't mean you're crazy. It just helps with the process."

"Really?" She looked skeptical.

"Really. It *does* help."

"Mas, I decided before last night, whatever happened, I wanted to stay here in San Francisco. I mean, if you want me to. I want what my sister had."

I narrowed my eyes at her. "Are you staying for Suzanne or staying for you? If it's for Suzanne, it's a mistake."

"No, I mean, I am staying for me and you. I want a relationship like she had. She wasn't perfect, but she worked at it. I haven't, and I want a meaningful relationship, not just a fuck and fly. I can honestly say I've never felt the way I feel about you with anyone else."

"We don't need to do this now. Wait a while. Take some time. You *need* time. San Francisco isn't a bad place to take some time off."

"Mas, are you pushing me away?"

"God, no. I want this as much as you, if not more, but you've just lost your sister and you've been through a lot of stress. You need time to heal. To be honest, I haven't properly grieved for Simon. I kept pushing it away. I need to deal with that."

She laughed sadly. "What a dysfunctional pair we make."

"But a good pair. Remember? Two sides of the same coin."

She leaned over and kissed me lightly on the lips, a kiss full of promise and hope.

We didn't go into the office that day, or the next, or the one after that. We called Marie so she wouldn't worry. We made love in the warm rays of sun, filtered through the window blinds. We visited the beach and wandered around San Francisco neighborhoods as the mood took us. I showed her my neighborhood and introduced her to all the people I knew.

She basked in their warm, friendly welcome.

The newspaper headlines blared out the capture of the Bodies in the Bay Killers. They got the story and at least a few details right. Soon, a new headline took over…a scandal in Silicon Valley. Two senior managers at Rant Applications had disappeared, along with a significant amount of money. No one connected the murders with the Rant Applications scandal, but we knew better.

Kenzo was a busy man, in and out of the DA's office. He left a message I didn't pick up for a day or two. I had other things on my mind.

It was Sophie who started the conversation. "Are you sure you want me to stay?"

I didn't need to think about that for even a second. "Yes, I want you to stay. I want you and me to become *us*…together. I felt something the first moment I saw you. I subconsciously recognized a connection. It wasn't just the kink. To me, you're the whole package. I've never had that feeling so completely before. So yes, I want you to stay."

"Then I'll stay, as long as you can recommend a good therapist."

We both laughed and held hands as we walked along the edge of Golden Gate Park. We talked about moving Sophie's business to San Francisco and sorting out the details of making us a partnership. We discussed dividing up the finders' fee for the funds skimmed by Howard and Gilbert and decided a three-way split was in order. Marie had been an integral part. It would be a nice surprise for her and her partner, Chung.

On the first day back into the office, we had a

message waiting for us from McCarrigan. Sophie delighted in explaining how he and Rant had been scammed by Jack Mellon and that the whole Dissolve program was junk. She promised to send him proof in the way of access to the program from the flash drives.

He was pissed at Jack Mellon and mad at himself for falling for the scam. He closed by asking if we'd be interested in working for him, if he had projects that needed our skill set.

The offer surprised us, and we decided to consider it, maybe.

The one thing Sophie didn't bring up—and I sure as hell wasn't going to—was Howard and Gilbert's fate. I was pretty sure she'd buried it, and I knew she'd have to face it to move forward when she was ready.

Life was complicated and busy. It felt good to share it with Sophie. She made several trips to the East Coast to clear up loose ends.

It was on our last trip to Philly she asked, "What do you think happened to them?"

Puzzled by her question, I suddenly realized she was talking about Howard and Gilbert. I took a moment to answer. "I don't know, but whatever it was, they deserved it. I'm positive no one will ever find them. They paid the required price, and we'll never have to worry about them again. Suzanne and all the others can rest easy, and so can their families. The police case against Smith and Haas is progressing. Those two will never see the light of day again. If they're lucky, they'll get eight life sentences. Those responsible for Suzanne's death are gone, and the actual killers are going away. Are you satisfied with that resolution?"

She looked at me, her eyes welling. "It helps we

got them, but I still miss her…and that's *so* hard."

"Yes, it's hard, and we'll deal with it together. I promise. I'm not going anywhere."

She smiled.

We heard the call for our flight and walked down the ramp, hand in hand, knowing in just a few hours, we'd be in San Francisco together. That thought made my heart jump.

Hammett and Chandler had a very bright future, indeed.

A word about the author…

Richard Albion lives in San Mateo, California, with his wife, the pillar who supports him, two grown children out of the nest, and multiple rescued animals making the nest better.

He is a European melting pot, writer of erotic Fem-Dom fiction, exceptional cook, clothing designer, and artist. Graduate of both UK and US colleges. Retired Sales professional now engaged in working on the artistic side of life, he enjoys travel, volunteering, martial arts, San Francisco, and NorCal weather. Cannot live too far from the ocean—it's genetic.

To chat with Richard Albion and other Wild Rose Press authors of erotic romance, join us at
www.groups.yahoo.com/group/thewilderroses.

Also Available
from The Wild Rose Press, Inc.
and major retailers.

What Wouldn't I Do
I Do Book Two
By Allie Fisher

My name is Alana Reed Master…

Doting wife and stay at home mom, that's what I was—desperately in love with my husband, a man whose bedroom eyes matched his bedroom expertise. A single mom when we met, I fell hard and never looked back until the day he asked me for a legal separation. He won't stop at divorce. He wants my girls, my home, and my life. And Dane Masters always gets what he wants.

I never expected a man like Sam Kealoha to enter my life. Recovering from his own heartbreak, he's got the body of a Polynesian God and a primal protectiveness that is sexy as hell. He's the man of my dreams, but I can't keep him. Now I'm forced to make choices that betray my heart while contemplating something I never thought I would do—getting rid of my husband.

Screwed
By Mike Owens

Somehow, it's always about the money. Sharon Saluda, in her junior year at Pisgah College, doesn't have nearly enough of it, and a diploma is her ticket out of the narrow confines of small town life in Jacob's Bluff, NC. A career as a stripper seems a promising solution, but when that ends badly, a desperate Sharon capitalizes on that most basic of needs—sex—by matching up college coeds with faculty clientele.

Her job description takes a dramatic uptick when Connor Shaw arrives and wants her as his own—for a very good price, of course. She takes the plunge, body and soul, because this man is gorgeous, ridiculously wealthy, and the sex is out of this world. But there's always a catch…right?

Thank you for purchasing
this publication of The Wild Rose Press, Inc.

For questions or more
information contact us at
info@thewildrosepress.com.

The Wild Rose Press, Inc.
www.thewildrosepress.com

To visit with authors of
The Wild Rose Press, Inc.
join our yahoo loop at
http://groups.yahoo.com/group/thewildrosepress/